MANIAC OR MONSTER?

"Hi, there," she whispered in a groggy voice. "Wha' took you so long?"

Roland said nothing, just squeezed her breast and took his hand away. He was shaking.

"Jason?" Celia asked.

"Jason's not here. Jason . . ." and Roland suddenly shrieked, *"had some dying to do!"* He grabbed her wrist and snapped a handcuff around it.

In an instant, before Celia could begin to struggle and scream, he whipped the other cuff around his own wrist.

Then he reached for the knife. He had work to do.

Also by Richard Laymon
published by Tor Books

NIGHT SHOW
TREAD SOFTLY

A TOM DOHERTY ASSOCIATES BOOK
NEW YORK

This is a work of fiction. All the characters and events portrayed in this book are fictitious, and any resemblance to real people or events is purely coincidental.

FLESH

A TOR Book
Published by Tom Doherty Associates, Inc.
49 West 24 Street
New York, NY 10010

ISBN: 0-812-52110-2 Can. ISBN: 0-812-52111-0

Library of Congress Catalog Card Number: 88-50476

First edition: October 1988

Printed in the United States of America

0 9 8 7 6 5 4 3 2 1

THIS BOOK IS DEDICATED TO
DEAN AND GERDA KOONTZ,
WHO CONSISTENTLY TOP
THE LAYMON TIMES
"BEST-PEOPLE LIST"

Chapter One

EDDIE, IN HIS VAN, HAD THE ROAD TO HIMSELF.

Except for the bicycle.

When he first saw the bike from the crest of the hill, it was below him and far ahead. At such a distance, he couldn't tell much about the rider.

He knew it wasn't a kid.

The bike was one of those high, streamlined jobs, not like you see kids pedaling around on. And the rider looked big enough to fit the bike.

Could be a teenager, Eddie thought.

Could be a gal.

Squinting, he leaned toward the windshield. The bottom of the steering wheel sank into his belly, filling the crease between his rolls of fat.

Could be a gal, he thought.

With the back of his hand, Eddie wiped his mouth.

He was halfway down the hill by now, picking up speed and closing the gap between his van and the bike.

The rider's brown hair was somewhat long. That didn't prove much. A lot of men wore their hair that long and longer.

But you don't see a lot of guys in red shorts.

Eddie sped closer.

Close enough to see how the rider's hips flared out from a small waist.

A gal, all right.

On both sides of the road were fields with trees here and there. No buildings. No people. The road ahead to where it curved and vanished was deserted. Eddie checked his side mirrors. Behind him, the road was clear.

"Her it is," he said.

He pressed the gas pedal to the floor.

Though the rider didn't look back, she must have heard the rising engine sound. Her bike moved to the right, gliding away from the middle of the lane and taking up a new position a yard from the road's edge.

Eddie bore down on her.

She was hunched over her handlebars. She kept pedaling.

Her T-shirt was so tight that Eddie could see the bumps of her spine. Bare skin showed between the bottom of her shirt and the elastic band of her shorts.

Her left arm swung out. She waved Eddie by.

At the last instant, she looked back. Eddie was near enough to see that her eyes were blue.

She was very pretty.

He turned his van toward her.

I like the pretty ones.

Her front wheel jerked right.

Pretty and young and tender.

He waited for her to meet the windshield.

But she was being hurled the wrong way—forward and to the right. She was no longer on the bike. She was above it, legs kicking overhead, as Eddie's van smashed through it.

No problem, Eddie thought.

She won't go far.

I'll get her. Oh, yes.

His right-side tires bounced over the gravel shoulder of the road and he was about to steer back onto the pavement when he came upon a bridge.

He hadn't even noticed it before.

He glimpsed the sign as he sped past it.

Weber Creek.

Not much of a creek.

Not much of a bridge—but it had a concrete guard wall four feet high.

Chapter Two

"ARE YOU ALL RIGHT?"

"Do I *look* all right?"

She was sitting on the ground with her back to the road, her head turned to look up at him. Above her right eyebrow, the skin was scraped off to her hairline. The raw place was striped with beaded threads of blood. It was dirty, and a few bits of straw-colored weeds clung to the stickiness.

Jake sat down beside her on the edge of the ditch.

Both her knees and the front of her right thigh were in the same condition as her forehead. Her right arm hung between her legs, knuckles against the ground. She held the arm with her other hand while it shook. She didn't appear to be trying to hold it still. The other hand seemed meant to soothe it the way someone might lay a hand on an injured pet.

"Do you think it's broken?" Jake asked.

"I wouldn't know."

Jake took out a notepad. "Could I have your name?"

"Jamerson," she said. The corner of her mouth twitched.

Jake wrote. "And your first name?"

"Celia."

"Thanks."

She turned her head to look at him again. "Shouldn't you be doing something about *that*?" Her eyes shifted toward the blazing van fifty or sixty feet to her left.

"The fire truck's on the way. My partner's keeping an eye on things."

"What about the . . . driver?"

"We can't do much for him."

"Is he dead?"

A shish kebab, Chuck had remarked when he saw the driver's remains hanging out the windshield.

"Yes," Jake said.

"He tried to hit me. I mean it. He had the whole road to himself. I'm over by the shoulder and I signal him to go around, and I look back and he's actually swerving right at me. He's grinning and he swerves right at me. Must've been going sixty." Her face had a puzzled expression as if she were listening to a bizarre joke and waiting for Jake to feed her the punch line. "That guy meant to kill me," she said. "He creamed my bike."

She nodded toward it. The bike with its twisted wheels lay in the weeds on the far side of the ditch.

"What happened, I turned quick to get out of his way and it flipped on me. Just before he hit it, I guess. The van never touched me. Next thing I knew, I was landing in the ditch and there was this crash. Bastard. That's what he gets, going around trying to . . . what'd I ever do to *him*?"

"Did you know him?" Jake asked.

"I've heard of these guys, they'll run down dogs just for laughs. Hey, maybe he thought I was a dog." She tried to laugh and came out with a harsh sobbing noise.

"Had you ever seen the man before?"

"No."

"Did you do anything that might've angered him?"

"Sure, I flipped him the bird. What is this? Is it suddenly my fault?"

"*Did* you flip him off?"

"No, damn it. I didn't even see him till he was about a foot off my tail."

"As far as you're concerned, then, his action was totally unprovoked?"

"That's right."

"You say that you heard the crash just after you landed in the ditch?"

"Maybe I hadn't hit yet. I really don't know."

"What happened next?"

"I think I conked out. Yeah, I'm pretty sure I did. Then what happened, I heard your siren. That's when I got up and . . ."

"Hey, Jake!"

Jake looked over his shoulder. Chuck, fire extinguisher in one hand, was standing by the open rear door of the flaming van and waving him over. "I'd better see what he wants. Sit tight, there should be an ambulance on the way."

Celia nodded.

Jake stood up, brushed off his seat, and walked over to his partner.

"Take a look-see here," Chuck said, pointing to the ground.

The pale dirt of the road's shoulder was speckled with a few dark blotches. Jake crouched for a closer look.

"Looks like blood to me," Chuck said.

"Yeah."

"Was the girl over here?"

"Not according to what she told me."

"We better find out for sure. Cause if she wasn't . . . know what I mean?"

Jake heard a distant siren. He saw a smear of blood on the gray asphalt of the road. The fire truck or ambulance wasn't in sight yet, so he rushed across both lanes. Chuck trotted along beside him, still hanging onto the fire extinguisher.

"How'd someone survive a crash like that?" Chuck said.

Jake shook his head. "Just lucky."

"Yeah, I guess it can happen. You hear about folks making it through airline crashes. *There.*" He pointed.

"I see it."

A slick of blood on a blade of crabgrass.

Jake stepped into the weeds. He scanned the ditch and the field beyond it. Both were overgrown with weeds that had flourished and bloomed under the recent spring rains. The uneven terrain of the field was dotted with clumps of bushes. There were a few trees scattered around.

He saw no one.

Chuck cupped his hands to the sides of his mouth and yelled, "Hello! Hey, out there!"

Jake, standing beside him, could barely hear his voice over the noise of the siren.

The siren died. Chuck called out again. Jake heard the groan of air brakes, the tinny crackle of a radio. He looked back and saw the town's bright yellow pump truck.

"How come you suppose he wandered off?" Chuck asked. "It was me got banged up, I'd stick around and wait for help."

"Maybe he's in shock and doesn't know what he's doing. More likely, though, he wanted to haul ass out of here. The girl says she was riding her bike along minding her own business and the van tried to run her down on purpose. Which would mean the guy's not a model citizen. You take care of matters here, I'll see if I can dig him up."

"Don't take all day, huh? I'm getting the hungries and my stockpile's dry."

The stockpile was the cache of Twinkies, chips and candy bars that Chuck kept in the patrol car.

"You'll live," Jake said. He slapped Chuck's paunch, then climbed down into the ditch.

After looking for traces of blood, he climbed out of the ditch on its far side.

Back on the road, the firemen were blasting at the flames with chemical extinguishers. Chuck was walking over to Celia, who was standing now, though bent over a bit and still holding her right arm.

Jake wondered if she was from the university. She was the right age, and he probably would've known her if she was a local. Also, there was her wise-guy attitude. *Do I look all right?*

Don't hold it against her, he told himself. She was hurting.

A good-looking woman, even with her face scraped up.

Came damn close to getting her ticket canceled.

He turned away and continued searching.

Two in the van, one bought the farm and the other guy got away. The dead guy was obviously the driver. The survivor must've been in the back of the van, or he would've gone out the windshield, same as the driver. And Celia didn't mention seeing anyone in the passenger seat.

If he was in the back, maybe he wasn't part of it.

No, he *was* part of it, or he would've stuck close to the van after the crash.

Wandering back and forth, Jake spotted a dandelion with a broken stem, a smear of blood on its blossoms. It was a few yards north of where he'd come out of the ditch. In his mind, Jake connected the two points and extended the line across the field. It led to a low rise a couple of hundred yards to the northwest. The high ground was shaded by a stand of eucalyptus trees. He headed that way.

From behind him came the blare of another siren. That would be the ambulance.

Nice response time, he thought.

He checked his wristwatch. 3:20 P.M. He and Chuck had spotted the smoke at 3:08. They'd reached the accident site two minutes later and called in. So the ambulance had taken ten minutes.

Good thing nobody's life was depending on it.

Jake waded into Weber Creek, peering up and down the narrow band of water. On the other side, he stopped long enough to check the area for signs. The weeds were nearly knee-high. He couldn't find any traces of blood or trampled foliage. Maybe the guy had changed course. Looking back, though, Jake could only make out the faintest sign of his own passage.

I'm hardly the world's greatest tracker, he thought.

And if the guy had made any effort to be careful, he could've skirted the places with high weeds and stuck to areas where the ground cover was sparse. Or maybe followed the creek.

Maybe I already passed him. If he stretched out flat . . .

Sneaking up on me . . .

Jake whirled around.

Nobody there.

His gaze swept over the field, then back toward the road. The van was still smoking, but he couldn't see any flames. Chuck was standing close to Celia. An ambulance attendant was heading their way.

Jake continued toward the rise, but he'd begun to feel that he'd lost the suspect. He didn't like that. In spite of the blood, it was apparent that the man hadn't been severely injured. Hurt, sure, but not incapacitated.

A potential killer.

Jake didn't want to lose him.

What kind of man pulls a stunt like that—tries to run down a total stranger in broad daylight? He wasn't driving, of course, but he was an accomplice, Jake was sure of that.

Maybe they never intended to kill her, just run her off the road, rack her up enough to take the fight out of her, and snatch her. That Jake could understand. A good-looking woman, get her into the van, have their fun with her, dump her later on, maybe dead.

If Celia's account was accurate, though, they actually tried to smash her with the van. It would've killed her for sure. And messed her up pretty good. Hardly your typical MO for a pair of traveling rapists.

They wanted her dead first?

Sick.

Outlandish, too. There just aren't that many necrophiles running around; the odds against two of them linking up must be staggering.

It could happen.

More likely, though, they just would have left her.

Thrill killers.

Combing the roads in a van, looking for suitable victims.

If I lose this guy . . .

Jake turned slowly, scanning the entire expanse of the field. He trudged to the top of the rise and made a quick circuit around the trees. Nobody there. On the other side, the ground sloped down to a narrow road. Beyond the road, the field continued. The foliage and trees were heavier on that side. Plenty of places for a man to conceal himself.

Jake spent a long time watching the area. Turning around, he gazed at the field he had crossed.

You lost him, all right.

Get up a search party, go over the area inch by inch. The logical step, but not very practical. How do you get together enough men on short notice to do the job properly?

He leaned against a tree. He kicked a small rock and sent it flying down the slope. It landed in a clump of bushes, and he imagined his suspect crying out, "Ouch!" and making a run for it.

Dream on, Corey.

Shit.

He looked up the side road. It led only to the Oakwood Inn. The old restaurant had been closed for years, but a couple from Los Angeles was planning to reopen it. He saw a station wagon parked in front. The folks must be there, fixing the place up.

I'd better warn them.

The damned restaurant only looked like it was a quarter of a mile away. Weary and discouraged—and gnawed by guilt for letting the creep slip away—Jake shoved himself away from the tree and made his way down the slope. He waded through the weeds. Once he reached the road, the walking was easier.

He kept a lookout, though he no longer expected to find the suspect.

Suspect, my ass, he thought.

This guy's into wasting random victims.

And I lost him.

Maybe the accident, losing his partner, took some of the starch out of him.

Right.

Goddamn it.

I lost him and it'll be my fault if he . . .

The distant sound of a car engine broke into Jake's thoughts.

Chuck coming to fetch him?

He turned and realized that the sound came from the direction of the Oakwood Inn. He remembered the station wagon.

Snapped his head forward.

He was standing in a dip.

He saw only the road.

From the noise, the car was speeding.

And he knew.

He'd been slow—he should've guessed it the instant he saw the car sitting there, vulnerable, in front of the restaurant.

Your van is totaled, you're on foot and hurt, you spot an unattended vehicle . . .

Heart racing, mouth gone dry, Jake Corey snatched out his .38, planted his feet on each side of the faded yellow centerline of the road, lowered himself into a shooting crouch, and waited.

He aimed at the road's crest fifty yards away.

"Come on, you mother."

Jake wished he had a .357 like the one Chuck carried. With that, he'd be able to kill a car.

Jake would have to go for the driver.

He had never shot anyone.

But he knew this was it. He couldn't let the bastard get away.

Six slugs through the windshield.

That should do it.

The car burst into view, bounced on loose shocks as it hit the down slope, sped toward him.

Wait till he's almost on you, blow him away, dive for safety.

Jake's finger tightened on the trigger.

Brakes shrieked. The car skidded, fishtailed, and stopped thirty feet in front of him.

Jake couldn't believe it.

"Let me see your hands!" he yelled.

The driver, a thin and frightened-looking man of about thirty, stared at Jake through the windshield.

"I want to see your hands *right now*! Grab the steering wheel *right now*!"

The hands appeared. They gripped the top of the wheel.

"Keep 'em there!"

Jake kept his revolver pointed at the man's face while he approached the car. The head turned, eyes following him as he stepped to the driver's door.

No one else in the car.

Jake pulled the door open and stepped back. Crouching slightly, he had a full view of the man.

Who wore a blue knit shirt, and Bermuda shorts, and who didn't appear to be injured in any way.

"What's going on, Officer?"

"Place your hands on top of your head and interlace your fingers."

"Hey really. . ."

"Do it!"

Why are you keeping this up? Jake wondered. Because you don't know. Not yet. Not for sure.

The man put his hands on top of his head.

"Okay. Now climb out."

As he followed orders, Jake got a look at his back. No blood or sign of injury there, either.

"Turn around slowly." Jake made circular motions with his left forefinger. The man turned. Jake looked for bulges. The knit shirt was skintight. The only bulge was at the rear pocket of his shorts—a wallet. Good. Jake didn't want to frisk him.

"Will you tell me what's going on?"

Jake holstered his weapon.

"Could I see your driver's license, please?"

The man took out his wallet. He knew enough to remove the license from its plastic holder. Probably been stopped for traffic violations.

Jake took the card. His hand was trembling. It reminded him of Celia's shaking arm. The name on the license was Ronald Smeltzer. The photo matched the face of the man in front of him. The home address was on Euclid, in Santa Monica, California. "Thank you, Mr. Smeltzer," he said, and returned the license. "I'm sorry about stopping you that way."

"A wave would've sufficed."

"I was expecting trouble. I assume you're the new owner of the Oakwood."

"That's right. Could you tell me what's going on? I realize I was taking the road a bit fast, but . . ." Smeltzer shrugged. He was obviously upset, but showing no belligerence. Jake appreciated his attitude.

"I was on my way to speak with you—to warn you, actually. We just had an incident over on Latham Road."

"We were wondering. We heard the sirens."

"On your way to investigate?"

"No, no. As a matter of fact, we haven't got ice. My wife and I have been working all day, trying to get the place in shape. No refrigerator, yet. It's supposed to be delivered tomorrow. We thought we'd relax over cocktails for a while, but . . ." He shrugged. He looked as if he felt a little foolish. "No ice. What can I say?"

"Your wife is back at the restaurant?" Jake asked. The man nodded. "I don't think you want to leave her alone just now. We've got a situation. Give me a lift to your restaurant and I'll explain."

The two men climbed into the car. Smeltzer turned it around and headed back up the road at a moderate speed.

"Pick it up," Jake told him. "I know you can do better than this."

Smeltzer stepped on the gas.

As the car raced toward the restaurant, Jake explained about the attempt to run down Celia Jamerson, the blood behind the van, and his search for the injured passenger. Smeltzer listened, asking no questions but shaking his head a couple of times and frequently muttering, "Oh, man."

The car lurched to a stop at the foot of the restaurant's stairs. Smeltzer flung open his door. At the same moment, a door at the top of the stairs swung wide.

A woman stood in the shadows. She stepped out onto the porch as Smeltzer and Jake climbed from the car. Her perplexed expression altered into a frown of concern—probably as she realized that Jake was a cop.

She had nice legs. She wore red shorts. This is my day for beautiful women in red shorts, Jake thought. The front of her loose gray jersey jiggled nicely as she trotted down the stairs. The jersey had been cut off, halfway up. Any higher, Jake thought, and he'd be seeing what made the jiggles.

"Ron?" she asked, stopping in front of the car.

"Honey, this is officer. . . ." He looked at Jake.

"Jake Corey."

"I ran into him on my way out. Almost literally." He gave Jake a sheepish glance.

"Some kind of trouble?"

Jake let Smeltzer explain. His wife nodded. She didn't say, "Oh, man," after each of his sentences. She didn't say anything. She just frowned and nodded and kept glancing over at Jake as if expecting him to interrupt. "Is this true?" she finally asked him.

"He covered it pretty well."

"You think there might be a killer hanging around here?"

"He didn't kill anyone today, but it wasn't for lack of trying. Have either of you seen anyone?"

She shook her head.

"But we've been working inside," Smeltzer added.

"You folks have a home in town, don't you?" Jake asked. He seemed to remember hearing that they'd bought the Anderson house.

"I was on my way there," Smeltzer said, "for the ice."

"It's certainly your decision, but if I were you, I'd close up here for today and go on back to your house. There's no point in taking unnecessary risks."

Husband and wife exchanged a look.

"I don't know," Smeltzer said to her. "What do you think?"

"We've got to get this place in shape before they bring in the equipment."

"I guess we could come in early tomorrow."

"It's up to you," the wife said.

"This guy does sound like he might be dangerous."

"Whatever you say, Ron. It's your decision."

"You'd rather stay," Ron said.

"Did I say that?"

"I think we'd be smart to leave."

"Okay. It's settled, then." She smiled at Jake. It was a false smile. *See? You got your way.*

Hey lady, he wanted to tell her, sorry. Just thought you might want to know there's an asshole in the neighborhood and maybe you're his type. Forgive me.

Smeltzer turned to Jake. "Could we give you a lift?"

"Yeah, thanks. I could use a ride back to the road."

"Fine. We'll just be a minute. We need to lock up."

He and his wife headed up the porch stairs.

Jake glanced at the woman's rear end. He didn't find it especially interesting. She was a fine-looking package, beautifully wrapped, but Jake had the idea that he wouldn't like what he found inside.

So much for lust.

They were inside the restaurant for longer than Jake expected. At first, he assumed they were probably delayed by a heated discussion about leaving ahead of schedule. Then he began to worry.

What if the guy from the van was in there and got them?

Not very likely.

But the possibility stayed with Jake. He counted to thirty, slowly, in his mind.

They still weren't out.

He went for the stairs, took them three at a time, and reached for the door handle.

The door swung away from him.

"Sorry it took so long," Smeltzer said. "Had to use the john."

"No problem." Jake turned away, not even trying for a glimpse of the wife, and trotted down the stairs.

From behind him came her voice. "This really *is* the pits."

"Better safe than sorry," Smeltzer said.

"Of course."

Chapter Three

A few classes were still in session and Bennet Hall had terrible acoustics that seemed to magnify every sound—especially on the stairways—so Alison climbed to the third floor with excessive caution, holding onto the old, wooden banister to keep herself steady.

Alison knew she was early.

She couldn't help it.

She'd tried to stay away until four, but Chaucer let out at two and she had no classes after that on Tuesdays and Thursdays, and it just isn't easy, killing two hours. The walk home only used up ten minutes. Neither of her roommates were there. Too bad. A conversation with Celia or Helen would've been good for making the time pass.

She'd tried to study, but couldn't concentrate. Not on the book, anyway. Just on the clock, the minute hand of which seemed to move one space every ten minutes. If she could just take a nap and wake up at a quarter to four . . . So she set her alarm clock and stretched out on the bed. Sure, sleep. She shut her eyes, folded her hands on her belly, and tried very hard. It was no use. She couldn't even lie still, much less sleep. Finally, she gave up on the idea, folded her waitress uniform into her flight bag, added a paperback, and left.

She had reached Bennet Hall at 3:20. That was early, even for her—a whole fifteen minutes earlier than her arrival time on Tuesday. So she took her usual seat on a concrete bench that encircled the broad trunk of an oak tree, and tried to read. Watched a squirrel eat a nut. Watched a couple of yelling lower classmen, probably frosh, toss a Frisbee around. Watched Ethel Something stroll toward the library holding hands with Brad Bailey. Tried to read. At last, it was ten till four. She couldn't wait any longer. Besides, she told herself, the class might let out early.

So she entered Bennet Hall and made her way as quietly as possible to the third floor. The hallway was deserted. She heard the slow tapping of a typewriter from a faculty office, and a few faint voices drifting into the hall from open classroom doors.

She stopped near the open door of the last classroom on the left. The students were out of sight, but her position gave Alison a clear view of Evan.

She'd been with him only last night, but she felt as if far too much time had gone by since then. Too much time with a hollow ache in her chest. The ache didn't go away. It seemed to get worse.

Come on, Alison thought. Dismiss the class.

Apparently, Evan hadn't noticed her arrival. He was looking forward, probably at the student who was asking about a minimum length requirement for the term papers.

"It should," he replied, "be like a young lady's skirt—

short enough to keep one's interest but long enough to cover the essentials.''

A few of the students chuckled.

''But how long does it have to *be*?'' the voice persisted.

Evan arched an eyebrow. Alison smiled. He was so cute, acting the pedant. ''Fifteen pages minimum.''

''Is that typed?'' inquired a different voice.

''Typed. Black ink. White paper of the 8½-by-11-inch variety. Double-spaced. One inch margins all around. If possible, refrain from using erasable paper—it makes my fingers sticky.''

They were freshmen. Probably taking notes on his every utterance.

Evan folded his arms. He was standing in front of his desk, its edge pressing into his rump. Taking off his wire-rimmed glasses, he asked, ''Any more questions?'' While he waited, he wiped the lenses on a lapel of his corduroy jacket. Without the glasses, his face looked bare and somehow childlike. He put them back on and became the scholar again. ''No? Your assignment is to read pages 496 through 506 in Untermeyer and come to class on Tuesday prepared to astonish me with your knowledge of Mr. Thomas's craft and sullen art. You are dismissed.''

Alison stepped away from the door. There was no stampede to leave the classroom. The students took their time departing, some coming out alone, others in groups of two or three. The bell rang. More students wandered out. Alison waited impatiently, then peeked around the door frame.

A girl in the fourth row was still in the process of stacking her books on top of her desk. Finally, she stood, cradled the precarious pile, and strolled toward the front. ''Have a nice weekend, Mr. Forbes.''

He grinned. ''I shall spend the weekend continuing my quest for naked women in wet mackintoshes.''

"Huh?"

"Have a nice weekend, Dana, and Friday, too."

Alison entered the room. The girl stepped around her and was gone.

"Naked women in wet mackintoshes?" Alison asked.

Evan grinned. He slipped a book into his briefcase. "A line borrowed from Mr. Thomas."

"Your friend Dana will think you're daffy."

"Daffiness is expected from English instructors."

Alison shut the door and went to him. He latched his briefcase, turned to her, and stared into her eyes.

"How you been?" she whispered. Her throat felt tight.

"Lonely."

"Me, too." She eased herself against him, arms moving beneath his jacket, head tilting back, lips waiting for his mouth.

He kissed her. He pressed her body closer and she snuggled against him. This was what she wanted, what she had longed for since last night—being with him again. If it could only go on and on. If they could only go from here to his apartment and be together, make love, eat supper, spend the evening and the night. But it couldn't be that way, and the knowledge was a whisper of regret that tainted the moments in his embrace.

Alison ended the kiss.

She pressed her mouth to the side of his neck, squeezed herself hard against him, then lowered her arms and slipped her hands into the rear pockets of his corduroy pants. "It feels so good," she said.

"My ass?"

"Just holding you."

"The clothes get in the way."

"It's still nice."

"Nicer still would be naked on the floor."

"Undeniable."

"How about it?" His hands went to her rump. They cupped her buttocks through her skirt, squeezed.

"Not a chance."

"Give me one good reason."

"The door doesn't have a lock."

"Aside from that."

She smiled up at him. "Isn't that enough?"

"A minor detail."

"You think so, do you?"

"It would be well worth the risk."

"No way, pal."

"A coward dies many times . . ."

"And discretion is the better part of valor."

"Methinks the lady doth not want to screw."

With a laugh, Alison pushed herself away from him. "Walk me to work?"

"Well, I don't know. One good turn deserves another, and . . ." He shrugged.

"You're kidding, right?"

"Nobody's going to come in here."

"How do you know?"

Evan reached out and opened the top button of her blouse. He started for the next button. Alison took him by the wrists and pushed his hands away. "I said no. I meant it. This isn't the time or the place."

He pressed his lips into a tight line and breath hissed from his nostrils. "If you say so," he muttered.

Alison looked into his eyes. His gaze, which before had seemed so deep and searching, now had a blankness to it as if something inside him had shut down and he no longer saw her at all.

He turned away. He opened his briefcase and took out a fat manila folder.

"Evan . . ."

"I guess I'll stay here for a while. I've got some papers

to grade. Besides, I want to see if anyone comes in during the next half hour or so. Call it curiosity.''

Alison stared at him a moment longer, not wanting to believe he was doing this to her. Then she walked to the door.

''Come on, Alison, what's the big deal?''

She didn't answer. She left.

In the corridor, then on the stairs, she expected Evan to hurry after her. He would apologize. *I'm sorry, it was a stupid idea. I shouldn't have brought it up.*

By the time Alison pushed her way through the main door, she knew he wasn't going to run after her. He'd meant it. He was staying. Still, she kept glancing back as she crossed the lawn.

How could he do something like this?

Evan had walked her to work almost every day during the past two weeks. A couple of times, he couldn't do it because of meetings or something. But this—this was just spite.

A punishment.

Because she wouldn't put out.

Put out. What an ugly term.

Put out or get out.

All day, she had been looking forward to seeing him. A hug and kiss in the classroom, holding hands as he walked her to the restaurant. Talking, joking, just *being* with him. And both of them knowing that he would meet her after work, that they would walk to the park or back to his apartment and then he would be inside her.

Not today, folks.

The sidewalk was blurry. She wiped her eyes, but they filled again.

If it was that important to him, maybe . . . it *shouldn't* be that important. What's the big deal? Well, it was obviously a very big deal to him.

I'm suddenly the bad guy 'cause I won't let him screw me on the classroom floor.

And you thought he loved you.

Well, think again.

He loved you all right—he loved putting it to you, that's what he loved.

Goddamn him.

Alison rubbed her eyes again. She sniffed and wiped her nose, and stopped at the curb. Gabby's was only a block away. She didn't want to walk in there crying.

She didn't want to walk in there at all.

Not today.

She wanted to shut herself inside her bedroom and stay there. And sleep, and forget.

But when the traffic signal changed, she stepped off the curb and continued toward the restaurant.

Maybe he'll show up later on, meet me at closing time just as if nothing had happened.

What then?

She walked past Gabby's, glancing in through the windows. Only a few of the booths were occupied. Still too early for the supper crowd. She hoped it would be a busy night, busy enough to keep her from having time to think.

The entrance was on the corner. She pulled open one of the glass doors. It seemed heavier than usual. Inside, she managed a smile for Jean who was heading her way with a tray of empty beer steins.

"Early today," Jean said.

All she could do was nod.

"You all right?"

"I'll be okay."

Jean stepped up close to her. "You need to talk, you give me a holler. I raised three girls, and it weren't always rosy, let me tell you. But you just name me a problem, you can just bet your tush I've run into it one time or another."

"Thanks."

"Get on along, now." Jean moved her head a fraction to the left. Taking the cue, Alison looked over Jean's left shoulder. "Careful Prince Charming don't follow you into the john."

Prince Charming sat alone at the last booth.

"Trying to cheer me up, are you?" Alison asked.

Jean winked and stepped around her.

Alison tried not to look at Prince Charming, but couldn't help glancing his way as she hurried toward the rest room. He was hunched over the table, pulling and twisting a long greasy hank of black hair in front of his face. Pasty skin showed through a hole in the shoulder of his gray sweatshirt. The sweatshirt looked as if he'd been wearing it for months.

A bowl of vegetable soup was on the table under his face.

Lucky Jean, getting to serve him.

Was he trying to wring something out of his hair and into the soup?

Alison averted her eyes. She caught a whiff of him as she rushed by.

Thank God he didn't look up at her.

She entered the rest room and locked the door.

Prince Charming, at least, had succeeded in taking her mind off Evan.

Evan.

The hurting started again.

If I want to feel bad, she thought, I should trade problems with Prince Charming out there.

She hoped he would be gone by the time she finished.

She put on her makeup slowly. Then she draped her

skirt and blouse over the door of the toilet stall and opened her flight bag.

Most of the other waitresses wore their costumes to work. Alison didn't like to wear hers on the streets, and especially not on campus. The yellow taffeta skirt was several inches too short and had a dainty, frilly-edged apron sewn to the front. The short-sleeved, matching blouse had her name stitched in red over the left breast. The fabric of both, thin enough to see through, had obviously been selected by someone who wanted to give the male customers an extra treat.

Alison put on a short slip, then the costume.

She folded her street clothes. Spreading open her flight bag to put them away, she saw her toothbrush and black negligee.

For later.

For Evan's place.

She might as well have left them home.

Squeezing her lower lip between her teeth, she stuffed her clothing into the flight bag and zipped it shut.

She stepped out of the rest room.

Prince Charming was gone.

My lucky day, she thought.

Chapter Four

"In a way, it's a relief," Ron said.

"You'll be singing out of the other side of your face, my dear, when we have to get up at five o'clock in the morning." Peggy sipped her vodka gimlet, being careful not to spill. She was at a bad angle for drinking, but it felt good to be leaning back against the sofa cushion, her legs stretched out and feet propped on the coffee table.

"I don't think we'll need to get up quite *that* early," Ron said.

"Think again. They're coming in at ten with the appliances, and the kitchen floor has to be stripped and waxed before they arrive."

"That won't take five hours, will it?"

"You don't think so?"

"I'm sure you know best."

Peggy nodded. An icy drop fell from the bottom of her

glass onto her bare belly below the cutoff edge of her jersey. She flinched a bit, then rubbed the glass against her shorts. It made a dark smear on the red fabric. She took another drink.

"We should've done the kitchen after lunch," Ron said.

"My dear, we'd planned to do it after supper—having no idea, of course, that the long arm of the law, so to speak, would reach out and fuck us over."

"He was just trying to help."

"I can live without that kind of help, thank you very much."

"We didn't have to leave."

"You couldn't wait to get out of there and you know it."

"I still think it was the wise thing to do. Why should we put ourselves in a possibly hazardous situation when it can be avoided?"

"Why, indeed?" she muttered.

"I really don't appreciate your attitude," Ron said.

"Too bad." She started to take a drink.

"Damn it, Peggy!"

Her hand jumped. The chill liquid sloshed, spilling down the sides of her chin. "Shit!" She sat up. It trickled down her neck. With her left hand, she lifted her jersey and blotted herself dry. "You didn't have to yell." Her throat felt thick and her eyes burned. "Now I'm all sticky. Jeez, Ron."

"I'm sorry."

She tugged the cutoff jersey down to cover her breasts, took a drink, then set her glass on a coaster. "Excuse me."

In the bathroom, she wiped her chin and neck with a damp washcloth. Ron appeared in the medicine cabinet mirror. His hands caressed her belly. "I am sorry," he said again.

"Me, too," Peggy said in a small voice. "I've been such a bitch. It's just that I wanted to get it over with tonight."

He lifted the jersey. His hands covered her breasts.

"I was worried about you," he said. "That's all."

"I know."

"If you want to stay here, I'll go back tonight and get a start on the floor."

"By yourself?"

"I could take the gun," Ron told her.

"I've got a better idea. Take the gun, and we'll both go."

Jake Corey, sitting with his back to the trunk of a eucalyptus tree, scanned the fields with the binoculars he'd brought from home.

It was dusk. A breeze had come up and it felt good, a real improvement over the afternoon heat that had punished him during the long trek after he'd left his patrol car.

He must've hiked two miles or more, searching, crisscrossing his way through the weeds before coming to the high ground to settle down and watch.

"Don't waste your time," Chuck had said at the shift's end.

"I haven't got anything better to do."

"Bullsquat. You oughta go out and get yourself some action, it'd do you good."

Jake was in no mood for the kind of action Chuck meant. If he didn't do this, he would spend the night alone in his small rented house, reading, maybe catching some TV, hitting the sack early. And he'd still feel guilty for letting the crash survivor slip away from him.

This way, at least, he was doing something about it.

The guy could be miles gone by now.

On the other hand, he might be nearby. The fields were

far from flat. He could've found himself a depression and stayed low, resting and waiting. Biding his time until he felt it was safe to start moving.

That was the scenerio Jake counted on.

That was why he waited, well concealed among the high weeds with the tree to his back, scanning the area through binoculars.

Especially the area near the deserted restaurant.

That's where you would head, he thought.

You're hurt. You've been lying low in the weeds for hours. You're hungry and parched. You're starting to want a glass of water more than just about anything in the world.

Well, there's the creek. You could get your drink there.

You'd still head for the restaurant.

You're not just thirsty, you're hungry, too. And this is, after all, a restaurant. You're not from around here, you've got no idea it's been closed for years. You only know that it isn't open tonight. So it's closed on Thursdays. You're in luck. Get inside, you can have a feast. Take enough when you leave so you'll be fixed up for days.

Jake's position on the high ground gave him a good view of the restaurant. At least of its front and south walls. The other side and rear could be approached by an army, and he'd never know. Not from here.

Maybe the guy's already inside.

Jake wished he had checked the place out before settling down for his vigil. At this point, he was reluctant to leave his cover.

Wait for dark.

That wouldn't be long, now. Color was already fading from the landscape, the bright greens and yellows dimming, turning shades of gray.

Dark in a few more minutes.

Like waiting at a drive-in for the movie to start.

Jake was in his Mustang. With Barbara. His window

was rolled down, the speaker hooked over its edge. Almost dark. Almost time for the movie. Kids were on the swings and teeter-totter of the play area under the screen.

Barbara. In a white knit shirt, white shorts, socks, and tennis shoes. Fresh and beautiful. Her skin dusky next to all that white.

A walk to the refreshment stand. It was always popcorn and soda during the first feature, then back at intermission for an ice cream sandwich or red vines. Usually red vines.

A lot of fooling around went on with the red vines. You could whip with them. Or tickle. Or tease. You could each take one end of the same vine in your mouth and chew your way toward the middle.

Until you met Barbara's mouth. Her cherry-flavored mouth.

The sound of a car engine snapped Jake back into the present, and he felt as if he'd awakened from a sweet dream.

Headlights appeared on the road to the restaurant.

The car approached. As it passed below him, Jake saw that it was a station wagon.

Terrific.

So much for his warning.

And so much for his plan to check the place out.

He watched the red taillights rise and fall with the dips in the road. When the brake lights came on, he raised the binoculars. A door opened. The car's interior light came on.

Smeltzer and Smeltzer. The dynamic duo.

Ron opened the rear door. He pulled out a double-barreled shotgun.

The door shut. Jake lowered his binoculars and watched the couple climb the stairs. They spent a few moments on the porch, Ron at the door. Then they both went in. Moments later, light appeared in the bay windows.

So what gives? Jake wondered. Why'd they come back?

Forgot something? If that's the case, they'll be out in a minute. Unless they get jumped.

Jake realized he was holding his breath, listening for a shotgun blast. Or a scream.

He got to his feet. He started down the slope to the road. Still listening. He heard his own heartbeat, the foliage crunching under his boots, the normal constant sounds of crickets and birds.

Maybe the guy doesn't jump them, Jake thought. Maybe he hides. He would've heard the approach of the car. An old restaurant like that, it must have plenty of good hiding places.

If he's in there at all.

He might just as easily be in the trees beyond the restaurant. Or two or three miles away. He could be anywhere. Hell, he could be lying in the weeds, dead from his injuries.

Or he might be crouched in a dark corner of the Oakwood Inn, watching for a good chance to pounce.

From a high spot on the road, Jake could see the station wagon and restaurant. But not the Smeltzers.

They didn't forget a damn thing, those idiots. They came back to work.

Not a big surprise.

Jake picked up his pace.

The woman, that afternoon, had obviously been reluctant to leave. Ron was the sensible one. But weak. The little wife must've pursuaded him that they shouldn't let a little thing like a possible killer in the vicinity stand between them and their chores. Scared? Take the shotgun. You stand guard while I sweep up the dust bunnies.

"Smart move, folks," Jake muttered.

He hoped they were smart enough, at least, to check the doors and windows carefully. Assuming they had locked up before leaving (and they'd certainly taken long enough, Jake remembered), then the guy probably couldn't have entered without breaking something.

Unless he was already inside before they secured the place. Hiding.

What if they know?

The thought astonished Jake. He stopped walking and stared at the restaurant. And toyed with the idea.

They weren't hostages—that didn't fit at all. But what if they were cooperating with the guy for some reason?

What reason?

Money? Maybe the guy's loaded and bribed them to help out.

Ron's story about going for ice always did sound fishy.

And they spent an awfully long time inside when they were supposed to be locking up. Maybe discussing the situation with their new friend.

They leave with me. Come back after dark. With a shotgun.

A shotgun for their pal.

Jake started walking again, frowning as he gazed at the restaurant.

What do I know about the Smeltzers? he asked himself. Next to nothing.

Hell, the van might've been on its way *here* when somebody got the bright idea of running down Celia Jamerson.

You're stretching it, aren't you?

Just covering the bases. Taking a good look at every angle. That's how you avoid surprises.

Do you really believe they've thrown in with the guy?

The wife, maybe. Yeah, I could believe that. But Ron?

Maybe Ron's a terrific actor.

Jake doubted it.

They had to both be in on it, or neither of them. So it was neither. Probably.

As Jake neared the restaurant, he decided that, in all likelihood, the two had simply decided to ignore the risk, bring a gun along for protection, and spend a while finishing up their chores. But he couldn't ignore the other possibilities, remote as they might be.

Better safe than dead.

He chose not to knock on the door.

Instead, he silently climbed the porch stairs and peeked through one of the bay windows to the right of the entrance. He saw no one. The area beyond the window would be the cocktail lounge. A long, dark wood bar with a brass foot rail ran the length of the room. It had no stools, but there were a couple of folding chairs and a card table in front of it, about halfway down. The card table held a small collection of bottles and cocktail glasses.

There's some evidence for you, Jake thought. They *had* been planning to drink here. Ron must've been telling the truth about going for ice.

Jake crept to the other side of the door. Through the window there, he had a full view of the main dining room. Without any tables or chairs, it looked huge. The dark paneled wall to the left had half a dozen windows. Sconces were hung in the spaces between the windows, between the windows at the rear, and along the wall to the right. The wrought iron sconces each held three imitation candles—white stalks with glowing bulbs at the top. Apparently, they didn't provide enough illumination for the Smeltzers. One table lamp rested on the floor, casting a pool of light across the glossy hardwood.

Next to the lamp stood a vacuum cleaner. A broom was propped against a stepladder. There was an open toolbox on the floor, and an assortment of rags and cans and bottles of substances to be used for cleaning and polishing.

Jake figured that the wall on the right must close off the

kitchen area. About halfway down it, light spilled out from bat-wing doors.

Jake climbed down from the porch. He made his way around to the right side of the building and approached one of the glowing windows toward the rear.

Quiet music came from inside, so he realized that the window was probably open. He crept toward it cautiously.

The window was open, all right.

It was high off the ground, its sill level with Jake's shoulders. Bracing himself with a hand against the rough wood wall, he peered in at a corner. He smelled the window screen and a faint odor of ammonia.

Ron, in a far corner of the kitchen, was bent over a bucket, levering dirty water out of a sponge mop with a long handle. He wore jeans and no shirt. His shirt was draped over the counter close to the radio.

Jake spotted the shotgun. It stood upright, barrels propped against the wall in a nook probably intended for a stove or refrigerator.

He couldn't see the wife.

Ducking low, he made his way along the side of the building. He stepped around the corner and peered through a rear window.

The wife was at the other end of the kitchen, down on her knees, scrubbing the floor. She still wore her red shorts. But nothing else. Her back was arched. She held herself up with one hand and scrubbed with the other. Her breasts shook as she worked.

Jake suddenly felt like a voyeur.

He stepped away from the window, leaned back against the wall, and stared out at the dark field and nearby woods.

So much, he thought, for checking out the Smeltzers.

It was pretty obvious they weren't harboring his fugitive.

Whether or not they were safe—that was anyone's guess.

But they had chosen to assume the risk, and they'd at least taken the precaution of bringing a firearm. Jake had done his duty; he'd warned them, even snuck around here to check on them. He couldn't see himself knocking on the door to warn them again—especially not after spying the half-naked woman.

He had an urge to look again.

Don't be a jerk, Corey.

He headed away.

"Did you hear that?" Peggy asked.

"Hear what?"

"Turn off the damn radio."

Ron dragged the sponge mop behind him to the counter and silenced the radio.

Peggy let go of her scrub brush. She straightened up, wiped her wet hands on her shorts, and stared at him.

"I don't hear anything," he whispered. He looked frightened. His eyes were wide and his mouth hung open a bit.

A drop of sweat trickled down from Peggy's armpit. She brought her arm against her side and rubbed it away.

"Maybe you just imagined it," Ron said.

"I didn't imagine anything."

Ron's head swiveled, eyes darting from window to window.

"Not out there," Peggy told him. Raising her arm, she pointed at the closed door to the cellar.

The color went out of Ron's face. "You're kidding," he muttered.

In a harsh whisper, she said, "I heard something, damn it, and it came from there."

"Oh, shit."

"Don't just stand there, get the gun."

He looked over at it, then back to Peggy. "What *kind* of noise was it?"

"A thud, a thump, I don't know. For godsake, Ron . . ."

"Okay okay." He tiptoed across the kitchen, lifted the shotgun, and held it at his side, barrels pointing at the cellar door.

Peggy glanced sideways. Her wadded jersey was on top of the counter, just out of reach. Bare to the waist, she felt very vulnerable. She watched the cellar door and inched her way toward the counter on her knees. She realized that she was afraid to make any quick movements. She couldn't take her eyes off the door. Reaching up, she patted the counter until she touched the jersey. She pulled it down. Holding it at her belly, she gazed at the door and fingered the jersey until she found its opening. She slipped her hands through the armholes, raised her arms high, and let the jersey drift down. For a moment, it blinded her. She tugged it quickly down off her face.

Gripping the countertop with one hand, she stood up. "Let's get out of here."

"You mean leave?" Ron asked.

"Yes."

"You must be kidding." The tone of his voice pried Peggy's gaze off the cellar door. She looked at him. His face was still pale, but a corner of his mouth twitched as if he were working on a grin. "We haven't finished the floor," he mocked her.

"Ron."

"I really do think we owe it to ourselves to finish the floor, don't you? Otherwise, we'll have to get up at the crack of dawn and—"

"There is someone in the cellar!" she hissed.

"Look who's the chicken now."

"I never called you a chicken."

"Didn't you? Seems like you did. Or maybe I just imagined it."

"This is no time to be . . . let's just get out of here, okay?"

"You're going to let a little noise scare you off? After you dragged me back here?"

"You want to stay, stay. Give me the car keys."

"And what am I supposed to do, walk home? Spend the night? No thank you. I've got a better idea. I'll go down and search the cellar, and when I come up you'll apologize. You'll repeat after me, 'Ron is not a wimp or a coward.'"

"You're not a wimp, you're not a coward. Now let's go. Please!"

He smirked at her. Then he stepped boldly toward the cellar door, lowered the shotgun, and wrapped his left hand around the knob.

"You idiot!" Peggy rushed forward, ready to grab him and stop the craziness, but her bare foot hit a slick patch and her leg flew up. She landed hard on her rump.

The mockery left Ron's face. "Did you hurt yourself?"

"I'll live."

"Here." He searched a pocket of his jeans, pulled out his key case, and tossed it to her. It thumped and jangled, striking the floor between her knees. "Go ahead and wait in the car." He pulled open the cellar door. "I'll come and get you after I've checked it out."

"Don't go down there. I know, you think I'm nuts. You think it was just a mouse or a rat or some damn thing, but—"

"Right."

He flicked a light switch and started down the cellar stairs.

Peggy snatched up the key case. She clutched it tightly as she listened to Ron's feet on the wooden treads. Slowly, quietly, she gathered in her legs and pushed herself to her knees.

The sounds of Ron's descent stopped.

"Ron?" she called. He didn't answer.

Peggy got up. She crept to the doorway and looked down. The cellar was lighted, but she could only see a small area at the foot of the stairway. Ron wasn't there. "Are you all right?"

"Yeah, fine."

She leaned against the door frame. "Why don't you come up now?"

"Just a minute. Haven't been down here before. This is kind of . . . *SHIT!*"

The jolt of the outcry jerked Peggy rigid and knocked her breath out. Stiff in the doorway, she gazed down. The thought flashed through her mind that if she had to run, she wouldn't be able to.

She tried to call down to him. Her voice seemed frozen.

God, oh God, what had happened to him!

"Damn thing," Ron said.

She felt relief, but not enough. She still couldn't speak. She gasped for air.

Ron stepped into view at the bottom of the stairway. He smiled up at her, looking rather pleased. "You should've seen it. Scampered out of nowhere, right in front of me." He started to climb the stairs. "Biggest damn rat I ever saw. Of course, I must admit, I've never *seen* a rat before."

Peggy staggered backward. Away from the door. A hand pressed to her chest.

She stopped when her rump pushed against a counter. She cupped her hands over the counter's edge to brace herself up.

Ron reached the top of the stairs. He frowned. "Are you okay?"

She took a few deep breaths. "You . . . scared the hell out of me . . . yelling like that."

"Sorry. The thing gave me quite a start."

"A rat."

"A rat. Didn't I tell you there was nothing to worry about?" Ron smiled and raised the shotgun.

"Hey, don't fool around with . . ."

Jake Corey, hiking up the middle of the road, having called it a night and taking the easy way back to his car instead of trudging through the dark fields, heard a gunshot.

He whirled around and ran.

Aw Jesus.

I knew it.

Aw Jesus, I shouldn't have let them stay. I knew it I knew it was wrong I knew he was there I knew it I should've forced them to leave. Those goddamn idiots I warned them so what more could I do plenty that's what I could've made them leave. They knew what they were doing like hell they did. Thought it couldn't happen to them it's always somebody else well maybe Ronnie boy blasted the bastard and not the other way around fat chance I'll just bet one of them's deader than cold shit maybe both of them by the time I get there can't you goddamn it run any faster!

The restaurant was ahead of him, jarring in his vision as he sprinted for it.

Past the car.

Up the stairs three at a time, snapping open the holster and drawing his .38, still at full speed when his shoulder hit the door.

Wood splintered and burst and the door flew open.

Nobody.

He ran for the bat-wing doors.

He dove through the doors, tumbled into the kitchen, came up in a squat and took aim.

He didn't fire.

He didn't know what he was seeing.

The woman in the red shorts was sprawled on the floor, faceup. Faceup? She didn't have a face. A chin, maybe.

Ron was hunched over her, his face to her belly.

No one else in the kitchen.

The cellar door stood open.

"Ron? Ron, which way did he go?"

Ron lifted his head. A bleeding patch of his wife's flesh came with it, clamped in his teeth, stretching and tearing off. He sat up straight. He stared back at Jake. His eyes were calm. He calmly chewed. Then he reached back for the shotgun.

Jake Corey's bullets slammed him down.

Chapter Five

ALISON FILLED TWO PITCHERS WITH DRAFT BEER AND carried them to a booth crowded with Sigs. Two of the guys were seniors: Bing Talbot and Rusty Sims. She'd dated Bing a few times her freshman year. She'd been in classes with him and with Rusty, and knew they were with the Sigma Chi house. The other four packed into the booth were undoubtedly also frat brothers—they had that look about them.

They'd already killed two pitchers and six Gabby-burgers. They were still working on the chili fries.

Alison set the two full pitchers down on the table.

One of the younger Sigs waved at her. "Hey, hey!" He pointed at the name stitched on her blouse above her left breast. "Wha's 'at say?"

"Alison," she told him.

"Wha' d'ya call the other one?"

"Herbie," she answered.

He fell apart, giggling and slapping the table.

Alison started to turn away, but Bing caught her by the skirt. Stopping, she smiled down at him. "You want it? It'd look good on you."

"Wait, wait," he said as if he hadn't heard her.

The others had definitely heard her. They were yucking it up, hooting and whistling over the remark.

"Wait," Bing said again. He let go of her skirt. "What'd the waitress say when she was sitting on Pinocchio's face?"

"Lie! Lie!"

Bing slumped. "You heard it b'fore."

"How 'bout joining us?" suggested a skinny guy who was squeezed between two of the huskier frat brothers.

"Not enough room."

"You can sit on my lap."

"No, mine!"

"Mine!"

"We'll draw straws."

"I'm not allowed to fraternize with the customers," Alision said.

"Awwww."

"Frat-ernize," Rusty said.

"I geddit, I geddit!"

She back-stepped quickly as Bing made another grab for her skirt. "Enjoy, fellows," she said, and turned away.

"Ah, what a lovely derriere." The voice was wistful.

Yes, indeed, Alison thought. And it's about time to haul that derriere out of this joint. She checked the wall clock behind the counter. Two minutes till ten.

Eileen, behind the cash register, looked up as Alison approached. "You taking off?"

"Yep."

Eileen, who was wearing red beneath her tight uniform,

glanced over at the Sigs then back at Alison. She grinned. "At last, my chance at table six."

"Enjoy," Alison told her. She went into the kitchen, said good night to Gabby and Thelma, and picked up her flight bag. When she came out, Eileen was already on her way to table six.

She went to the rest room, intending to change into her street clothes, but the door was locked. With a shrug, she left. She didn't mind walking home in the uniform. At night, it didn't seem to matter so much.

She started down the sidewalk, coins from tips jangling in her apron pocket. After a few steps, she crouched, opened her flight bag, and took out her purse. She was transferring handfuls of change from her apron to a side pocket of the purse when someone approached.

And stopped in front of her.

She recognized the beat-up, ankle-high boots.

Her heart quickened.

She looked up at Evan.

"So," she said, "you came after all."

"I never said I wouldn't."

"I guess not." She finished emptying her apron, buckled down the purse flap, shut the purse inside her flight bag, and stood up.

"Can I carry that for you?"

"If you like."

She handed it to him. Evan pretended it was too heavy, gasped with surprise and staggered sideways. "Whoa! *Mucho* tips, huh?"

Alison found that she couldn't smile.

"Hard night?" he asked.

"Hard afternoon."

"Oh." He took her hand and they started walking. "Nobody came into the room, by the way. I stayed until after five."

"So it would've been perfectly all right, is that it?"

"Yeah. I knew it would be."

"Good for you."

"Hey, come one. We didn't do it, okay? You won. So what's the big deal?"

"No big deal," Alison muttered.

They waited at a street corner for the light to change, then started across.

"Am I some kind of creep because I wanted to make love with you?"

"Not exactly."

"Hell, we've done it in the park. Not just at night, either. What about Sunday afternoon?"

She remembered the bushes, the sunlight, the feel of the blanket, the feel of Evan. It seemed a long time ago.

"I don't happen to see the big difference," he said. "A park, a classroom."

They stepped onto the curb and started down the next block. They passed closed shops, a bar with the sounds of clacking pools balls and jukebox music drifting from the open door, more deserted stores.

"So what's the big difference?" Evan asked.

"There's not that much," Alison told him. "It doesn't have to do with that."

"You lost me."

"It doesn't have to do with the difference between the park and your classroom."

"I still don't get it."

She looked at him. He was frowning. "The thing is, you dumped on me."

"I see."

"It didn't bother me that you wanted to have sex. It was your reaction when I said no."

"Just because I wouldn't walk you to Gabby's?" He sounded as if he considered that a silly reason to be upset.

"Sort of," Alison said.

They reached the corner of Summer Street's intersection with Central Avenue. Evan's apartment was four blocks to the right, just off Summer. The house where Alison lived was straight ahead, two blocks past the end of the campus, on a road off Central. As she expected, Evan led her to the right.

She didn't resist.

Her heart pounded harder.

Earlier, she had made up her mind against going to his apartment tonight. She had doubted that he would meet her after work, anyway, but if he did come, she would simply have to tell him no.

That kind of decision was easy, she realized, with Evan nowhere around and the confrontation sometime in the vague future.

It wasn't so easy when the time came.

And it would get more difficult with every step. Before long, they would be at his apartment.

"Wait," she said. Stopping, she pulled her hand free.

Evan looked at her.

"I don't think so," she said.

"You don't think what?"

"Not tonight."

In the dim glow from the street lamp, she saw his brow crease. "You don't mean it."

"I mean it."

A side of his lip went up. He looked surprised, annoyed, disgusted—as if he had stepped on a mound of dog waste. "What is it with you?"

"I don't like what happened, that's all."

"Christ," he muttered.

"It changed things. It made me think. It made me wonder if all you really care about is the sex."

"That's crazy."

"I don't know—is it?"

"Of course."

"Then you won't mind too much if we . . . abstain."

"You don't want to make love tonight," he said quietly, as if explaining the situation to himself.

"It's not that I don't want to."

"But."

"But I won't."

"I didn't walk you to work, so now you're going to punish me by holding out."

"That isn't why."

"No? That's how it sounds."

"I'm 'holding out,' if you have to call it that, because I need to find out what's there—what's there without the sex. I mean . . ." Her throat tightened. "Do you drop me, or what?"

"Alison."

"Do you?"

Evan looked confused and hurt. Raising a hand to the side of her head, he gently stroked her hair. "You know better than that."

"I wish I did."

"I love you."

"Even without sex?"

"Of course. Come on now, let's go to my apartment and you'll see that I'm a marvel of restraint." He took her hand.

"No, not to your apartment. We both know what would happen."

"We'll just sit down and talk. On my honor." He smiled. "Unless, of course, you should happen to change your mind, in which case . . ."

"I'm going back to my place," Alison told him. "Are you coming?"

"You've got *roomies*."

She reached for her flight bag.

''Never mind, I'll come along. Can't have you wandering the streets alone—not with all these tips.''

The returned to the corner and crossed Summer Street.

''Another thing,'' Alison said.

''You mean there's more?''

''It's not just for tonight.''

''This celibacy kick?''

''It wouldn't mean anything, just one night.''

''Hey, it means a lot to *me*.''

''Obviously.''

''Come on, I'm just joking around.''

They walked in silence for a while. Finally, Evan asked, ''About how long do you have in mind?''

''I don't know.''

''A week, a month, sixty years?''

''It'll depend on how things go.''

''What, exactly, do you hope to accomplish by this little maneuver?''

''I thought I already explained that.''

''You want to see what sort of relationship we have without sex?''

''That's about it.''

Evan shook his head. ''Can't we vote on this?''

Encouraged by his light tone, Alison said. ''It doesn't have to be so bad. We'll still see each other. Won't we? You said . . .''

''We'll still see each other.''

''We'll find other things to do when we're together.''

''No more idiot box—no pun intended.''

''What do you mean?''

''One time in high school, my folks got the bright idea I was spending too much time in front of the idiot box—the television. They said there's more to life than watching

TV. So they cut me off. I was supposed to broaden my horizons and forget the tube."

"And did you?"

"Sort of. I read a lot of books. I played cards—solitaire. I spent more time on my homework. My grades improved. I did all kinds of stuff."

Alison smiled. "We can read to each other, play cards, study . . ."

"Strip poker?" He squeezed her hand. "There's a side effect that I haven't yet mentioned. I became obsessed with television. Whenever I could, I finagled my way over to friends' houses to watch theirs. And sometimes I even snuck downstairs after my folks were asleep. I'd turn on the TV in the family room and sit in the dark about a foot in front of the screen with the volume so low I could hardly hear the voice over that humming noise you get. It was pretty neat, actually. I was like a starving man at a feast."

"Stolen sweets."

"Precisely."

"And you think being deprived of sex will have a similar effect?"

"It's bound to."

"What are you going to do about it?"

"You don't leave me much alternative. I guess I'll just have to jack off with your yearbook pictures."

"Evan!" Laughing, she shoved her elbow into his ribs. He stumbled off the sidewalk.

"You got a better idea?" he asked.

"How about cold showers?"

"I hate cold showers." He took her hand again. "It is all right, I take it, to hold your hand?"

"Don't be silly."

"What about kissing?"

"We'll see."

"Ah, the prices we pay for our tactical errors."

At the south end of campus, they waited while a car approached on Spring Street. After it turned onto Central, they crossed. They walked past the root beer stand where Alison had first met Evan.

She remembered that rainy evening, standing at the counter while she waited for her order and hearing a voice behind her intone, "She walks in beauty like the night."

A glance back.

Evan Forbes gave her a smile.

"Talking to one's self is a sign of madness," she informed him.

"Ah, but I was talking to you. Is that also a sign of madness?"

"Could be."

She had seen Evan around campus, knew that he was one of the small cadre of graduate students in English, and had noticed the way he watched her the previous night when she'd served him at Gabby's.

She picked up her hamburger, fries, and root beer.

"Do you mind if I join you?"

"No, fine."

Evan followed her to a table.

"Aren't you going to order something?" she asked.

Shaking his head, he sat across from her and took one of her french fries. "I'll eat yours."

"Oh."

"As a matter of fact, I've already eaten. I spied you leaving the library and tailed you here."

She felt a blush warm her face. "That's a lot of trouble to mooch a french fry."

Remembering, Alison found herself smiling. "You ate *all* my fries," she said.

"Nerves. The fries kept me from biting my fingernails."

"Probably tasted better, too."

They crossed the railroad tracks, walked past the Laundromat where Alison took her dirty clothes once a week, and turned down Apple Lane. Professor Teal's house was third from the corner. Its porch light glowed, but the ground floor windows were dark. The front windows upstairs were bright, however, so Alison assumed that at least one of her roommates was in. Helen, probably. Celia would still be at Wally's, more than likely, raising hell and soaking up beer.

A wooden stairway angled up the side of the house to the upstairs door. The light above the door was off.

Evan stayed beside her on the walkway across the yard and remained at her side, though it meant walking on the dewy grass, as she followed the flagstones past the front of the house. They climbed the stairs together. At the top, he set down her flight bag.

"Are you going to ask me in?"

"I don't think so."

The quiet, mellow sound of a Lionel Richie song came from inside.

"One of your roomies is here to protect your virtue."

Alison squeezed his hand. "I'm tired. I just want to go to bed."

"Sans Evan."

"Will I see you tomorrow?"

He nodded. "What now? Am I allowed to kiss you good night?"

"I think that's allowed."

In the moonlight, she saw him smile. He lifted her hand to his mouth and kissed the back of it. "Until tomorrow, then." He released her hand and turned away.

"Evan."

He glanced around. "Yes?"

"Don't be this way," she murmured.

"Fare thee well, chaste maiden."

Alison leaned against the door frame and watched him descend the stairs. The planking creaked under his weight. At the bottom, he didn't turn to follow the flagstones, but headed straight across the lawn toward the sidewalk.

Alison yelled, "You snot!"

Then he was gone.

She unlocked the door. As she entered, Helen peeked out of her bedroom. "It's okay," Alison told her. "The coast is clear."

"What happened?" Obviously, she had heard the parting shout.

"A little disagreement."

"Little?" With a glass of cola in her hand and a bag of potato chips tucked between her arm and side, Helen went over to the recliner and sat down. She was wearing her bathrobe and sagging purple socks. "I heard you come up the stairs, so I made myself scarce. I thought you might bring him in."

"Nope." Alison set her flight bag on the coffee table. She sat on the sofa, kicked her shoes off, and swung her legs onto the cushions. Sitting down felt great. She sighed.

"Want a soda or something?"

"No thanks."

"Chips?" Helen lifted the bag. "They're sour cream and onion."

"I'm too upset to eat."

"That's when food is best. Fills up that empty feeling."

"If I ate every time I got upset . . ."

"You'd be a tub like me," Helen said, and poked a potato chip into her mouth.

Alison shook her head. "You're not so fat."

"I ain't skin and bones."

Helen might have been described as "pleasingly plump," Alison thought, if she'd had a cute face, but she didn't even have that going for her. She had a pasty complexion, a broad forehead, buggy eyes behind her huge round glasses, an upturned nose that presented a straight-on view into her nostrils, heavy lips, and a neck so thick that it enveloped whatever sunken chin she might have.

"So, you want to tell me about it?" Helen asked as she chewed.

"Evan's ticked at me because I wouldn't put out."

"Figures. He's a man. A man's an ambulating cock looking for a tight hole."

"Real nice, Helen."

"Real true. Take it from me."

"You've had some bad experiences."

"So you think I'm wrong?"

"I'd be hard-pressed to argue it," Alison said, "the way I'm feeling right now."

"I've never in my life been out with a guy who cared about anything but getting into my pants. Never. And that's saying something. I mean, take a look at me. You'd think they wouldn't want to touch me with a ten-foot pole. A six-inch pole, that's another story." She gasped a short laugh, blowing out a few crumbs of potato chips.

Alison had heard all this, and more, on numerous occasions during the time when she had been rooming with Helen. The young woman was bitter, and with good reason. She had been sexually used and abused by many men, including her stepfather.

Before meeting Helen, Alison had assumed that men would tend to stay clear of someone with Helen's looks. Not so.

If Helen understood why she was frequently targeted by men, she never let on. But she rarely dated anymore, so maybe she had reached the same conclusion as Alison; that the men saw her as easy prey—that anybody with a face and body like Helen's had to be hard up—that she would gladly spread her legs and be grateful for the attention.

"I take it back," Helen said after washing down a mouthful of potato chips with cola. "I did go out with a guy once who didn't try to make me. He turned out to be a homo."

"I want a man who will be my friend," Alison told her.

"Gotta find yourself a homo, then."

"But I like sex, too.'

"Then what's your beef with Evan?"

"It's turned into too big a deal. I don't want sex to be the only thing. Maybe not even the *main* thing."

"Yeah, you and me both. I used to think, if I could just find some guy who looked like he got beat over the head with an ugly stick. But that hasn't worked out, either. The ugly ones are just as messed up as the handsome ones—maybe even worse."

"The pits," Alison muttered.

"So did you and Evan break up, or what?"

"Not exactly. I just told him we need to abstain for a while and see how it goes."

"Oh, boy."

"Oh, boy?"

"I bet he wasn't too crazy about that idea."

"He didn't take it very well."

"Surprise, surprise."

"If he dumps me over something like this, I'm better off without him."

"Don't worry, he won't dump you."

"I don't know. He was acting . . . pretty spiteful."

"Sure. He was looking forward to some whoopy. Major disappointment, sob, sob. By tomorrow, though, he'll be telling himself you just had a bad night, and he'll be expecting you to come to your senses by the next time he sees you. He'll probably treat you extra nice, just to be on the safe side."

"He'll be in for another disappointment."

"How long are you planning to hold out?"

"Just long enough to see what happens."

"Know what I think?" Helen asked, brushing some crumbs off the front of her robe.

"What?"

"I think you've just had a bad night, and tomorrow you'll come to your senses and put out for the guy."

"You on his side?"

"I know you. You're angry at him right now, but anger has a way of softening pretty fast and you're an easy mark. First thing you know, you'll be feeling sorry for him—and feeling guilty because you're the reason he's so miserable. Then you'll do what's necessary to cheer him up. This time tomorrow night, you'll be in the sack with him."

"No way."

"You'll see."

Alison heard the faint, scuffing sound of footsteps. Someone was climbing the outside stairway. Very slowly. Helen stopped chewing and raised her thick eyebrows.

Alison's heart pounded hard. "Maybe it's Celia," she whispered.

Helen shook her head. "Try again. Wally's doesn't close till two."

"Oh, God. I don't need this."

"Want me to tell him you're in the shower, or something?"

The footsteps came to a stop on the landing just outside the door. "No, I'd better . . ."

A key snicked into the lock. Alison's stiff body relaxed, sinking back into the sofa. Mixed with her relief was a hint of disappointment.

Then Celia came in, and Alison jerked upright.

Celia's right arm was held across her chest by a sling. A bandage covered the right side of her forehead from her eyebrow to her hairline.

"Whoa," said Helen.

"What *happened*?" Alison asked.

"I got creamed, that's what." With her left hand, Celia swept the jacket off her shoulders. She dropped it, along with her purse, onto the floor beside the door. "Some bastard tried to turn me into a road pizza."

She limped toward the sofa, wobbling a bit, apparently not only injured but somewhat drunk. After easing herself down beside Alison, she carefully raised her legs onto the coffee table, stretched them out, and moaned.

"You and that stupid bike," Helen said. "I *told* you you'd get nailed."

"Take a leap."

"You were on your bike and a car hit you. Tell me that I'm wrong."

"How about getting me a drink?"

"Don't you think you've had enough?"

"It helps the pain."

"I'll get you something," Alison offered. "What do you want?"

"Anything but beer. I couldn't look another beer in the face. Bring me some whiskey, okay?"

Alison hurried into the kitchen. She grabbed a bottle of Irish whiskey from the cupboard, got a glass, and returned to the living room. She filled the glass halfway and handed it to Celia. "You're a bud," Celia said.

"How'd it happen?" Alison asked, sitting down again.

"Some bastard tried to run me down. I was over on Latham Road, you know? On my way back from Four Corners. And this van came down on me. The guy had all kinds of room to go around, but he steered right *at* me. He *intended* to hit me. Some kind of a nut. Anyhow, I tried to get out of his way and the bike flipped. That's how I got busted up.'' She sat up slightly, wincing, and took a drink. Then she settled back. She rested the glass on the lap of her sweatpants.

''He *intended* to hit you?'' Helen sounded skeptical.

''You bet your buns.''

''Why would someone—?'' Alison began.

''Cause he was a fuckhead, that's why. And no, I didn't flip him off. I didn't do *anything*.''

''I'll just bet,'' Helen said.

Celia glared at her. ''What's your problem, your vibrator go on the fritz?''

''Matter of fact—''

''Come on, Helen,'' Alison said. ''Lay off. She's hurt, for godsake.''

''I'm pulverized.'' Celia took another drink.

''Anything broken?'' Alison asked.

''No bones. I've got sprains, strains, contusions, abrasions, and general fucking mayhem from head to foot. I was in the emergency room about two hours. On the bright side, my doctor was a hunk. A guy that really enjoyed his job. He checked me out where I wasn't even hurt.''

''Every cloud has its silver lining,'' Helen said.

''Yeah. I'll probably be hearing from him.'' She lifted her glass, held it in front of her eyes, and stared at the amber liquid. ''You wanta hear the good part?'' she asked. From the tone of her voice, she didn't sound overjoyed by ''the good part.'' Helen frowned. Celia kept her eyes on the whiskey. Her jaw moved slightly from side to side, rubbing her lower lip across the edges of her teeth. ''The guy that did this to me . . . he bought the farm.''

''What?'' Alison asked. ''You mean he—?''

''Crumped, croaked, bit the big one. His van went onto the shoulder of the road after he tried to hit me, and plowed into the guard wall of a bridge. Killed him dead. Then he got his ass cooked.''

''Holy Jesus,'' Helen muttered.

''Served the bastard right,'' Celia said, and drank her glass empty. ''I didn't even know the guy. So what's he doing, trying to kill me? Huh? Can't even go riding my bike without some nut trying to murder me. Served him right. What'd he wanta do that for? He didn't even know me. But he sure paid. He paid. Wish I coulda seen the look on his face when he hit the wall. Boy, I bet he was surprised.'' She smiled and her chin trembled and she began to weep. She lowered the glass to her lap. It fell over. A few drops of whiskey trickled onto her sweatpants. Squeezing her eyes shut, she pressed her head back against the sofa cushion and sobbed.

Alison put a hand on Celia's thigh. ''It's all right,'' she whispered. ''It's all right.''

''Christ.'' Celia sniffed. ''The guy got cooked.''

Chapter Six

THE BUZZ OF THE ALARM CLOCK STARTLED JAKE OUT of sleep. He killed the noise and pushed himself up on one elbow. Ten o'clock. He'd slept for seven hours. So how come he felt like death warmed over?

Because of yesterday.

Groaning, he swung his legs off the bed, sat up, and rubbed his face.

Yesterday. One charbroiled man hanging out the windshield. One woman with pieces of her brain and skull clinging to the wall and spread around in clumps on the kitchen counter. One man munching on her flesh.

Jake felt sick, remembering.

Then his sickness changed to fear as his mind did a slow-motion replay of Smeltzer going for the shotgun. The patch of skin in Smeltzer's teeth flapped lazily, sprinkling blood, as he turned and reached. Jake thought, *He's going for it!* He thought, *This is it!* He fired, feeling the revolver jump, feeling the blasts slap his ears, smelling the pungent smoke, watching Smeltzer jerk each time a bullet kicked into him, saw again how one slug opened his throat and how he drifted backward, hosing Jake with blood, the skin still clamped in his teeth, his body twitching after he hit the floor, the blood raining down on him.

Jake took a deep, shaky breath, and got to his feet.

I had to do it, he told himself. I'd be dead if I hadn't dropped him.

It wasn't an excuse; it was the truth. And he had reminded himself of that truth so many times since last night that he was tired of it.

He went into the bathroom and turned on the shower.

Last night, the water going down the drain had been pink from Smeltzer's blood. He'd showered until the hot water ran out. Then he had waited half an hour, and taken a second shower. This would be number three.

He stepped under the hot spray and began to soap himself and saw Smeltzer look up at him, ripping a patch of flesh from the woman's belly. The flesh tore away and he started to turn. *He's going for it!*

"Turn it off!" he snapped. "We've seen it, we've seen it a hundred times, thank you very much. What is this, the goddamn network?"

Just what it's like, he thought. How many times had they shown the footage of Hinkley blasting away at Reagan, or the *Challenger* rising beautifully into the sky and blowing up? And each time they show it, you hope it'll be different this time, you hope they rewrote the script and Hinkley waves instead of shoots, and the *Challenger* makes it into orbit, and you go charging into the kitchen and Smeltzer and his wife are busy mopping the floor and they look at you as if you're nuts. But the script never changes.

Each replay is identical to the last one, no matter how hard you wish it different.

They aren't mopping. She's on the floor with just her chin on the end of her neck, and Smeltzer is down on her. *My God what is he doing!*

Oh, I do not need this not one little bit. It's my day off, how about my memory taking the day off, too? Pick up Kimmy in about an hour. That should help. A lot. Call Applegate first, though, find out when he'll be winding up the autopsy on Smeltzer—guy must've been drugged out, probably angel dust, which is about the only logical explanation for what he did. Eating her. Jesus! Had to be angel dust.

But how does angel dust connect with the van? The two incidents had to be related, somehow. Didn't they?

When he finished showering, Jake got dressed and made a cup of instant coffee. Then he dialed the morgue. "Betty? It's Jake."

"How you doing, fella?"

"Hanging in."

"I heard about last night. Pretty rough, I guess."

"I've had better times."

"I'm free tonight, just in case you could use a little loving."

"Thanks for the offer," he said. Betty's idea of a little loving was a lot of hard work. She was a twenty-two-year-old blonde beauty. She had been a champion gymnast in high school, and now her performances were confined to the bedroom. She was truly awesome. Jake's several encounters with her had been real adventures, but exhausting, and afterward he had always somehow regretted the time spent with her.

He was glad, now, that he had an honest excuse for avoiding Betty. "Afraid I can't, tonight. This is my weekend with Kimmy."

"Just let me know."

"I'll be sure to. Is Steve around?"

"He's out for the day."

"You're kidding."

"I wouldn't kid you, fella. He got a call first thing this morning from Dr. Willis—the coroner over in Marlowe? Willis wanted him to take a look at some stiff they turned up."

"We've got stiffs of our own."

"Willis and Steve are old pals. And Willis has a country club in his backyard. I think there was more to it than just a professional consultation. Steve took his golf clubs."

"Great. And tomorrow's Saturday."

"He told me you'd be calling. He said to tell you he'll be in tomorrow, for sure, and do his number on your guy first thing."

"Okay."

"You sure about tonight? What time does your kid hit the sack?"

"I wouldn't be much fun, anyway."

"Sure you would. But hey, it's up to you."

"I'll be in touch," he said. "Take it easy now."

"You, too, Jake."

He hung up.

Fifteen minutes later, he swung his car onto the circular driveway and stopped it behind a red Porsche with the cutesy license plate, BB'S TOY.

BB's toy would look best, Jake thought, wrapped around a tree. Then he felt guilty. After all, she was Kimmy's mother. Kimmy loved her. Poor taste on the kid's part, but you love the mother you get, even if she is a slut.

His chest felt tight, his mouth dry, as he stepped onto the front stoop and pressed the doorbell. From inside came the faint sound of chimes playing the opening bars of Beethoven's Fifth.

Harold Standish opened the door, stepped back, raised his hands high and said, "Don't shoot."

Jake stared at him. The man's routine hadn't been amusing the first time he pulled it, over a year ago. It had become less amusing with each repetition. This morning, it gave Jake an urge to tear off Harold's trim little mustache.

"Just pulling your leg, Jako. Come on in. The little woman's getting the Kimmer ready for her big day."

Jake stepped onto the marble foyer.

Harold headed for the living room, walking sideways and smiling, keeping his eyes on Jake—apparently afraid to turn his back. Jake had never spoken a sharp word to the man, had certainly never threatened or assaulted him. But Harold knew what he had done. And, quite obviously, he knew what he deserved.

What Harold did not know was that Jake had never blamed him for the situation. It might have been different if he'd seduced Barbara with good looks and charm, but Harold was a skinny guy with a receding hairline, a nose like a turkey's beak, and all the charm of a field mouse. He was a wimp. A wimp who made big bucks filling teeth. And Barbara, not Harold, had been the seducer.

She hadn't dumped Jake for a man. She'd dumped him for a handsome bank balance and plastic cards with dreamy credit lines. Harold was a piece of excess baggage that came along with the good stuff.

If it hadn't been Harold, it would've been someone else.

Barbara was the one who deserved . . .

"Could I get you some coffee, a sweet roll?" Harold asked.

"No thanks."

Harold sat on a recliner, but didn't settle back. He stayed on the edge of the seat as if ready to rush off, and cupped his hands over his knees. "So," he said.

Jake sat on the sofa.

"So, how are things in law enforcement business? Keeping the criminals in line?"

"We try." Apparently, Harold hadn't heard about last night. That was fine with Jake.

Harold nodded as if pondering the response. He gazed at the floor. He seemed nervous about the silence. Afraid Jake might take the opportunity to bring up an unpleasant topic, such as adultery? Ah, he must've thought of something. His eyebrows lifted and he looked at Jake. "How do you feel about the handgun initiative?"

"I'm against it."

"One would think that a man in your line of work, who sees the tragedies caused by private ownership of guns—"

"We had a seventy-two-year-old widow, last month, who woke up to find a stranger in her bedroom with a knife in one hand and a hard-on in the other. She shot him four times with a pistol she kept on her nightstand. Me, I'm glad she had the gun."

"But statistics show—"

"Save it, Harold. You want the bad guys to win, that's *your* business."

Harold dared a condescending smile. With a shake of his head, he stood up. "I'll see what's keeping the ladies," he said, and backed out of the living room.

He was no sooner gone than Barbara came in.

"Tag team?" Jake asked. He felt sick. He always felt sick when he saw her, but this morning was worse than usual because of what she wore.

"Kimmy's almost ready," she said.

"Fine," he muttered, staring at Barbara and wondering what the hell she was trying to do.

She wore a blue silk kimono. Its front was open, showing a long V of bare skin all the way down to the sash at her waist. The glossy fabric shimmered from the motion of her breasts. Turning away from Jake, she crossed the living room. The kimono was very short. At the far side of the draperies, she reached high to pull the draw cord and the garment lifted above the pale curves of her buttocks. The draperies skidded open. She lowered her arms, and the fabric drifted down.

"Real cute," Jake said.

Whirling around, she glared at him.

Jake smiled. His mouth felt rigid. His chest ached.

"Problem?" she said.

His smile died. "You're some piece of work, woman."

"You better believe it."

"What're you trying to pull?"

"I'm not trying to pull a thing, darling. Do I take it that you don't approve of my attire? It's an early birthday present from Harold. Isn't it heavenly? And it *feels* so scrumptious." Staring at Jake, she smiled lazily and half shut her eyes. Her hands started high and glided downward, caressing the kimono, rubbing the fabric against her breasts. "Scrumptious," she whispered.

"If only Harold could see you now."

"So what if he did." She squirmed slightly as she rubbed her breasts. Her motions had loosened the front of her kimono, widening the opening. It was open all the way down.

"For godsake!" Jake snapped in a hushed voice.

She smirked. "Turning you on?"

"I get turned on better scraping dog shit off my boot."

Barbara's eyes went wide. Her face colored. Her back went stiff. She tugged the kimono shut. "You bastard." Her voice trembled when she said it. Her chin started to shake.

Astonished, Jake realized she was about to cry.

She pivoted away from him. "Kimmy!" she shouted. "Get your ass down here!"

"Barbara!" Jake snapped.

"Fuck you." She hurried from the room.

Jake stayed on the sofa, stunned and angry and confused. What the hell had just happened?

Normally, when he came to pick up Kimmy, Barbara acted as if he were a visiting peasant: haughty, sarcastic, delighted by the opportunity to rub his nose in the lifestyle she had achieved by dumping him for Harold.

What was this, today?

Acting like that with Kimmy and Harold in the house.

Harold had to know she was dressed that way.

What was she trying to prove?

That's pretty obvious, he thought. She was trying to prove she could turn me on.

Look how she flew apart when I put her down.

The gal's got a major-league problem.

Off the deep end, or she wouldn't be pulling that kind of stunt.

Troubles with Harold?

Oh, wouldn't that be a shame.

Golly, I'm so sorry. It breaks my heart, you slut.

The harsh thoughts made Jake feel a little guilty. He told himself that he had loved her once, that it was wrong to wish misery on her.

What about Kimmy? If Barbara and Harold were having problems, she could certainly be affected. He didn't want that. If Kimmy had to live with her mother—and there was no real alternative as long as Jake remained unmarried—then he wanted her to be in a home where there was love and happiness.

The situation was only tolerable as long as he could be sure that Barbara was taking good care of her. If this morning was any indication, however, Barbara was losing her grip.

Maybe it's nothing, he told himself. Just a fleeting aberration. Tomorrow's Barbara's birthday. She would only be twenty-seven, but he remembered her saying, when she hit twenty-one, that it was all downhill from there. She apparently believed it, too. Each year, after that, she had fallen into a pit of depression around birthday time.

That must be it, he decided.

Flaunts her stuff in front of her ex-husband to prove to herself that she's still got something to flaunt.

And he smashes her down.

Shit.

At least it was good to know that her bizarre behavior was nothing more serious than the birthday blues.

If that's what it was.

"Hi, Daddy!"

He stood up, suddenly feeling good as Kimmy came toward him, smiling. As always, after going days without seeing her, he was amazed by her beauty. A gorgeous four-year-old kid with big blue eyes and a great smile, she couldn't go anywhere without people taking a second look.

Harold stood in the entryway, holding her overnight bag. Kimmy had Clew, her tiny stuffed kitten, clutched in one hand. She raised her arms, and Jake picked her up and kissed her. "How's my baby?" he asked.

"I'm not a baby, I'm a little girl."

"Oh, well excuuuuuse me."

Leaning back and grinning, she poked a finger against a button of Jake's shirt. "You have a spill, Daddy."

"I do?" He looked down.

Kimmy darted her finger up and poked his nose.

"Oow! Y'got me!"

Laughing, she sucked on her forefinger. Her eyes were eager with mischief. A Wet Willy was on its way.

"Oh, no, you don't," Jake said, forcing her away before she could twist the wet finger in his ear. She giggled and tried to hold on, but he freed himself and put her down.

Not in front of Harold, he thought.

Then he wondered, with a tug of pain, if she ever gave Wet Willies to Harold.

"Let's get the show on the road," he said.

He reached down his hand. Kimmy took a firm grip on his forefinger and led the way.

"You two have a good time," Harold said as they approached him. He gave the overnight bag to Jake. His smile looked strained. "You'll have her back tomorrow?"

Jake nodded.

They left. It was good to get out of the house. He smiled down at Kimmy.

Her smile was gone. "Don't I get to stay by you tomorrow?"

"Not this time. Tomorrow's Mommy's birthday."

"I know that." She gave him an annoyed look. She did not approve, at all, of being told what she already knew. Clearly demeaning.

"Well, you want to be there for her party, don't you?"

"I s'pose."

"It'll be fun."

He opened the passenger door for Kimmy, and lifted her onto the safety seat. While he strapped her in, she tucked Clew into the top of her bib overalls so the tiny gray head poked out like a kangaroo in its mother's pouch.

Then she stuck her forefinger into her mouth.

"Oh, no, you don't!"

"Yes, I do!"

Jake grabbed her wrist, but let himself be overpowered. The wet fingertip pushed into his ear and twisted. "Eaah!

You got me!'' Before she could get him again, he ducked out of the car.

He hurried around and climbed in behind the steering wheel. Kimmy was ready to bestow another Wet Willy. She strained to reach him, but it was no good.

''Saved by the car seat,'' he said.

''C'mere.''

''Not a chance. Think I'm dumb?''

''Uh-huh,'' she said, nodding.

''Wiseacre,'' He pulled into the street. ''So, what would you like to do today?''

''Go to the moojies.''

''The moojies it is. Anything special you want to see?''

She made an eager face with her eyes wide and her brows high. ''*Peter Pan*.''

''We saw *Peter Pan* last week.''

''I really want to see *Peter Pan* again.''

''Sure, why not. Maybe this time the crock will gobble up Captain Hook . . .''

Gobble up.

Ronald Smeltzer.

Could've gone all day without thinking about that.

''Can we eat at McDonalds?''

''No.''

''Daddy!'' She shook her fist at him, grinning over the tiny knuckles.

''Well, if you insist.''

''Daddy, can I talk to you?''

''Sure. Isn't that what we've been doing?''

She braced an elbow on the padded armrest of her seat, and leaned toward him. She looked serious. ''There isn't any such thing as crocodiles, is there?''

''What makes you think that?''

''Well, because it's just a moojie.''

''That doesn't mean they don't exist.''

"Dracula and werewoofs and the mummy aren't really real, you said so, so crocodiles aren't really real, are they?"

"Gotcha worried, has it?"

"This is not funny."

"Crocks are real, but I wouldn't worry about them."

"I do not want to get eaten."

Jake felt as if he'd been kicked in the stomach. "Well, you'll just have to keep your eyes open. If you see a crock waddling your way, toss it a Twinkie and run. It'd much rather eat Twinkies than you."

"I'm not so sure."

Chapter Seven

WITH A FRESH CUP OF COFFEE, DANA NORRIS RETURNED to her table in a corner of the student union. She read the poem again, wrinkled her nose, and sighed.

Why couldn't this guy write stuff that made sense?

"Salutations."

She looked up and found Roland standing in front of her table.

Roland the Retard.

He wasn't actually retarded—brainy, in fact, but nobody would guess that by looking at him.

His black, slicked down hair was parted in the middle like Alfalfa of the old Our Gang films. The style, he liked to explain, was his tribute to Zacherle, who used to host a late-night horror show on television.

Today, he was wearing a bright plaid sport jacket and one of his assorted gore-shirts. The skin colored T-shirt featured a slash wound down its midsection and a bright array of blood and guts spilling out.

"May I join you?" he asked.

"I'm trying to study."

Nodding, he pulled out an orange, molded-plastic chair and sat across the table from her.

Dana looked down at her book. "What the hell is a force in a green fuse?"

"Sounds like a slimy wick to me."

"You're a big help."

Roland leaned forward, elbows on the table. "Did you hear what happened out at the Oakwood Inn?"

"Why don't you go away and get yourself something to eat. You look like—"

"A cadaver?" he suggested.

"Exactly."

"Thank you." He grinned. His big, crooked teeth looked like a plastic set you might buy at a gag shop the day before Halloween.

Dana didn't know how Jason could stand to room with this guy, much less be friends with him.

"So," he said, "I guess you didn't hear."

"Hear what?"

"About the massacre."

"Ah. A massacre. That explains the gleam in your eyes."

"It happened right outside town. There's that old restaurant, the Oakwood Inn. This couple came up from LA planning to open it again. The place had been closed for years—apparently shut down after several of the patrons turned toes up when they ate there. Food poisoning." Roland wiggled his thin black eyebrows. He looked absolutely delighted. "So last night they were in the place fixing it up and the husband went totally berserk and blew off his wife's head with a shotgun. Then a cop showed up and blew away the husband."

"Just your cup of tea," Dana said.

"Outrageous, huh?"

"Too bad you couldn't have been there to enjoy it."

"Yeah, well, those are the breaks. I drove out there this morning, but the cops have it all blocked off." He shrugged. "The stiffs were probably gone by then, anyway."

"More than likely."

"I sure would've like to get a look inside, though. I mean, maybe it hadn't been cleaned up yet. Can you feature the mess it must've made, a gal catching a twelve gauge in the face? Pieces of her brain and skull sticking to the walls . . ."

"You're revolting."

"Anyway, I thought I'd go back later. Maybe the cops'll be gone by then. Do you mind if I borrow your Polaroid?"

Dana stared at him. She felt a rush of heat to her face. "What makes you think I've got a Polaroid?"

"I just know. How about it?"

"That shit. He showed you the pictures, didn't he."

"Sure. We're roomies."

Her mouth was dry. She lifted her coffee mug with a shaky hand and took a drink. She should've known that Jason wouldn't keep his word. Who else had he shown them to? Everyone in the dorm? She'd wanted to burn the things, but Jason had promised he would hide them, never show them to another soul.

She could just see Roland the Retard drooling over them.

"How about it?" he asked. "Can I borrow the camera?"

"I'm gonna kill that shit-head."

Roland giggled. "If you do, let me watch."

On second thought, Roland probably hadn't drooled—

probably he hadn't even found the photos particularly interesting, since they showed no entrails or severed limbs. Unless he supplied all that with his sick imagination, which seemed more than likely.

"Have you seen a shrink about this problem of yours?" Dana asked.

"A shrink? A *head* shrinker? Do you know how they do that, by the way? First, they split the scalp so they can peel it off the skull, then—"

"Knock it off."

Roland's mouth snapped shut.

"What is it with you? I know you're Jason's roommate and buddy and I'm supposed to be nice to you and treat you like a human being, but he's not here, so forget that shit. What is it with you, huh? I'm curious. Either you're totally deranged, which I doubt, or this whole obsession with blood and guts is some kind of game. If it's a game, it's something you should have outgrown at least five years ago."

During her outburst, Roland had taken his elbows off the table and pressed himself into his chair. He looked stunned. His tiny eyes were wide open, his jaw hanging down.

"Do you know *why* you're this way?" Dana continued. "Well, I've got an idea on that subject. It boils down to this—you're scared."

Roland glanced over his shoulder, apparently to see who might be within earshot. Nobody was at the nearby tables.

"You're scared that nobody will know you exist if you don't go around acting like a weirdo. This way, people notice you. They don't *like* what they notice, but they do notice you. That's number one. Number two is, you latched onto this blood and guts crap because it makes a joke out of what scares you more than anything—death.

You make a mockery out of pain and death to keep it from being real, because the real thing has you terrified.''

Dana stopped. She leaned back in her chair, folded her arms beneath her breasts, and glared at him.

''You're crazy,'' he muttered.

''People were really truly killed out at that restaurant last night,'' she said, forcing herself to speak in a calm voice. ''It was real—if what you told me is true.''

''Yeah, it—''

''Real, Roland. Not one of those splatter movies you love so dearly. And it's got you scared pissless, so you have to defend your fragile psyche by trivializing it.''

''You're a regular Sigmund Freud.''

''The truth is, you probably drove out there in the full expectation that you'd be turned away by the cops. You knew you wouldn't get to see the bodies or the brains sticking to the walls. The only reason you went out there was so you could brag about it. If you make it part of your weird-guy act and it gets you attention, it isn't so real anymore, isn't so scary.''

''That's not true.''

''You creep, you're scared of your own shadow.''

''I am not. I *wanted* to see the bodies. It's not my fault the—''

''A coward, Roland. You're a coward.''

''I would've gone in if—''

''Sure. If the cops hadn't shooed you off. I'll bet. As a matter of fact, I *will* bet. A hundred bucks. Imagine the neat T-shirts and masks you could buy with a hundred bucks.''

A corner of Roland's mouth curled up. ''You're betting me a hundred dollars I won't go inside the restaurant?''

''I sure am.''

''You're nuts.''

''Have you got a hundred to put against mine?''

Roland hesitated.

"Didn't think so."

"That's a pile of money."

"I've got a deal for you. If you lose, you don't have to pay me a cent. But you drop this gore crap. You stop wearing those stupid T-shirts and start acting like a human."

He frowned. "I don't know. That's—"

"Trying to worm out?"

"No."

"How about it?"

"All I have to do, to win, is go inside the restaurant?"

"At night," Dana added.

"No sweat."

"You go in tonight, and you stay *all* night. Alone."

His smiled started to slip.

"As for my Polaroid, you may take it along."

"How are you going to know if I stay all night? I mean, I could sneak out. Not that I *would*, but—"

"I'll be right outside in my car. And who knows, maybe I'll come in to check on you from time to time just to make sure you're still there."

"You've got a deal."

"I'll pick you up at nine behind your dorm."

Chapter Eight

"SO MAYBE I WAS WRONG," HELEN SAID.

"Huh?" Alison asked.

"You haven't given *King Lear* a glance in the past half hour, just been staring at the phone."

"I thought he might call," she said.

"So did I. Maybe we misjudged him. I figured he'd make a grand play for you, but . . ."

"I think his grand play is to ignore me."

Celia, lying on the sofa, pulled the stereo headphones off her ears and said, "Am I missing something?"

"Alison's getting anxious."

"So call the guy," she advised.

"I can't do that."

"She can't do that," Helen repeated. "She's laid down the terms. The next move is up to Evan."

Groaning, Celia eased her feet off the sofa and sat up.

"You don't want to just sit around all day hoping he'll call," she told Alison. "You need to do something to take your mind off him. I need to get out, myself."

"Try going to your two o'clock," Helen said.

"That seminar's the shits. Besides, it's been three weeks since my last cut. I need a break. Especially after yesterday."

"We *told* you you'd be sorry," Helen said, "signing up for a Friday afternoon class."

"Take a hike." She looked at Alison. "How about we go over to the mall?"

Alison liked the idea. "Are you up to something like that?"

"A walk'll do me good, get the kinks out."

"How about it, Helen?" Alison asked. "Want to come along?"

"Nah."

"Come on," Alison urged her. "You're turning into a hermit."

"I had three damn classes this morning. How does that make me a hermit?" She got up and went to the window. "Anyway, it's going to rain."

"What's a little rain," Alison said.

"Besides, I'd have to change back into something."

"Aw, go as you are," Celia told her.

Helen turned around and looked down at herself as if considering Celia's suggestion. She was wearing a housedress that looked like an old tablecloth, complete with food stains. She fastened a snap that had come loose between her heavy breasts. "I guess, if I keep my raincoat on . . ."

"Get serious," Celia said.

"I'll just stay here."

"No, come on," Alison said. "You don't want to spend all afternoon cooped up in the house. If you wear your raincoat, nobody'll know what you've got on. The dress isn't so bad, anyway."

Helen looked at Celia.

"I don't care. Wear whatever you want. Let's just get going."

"I'll just be a minute," Alison said.

As she headed for the hallway, she heard Celia say, "For godsake, at least put on some underpants. You fall on your ass, you'll be flashing beaver."

Helen's response, if any, was inaudible.

Smiling, Alison began to climb the stairs to her attic room. The staircase had barely enough light to see the steps, so she ran her hand along the banister as she hurried to the top. Her room was not much brighter than the staircase. Not bothering with a lamp, she stepped over to the single window and looked out.

Pretty gloomy out there, all right. A storm was certainly on the way, but she guessed that it might hold off for a while.

It'll probably start up, she thought, just in time to catch me walking to Gabby's.

She could get a ride from Evan. He'd be glad to . . .

She remembered. The hollow ache came back.

What have I done?

It's okay, she told herself. It's okay. If he's through with me over something like this, fine.

She crossed the small room to her dresser and took out her blue jumpsuit. The one-piece, velour outfit would feel soft and cozy, perfect for this kind of weather. Getting into it would be the problem. She had turned the heater off before leaving for her morning classes, and the room was chilly.

As fast as she could, she jerked her flannel shirt over her head, flipped off her slippers, tugged her jeans down her legs, kicked the jeans away, stepped into the jumpsuit and pulled it up. Shivering, she thrust her arms into its sleeves. She raised the zipper to her neck, and sighed with relief as the chill was shut out.

Quickly, she put on a pair of wool socks and stepped into her sneakers. Then, she snatched her windbreaker from the closet, grabbed the strap of her shoulder bag, and hurried downstairs.

Helen, waiting in her sou'wester and boots, looked ready for a typhoon.

"Ahoy," Alison said.

"We're *waiting* for you, Celia!" Helen called from somewhere inside her rain gear.

"Patience," Celia called from her room. "I'm a crip, remember?" A few moments passed, and she came out clutching a snap-brim cap in her teeth while she adjusted her sling. She had changed into a bulky, cable-knit pull-over that she'd bought on a trip to Ireland. Her pants were loose-fitting corduroys with deep pockets, cuffs tucked into snakeskin boots.

"You look smashing," Alison told her.

"Smashed up is more like it," she said, taking the cap from her teeth and flipping it onto her head at a rakish angle.

"Where's your raincoat?" Helen asked.

"My raincoat is a poncho. I'm not gonna fool with it."

"You'll get soaked."

"If it rains, which I doubt, you'll stay dry enough for the three of us."

A cool wind hit Alison when she opened the door. She fastened the snaps of her jacket. Halfway down the stairs, she looked back. Celia was using her good hand to keep the cap on her head. "Are you going to be warm enough?"

"You kidding? This is an Aran sweater."

"Whatever you say."

Helen, higher on the stairs, turned up the broad brim of

her rain hat. Her face appeared, and she smiled as if pleasantly surprised to find herself in the company of others.

Three steps from the bottom, Alison leaped. Her bent knees absorbed the impact.

"Gimme a break," Celia called.

Grinning, Alison walked backward. "This is neat weather," she said. "Invig—"

"L'gout, now."

Something prodded her spine.

Celia started to laugh.

Whirling around, Alison found a knotty cane leveled at her belly. At the cane's other end stood Dr. Teal, a grocery bag in his free hand. He swung the cane back, resting it on his shoulder. As he looked at the three, his eyebrows lifted, crinkling his brow. "Setting out, I see. A fine day for an excursion."

"A blustery day," Alison told him. He was a man who appreciated allusions.

"Keep a sharp eye out for Eeyore's tail," he said.

"Want a hand with the groceries?" Alison asked.

"Thanks for the offer, but I must not keep you from your expedition. Proceed!" He stepped off the cobblestones into the wind-bent grass, and made a sweeping gesture with his cane.

Alison stepped past him and turned around. Celia tipped her cap to the professor.

"You, my dear, have looked better."

"I got a little banged up."

"I'm very sorry to hear it."

"You oughta see the other guy."

Shaking his head, the old professor patted her gently on the shoulder as she stepped by.

"Say-hay," Helen greeted him.

"Say-hay." He leaned close to her and said something Alison couldn't hear. Then he walked around the stairway, stopped at his side door, and propped his cane against the wall.

Alison walked a little farther, then waited for the others to catch up. "What'd he say?" she asked Helen.

"I don't know, some nonsense. That guy's battier every time I see him."

"But what did he say?" Alison persisted.

" 'Let the albatross live.' Whatever that's supposed to mean."

"I think," said Alison, "he was saying he liked your outfit."

As she reached the sidewalk, she saw a man on the next block. He was leaning into the wind, clutching his tan jacket shut. He had light brown hair like Evan. Alison felt her heart quicken. She squinted, trying to see him better.

They'll just have to go on without me, she thought. They'll understand.

He's come back to me. In spite of my ultimatum.

She'd almost given up hoping, but Evan must've decided to try the new arrangement.

She was glad she was wearing the jumpsuit. Of all her outfits, it was Evan's favorite. The zipper down the front drove him wild.

As she walked toward him, she popped open the snaps of her windbreaker and lowered the jumpsuit zipper a few inches.

She could take him to the house. It would be warm and cozy, and they would have the place all to themselves until Celia and Helen got back.

Not such a great idea, she thought. It'd be asking for trouble.

On the other hand, it would be a good test. If Evan could resist temptation under those circumstances . . .

The man was closer, now.

He didn't look so much like Evan, anymore.

He turned away at the corner, and his profile was all wrong—his nose too long, his chin too weak.

"That guy looked a little like Evan," Celia said.

Alison shrugged. She felt cheated and empty. "Evan can take a flying leap," she muttered.

The warmth of the enclosed shopping mall felt good. Alison's windbreaker was light enough so that she wasn't bothered by keeping it on, but she pitied Helen. The poor gal had to feel stifled under the heavy raincoat.

Don't feel too sorry for her, Alison thought. She could've put on decent clothes if she hadn't been so lazy.

The three wandered along the concourse, close to the left side. While Celia and Helen looked into shops, Alison scanned the other shoppers. Many of them were students. One of them might be Evan.

At Contempo Casuals, Celia stopped and gazed at the mannequins near the entrance. "I want to check it out," she said, and they entered.

Helen took off her huge, floppy hat. Her round face looked moist and florid. She opened the top buckle of her coat.

"Better stop there," Celia warned. "They'll sound the slob alarm."

"Eat it," Helen said. But she left the lower buckles alone.

They followed Celia to the rear of the store, where she began looking at negligees.

"You're not getting *another*," Helen said.

"Oh no?"

"What've you got, twenty of them? And at the rate you go through guys, none of them gets a chance to see more than one, anyway."

"Jealous?"

Helen just shook her head.

Celia took her time studying the selection, lifting various garments on their hangers and inspecting them, pondering, putting them back. She went about the task one-handed, so after a while Alison began to help by returning the rejected garments to the crowded racks. At last, Celia found one she seemed to like. She turned to Alison, holding it up. "What do you think?"

It was a backless nightie, very short, of glossy royal blue. It had spaghetti straps which tied at the back of the neck, and an open, plunging front. The cups were wisps of blue gauze.

"Figures you'd pick a thing like that," Helen said.

"Looks fine to me." Alison wondered if there was another one just like it. If Evan saw her in something like that . . .

Forget him.

"I wouldn't get it," Helen said.

"Of *course* you wouldn't."

With one side of her lip curled up, Helen flicked the sheer gauze. "You don't want that. And I'm not talking modesty here. I realize you're far beyond such things."

"Then what *are* you talking about?"

"That color. It'll make your titties look sick. You want to look like you've got blue boobs and purple nips?"

Celia raised her eyebrows. She looked at Alison.

"I hadn't thought of that," Alison admitted.

"See if they've got the same thing in black," Helen suggested.

"Good idea." She smiled. "Thanks."

"Though, if you ask me, you'd be better off putting your money in potato chips."

Alison held the blue nightie until Celia, searching the rack, came up with a black one in the same style. "Great," Celia said. "Perfect."

Alison hooked the hanger over the rail, then unhooked

it and looked again at the garment. The blue was deep, bright, and shiny. She caressed the fabric. It felt slick, and clung to her hand. She wondered how it would feel on her, how it would look. She had never owned anything like this. She raised her eyes. Celia and Helen were both staring at her. She grinned.

''Blue boobs,'' Helen warned.

''I can live with it,'' she said.

Celia grinned. ''A little something just in case Evan comes through?''

''What happened to your vow of chastity?'' Helen asked.

''This has nothing to do with it,'' Alison said.

''Oh, no?''

As they left the shop with their purchases, Alison offered to carry Celia's bag.

''Yeah,'' Helen said. ''Take it off her hands. Something like that, it must weigh a ton.''

''Maybe you should've bought one,'' Celia told her.

''Ready to go?'' Helen asked, ignoring the remark.

''We just got here.''

She curled her upper lip. There were sparkles of sweat above it. She had to be suffering, Alison thought, trapped inside that heavy raincoat.

''Maybe we should go,'' Alison said.

''I just want to be fair to you guys,'' Celia explained. ''Poor Helen needs to ogle the puppies and hit the doughnut shop, and you want to check out the bookstore, don't you?''

''It doesn't matter,'' Alison told her. ''I think one of us is melting.''

''I'm all right,'' Helen said, though clearly she wasn't.

Celia grinned. ''That perked you up—doughnuts, maple bars, bear claws, chocolate eclairs . . .''

''I could sure use a soda,'' she admitted.

With Helen in the lead, they headed across the concourse toward the wing of the mall where the food stands were located.

"Salutations," someone said from behind them.

They turned around.

It was the weird kid. Though Alison didn't know his name and had never spoken with him, she had noticed him around the campus. He was impossible not to notice, the strange clothes he wore and the way he parted his hair in the middle. Right now, he was wearing a garish sport jacket and a T-shirt with a gash spilling blood and entrails printed on its front. He was clutching a bag from Spartan Sporting Goods.

"You're Celia Jamerson, right?" he asked. "I saw you in *The Glass Menagerie*. You were great."

"Thanks," Celia said.

"You probably don't remember me."

"You're Jason's friend, aren't you?"

He grinned, his thin lips stretching away from big, crooked teeth. "I'm his roommate, Roland. Anyway, I was just wondering if you're okay. What happened, were you in an accident?"

"I had a little mishap on my bike."

"Gosh, I'm sorry." His gaze traveled sideways to Alison and slid down her body, then returned to Celia. "I hope it wasn't serious," he said.

"Well, thank you. I'll be all right. How's Jason?"

"Oh, he's fine. He'll be trying out for the spring play. I know he's hoping you'll be in it."

"I don't know. Auditions are next week. I'm pretty banged up."

"That's awful." He looked again at Alison. She felt an urge to pull her jacket shut. "Anyway, I'd better get going. Hope you're feeling better."

"Thanks," Celia said. "See you around."

He turned and walked away.

Alison realized she had been holding her breath as if afraid of inhaling a disease.

"What a dream boat," Helen said.

"A nightmare boat," Alison muttered. "I feel like I need a bath."

"He sure looked us over."

Alison hadn't seen him looking Helen over, but she kept her mouth shut.

Celia shrugged. "It was nice of him to be concerned about me."

"Play your cards right," Helen told her, "maybe he'll ask you out. How'd you like to model your new nightie for him?"

"Gimme a break."

With Helen in the lead, they walked toward the food area. Alison still felt a little squirmy. Though there wasn't much similarity between them, Roland somehow reminded her of Prince Charming, the crazed, filthy man she'd seen yesterday afternoon at Gabby's.

They stopped at one of the refreshment stands. Helen ordered a drink and a hot dog. Alison and Celia each ordered sodas. They found a vacant table in the middle of the concourse and sat down.

Poking her straw through the plastic lid of her drink, Alison could almost see Roland leering at her. "What a creep," she muttered.

"He gives new meaning," said Helen, "to the expression 'nasty slimy yuck.' "

Celia grinned. "Yeah, but his roomy's not half bad."

"He the guy who played the gentleman caller?" Alison asked.

"That's the one."

"If he's so wonderful," Helen asked, squeezing a thick

trail of mustard across her hot dog, "how come you haven't added him to your list?"

"For godsake, he's a *freshman*."

"Shouldn't let a little thing like that stop you."

"You kidding? I'd never live it down, it got around I was seeing a frosh. Besides, he's already going with some gal."

"So," Helen said, "it's not that he's a freshman. Just that somebody else has dibs on him."

"Gimme a break. He'd drop her like a hot spud if I gave him the ol' look."

Helen took a big bite out of her hot dog. Mustard dribbled down her chin. Wiping the mustard off with the back of a hand, she said to Alison in a muffled voice, "Don't you just adore modesty in a person?"

"Hell," Alison said, "she's probably right."

"Not that I intend to give Jason the ol' look," Celia pointed out. "Like I said, he's a freshman.

Helen licked the mustard smear off the back of her hand. "Maybe you could date him incognito. Wear Groucho glasses."

"He's got to have a personality defect," Alison said, "if he pals around with that weirdo."

Celia grinned. "Can't judge a person by his roommates. Shit, look at *mine*."

Chapter Nine

Roland waited alone. He wished Jason were here, not off in Weston for his sister's wedding. They could talk about the bet, make jokes. It wouldn't be nearly so bad.

It wouldn't be happening at all if Jason were here. Dana wouldn't have crapped on him.

The bitch.

She'd always despised him, he knew that. But she never let it show much until today.

She was probably ticked because Jason left without her. They always went to the movies on Friday nights, then parked somewhere to screw around.

But not tonight.

No fun and games with Jason tonight, so take it out on Roland.

He stepped to the windows.

It was raining like shit out there.

A car came in off Spring Street, its headlights making slick paths on the pavement of the parking lot. Roland's stomach twisted. As the car neared the rear entrance to the dorm, however, he saw that it wasn't a Volkswagen.

The clock on his desk showed a quarter till nine. If Dana was on time, she wouldn't be here for another fifteen minutes.

Fourteen.

His stomach stayed tight.

That bitch, why is she doing this to me?

Did it have to do with the Polaroids? That's when she went haywire, after she realized he must've seen them.

Crouching at Jason's desk, Roland slid open the bottom drawer, lifted out a stack of *Penthouse* and *Hustler* magazines, and pulled out the envelope. He took it to his desk. Sitting down, he turned on his gooseneck lamp. He removed the ten photos from the envelope and spread them across his desktop.

Two of them were overexposed.

Another shot, this one a real close-up apparently taken from between her knees, was blurry. Jason must've been so excited he forgot to adjust the distance setting. But he'd tried again and gotten it right.

Yeah, Dana probably wasn't very happy at all that I got a look at these.

Roland unsnapped the case on his belt and pulled out his folding Buck knife. He pried open the blade. Touched its point to the glossy surface between her thighs. "How do you like *this*?" he whispered in a shaky voice. He felt an urge to shove the knife in, but didn't dare. Jason would know he was the one who'd done it.

Pressing the flat of the blade against his chin, Roland stared down at the photos.

What if I give them to her? Maybe she'd let me off the hook.

If I try that, she'll know I'm scared.

I'll spend the night in that fucking restaurant and I'll make a hundred bucks. A cinch. Might even be fun.

Fun. Like hell.

But he didn't have any choice. If he backed out, Dana would tell everyone he's a chicken and a phony.

Maybe I can find a way to get back at her.

He slipped the photos into the envelope.

The faint beep of a car horn made him flinch. He stood up, saw his reflection in the window, and turned off the lamp. Looking down through the darkness, he saw a VW bug at the curb. It was Dana's all right. He recognized the banner on its aerial.

Roland pushed open the glass door and jogged toward the car. He was hunched over as if the rain were a heavy weight. His shoes slapped water off the pavement. He wore a dark stocking cap and a windbreaker. A sleeping bag was clutched to his chest.

Dana leaned across the seat to open the door for him.

After climbing in, he dropped the sleeping bag to the floor between his feet, pulled the door shut, and struggled out of a small backpack.

"A beautiful night for your adventure," Dana said.

"Yeah. Too bad there's no thunder and lightning." He chuckled. He sounded nervous.

Dana pulled away from the curb and headed across the parking lot. "You'll have to give me directions."

"Take a right on Spring. I'll let you know when to turn off."

She stopped at the parking lot exit, waited for a few cars to swoosh past, and turned onto Spring Street. The rain was coming down hard. She leaned forward, trying to see better.

Roland was silent.

Usually he talked nonstop.

"Scared?" Dana asked.

"Yeah, I'm scared. Your wiper blades aren't worth shit."

"Tell me about it," Dana muttered. Instead of sweeping the water aside, they seemed to smear it and leave trails across the windshield.

"I didn't come out tonight to get killed in a car wreck."

"I know. You came out to get killed in a haunted restaurant."

"Haunted. That's a good one."

"Don't you think so? Aren't you the guy who told me and Jason that ghosts happen when people get croaked too fast?"

"Maybe," he said.

"Sure. We were walking back from that midnight show of *The Uninvited* and you said a ghost gets started when someone doesn't know he's dead yet. His spirit, or whatever, thinks he's still alive. Isn't that how you explained it?"

"Well, that's a theory, anyway."

"These two people got *blown away* last night. Can't be much more sudden than that. So their ghosts must be hanging around, don't you think?"

Roland didn't answer.

"My camera's in the backseat. Maybe you can get some snapshots of them."

"Make a left at the traffic light," he muttered.

There was no turn pocket. Dana checked the rearview mirror. The road behind her was dark, so she slowed. A pickup truck approached from the front. She squinted against the glare of its headlights. The truck sped by, spray from its tires splashing her door and window. Dana made the turn, then took a deep breath. The road ahead was dark except for a few streetlights. There were houses on both sides. She knew that the road led out of town, but couldn't remember a restaurant along the stretch.

"You don't believe in ghosts," Roland said.

"Ah, but you do. Or is that just part of your act?"

"They don't scare me."

"Ever seen one?"

"No."

"Not yet, huh?"

"If ghosts exist, they're harmless. They can't do anything to you."

"Such as cut your throat or something?" Dana asked, glancing at him and grinning.

"They wouldn't be able to hold a knife. Or anything else, for that matter. They don't have any substance. All they can do is appear."

"And turn you into a raving lunatic."

"Only if you're scared of them."

"Which you aren't, of course."

"There's no reason to be."

"Who are you trying to convince?"

Roland said nothing.

"The gal got her head blown off, right?" Dana said. "Does that mean her ghost won't have a head?"

"I'm not sure."

"I thought you were supposed to be an expert."

Dana saw no more houses ahead. On both sides of the road were fields, barren except for scattered trees. "Where *is* this place, anyway?"

"We're almost there."

"Seems like a queer place for a restaurant, this far out."

"The turnoff's around the next bend. You'll want to go right."

"I don't know much about these things," Dana said, "but I'd bet the babe's ghost is missing its noggin. Just a guess, you understand."

"You'd better slow down."

There were headlights near the crest of the hill far ahead. Her rearview mirror was dark. She eased down on the brake but couldn't see the side road. "Where?"

Roland pointed.

It was a narrow low space that looked more like a driveway than a road.

Dana slowed almost to a stop. As she turned, the VW's headlights swept across a large, dark, wood sign. She tried to read the sign's carved words, but they were a blur through the water streaked and splattered on her windshield. The wipers beating back and forth were no help—just another distraction. The headlights left the sign. Squinting, Dana saw the falling rain, the slick trails her head beams made on the pavement, and land rising on both sides of the road.

"Have you got the money?" Roland asked.

"In my purse." She grinned at him. "Not that you'll be getting it."

"I'll get it, all right."

"I'd be surprised if you last ten minutes."

"You're going to come in at dawn, right?"

"Wrong. We'll both be back in town snug in our beds before midnight."

"I mean, just assuming I don't chicken out. Which I won't. You'll come in at dawn?"

"Just come out."

"You want to see inside the place, don't you?"

"No."

"Well, come in anyway."

"Forget you."

The sides of the road were gone, and Dana realized she had entered the parking area. She kept driving straight ahead. At first, she couldn't see the restaurant. Then the head beams found its stairs, porch, and door. The pale band of a police line ribbon was stretched across the porch posts at the top of the stairs. The door was crosshatched with boards.

Dana stopped directly in front of the stairs and killed the headlights. "Whoops," she said. "Where'd the restaurant go?"

"How am I supposed to get in?"

Dana bent over, head against the steering wheel, and reached down between her knees. Her fingertips combed the gritty floor mat until they found the pry bar. She picked it up and gave it to Roland.

"You thought of everything," he muttered.

Twisting around, Dana knelt on her seat and got the camera out of the back. "Take some good ones," she said. "Especially of the gal. No head. Should be nifty."

Roland put the camera into his pack. Leaning forward, he swung the pack behind him and struggled into its shoulder straps. He hugged the sleeping bag against his side and gripped the pry bar. "How about turning on the headlights till I'm inside?" he asked.

"Why not." The lights tunneled into the darkness. "Have fun."

"You'll come in for me at dawn," he said. It was not a request.

"I'm not going inside that place."

"I think you will." He opened the door and climbed out. Standing in the rain, he leaned inside. "I've got the pictures with me."

"Give them here," Dana snapped.

"You may have them in the morning. If you *don't* come in after me, you'll never see them again. But everyone else will."

"You shit!"

He slammed the door.

When he was in front of the car, Dana blasted the horn

and he jumped. He turned around. Glared at her. Then curled his lip above his crooked teeth and turned away. At the top of the stairs, he broke the police ribbon and stepped to the door. He started to pry the boards off.

Dana, furious, watched him. Her heart was beating fast, her breath hissing through her nostrils. She saw herself rush up behind Roland and slam his head against the door until he was senseless. Then she would search him and find the pictures.

But she didn't move.

Her luck, the creep would probably hear her coming.

In her mind, she saw Roland whirl around and lay open her head with the bar.

She wouldn't put it past him.

He's a fucking wimp, she thought, but he's not exactly stable.

She saw him drag her body into the restaurant.

The thoughts began to frighten her.

Roland got the door open. He lifted his sleeping bag off the porch, glanced back at Dana, then went inside. The door swung shut.

Dana shut off the headlights.

Leaning across the seat, she locked the passenger door.

She reached for the ignition key, intending to turn the engine off. But she changed her mind, shifted to reverse, and slowly backed the car away. She considered leaving. It would serve the shit right, getting stranded out here. If he realized she was gone, however, he might decide to spread out his sleeping bag on the porch. He had to spend the night inside. That was the bet. That was the punishment, the price he had to pay for being such an asshole.

And for looking at the pictures.

He has them *with* him.

Dana, suddenly realizing she might be dangerously close to the rear of the parking area, hit her brakes. The car jolted to a stop. She set the emergency brake and killed the engine.

When her eyes adjusted to the darkness, she found that she could see the restaurant. It was about fifty years ahead of her, a low dark shape the width of the parking lot, black beneath its hooded porch.

It looked forbidding.

And Roland was inside.

Dana smiled. "You'll have a *real* good time," she muttered.

When Roland closed the restaurant door, he stood motionless and scanned the darkness. He could see nothing. He heard only his own heartbeat and quick breaths and the sounds of the rain.

There's nothing to be afraid of, he told himself.

His body seemed to believe otherwise.

He knew what he wanted to do. He wanted to drop the sleeping bag, take off his pack, and get his hands on the flashlight. But he couldn't move.

Go ahead and do it.

He was sure it would be all right, but part of him knew with absolute certainty that something was hunched silent in the dark nearby. Aware of his presence. Waiting. If he made the slightest move, it would come for him.

The quiet whinnying of Dana's car engine broke through his fear. He turned around and opened the restaurant's door. The Volkswagen was backing away.

She's leaving?

The thought alarmed him at first, then filled him with relief. If she actually drove off, he wouldn't need to stay inside. Spend the night on the porch, maybe. Keep a lookout and make sure he was back inside when she returned.

If she returned.

And if she didn't come back in the morning, the hike

back to town was only a few miles and he'd still win the bet.

The car didn't turn around. Near the far end of the parking lot, its red brake lights glowed briefly.

It stopped.

The engine went silent.

Roland's hope died. Dana wasn't leaving, after all, just putting some distance between herself and the restaurant. She must've been nervous about being close to it.

He watched for a while, but the car didn't move again.

Leaving the door open for a quick escape, Roland dropped his sleeping bag to the floor. He took off his pack and removed the flashlight. With his back to the doorway, he thumbed the flashlight switch. The strong beam shot out. He whipped it from right to left. Shadows jumped and writhed, but no foul shape was lurching toward him.

Roland allowed himself to breathe. He wished his heart would slow down. It felt like a fist punching the insides of his chest.

He shut the door and sagged slightly against it. He locked his knees to keep them from folding under him. His kneecaps began to flutter with a spastic, twitching bounce, as if they wanted to jump off his legs.

Roland tried to ignore them. Aiming the flashlight ahead, he took several steps until he could see around the corner of the wall. The wall extended down the right side of the main dining room. Something just beyond the corner caught his eye. He held his breath until he identified the objects as a stepladder, a lamp, and a vacuum cleaner. On the floor near them were a toolbox, some jars and bottles and rags. He moved the beam away.

A bright disk at the far end of the room startled Roland, but it was only his own light reflecting off a window. He wasn't alarmed when his light hit the other windows.

Except for the clutter near the one wall, the dining room

was empty. He swept his beam back across it, to the wall ahead of him, and to the right. A few yards away was the corner of an L-shaped bar counter. The shelves behind it were empty. There were no stools in front of the counter. A brass foot rail ran its length.

Turning slightly, Roland played his beam over the space between the bar counter and the front wall of the restaurant. A card table stood near the wall. Bottles and a few glasses gleamed with the light. There were two folding chairs at the table.

Crouching, he shined his flashlight beneath the card table.

He stood up. Beyond the table, at the far end of the room, was an alcove. A sign above the opening read, "Rest rooms."

Roland moved slightly forward until he could aim his light into the space behind the counter.

Returning to his backpack, he took out two of the candles he had purchased that afternoon. He went to the table, and lit them. He let the wax drip onto the table, then stood the candles upright in the tiny puddles. He stepped back. The two flames gave off an amazing amount of light, their glow illuminating most of the cocktail area.

Comforted somewhat by the light, Roland walked past the table. He noticed bat-wing doors behind the bar, probably to give the bartender access to the kitchen.

The kitchen.

Where the killings happened.

The areas above and below the doors were dark. He didn't shine his light inside. Instead, he entered the short hallway to the rest rooms. A brass sign on the door straight ahead of him read "Ladies." The door marked "Gentlemen" was on the right.

He needed to check inside each, but the prospect of that renewed his leg tremors and set his heart sledging again.

He didn't want to open those doors, didn't want to face whatever might be lurking within.

It'll be worse, he told himself, if I don't look. Then I won't know. I might get a big surprise later on.

He took the flashlight in his left hand, wiped the sweat off his right, and gripped the knob of the ladies' room door. The knob wouldn't turn. He tried the other door. It, too, was locked.

For a moment, he was glad. He wouldn't be opening them. It was a great relief.

Then he realized that the locked doors didn't guarantee that the rest rooms were safe. Probably, the doors could still be opened from the inside.

He shined his light on the knob of the men's room door. It had a keyhole. A few times in the past, he had gotten into toilets simply by inserting a pointed object into the lock hole and twisting. He pulled up the leather flap of his knife case.

The snap popped open.

Christ, it was loud!

Whoever's behind the door . . .

Calm down.

. . . heard it.

There's nobody inside the goddamn john.

Roland stared at the door.

He imagined a sudden, harsh rap on the other side.

Gooseflesh crawled up his back.

Leaving his knife in its case, he backed away.

The candlelight was comforting.

He picked up the folding chairs one at a time and carried them to the entryway beneath the Rest rooms sign. Back-to-back, they made a barrier that would have to be climbed over or pushed away. He placed a cocktail glass on the seat of each, near the edge. If the chairs moved, the glasses should fall.

Pleased with his innovation, Roland returned to the card table. He picked up one of the bottles. It was nearly full. With a candle behind it, he saw that the liquor was clear. He turned the bottle until he could read its label in the trembling light. Gilbey's Vodka.

Great.

He twisted off the plastic cap, raised the bottle, and filled his mouth. He swallowed a little bit at a time. The vodka scorched his throat and ignited a fire in his stomach. When his mouth was empty, he took a deep breath and sighed.

If he drank enough, he could numb himself to the whole situation.

But that would make him more vulnerable.

One more swig, then he recapped the bottle.

Crouching over his pack, Roland lifted out Dana's camera and folded it open. A flash bar was already attached to the top. He stood up and took another deep breath. It felt good inhaling, filling his lungs. They didn't seem tight like before. In fact, he realized that he was no longer shaking. There was a slightly vague feeling inside his head. Had the vodka done this?

Back at the table, he set down the camera and took one more swallow.

Then one more.

Picking up the camera, he went to the end of the bar. He lifted the hinged panel, tipped it back so it would stay upright, and stepped through the opening. He stopped in front of the bat-wing doors. Beyond them was darkness.

The kitchen.

"Anybody . . ." He almost said, "here?" but that word wouldn't come out. He wished he'd kept quiet. His fear had come back with the sound of his voice, a tight band constricting his chest.

He raised the flashlight above the doors. Its beam spilled along the kitchen floor, shaking as it moved.

He smelled the blood before he saw it. He knew the odor well, having collected some of his own in a mayonnaise jar and smeared it over his face on Halloween to gross out the guys in the dorm. His blood had smelled just this way—metallic, a little like train rails.

The flashlight beam found the blood. There was lots of it, all over the floor about halfway across the kitchen. It looked brown.

There were pale, tape outlines showing the positions of the bodies.

This is getting real, he thought.

Shit.

This is getting very real.

He'd made a big mistake. He had no business here. He was a dumb-ass kid intruding where he didn't belong.

He lowered the flashlight. Backed away. Felt someone sneaking up on him and whirled around. Nobody there. He hurried to the other side of the bar.

I don't need this. I don't need to prove anything. I don't need Dana's money.

Near the door, he dropped to his knees and stuffed the camera into his pack.

Take pictures. Sure.

He stood, lifting the pack by one strap and hooking a finger of the same hand through the draw cord of his sleeping bag.

Shit, the candles.

The bundles swinging at his side, he rushed to the card table. As he puffed one candle out, he spotted the chairs he'd set up to block the hall to the rest rooms.

Leave them. Who cares.

He blew out the other candle. Followed the beam of his flashlight to the door. Opened the door.

The night breeze, smelling of rain, blew against his face.

He stared through the downpour at Dana's car—a small, dark object waiting at the far edge of the lot. The plastic banner on its aerial waved in the breeze.

I'd be surprised if you last ten minutes.

The bitch, she'll never let me live this down. She'll tell everyone. I'll be a joke.

Roland kicked the door shut.

"I'm staying!" he yelled. *"Fuck it!"*

He stepped close to the bar. He unrolled his sleeping bag, took off his cap and jacket, and sat on the soft, down-filled bag.

I should've done it like this in the first place.

Shouldn't have snooped around.

Should've done it the way I'd planned.

Reaching deep into his pack, pushing aside the candles and camera, he touched steel.

The handcuffs rattled as he pulled them out.

He snapped one bracelet around his left wrist, the other around the brass foot rail of the bar.

Flashlight clamped under his left arm, he aimed it at the card table and gave the handcuff key a toss. It clinked against one of the bottles and dropped onto the table.

Out of reach.

We'll see who chickens out, he thought.

We'll see who lasts the night.

Chapter Ten

IT WAS ALMOST QUITTING TIME, AND THE RAIN OUTSIDE Gabby's showed no sign of letting up. Alison backed away from the window. She was glad that she'd borrowed Helen's rain gear; she would have gotten drenched if she'd worn her windbreaker to work.

Not if Evan picks me up, she thought.

Fat chance.

Who knows, maybe he'll surprise you. After all, he showed up last night when you didn't think he would.

Alison went to a table that had just been vacated. She dropped the tip into her apron pocket and began to clear off the dirty plates and glasses.

If Evan cares at all about me, she thought, he'll pick me up. He knows it's pouring outside and I'll have to walk home unless he gives me a ride. Coming to my rescue about now would go a long way toward getting back on my good side. He has to know that.

After wiping off the tabletop, she lifted the heavy tray and carried it into the kitchen.

Maybe he'll show up, she told herself. And if he does, maybe he'll be in for a surprise.

Before leaving the house that afternoon, Alison had tucked her toothbrush and her new nightie into the bottom of her flight bag. Then she had taken them out. She would have no use for them even if Evan should make an appearance. After all, she hadn't changed her mind about sleeping with him. It was silly to prepare yourself for something that just wouldn't happen.

But she thought about last Friday night. He had come into Gabby's after the movie let out at the Imperial, sipped a beer while he waited for her to finish the shift, and they had walked back to his apartment. She hadn't expected to spend the night. It was so wonderful, though, that she couldn't force herself to leave and they had made love almost till dawn. That had been her first whole night with him.

If they could have another night like that . . .

We won't, she told herself. Too much has changed.

But she'd gone ahead and put her toothbrush and nightie back into the bag. You never know. Maybe, somehow, everything would suddenly be right again.

She wanted it all to be right.

As she unloaded the dirty dishes in the kitchen of Gabby's, she imagined Evan coming for her. "I just couldn't stay away from you any longer," he would say. "I tried to stay away and punish you, but I couldn't. I've given it a lot of thought, Alison. Sure, I'd like to make love with you. I'd like nothing more, because it makes us part of each other, as if, for a little while, we're one person. But I can live without that if I have to. The main thing, really, is just to *be* with you. I would be happy just looking into your eyes, just hearing your laughter, just holding your hand."

And maybe she would go back to his apartment, after all. While he waited on the sofa, she'd close the door to his bedroom and slip into the negligee . . .

"Al!"

Startled, she turned around. Gabby, standing at the grill, was looking over his shoulder at her. "Go on and get out of here. Have a good weekend."

"Thanks," she said. "You, too."

At the rear of the kitchen, she scooped her tips out of the apron and into her bag. She struggled into Helen's heavy raincoat, put on the strange hat, and lifted the bag. "See you Monday," she called, and pushed her way through the swinging door.

The table that she had just cleared was no longer deserted.

Evan sat there.

His arm was around Tracy Morgan.

More-Organ Morgan, Mouth-Organ Morgan, also known as Tugboat Tracy for reasons that had always been unclear to Alison.

Alison felt herself shrivel inside.

Evan, as if sensing her presence, looked around at her. His glasses were spotted with rain. One side of his mouth twitched upward.

Alison rushed for the door, shouldered it open, and lurched into the pounding rain.

She looked sideways.

Behind the lighted window, Evan watched her and calmly stroked Tracy's long, auburn hair.

Chapter Eleven

ROLAND HAD PURCHASED THE HANDCUFFS THAT AFTERnoon at Spartan Sporting Goods for $24.50.

He had wanted to buy the cuffs when he'd first seen them a few weeks ago. Staring through the display case at the shiny bracelets, he'd been excited by thoughts of what he might do with them. Not that he would ever do such things. Still, just owning them would be nice, the same way it was nice to own a few knives even if you didn't actually plan to run around carving up women with them. He'd bought the Buck knife that day. It wasn't embarrassing, buying the knife, because people bought knives for camping, fishing, hunting. But if you're not a cop, why do you need handcuffs? What would the salesperson think? It would be like buying a pack of condoms.

Roland had never bought condoms, even though he wanted them. And he hadn't bought the handcuffs, either.

Until today.

When Dana challenged him to spend the night in the restaurant, he immediately remembered the cuffs and he knew how to win the bet. The cuffs would guarantee it. His courage, or lack of it, would be irrelevant once he had anchored himself to something in the restaurant. No matter what, he would win the bet.

With a hundred dollars and his reputation riding on the bet, he had returned to the store. He could feel himself blushing as he peered through the counter glass.

"Can I help you with something?" asked the clerk.

Roland kept his eyes down. "I'd like to see the handcuffs."

"Black or nickle finish?"

"Nickle."

Crouching, the man slid open the back of the counter and reached inside. He was heavyset, his brown hair long around the sides of his head as if to make up for what was lacking on top. He put the cuffs on the counter.

Roland picked them up. They felt heavy.

"Grade A tempered steel. The links'll withstand a direct pull of twelve hundred pounds."

Nodding, Roland tugged the bracelets. The connecting chain snapped taut. "Fine," he said. "How much are they?"

"Twenty-four fifty. Interested in a case?"

"No, I don't think so."

"Anything else? We've got a sale on the Navy MK.3 Combat knife, regularly forty-nine ninety-five. A real beaut of a knife. Like to see one?"

Roland shook his head. "No, this'll do it."

"Cash or charge?"

That was all there was to it. No embarrassing questions, no snide remarks. Relieved, Roland left the store with his purchase.

And spotted Celia. Now, there was a gal he wouldn't mind trying the handcuffs on. That other gal, too—the one in the jumpsuit. Looking at that one, he could see himself cuffing her hands behind her back and pulling down that zipper all the way past her waist.

Oh, yes. Either one of those gals. Cuff them, and they'd be at his mercy.

But he hadn't bought the cuffs for that. He would never have the guts, anyway.

I'm not crazy, he had told himself.

He'd bought the handcuffs only because of the bet. With them, nothing could prevent him from winning, as long as the restaurant had a secure fixture to which he could fasten one bracelet. It was bound to.

A door handle. A pipe. Something.

A brilliant idea.

Sitting in the darkness cuffed to the bar rail, however, Roland wasn't quite so sure the idea was brilliant. What if something happened and he *had* to get out?

Like a fire, for instance.

Good thing he had blown out the candles.

The place isn't going to burn down, he told himself. Don't worry about it.

He couldn't help worrying about it.

Suppose Dana started the place on fire to drive him out so he'd lose the bet? No. She's not that crazy. A little crazy. That time at the movies when he reached across to get the popcorn from Jason and accidentally brushed her breast with his arm, she'd dumped her drink on his lap. Once when they went to the drive-in, she made him get in the trunk of Jason's car so he could sneak in without paying, then she had talked Jason into leaving him there for almost an hour.

She really hates my guts, Roland thought. But she won't burn the place down. That was too crazy even for Dana.

Probably.

What she might do is leave.

No, she wants the Polaroids. She'll come in for them.

That doesn't mean she'll give me the key.

When she finds me cuffed here, she might just take the photos and go. Or worse.

Roland's mouth went dry. A cold hand seemed to clutch his stomach.

I'll be at her mercy.

Oh, shit what'll she do to me?

It wasn't a question of *whether* Dana would do something to him—it was a question of *what.*

You've got all night to wonder about that one.

Why didn't I think of that before I cuffed myself to this fucking rail?

He jerked his left hand. The steel clattered and the edges of the cuff dug painfully into his wrist.

A twelve-hundred-pound pull. That's what the salesman said it would take to break the links.

Roland felt along the floor at his side. He touched the flashlight, picked it up, and shined it at the card table. The bottles glinted in its beam. The key was up there, out of sight.

The table was eight or ten feet to his left.

With his cuffed left hand, he slid the bracelet along the rail. It made an awful, metallic scraping sound that sent a shiver through him. But it did move. Sliding it, he would be able to move sideways until he was close to the table. Then maybe he could hook a foot around one of the table legs and drag the thing over to him—and get the key.

Worth a try, he thought.

What about the bet?

No problem.

Roland grinned.

Just let me get the handcuff key, I'll stay. A cinch.

A cinch because he realized that the restaurant no longer frightened him much. What really frightened him was knowing that Dana, at dawn, would come in and find him handcuffed.

I'll get that damned key, he told himself.

He squirmed sideways off his sleeping bag, his back rubbing the smooth wood of the bar counter, his left hand scooting the cuff along the brass rail with that awful grating noise. A noise that made his teeth ache. A noise that tormented him like the scrape of fingernails down a blackboard.

He stopped to rest.

The silence was soothing.

Just a little more distance to go, and . . .

Roland heard a sound.

It was a soft thump, such as a rope might make dropping from a height onto the hardwood floor.

It came from . . . where?

Off to the right.

Roland's flashlight was aimed in the general direction of the table. The bright center of the beam shook.

He listened. He heard his heartbeat and the rain and nothing more.

What could *make* a sound like that?

A snake? A snake flopping off the bar?

His skin suddenly crawled with goose bumps.

How could a snake get in here?

Hell, the place had been deserted for years. Maybe it fucking *lives* here.

Or Dana snuck it in. She might do that. Pick one up at a pet shop.

The bitch.

Dana bought a snake to scare him out, and Roland bought cuffs to keep himself in.

If she bought the thing, it's harmless. They don't sell poisonous snakes. Do they?

Roland needed to see it—to see what it was, and *where.*

Maybe the light'll drive it off, he thought.

He swung the beam sideways, planning to check the floor to the right. It passed in front of him and had already moved on before he quite realized that he'd seen something between his feet. The beam jumped back to it.

Roland lurched. The back of his head thumped the bar. Urine sprayed his thigh, filled his jeans as he jerked his hands back.

The thing was fast. It squirmed like a sidewinder going for his right foot.

But it wasn't a sidewinder.

It wasn't a snake.

Roland lifted his right foot off the floor, away from its head, and shot his left at it. His heel caught the thing and sent it skidding and flipping away. It came straight back at him.

It had slimy yellow flesh webbed with red and blue veins. Its eyes had the dull gray look of phlegm. Its head—or mouth—made wet sucking noises as it flattened then spread open.

Roland raised both legs as high as he could. He was still urinating, the stream hitting the inside of his jeans and splashing back, showering his genitals and running down his buttocks. He kicked down hard with his right heel, but missed the thing and flung his leg high again.

It didn't try to leap for his upraised foot. Instead, it darted forward and hit the back of his leg just to the right of his groin.

Roland's throat constricted, ready to emit a cry of agony and horror.

But he felt no pain.

Only a hot, tingling pressure that sent a delicious shiver through his body.

He grabbed the thing, but didn't try to tug it off. Instead, he held it gently. It felt warm and powerful. Soon it was gone, leaving a hole the size of a quarter in the leg of his jeans.

And in his leg.

The wound didn't bother Roland.

He opened his waist button, lowered his zipper, and curled onto his left side. He slid his hand inside the seat of his jeans. He wore no underpants. The denim was sodden against the back of his hand, and the skin of his rump was wet.

The creature moved inside him, just beneath his flesh. With a hand pressed to the mound it made, he could feel it sliding along. His skin sank into place again after it had passed. He felt it turn toward his spine. Bending his arm behind him as much as possible, he caressed it through his skin until it was too high up to reach.

He put his hand to the back of his neck in time to feel the skin rise beneath his palm. Moments later, the thing stopped moving.

A sudden jolt hit Roland—pleasure so fierce it made him squirm and moan for release.

Chapter Twelve

ALISON HUNG HER DRIPPING RAINCOAT AND HAT ON A rack near the door of Wally's Saloon. Fortunately, the rest rooms were just off to the side; she could change out of her waitress costume without having to pass through the crowd of drinkers.

In a toilet stall, she took off the uniform. She took off her slip and bra. Crouching, she removed her jumpsuit from her flight bag. Beneath it was the negligee. The sight of the royal blue fabric made Alison ache as if all her insides, from throat to bowels, were being squeezed and wrung.

That bastard. Oh, that bastard.

Screw him. Who needs him.

She stepped into the jumpsuit, pulled the soft fabric up her legs, pushed her arms into the sleeves, and raised the zipper. Then she stuffed her bra, slip, and uniform into the bag, and left the stall.

She leaned close to a mirror. Her short hair was matted down somewhat from the rain hat. She ran her fingers through it, shook her head, and it looked okay. Her eyes were still a little red from the crying she'd done after leaving Gabby's. The hike through the rain, however, had left her cheeks with a rosy glow.

The jumpsuit clung to her breasts. Her nipples made the fabric jut. She wondered if she should put her bra back on. Did she really want to go into the bar this way?

Hell, why not? Give the guys something to look at.

Besides, the soft warm fabric felt good against her bare breasts.

She trembled as she slid the zipper down. In the mirror, she saw the pale skin below her sternum throbbing from her heartbeat.

She stared into her eyes.

Are you really going to do this? she wondered.

Damn right. Two can play this game.

This is crazy.

No, it's not. Evan doesn't want me, somebody else will. It'll serve the bastard right.

But the zipper really was too low. If she bent over, everyone in the vicinity would get an eyeful. So she raised the zipper a couple of inches, then left the rest room, flight bag swinging at her side.

As usual, Wally's was crowded and noisy. It was the university's watering hole, so she recognized most of the patrons. She greeted a few friends on her way to the bar. Some asked where Evan was, and she answered, "Busy." Which was, she thought, the plain truth.

She dodged Johnna Penson as the girl backed away from the bar with a pitcher of beer. Johnna saw her and grinned. "Hey-ho, what's up?"

''Not much.''

''Where's lover boy?''

''Scared to come out in the rain. You seen Celia?''

''Just missed her. She took off with Danny Gard and some other guy. See ya.'' Johnna squeezed past Alison.

Alison stepped up behind a guy who was waiting to order.

She realized that she had expected Celia to be here. The support of a friend would've been welcome. On the other hand, she could just imagine Celia's reaction. ''You don't want to do it, pal. It isn't you. You're hurting, but you aren't gonna solve anything by putting out for the first guy who smiles at you. Believe me, you'll regret it.''

So what if I regret it?

You just want to pay him back, she thought. You're stooping to his level.

Maybe I'll just have a beer or two, and go home.

Who you trying to kid?

We'll just see what happens, okay? Any objections?

The man in front of Alison stepped out of the way, and she moved in against the bar. ''A mug of draft. No, make it a pitcher.''

She set her flight bag onto the counter and dug out her purse while the bartender filled her order. After paying, she slung the strap over her head to free her hands, picked up the pitcher and frosty mug, and turned away.

Moving through the crowd was an ordeal. Alison nodded, smiled, said ''Hi'' to people she knew, said ''Excuse me'' to strangers, squeezed between people, trying not to bump her drink or theirs, and finally found a deserted table near the front wall. It was a small, round table with two chairs. She put down her load and sat facing the mob.

No sooner had she filled her mug and taken a sip than a man walked toward her, smiling nervously.

That sure didn't take long, she thought.

Her heart thumped faster as he approached. She had seen him around campus, but didn't know his name. He was tall and lean, with a boyish face and a scrawny, pale attempt at a mustache.

Not wanting to appear interested, Alison lowered her gaze to her beer.

I'm not so sure about this, she thought.

"Excuse me?" he said.

She looked up. Smiled. Said, "Oh, hi."

He patted the back of the unoccupied chair. "Anyone sitting here?"

She shook her head.

"Mind if I borrow it, then?"

Feeling foolish, she shook her head again.

"Thanks a lot," he said.

Alison watched him carry it to a nearby table, where he joined a couple of friends. Her face burned.

"Terrific," she muttered.

All he wanted was the goddamn chair.

And now I'm without it, so if some guy *does* come along he won't have anywhere to sit.

I ought to get out of here.

Can't leave all this beer behind.

Give the pitcher to someone, make a gift of it.

Pour it over that dork's head.

Instead, she drank what was in her mug, refilled it, and warned herself not to guzzle. This whole deal, she thought, is iffy enough without getting smashed. Take it easy.

She sipped slowly.

At the far end of the room, just beyond the dance floor, a huge television screen was suspended from the ceiling. It showed music videos, the volume so high that it could drive you mindless if you were near the speakers.

The noise had never seemed to bother Evan. It had driven Alison nuts, but she'd suffered with it, time and again, just to keep him happy. He loved to watch her dance—always looked as if he wanted to reach out and tear her clothes off.

What the hell am I thinking about *him* for?

What if he shows up?

Alison looked toward the entrance.

Suppose he shows up with Morgan the Organ-grinder and sees me sitting here alone like a fucking wallflower. Wouldn't that be cute?

One more good reason to am-scray.

She refilled her mug.

Better take it easy.

Alison looked again at the video screen. A hairless woman wearing a loincloth and skimpy top of leopard skin was twisting and writhing to the music. She had shiny blue skin (same color as my nightie, Alison thought, the one that Evan, the shit, will never be lucky enough to see me in). The gyrating blue woman had a snake around her leg. Its head vanished behind her thigh, then reappeared against her groin. The snake slid higher, angling toward a hip, its thick body rubbing her through the loincloth as she writhed in apparent ecstasy.

Lord, Alison thought.

She took a sip of beer, her gaze fixed on the screen.

The snake curled around the woman's bare torso, circling higher. Its head came out beneath her armpit. It moved slowly across her breasts. Its tail was still flicking across her left breast when the head showed up beside her neck. The woman, squirming and rubbing her sides and belly (in lieu, Alison thought, of where she'd be rubbing if the producers weren't worried about taking a final step out of bounds), turned her face toward the head of the snake and pursed her thick, shiny lips.

"Excuse me?"

Alison flinched.

A young man was standing in front of her, just off to the side. She was surprised that she hadn't noticed his approach.

"Sorry if I startled you," he said.

"It's all right."

"That's quite a video, huh?"

She felt herself blush. Her mouth was dry. She took a sip of beer. "Pretty far out," she said.

"Are you with someone?"

"Uh, no."

"Mind if I join you?"

He didn't look familiar to Alison. He appeared more mature than most students, and better dressed in his slacks and white, crewneck sweater. His black hair was neatly trimmed. Instead of a beer, he had a cocktail in his hand—probably a martini.

She pegged him as a law student.

"Some guy made off with the other chair," she said.

"No problem." He wandered away. A few moments later, he came back with a chair and sat across from her. "I'm Nick Winston," he said, and offered his hand.

"Alison Sanders." She shook his hand. "Law student?" she asked.

"How'd you guess?"

"You have that look."

"Old, you mean?" he asked, grinning.

I prefer older men, she thought. But she stopped herself from saying it. "Just more together than the rest of us," she told him.

"You a psych major?"

"What makes you think so?"

"You have that look," he said.

"Neurotic?"

"Introspective."

"Nah, I'm not introspective, just depressed."

"And what, may I ask, could cause a beautiful, obviously intelligent young woman like you to be depressed?"

" 'I see myself dead in the rain.' "

"Ah, an English major."

She smiled. "Right."

"Do you really?"

"What?"

"See yourself dead in the rain?"

"Nope. Just felt like spouting some Hemingway."

"Don't you find his outlook rather juvenile?"

Her appreciation of Nick Winston slipped a notch. "What do you mean, juvenile?"

"Well, in particular, his portrayals of women. They're like the fantasies of an adolescent. Maria, for instance."

"I love that sleeping bag scene."

Nick raised an eyebrow. "Well, now."

Alison found herself blushing again. "I just mean, I think it's very romantic."

"Romantic, perhaps, but idealized to a ludicrous extent. Have you ever experienced intercourse in a sleeping bag?"

"Maybe."

"Ah, we're being coy."

Alison shrugged and took a drink. When she looked again at Nick, he was gazing into her eyes.

This is certainly progressing apace, she thought.

What the hell am I getting into?

"If you *have,* I'm sure you found it confining and the ground very hard and the entire experience barely tolerable."

I didn't find it that way at all, she thought. But that's my business, Nick old sport.

"I find a king-sized bed to be the ideal setting for such encounters, don't you?"

"I thought we were discussing Hemingway."

"And so we are. I believe that I was explaining my theory that the sleeping bag scene in *For Whom the Bell Tolls* presents a false, idealized view of—"

"I think it's nice."

The corners of Nick's lips curled up. "I don't think it would be so nice in a rain storm."

"If you had a tent—"

"Unfortunately, I have neither a tent nor a sleeping bag. I do, however, have a Trans Am which could transport us in comfort to my apartment."

"Where, no doubt, you have a king-sized bed."

He lifted his glass and took a sip, staring at Alison over the rim. He looked as if the stare were well practiced. Setting down his drink, he leaned forward. He folded his arms on the table and gazed steadily into Alison's eyes. "As a matter of fact, yes, I do have a king-sized bed. Whether or not we use it, however, is entirely up to you."

"Thanks."

"I realize that we've just met, and I would understand a certain hesitancy on your part to indulge in . . . intimacies. I certainly wouldn't want you to feel any pressure from me in that regard."

"I don't know, Nick."

You don't know? she asked herself. Isn't this exactly what you were looking for?

Maybe, maybe not.

"I'll drive you over to my place. We'll have a drink or two to take off the chill, listen to some good music. Nothing more than that, unless, of course, you insist."

"I see. You'll be a perfect gentleman."

He shrugged elaborately. "Of course, if you would rather not."

"I didn't say that."

"Ah, but you have your doubts."

"I'm not exactly in the habit of rushing over to a guy's apartment after I've known him for about five minutes."

"I'm not exactly in the habit of *asking* after five minutes." He took another small sip of his cocktail. He set it down. He gazed into her eyes. "To be quite honest, Alison, there's something . . . special about you. I felt it the moment I saw you sitting here . . ."

"Gaping at that erotic video," she added.

"It wasn't that. It's just that, when I saw you, it was as if we weren't strangers, as if I'd known you for a very long time."

Might've been a good line, except that it sounded so trite.

Trite or not, what if he actually meant it?

"I want to know you better," he said.

"I don't—"

"A couple of drinks, that's all. We'll listen to music, we'll talk. We'll get to know each other. What've you got to lose?"

Good point.

"If you're afraid I might *attack* you, or something . . ." He shook his head, smiling at the ridiculous suggestion.

"It isn't that."

"What, then?"

"I don't know."

"Then let's give it a try. We owe it to ourselves."

"Give me some time to think about it. Meanwhile, I've got to use the john. I'll be right back."

In a pig's eye, she thought.

She left the table, taking her flight bag with her. Unfortunately, she really *did* need to use the toilet. The homeward hike would take a good fifteen minutes. In her condition, she'd never make it without exploding.

She rushed into the rest room. Her jumpsuit made matters difficult, but finally she finished and left the stall.

She stepped to one of the sinks. Slowly, she washed her hands.

You *could* go with him, she thought. Isn't that why you came here tonight?

Her heart pounded so hard that it made her chest ache.

Forget it. Grab the rain duds and pull a disappearing act.

In the mirror above the sink, her eyes looked wide and frantic.

She dried her hands on a paper towel, then walked to the rest room door. She opened it.

Nick stood in front of the coat rack, wearing a clear plastic slicker and a tennis hat. He smiled when he saw her. "All set?" he asked.

Oh, God.

Nodding, she pulled Helen's rain gear off the hanger. Nick held the heavy coat while she struggled into it. She put on the hat. Nick pushed open the door, and she stepped outside. The rain was still coming down hard.

Nick took hold of her hand.

They walked across the parking lot, Nick leading her around puddles.

At the passenger side of his car, he released her hand and bent over the door to unlock it.

"Nick," she said.

"Yeah," he called without looking back.

"I don't think so."

"What?" He forgot about the door. He whirled around and scowled at her. "What did you say?" he asked over the noise of the storm.

"I'm not going to your place. Not tonight. Thanks for asking, though. I'm sorry."

"Got a car?"

"What?"

"A car. Did you drive here?"

"No."

"Get in, then. I'll drive you."

"I told you—"

"I heard, I heard. To your place. You don't want to walk in this mess." Turning away, he bent over and unlocked the door. He opened it for her.

Alison hesitated.

"Get in or don't. It's up to you."

"Okay. Well. Thanks." She climbed in, and Nick shut the door. She took off the rain hat and opened the coat.

Now what, she wondered.

Nick slid in behind the wheel and started the car. He looked across the darkness at her. "A long time," he said, "since anyone's tried to ditch me." He sounded amused, not angry.

"I'm sorry. It's been a bad night."

"My fault," he said. "I picked up on your reluctance, but I persisted, anyway. I should have backed off, I realize that now." He turned on the headlights and windshield wipers, and backed the car out of its space. "I suppose I can lay some of the blame on conditioning. So often, women play games. They make a show of pretending not to want something, while in point of fact they do want it." He drove slowly toward the road. "Apparently, they take some sort of bizarre delight in watching men struggle to win their consent."

"I guess that happens," Alison said. "I suppose I've done it myself. It isn't always a game, though. Sometimes, you just don't know what you want. You could go either way."

Nick glanced at her. "Is that how it was with you, tonight?"

"Pretty much."

He stopped at the edge of the parking lot. "Which way?"

"Right."

He waited for a car to pass, then swung onto the road. "Therefore, you're suggesting that a different approach on my part might have succeeded."

Alison smiled. "Could be."

"I should've played hard to get."

"Maybe."

"Damn it," he muttered. "I'm always striking out."

Alison found herself liking him better. Without the cool posing, he seemed like a different person. "Maybe next time at bat," she said, "you'll do better."

He sighed.

"A left at the next corner."

He nodded. After making the turn, he said, "Anyway, I'm glad we met. Even if I did make a mess of things."

"It's not your fault. It's me."

"No. You're terrific. God knows, the way I was acting *I* wouldn't have gone off with me."

"You can let me out here," she said.

He swung his car to the curb, stopped it, and set the emergency brake. Leaning forward, he peered out her window. "You live in that house?"

"Upstairs. With a couple of roommates. Thanks a lot for the ride."

"No problem. I'm glad we . . . had this chance to talk. God only knows why, but it makes me feel a little better about things."

"Me, too." Leaning toward him, Alison slipped her fingers behind his head. His face was a dim blur in the darkness, moving closer. She pressed her mouth gently to his, then eased away. "See you around," she whispered. "Okay?"

"Okay."

"You in the student directory?" she asked.

"Yeah."

"Me, too. You going to call?"

"You bet."

Then Alison was out of the car and striding through the rain. She knew that she had almost stayed. She was glad that she hadn't. She felt lonely and hurt, but strong. She had lost Evan. Maybe she had made a new friend tonight, but that didn't matter so much as knowing that she had won against herself.

Chapter Thirteen

DANA WOKE UP AGAIN, CRAMPED IN THE BACKSEAT OF her Volkswagen. This time, her right arm had fallen asleep. Before, it had been a leg, a buttock, a foot. No matter what her position, one part or another of her body got its circulation cut off.

Right now, she was lying on her side with her knees bent, using her right arm for a pillow. The arm had no feeling at all. With a struggle, she managed to sit up. She shook her arm, grimacing as the numbness became an aching tingle. The tingle was like a thousand stabbing needles. But soon it went away and her arm felt almost normal.

She reached to the floor and picked up her travel clock. Pushing a button on top, she lighted its face. The digital numbers showed 2:46 A.M.

The alarm had been set for 3:00 A.M.

She wouldn't be needing it.

When she'd set the alarm, she hadn't realized that she would be waking up every fifteen or twenty minutes.

She flicked a switch sideways to deactivate the alarm, then put the clock down.

The rain still pounded down making an endless rumble hitting her car.

Might as well go ahead now, Dana thought.

She began to shiver.

It'll be fabulous, she told herself.

She didn't want to go out in the rain. But this was too good an opportunity to miss, and she'd already gone to so much trouble. What's a little rain?

I'll get soaked.

But I'll scare the hell out of Roland.

Besides, he had stuck it out this long. Left alone, he might very well make it till morning.

Dana didn't want to lose the bet.

The money was no big deal, but the whole idea was to humiliate and destroy Roland. If he didn't come running out of the restaurant in terror . . .

I'll do it.

She struggled into her poncho, flipped up the hood to cover her head, and left the car. She shut the door quietly.

The rain pattered on the plastic sheet as she stepped to the front of her car and opened the trunk. She slipped the screwdriver and knit cap into her pockets, and clutched the five-pound sack to her belly underneath the poncho to keep it dry. Then she closed the trunk and headed for the restaurant.

If Roland is watching from a window, she thought, I'm sunk.

That wasn't likely, though. If he was awake at this hour, he was probably hiding in a closet—and scared out of his gourd.

But not half as scared as he'll be in a few minutes.

Dana crossed the parking lot at an angle.

She was pleased with herself. She'd made a pretty good show of being afraid of the restaurant, so Roland would never suspect a trick like this.

At the corner of the lot, she waded through some high grass to the restaurant wall. The grass was wet, soaking through her running shoes and the cuffs of her jeans.

She stayed close to the wall, heading for the back of the building, ducking under the windows.

There were no doors along this side of the restaurant. In the back, however, she found one. The upper portion had four sections of glass.

Dana crept up the wooden stairs and pressed her face to one of the panes. Dark in there. A lot darker than outside, but patches of the counters and floor were pale gray with light from the windows.

This obviously was the kitchen. This was where the killings had supposedly taken place.

She couldn't see Roland.

The kitchen wouldn't be at the top of his list of places to spend the night. Anywhere *but* the kitchen.

Dana set the sack down between her feet. She tried the knob. When it didn't turn, she began to work her screwdriver into the crack between the door and its frame, directly across from the knob.

She widened the gap. Splinters of wood broke off. She kept digging and prying. At last, the lock tongue slipped back and she carefully opened the door.

Picking up the sack, she entered the kitchen. The sounds of the storm were muffled when she shut the door. The fresh air also went away. There was a heavy, unpleasant odor.

Motionless, she listened. Water dripping onto the floor from her poncho, nothing else. Except her heartbeat.

Roland won't hear that.

He obviously wasn't in the kitchen. The rain pounding on the roof provided enough steady noise to cover any sounds Dana might make.

As long as she was careful.

Very slowly, she pulled the poncho over her head. Its plastic made quiet rustling sounds. She lowered it to the floor.

Listened.

Balanced on one foot at a time, she pulled off her shoes and socks.

She realized that she was gritting her teeth and trembling.

Excitement, not fear.

Poor Roland, he'll have a cardiac arrest.

Wouldn't *that* be a pity.

Dana unbuttoned the waistband of her jeans and lowered the zipper. Thumbs under the elastic of her panties, she drew down both garments at the same time and stepped out of them. Then she pulled her sweatshirt off.

She took a deep, shaky breath.

This'll be quite a treat for you, Roland old pal. You wanted to look at the bod, you'll get it. The real thing, this time, not some fucking snapshots.

Hope you enjoy it.

Squatting, Dana folded open the sack. She scooped out a handful of flour. It seemed almost iridescent. She spread the powder over her skin from shoulder to shoulder. Streams of it trickled down her breasts. Coating her left arm, she noticed that her skin was pebbled with goose bumps. She filled her other hand and covered her right arm. Then she scooped up flour in both hands and spread it over her chest and belly. Her nipples were stiff. Touching them sent warmth down her body. She rubbed flour over her thighs, hands gliding, feeling her gooseflesh through the thin layer of powder, feeling her slick wetness when she patted the flour between her legs. With her hands full again, she coated her feet and shins and knees.

Then she straightened up. Shoulder to feet, she was white except for faint areas where the flour had been rubbed thin from the way she had squatted. She dug more powder from the sack, spread it over her thighs and hips and belly, and emptied her hands by swirling the last of the flour over her breasts.

She looked down at herself again.

Some ghost.

Roland wouldn't know whether to get a hard-on or a heart attack.

The floor around her feet was dusted white.

Dana wrung her hands, trying to get the flour off them. They remained white. She reached back and rubbed them on her buttocks. That got most of it.

Turning toward her pile of clothes, she bent from the waist to avoid smearing the powder, and pulled her knit cap from the pocket of her jeans. It was navy blue, but it looked black in the darkness. Holding the cap away from her body, she felt for the eyeholes she had cut that afternoon. When she found them, she pulled the cap over her head, drew it down to her chin, and tucked her dangling hair up the rear of it.

Dana wished she could check out the effect. Maybe tomorrow night. Do it again, only in Jason's room. He had a full-length mirror. Maybe have *him* spread the flour on her. And she would do the same for him. And then they'd make it.

Only one problem. Jason might not be overjoyed that she had paraded in front of Roland bare-ass naked.

He should complain, the shit. He's the one showed Roland the Polaroids.

Dana took a trembling breath through the wool cap.

Time to get going and give Roland the thrill of his life.

She started across the kitchen. After a few steps, one of her feet landed on something sticky, like paint that hadn't quite dried.

Her nose wrinkled.

Hadn't they cleaned up the mess from last night?

She sidestepped and got out of it, but her foot made a quiet snicking sound each time she lifted it off the linoleum.

With her back to the kitchen windows, she couldn't see much.

Blindman's buff.

Hands out, she finally touched a wall. She made her way slowly along it, and found a door. When she opened the door, a cool draft wrapped her skin. Something wasn't right about this. Clutching the door frame, she slipped her right foot forward and felt the floor end.

Stairs?

Maybe a stairway leading down to the wine cellar, or something.

Roland might be down there.

Not a chance.

Dana shut the door and continued following the wall. Soon, she touched another door frame. Reaching past it, she felt wood. Ribbed wood. A louvered door of some kind.

Moving in front of it, she gently pushed. The hinges creaked slightly.

That's okay. Let Roland hear it. Give him something to think about.

Holding the door open, she stepped through. Her side hit something that squeaked and wasn't there anymore, then bumped her again from armpit to hip. Even without being able to see, she knew what must have happened;

they were double swinging doors, and she'd only opened one side before trying to go through.

Roland *must* have heard that.

Give him a little more?

She considered moaning like an anguished spirit. But maybe spirits don't moan. Besides, he might figure out who it was from her voice.

Dana stepped through the doors, eased them shut, and stood motionless.

It was a big room.

Roland might be here. Might be looking at her right now. Frozen with terror.

This is it.

Dana's heart pounded furiously. Tremors of excitement shook her body. Drops of sweat slid down her sides, tickling.

Several windows along the three walls let in hazy gray light, but vast areas of the room were black.

Dana looked at herself through the fuzzy holes of her cap. The flour gave her skin a dull gray hue, not the glow she had wanted. But good enough. Maybe better, in fact. Bright enough to let her be seen, but only dimly.

What you can't quite see—that's what is really scary.

So how does a ghost walk? she wondered. They probably don't. In movies, they generally swoop through the air. But zombies kind of stagger around with their arms out.

Dana lifted her arms as if reaching for her next victim and took long, stiff-legged strides toward the center of the room.

Shit, this isn't a zombie walk, it's Frankenstein.

Frankenstein's the scientist, stupid, not the monster.

Yes, Roland.

She stopped strutting and changed her gait to a slow lurching stagger.

Perfect.

So where the fuck are you, Roland? If you're too scared to scream, let's at least have a few gasps or whimpers.

Are you crouched in a corner, wetting your pants?

Dana slowly turned around, searching for his huddled shape in the gray near the windows, trying to find him in the black areas.

He isn't here, she decided. Even if I can't see him, he for sure would've seen me by now. He would've done something—yelled or maybe run for it.

Dana turned toward the front of the restaurant, lowered her arms for a moment to smear the sweat rolling down her sides, then raised her arms again and shuffled forward.

Over to the left, the room branched out. Dana saw a vague shape that might be a bar.

He's probably hiding behind it.

She took a few steps in that direction and a rush of excitement stopped her.

Roland's sleeping bag.

Mummy bag.

One dark, puffy end of it was barely visible in the gloom from a front window.

I can't see him, but he can see me. If he's looking this way. If he's awake.

For a few seconds, Dana couldn't force herself to move. She stood there, shaking and breathless, feeling as if her legs might give out.

This'll be good, she thought. This'll get him. The shithead'll wish he'd never been born.

Go for it, she told herself.

She lurched toward the sleeping bag. Her legs felt like warm liquid, but they held her up. She let out a low moan.

That'll get his attention.

When she stopped moaning, she heard him.

He was taking quick, short breaths.

Awake, all right.

She stood over him, no more than a yard away, peering down but still unable to see anything in the darkness. No, maybe that was a face—that oval blur. If so, Roland was sitting up.

Bending at the waist, she reached toward him.

A shriek blasted her ears.

Every muscle in Dana's body seemed to jerk, snapping her upright, hurling her backward. She waved her arms, trying to stay up, then fell. The floor pounded her rump.

A light beam stung her eyes.

She shielded her eyes with a hand. "Take it out of my face." The beam lowered. She pulled off the cap. The light was on her chest, moving from one breast to the other. It dropped, streaking down her belly and shining between her legs. She threw her knees together, blocking it. The light returned to her breasts. She covered them with one arm and used the other arm to brace herself up. Her chest heaved as she struggled to catch her breath.

"So," she gasped, "did I scare you, or what?"

In answer, the light tipped downward. Roland was sitting on top of his mummy bag, his legs stretched out. The lap of his faded blue jeans was stained dark.

Dana grinned. "You wet your pants."

"I wanta go," Roland said in a shaky voice.

"Hell, you already *went*."

"You won, okay? You won. Let me loose." He turned his light toward a nearby card table with bottles on top. "The key's up there."

"Key?"

The beam moved again, this time to his left hand. It was cuffed to a metal rail near the bottom of the bar.

"Holy shit," Dana muttered.

"My insurance. That's how I knew I'd win."

"You *cuffed* yourself?"

"Get the key, okay?"

So that was why Roland had insisted that she come in at dawn to get him—so she could unlock the handcuffs.

"Where are the Polaroids?" she asked.

"In my pack."

"Give me the flashlight."

Roland didn't argue. He lowered it to the floor and pushed. It skidded toward her feet. Dana sat up, stretched forward, and grabbed it.

Getting to her knees, she shined the beam on Roland. His gaunt face, dead pale, looked even more cadaverous than usual. Squinting, he turned away from the glare.

She aimed the light at his crotch.

"Peed your fucking pants," she said. "Did you really think I was a ghost?"

"I don't know," he mumbled.

Dana chuckled. Then she crawled to the pack, searched it, and found an envelope. Inside the envelope were the photographs. She flicked through them, counting. All ten were there. She set the envelope on the floor and took her camera from the pack.

"What're you doing?" Roland asked.

"Just recording the moment for posterity." Standing up, Dana faced him and clamped the flashlight between her thighs aiming it so the beam lit his wet jeans. She raised the camera to her eye. "Say 'cheese.' " She took three shots, the flash bar blinking bright. "Now take off your pants."

He shook his head.

"Want me to leave you here?"

With his one free hand, Roland opened his jeans and tugged them down to his knees.

"You don't believe in underpants?"

Dana snapped three more shots, then gathered up the photos that had dropped to the floor. She tucked them inside the envelope and put the envelope and the camera into his pack. She put her stocking cap in with them, swung the pack up and slipped her arms through the straps.

She shined the beam on Roland, who had pulled up his pants and was zipping the fly. "Adios."

"Unlock me," he said, squinting into the light.

"Do you think I'm nuts?"

"I went along with it. You promised. Now come on." He wasn't pleading. He sounded calm.

Dana thought about it. She really wanted to leave him here. But that would mean coming back tomorrow or sending Jason over to set him free. Also, he would end up winning the bet. A hundred bucks down the toilet.

"I don't care about the pictures," he said. "You can keep them."

"Mighty big of you. I'd like to see you just *try* to take 'em off me."

"Then what's the big deal? Get the key."

"Maybe. Stay put while I get dressed."

"Very funny."

She left him there. With the aid of the flashlight, her return to the kitchen was easy. Her foot had left smudges of blood on the linoleum. She wrinkled her nose at the sight of the mess she had stepped in.

Using the wool cap, she began to brush the flour off her body.

The gag had certainly worked.

Scared the hell out of Roland.

Wet his pants.

Funny how he hadn't tried to hide that, just flashed the light down there to show her the damage as if it were nothing.

In fact, he'd been awfully calm about letting her take the pictures. Even pulled his pants down without much protest.

After having the headless ghost come at him, everything else must've seemed easy.

Maybe he's in shock, or something.

Probably is.

On top of which, he's scared shitless I'll drive off and leave him. He knows he damn well *better* cooperate. Without the key, he's stuck and he knows it.

Dana shined the light down at her body. Most of the flour was off, but her skin was still dusted white. She would need to take a shower when she got back.

After dressing, she slipped the envelope containing the photos into a rear pocket of her jeans. She pulled the poncho over her head and picked up Roland's pack.

Her dorm room was without a kitchen, so she had no further use for the flour. She left the open bag on the floor and returned to the cocktail area.

Roland still sat with his back against the bar and his legs stretched out. He looked as if he hadn't moved at all while she was gone.

"So," Dana said. "I guess you're ready to leave."

He nodded.

"I don't want pee on my car seat."

"I'll sit on my sleeping bag."

"I've got a better idea. How about if you walk back to campus?"

"It's raining."

"Yeah, well, you can use a shower."

"Just give me the key."

Dana stepped to the table. "I knew you wouldn't last out the night," she said. The small key to the handcuffs glinted among the bottles and glasses. She picked it up. "The cuffs were a pretty neat idea, though. You would've won for sure if I hadn't come along. But you lost, all right. I always knew you were a chicken. I guess you knew it, too, or you wouldn't have cuffed yourself in. Huh? You *knew* you didn't have the guts to stick it out."

She twisted the cap off a bottle of vodka. They key was small enough to fit through the bottle's neck. She dropped it. The key made a quiet splash. A moment later, it clinked against the bottom. She screwed the cap back on and tightened it with all her strength.

"Do yourself a favor," she suggested. "Drink your way down to the key. It'll help take the sting out of your hike."

Dana tossed the bottle onto his lap.

At the door, she smiled back at him and said, "Cheers."

The door bumped shut. Roland, in the darkness, clamped the bottle between his legs and twisted the cap off. He tugged his T-shirt up. Dumped vodka onto his belly until the key fell onto his bare skin. Flung the bottle away. Peeled the key off his belly and unlocked the cuff at his wrist.

Dana, walking quickly through the rain, was only a few yards from her car when she figured that Roland had probably succeeded, by now, in removing the handcuffs. It would still take him a while to gather up his sleeping bag. She glanced back, anyway.

Roland!

He looked crazy sprinting toward her, his head thrown back and his mouth wide, his arms windmilling as if he were trying to swim, not run.

In his right hand was a knife.

Dana raced for the car.

She thought, that was damn quick of him.

She thought, what's he doing with that knife?

Where are my keys?

In the ignition.

Lucky. No fumbling.

She grabbed the door handle and pulled. The force of her pull ripped her fingers from the handle and she remembered she had left the car by its passenger door.

She whirled around.

Roland was almost upon her.

"Okay, look, you can ride back with me!"

He stopped. His lip curled up.

"Hey, Roland, come on."

He clutched the front of her poncho, jerked her forward, and rammed the knife into her belly.

Roland pulled the knife out. He shoved Dana backward, keeping his grip on the poncho, and lowered her to the pavement. She sat there, moaning and holding her belly.

Roland sat on her legs.

He punched her nose and she flopped back. Her head thumped the pavement. She didn't lose consciousness, but she didn't struggle. Rain fell on her face. She blinked and gasped for air.

Straddling her, Roland plucked the front of the poncho away from her body, poked his knife through it, and sliced the plastic sheet open to her throat.

"Plea—" she gasped.

He cut open the front of her sweatshirt and spread it apart.

Rain sluiced away the blood on her belly, but more blood poured from the gash. Her chest rose and fell as she panted. Roland stared at her breasts. Then he put his knife away.

Bending low, he stretched out his arms. He held her breasts. They were wet and slick, warm beneath the wetness.

He kissed the gash on her belly.

He sucked blood from it.

Dana shrieked and jerked rigid beneath him when he bit.

* * *

She stayed alive for a long time. It was better that way.

Her heart still throbbed when Roland tore it from her chest cavity.

He was almost full, so he didn't eat much of it. He stuffed what was left into her chest, then crawled to her head.

He scalped her, cracked open her skull with the pry bar, and scooped out her warm, dripping brain.

The best part.

Chapter Fourteen

JUST AFTER SUNRISE, ROLAND RETURNED TO CAMPUS. He left Dana's car in the lot behind his dorm, and hurried into the lobby. He rushed upstairs, along the quiet corridor, and got inside his room without being seen—lucky, since he was naked except for his windbreaker.

He dropped his backpack to the floor, then took off his windbreaker and inspected it for blood. He'd been very careful with it, knowing that he would need to wear it back to the dorm after getting rid of his other clothes.

They were with Dana, stuffed inside his mummy bag and hidden in bushes about ten miles south of the restaurant.

The windbreaker, inside and out, looked spotless. He dropped it over the pack, then checked himself. The rain had done a good job of cleaning him. Though all his fingernails had blood caked under them, he looked fine otherwise.

Roland put on his robe, gathered what he needed for a shower, put his room key in his pocket, and hurried down the corridor.

The rest room was silent. He made sure the toilet stalls were vacant, then unloaded his stuff onto a bench in the dressing area of the shower room and approached the sinks. Taking off his robe, he inspected himself in the mirrors above the sinks. At the back of his leg was a crust of dried blood in the shape of a circle where the thing had chewed its way into him. From there, a bluish bruise extended upward, angling across his right buttock to his spine, then straight up his back to the nape of his neck. His hanging black hair, he thought, was long enough to cover the neck area when he was dressed.

He stepped closer, shivering as the cold edge of the sink met the back of his legs. Turning sideways, he twisted his head around. He could see a slight hump at the back of his neck. It continued to about halfway down his spine.

Roland fingered the distended skin behind his neck. The lump felt much larger than it looked. He stroked it. The thing writhed a bit, and gave him a mild tingle of pleasure—only a hint of the ecstasy it had bestowed when he had fed it.

Worried that someone might come through the door, Roland draped the robe over his shoulders and returned to the dressing area. He dropped his robe onto the bench, gathered up his washcloth, soap, shampoo and toothbrush, and entered the shower room.

The hot spray felt wonderful on his chilled skin. He lathered himself and scrubbed. He washed his hair. After rinsing, he found that much of the blood was gone from under his fingernails. But not all of it. He used his toothbrush to get rid of the rest.

Back in his room, Roland stood in front of the built-in bureau and combed his hair straight forward as he always did before parting it down the center. This time, he parted it on the left. It made him appear more normal. Good. He no longer cared to draw attention to himself by looking weird. He wanted to blend in with the student body. At least until it was time to find a new van and hit the road.

No. Too soon.

You'd attract more attention if you suddenly changed.

For now, do everything the same as always.

Roland nodded and moved his part to the center where it belonged.

He put on a clean pair of jeans and socks, then a yellow T-shirt with bloody bullet holes printed across its front as if he'd been stitched by a machine gun. The T-shirt, however, let too much show. He put on another shirt over it—a black sports shirt with a collar high enough to conceal the back of his neck.

Roland yawned. He ached to sleep. Plenty of time later for that. Just a couple more things to do.

He removed the handcuffs and key from his pack, and hid them under some socks in his bureau.

Then he took out the envelope with the photos. The envelope was smeared all over with bloody fingerprints.

"Not too cool, Roland, old man," he whispered.

He opened it. The photos weren't stained. He separated them, slipping the shots of Dana into a fresh envelope, and returned them to Jason's drawer.

He flipped through the remaining photos and grinned. Dana would've been pleased by the way they turned out. Roland in his pissed jeans. Roland naked from waist to knees. She would've had fun with these, using them to humiliate Roland.

Roland?

Me.

He frowned, puzzled that he had been thinking of himself by name.

After tearing the photos and envelopes into tiny pieces, he returned to the rest room and flushed them down a toilet.

Back in his own room, he stretched out on his bed and slept.

The door bumped shut, waking him. Sitting up, he rubbed his face while Jason tossed an overnight bag onto the other bed and hung up his suit.

"How was the wedding?" Roland asked.

"Not bad. The groom's a real dork, but that's her problem. Man, did I tie one on." He sat on his bed and made a sour face. "What gives, anyway?"

"Huh?"

"I saw Dana's car in the lot."

"Yeah."

"Where is she?" Jason lowered his head slightly. "Hiding under the bed? You been slipping it to her?"

"Oh, sure."

"So what's her car doing out there?"

"It's a long story."

"So? Spill it." Jason opened his bag, removed a pint flask, and took a swig. "Hair of the dog," he muttered.

"She's probably all right," Roland said.

"Yeah? What do you mean, probably?"

Roland got up. He found the newspaper story about the killings at the Oakwood Inn, and handed it to Jason. "Read this."

Waiting, Roland glanced at the clock. Almost noon. He'd been asleep for nearly six hours. He felt good.

Jason looked up. "Yeah? What's this got to do with Dana?"

"We went over there last night. To the restaurant."

"For dinner?" He looked at the paper. "Who opened it?"

"No, it wasn't open. It was deserted, locked up."

"Then what were you doing there?"

"Dana got this thing into her head about me not having any guts. She dared me to spend the night in the restaurant. She bet me a hundred bucks I wouldn't."

A grin spread over Jason's face. "Yeah, that's Dana, all right. I was gone, so she figured she'd use the opportunity to stick it to you."

"She doesn't like me much."

"Sure she does. She just gets a kick out of tormenting you, that's all."

"Well, whatever. Anyway, I said I'd spend the night there, and that I had more guts than she did."

"Wrong move, buddy."

"So the way it turned out, we both went into the place. The deal was, whoever chickened out first and split, would lose."

Jason shook his head slowly. "Christ, and to think I missed out on all this. So what happened, you turned tail, she stayed, and you drove her car back here?"

"There was more to it than that."

Jason took another drink from his flask.

"Around midnight, we heard a noise. Kind of a bumping sound. Scared me shitless."

"Yeah, I bet it did."

"I was ready to get the hell out, and Dana told me to go ahead and kiss the hundred bucks good-bye. So I stayed. She went exploring to find out what made the noise."

Jason began to look concerned. "You let her go off alone?"

"I *told* her not to."

"You could've gone with her."

"Anyway, the thing is, she didn't come back. I stayed

by the front door, near the bar. I heard her wandering around. After a while, she called out and said she'd found the wine cellar. I guess she went down there. I waited a long time, Jase, but she didn't come back."

"So you ran off and left her?"

"No. Not then, anyway. I went to the kitchen. It was . . . that's where those two people got killed. There was blood. Lots of it."

"You must've felt right at home," Jason muttered. There was no humor in his tone. He sounded annoyed and worried.

"It was pretty disgusting. Anyway, I found an open door with stairs leading down to the cellar. I shined my flashlight down, but I couldn't see her. Then I called her name a few times. She didn't answer. Finally, I started to go down. I was pretty damn scared, but I'd made up my mind I *had* to find her. I'd just gone down a couple of stairs when I heard someone laugh. It was a real quiet, nasty laugh. *That's* when I got the fuck out of there."

Jason's mouth hung open. He gazed at Roland with wide, bloodshot eyes.

"I ran out and got in the car. She'd left the keys in it. I thought I'd go for the police, and then I realized it must've been Dana who'd laughed that way."

"Did it sound like her?"

"God, who knows? When I heard it, I thought it sounded like a man. Then I got to thinking, and I was sure it must've been Dana. She did it to scare me off. You know? To win the bet. So I was sitting in her car and she'd won the hundred bucks by pulling that stunt and scaring me off, so I got kind of pissed at her and I figured it'd serve her right if I just took off with the car and left her there. So that's what I did."

"Jesus."

Roland shrugged. "It's just a few miles out. I figured, let her walk. She's probably back at her dorm by now."

Jason got up without another word and left the room. Roland went to the door and watched him stride down the corridor—heading for one of the pay phones near the exit door.

Roland sat on his bed and waited. His story had sounded quite convincing, he thought. He forced his smile away in time to greet Jason with a somber face.

"I talked to Kerry. Dana isn't back yet. She sounded pretty worried."

"Maybe Dana got a late start. Like I said, it's a few miles. If you want, we could drive out that way and give her a lift."

"Let's go."

Jason's car was low on gas, so he said they should take Dana's Volkswagen. He told Roland to drive. Then he settled in the passenger seat and shut his eyes. "Tell me when we get there," he said.

He wished he'd taken it easy on the booze, yesterday. All that champagne at the reception, then dinner with his folks—cocktails, more champagne, brandy afterward. Great fun at the time, but now he had a headache and his stomach felt as if he'd been eating rotten eggs. And his body seemed to buzz.

Should've skipped the whole deal, he thought. Could've been here last night, instead, making it with Dana. Then none of this would've happened.

What did those two think they were doing, going out to some damn empty restaurant like that?

Easy to figure. Dana wanted to mess with Roland's head. Never could stand the guy. As for Roland, he probably had some fancy hopes of putting it to her. Lotsa luck on that one, pal. You were the last guy on earth, you wouldn't stand a chance. Hates your guts, pal.

What if he tried and she told him to fuck off and he went ape and nailed her?

The thoughts made Jason's heart pound harder, sending jolts of pain into his head.

Roland might be a little peculiar, he told himself, but the guy wouldn't pull something like that. He might want to, but he didn't have the guts. Especially not with Dana.

But it could've started with a small disagreement. Dana turned mean, lashed out at him with that tongue of hers. Next thing you know, Roland strikes back.

If he hurt her, I'll kill him.

Jason rubbed his temples. He remembered a talk with Roland, late one night in the darkness of their room when they both were lying awake.

> Jason: If you could fuck any girl on campus, who'd it be? Aside from Dana.
>
> Roland: I don't want to fuck Dana.
>
> Jason: Oh, sure.
>
> Roland: Geez, I don't know.
>
> Jason: Just one. Who'd it be?
>
> Roland: Mademoiselle LaRue. (His French teacher.)
>
> Jason: You're joking. She's a bitch.
>
> Roland: She's a real piece.
>
> Jason: She's a bitch. What are you, a glutton for punishment?
>
> Roland: First, I'd tie her up. I'd throw the rope over a rafter or something, so she's hanging there. Then I'd take out my knife and cut off all her clothes. When she's all naked, I'd start cutting on her.
>
> Jason: Pervert. I said "fuck," not "torture."

Roland: Oh, I'd get around to that. Eventually. But I'd want to have some fun with her, first.

Jason: Fun? You are warped, man. Definitely warped.

Just a fantasy of his, Jason told himself. The guy's a chicken. He'd never actually try to *do* anything like that, not with Mademoiselle LaRue or Dana or anyone else. All just talk.

Better be.

He opened his eyes and looked at Roland.

"Almost there," Roland said. "I've been watching the road. Surprised we haven't run across her walking. But you know, she could've been getting back about the time we started out. Maybe we just missed her."

Or maybe she's at the restaurant, tied up and hanging from a rafter, stripped and cut up . . .

"She better be all right," Jason muttered.

"God, I hope so," Roland said. "I keep thinking about that laugh I heard in the cellar. I mean, suppose it *wasn't* Dana?" His lips pulled into a tight line. He looked in pain. "If anything happened to her, it's all my fault. I should've gone down there. I should've."

Ahead, on the right, was a sign for the Oakwood Inn. Roland slowed the car and swung onto a narrow road in front of the sign.

"What if someone was down there?" he said. "Like a pervert or something, and he got her? Maybe he hangs around the place, just waiting for people to come along."

"You've seen too many of those splatter movies," Jason told him.

"That kind of thing happens, though. In real life. Look at *Psycho* and *Texas Chainsaw Massacre.* They were both based on real life, on that Ed Gein guy in Wisconsin.

Know what he used to do, he used to *dress up* in the skins of his victims—wear 'em like clothes.''

''Hey, come on. I don't want to hear this.''

''All his neighbors thought he was a real neat guy because he'd bring them gifts of meat. What they didn't know, the meat was human.''

''For Christsake, cut it out.''

''I'm just saying it's not just in movies. Weird shit happens.''

Roland stopped the car in front of the restaurant. He turned off the engine. He frowned at Jason. ''Wish I'd brought my knife,'' he whispered. ''I mean, there's probably nobody in there, but . . .''

''Wait in the car if you're scared.'' Jason threw open the door and climbed out. He walked straight to the porch stairs. He took them two at a time.

Bad enough, he thought, without Roland talking about that stuff and acting like he's scared some nut might be hiding in the restaurant.

In front of the door, Jason hesitated. Nobody's in there, he told himself. Except maybe Dana.

She'll be standing inside, a hip thrust out to the side, hands on her hips and a smirk on her face. ''So, my ride is here at last. Took you dorks long enough. If you thought I was gonna *walk* back, you were nuts.''

She won't be in there.

Maybe her body. Hanging naked, all cut up.

She's probably back on campus by now.

She'll get a big laugh when she hears about this. Our rescue mission.

She won't get a big laugh. She's dead.

Jason looked over his shoulder. Roland was coming, so he waited. He rubbed his sweaty hands on his jeans. He tried to take a deep breath, but there was a hard, tight place below his lungs that wouldn't let them expand enough.

Roland climbed onto the porch. Crouching, he picked up a board with nails at both ends. There were several such boards lying around. Apparently, they'd been used to barricade the door. "Why don't you get one?" Roland whispered.

Jason shook his head. He didn't need a weapon unless he believed there was danger inside; he didn't want to believe that.

He pushed on the door. It swung open. Cool air from inside breathed on him, raising goose bumps. He took a single step forward.

Enough light entered the restaurant through the doorway and windows for him to see the cocktail area to his right, the big dining area to his left. He stepped toward the dining room. It looked empty except for a ladder, an open toolbox, some cans and jars, a vacuum cleaner and broom, all clustered near the right wall. Nothing moved.

"Dana!" he called out. His voice sounded hollow, as if he'd yelled the name into a cave.

No answer came.

Did you really expect one? he thought.

He looked to the right. On the floor in front of the long bar was an empty vodka bottle. Had Dana and Roland been drinking? Maybe they both got drunk. Maybe that's how it started.

He could ask Roland about the bottle. But he didn't want to hear his voice again—didn't want anyone else to hear his voice again.

With Roland at his side, he walked into the dining area. Along the wall beyond the ladder was a double door—the kind that saloons always had in westerns. He pushed through it and entered the kitchen.

The linoleum floor had footprints, maybe a dozen of

them, rust-colored stains made by a bare left foot. A small foot. Dana's foot? The tracks began at a dried puddle of blood near the far side of the kitchen and became fainter as they approached the place where Jason was standing.

Near the blood puddle was a sack of flour. The floor directly behind the sack was coated with the white powder.

"What's all this?" Jason whispered.

"The blood's from those two who were killed Thursday night."

Christ, he thought, don't the cops clean it up? If they don't, who does?

"What about the flour?"

"It was here when we came," Roland answered in a voice as hushed as Jason's.

"The footprints?"

"I don't know."

"They weren't here?"

"I don't think so."

"Was Dana wearing shoes?"

"Sure. Anyway, she had shoes on last time I saw her." Roland pointed with his board at an open door. "The cellar's down there."

Jason walked slowly toward it, rolling his feet from heel to toe so he wouldn't make any noise though he knew that anyone down there—anyone alive—would've heard him call out Dana's name and maybe even heard the quiet conversation in the kitchen.

He peered down the steep wooden stairway.

Dark as hell down there.

He hoped that the restaurant had electricity, then recalled that there'd been a lamp and vacuum cleaner with the ladder and things in the other room. He flicked a switch on the wall beside the door. A light came on below.

"Want me to stay up here and keep watch?" Roland whispered.

"Keep watch for what? Come on."

He started down the stairs. They groaned under his weight. He pictured breaking through one, falling. Worse, he pictured someone hiding behind the stairway, grabbing his ankle from between the boards.

Partway down, he stopped and ducked below the ceiling. From here, he could see most of the cellar. Straight ahead were several sections of empty shelves, some made for holding wine bottles and others apparently intended for the storage of other restaurant supplies. Off to the left was a vast area with pipes running along the ceiling, a furnace near the far wall.

No Dana.

No one else.

That he could see.

Jason rushed to the bottom, got away from the staircase and looked back. Nobody behind it.

His tension eased a little. Even though the cellar had plenty of places where someone might be hidden, he doubted that anyone, alive or dead, was down here.

Just me, he thought. And Roland.

Nevertheless, he began to search. Roland stayed behind him as he walked through the aisles between the shelves.

Roland. Behind him. Carrying that board with the nails in it.

And I'm probably the only one who knows he was here last night with Dana.

If it *was* Roland who . . .

He could almost feel those nails piercing his skull.

He turned around. Roland, with the board resting on his shoulder, raised his eyebrows. "You want to take the lead for a while?" Jason whispered.

Roland's lip curled up. "Thanks anyway."

"I'm going first, I ought to have the weapon."

"Could've got one for yourself."

"Don't give me shit."

"What'll *I* use?"

"Don't worry about it, huh? Anything happens, I'd be better with that thing than you."

Roland's eyes narrowed. For a moment, Jason half expected Roland to swing the thing down at him. Wouldn't dare, he thought. Not with me facing him. Knows he wouldn't stand a chance. I'm bigger, stronger, quicker. By a long shot.

"Guess you're right," Roland said, and handed the board to him.

They resumed the search. Now that he had the weapon, Jason wondered about himself. He must've been crazy to think that Roland might try to kill him.

The kid's more scared than me about being down here.

He didn't lay a finger on Dana.

He's sure, in that twisted mind of his, that some maniac right out of a slasher movie was down here last night and did a number on Dana.

What if he's right?

No, please. Nobody got her. She was down here alone, she did that laugh herself to scare Roland off, she's probably back at her dorm by now.

She's dead, whispered Jason's mind.

But he didn't find her body in the cellar. He didn't find a pool of blood. He found none of her clothes. He found no signs of a struggle. He found nothing at all to indicate that Dana had ever been in the cellar, much less murdered there.

He was glad to get out of the cellar. He shut the door and leaned against it.

"What do you think?" Roland asked.

"I don't know."

"Why don't we get out of here?" Without waiting for a reply, Roland walked to the rear door of the kitchen and swung it open. He stopped. "Hey."

"What?"

"Take a look at this."

Jason hurried over to him. Roland was fingering the edge of the door. The wood on its outside, near the latch, was gouged and splintered. "Someone broke in," Jason said.

"Not me and Dana. We came in the front way."

"Christ."

Roland whispered, "There *was* someone else."

Jason tossed the board aside and stepped through the doorway. Beyond the rear of the restaurant a vast, rolling, weed-covered field stretched to the edge of a forest.

He stepped down from the porch. He walked through the tall grass and weeds of what had once been a lawn. The edge of the lawn blended in with the start of the field, only different in that the lawn was flat and the field began with a small rise. He climbed the rise.

Roland came up behind him and stood at his side while Jason shielded his eyes against the sunlight and scanned the area.

"What now?" Roland asked. "Search in the weeds?"

"I don't know." There were acres and acres, and then the forest. The idea of trying to find Dana out there seemed overwhelming and futile.

If she's in the weeds, he thought, she's dead.

"Maybe the guy has a place in the woods," Roland said. "A shack or something, you know? That Ed Gein I was telling you about—"

"We'll never find her," Jason said.

"Maybe . . ." Roland didn't continue.

Jason looked at him. "Maybe what?"

Roland shrugged. "It's probably a dumb idea. But if we

go back to campus and she still hasn't shown up and we figure maybe she really did get snatched by some kind of a nut . . ."

"Then we'll go to the police."

"Hell, shit, they'll think *I* had something to do with it. Man, I was the last one with her last night. They'll blame *me*, and then we'll never get the guy that did it. I mean, she might still be alive. If some crazy guy got her, maybe he's keeping her alive. Maybe he doesn't want to kill her till after he's done . . . messing with her. You know?"

"Guy sounds a lot like you," Jason said.

Roland made a nervous laugh. "Yeah. Takes one to know one. Shit, though, I'd never *do* anything like that. I just think about it, you know? But that gives us an advantage, right? I can like imagine what he might do. And that's why I've got this idea."

"What idea?"

"How to get him. And how to find Dana."

"Yeah? Let's hear it."

Chapter Fifteen

"HOW YOU DOING, FELLA?"

"Just fine," Jake said into the phone. He didn't feel fine at all, he felt depressed. As soon as he hung up, he would be taking Kimmy back to her mother. "Did Steve get in?"

"Sure did. He wants to talk to you. Hold on a sec."

Moments later, Steve Applegate came over the line. "Jake? I finished up on Smeltzer. I want you to get over here."

"Find something interesting?"

"Interesting? Yes, I'd say interesting. How soon can you be here?"

"Fifteen, twenty minutes."

"Higgins should be in on this."

The Chief? "What is it?"

"Whetted your curiosity, have I? Well, then you'd better

get moving. I'll phone Higgins.'' Without another word, he hung up.

Jake put down the phone.

Kimmy was huddled in a corner of the sofa, watching television. The Three Stooges. Curly saluted his nose to block a two-fingered eye jab from Moe, then went ''Nyar-nyar-nyar!''

''Hon,'' Jake said, ''we'd better hit the road.''

''Do we have to?''

''You giving me back talk?'' he snapped. ''Huh?'' He rushed over to Kimmy. Eyes wide, she clamped her arms to her sides. Jake pushed his fingers under them, digging into her ribs. She laughed and writhed. ''I'll teach you! Sass me, will you?'' Rolling on her back, she kicked out at him. The sole of her shoe pounded his thigh. ''Owww!'' Clutching his leg, he staggered backward and fell to the floor.

Kimmy grinned down at him from the sofa. ''That's what you get,'' she said, ''when you mess with She-Ra.''

''Jeez, I guess so. You discombobulated me.''

She waved a fist at him. ''Want some more?''

''No, please.'' Jake stood up. ''Anyway, we really do have to go.''

The joy went out of her face. ''Do we *have* to?''

''I'm afraid so, honey. Mommy's expecting you, and besides, I have to go to work.''

''I'll go to work with you, okay?''

''I don't think so.''

''I won't make the siren go,'' she assured him, looking contrite and hopeful. ''Really I won't. Can't I go with you?''

''I'm sorry, honey. Not today. Besides, I won't be using the siren car.''

''I want to go with you, anyway.''

"You wouldn't want to go where I'm going. I have to see a guy who's toes up."

"Oh, yuck. Really?"

"Yep."

She made the kind of face she might have made, Jake thought, if somebody stuck a plate of beets under her nose. "Well, don't touch him," she advised.

Stopping behind BB's Toy, Jake got out and opened the passenger door for Kimmy. She watched him with somber eyes. When the safety harness was unsnapped, she didn't throw the straps off her shoulders in a hurry to climb out. She just sat there.

"Let's see a smile," Jake said. "Come on, it's Mommy's birthday. She'll want to see a smile on that mug of yours."

"I don't feel good."

"Are you sick?"

"I am not happy."

"Why not?"

"You're making me go away."

"I'm sorry."

"No, you're not."

Jake lifted her out of the car seat. She wrapped her arms and legs around him. "You'll have a good time today," he said as he carried her toward the house.

"No, I won't."

"And I'll be back on Friday and we'll have two whole days together like we're supposed to."

Kimmy squeezed herself more tightly against him. He could feel her begin to shake, and he knew that she was crying. She didn't bawl; she cried softly, her breath making quiet snagging sounds close to his ear.

"Aw, honey," he whispered. And struggled not to cry, himself.

* * *

Jake swung his car into the lot beside the Applegate Mortuary. The town of Clinton wasn't large enough to justify a city morgue, but Steve, whose brother took care of the funeral parlor side of the business, had spent twelve years as a forensic pathologist with the Office of the Medical Examiner in Los Angeles—resigned in a huff after Thomas Nogushi got canned—and had come back here to practice in his hometown.

Clinton didn't do a booming business in autopsies, but there were evidently enough to keep Steve happy. An autopsy was required for everyone who died as the apparent result of an accident, suicide, or homicide, under any kind of circumstances in which the death was not pretty much expected by the deceased's physician. An autopsy was also required for every corpse headed for the crematory instead of the grave. With all that, even a small, peaceful town like Clinton provided quite a few opportunities for Steve to practice his art.

Three new customers Thursday alone, Jake thought as he climbed from his car. Steve must think he's back in LA.

Jake entered through a rear door that opened into Betty's office. She looked away from her typing, smiled when she saw him, and swiveled her chair around. "Been a while, Jake." Tipping back her chair, she folded her hands behind her head—a posture that seemed designed to draw Jake's attention to her breasts. Betty's job didn't require her to face the public, so she was allowed to dress as she pleased. She was wearing a T-shirt with the slogan, "Make My Day." It clung nicely to her full breasts. Her nipples pointed at Jake through the fabric.

"Looking good," he said.

"Natch." She stared at his groin. He didn't look, himself, but he could feel a warm swelling down there.

"Well," he said, "Steve's waiting for me."

"No hot hurry. Higgins isn't here yet." She looked up at his face. Her eyes widened a bit. "So what's the story?"

"What story?"

"Got a new friend?"

Jake shook his head.

"Taken a vow of celibacy?"

"Just busy, that's all."

A smile tilted her mouth. "Well, if you ever happen to get unbusy, I just bought a rubber sheet for my bed and I've got a great big bottle of slippy-slidy oil we can rub all over each other. You oughta just see how it looks on me in candlelight."

Jake could imagine. He pursed his dry lips and blew through them. "I'll keep it in mind," he said.

"Just in case you find some free time on your hands."

"Yeah."

She nodded. Again, her gaze lowered to his crotch. "I'd be glad to take care of *that* for you right now, if you'd like. Plenty of empty rooms around here. How about it?"

"You're kidding." He knew she wasn't. "We're in a morgue," he reminded her.

"Just the place for taking care of stiffs, and I'm looking at one." She rolled back her chair and stood up. She was wearing a short, black leather skirt. Her bare legs were slender and lightly tanned.

"This is crazy," Jake muttered. He felt shaky inside. Was he really going along with this?

Then the rear door opened and in stepped Barney Higgins, Chief of the Clinton Police Department. Betty rolled her eyes upward. She turned to Higgins. "Hi-ya, Barn."

"Hey, Betts." The small, wiry man winked and snicked his tongue. "What's that y' got in yer shirt?"

"Your guess is good as mine, Barn."

"Where'd you pick 'em up? I'd like to order a set for

the wife." He laughed and slapped Jake's shoulder. "Let's get a move on, I got a hot poker game back at the house." He turned to Betty. "Where's the Apple, down in his butcher shop?"

"B-1," she said. "Have fun, boys."

Leaving her office through a side door, they started down a flight of stairs toward the basement. "You get a good look at that gal?" Barney asked.

"Sure did."

"Prime. *Ooo!* How'd y'like playing some hide-the-salami with a prime thing like that? Yeah!"

"She's a knockout, all right."

At the bottom of the stairs, Jake pulled open a fire door. Directly across the corridor was B-1, the autopsy room. His stomach fluttered as he walked over and opened the door. From the room came a high whining buzz like the sound of a dentist's drill.

Steve Applegate, a cigar stub clamped in his teeth, squinted down through the smoke at what he was doing. Whatever he was doing, it involved the head of a naked woman who was stretched out on one of the tables. And it involved the small buzz saw that was making such a racket.

Jake chose to watch his shoes as he walked across the polished linoleum floor.

The saw went silent.

"Who y'got there?" Barney asked.

"Mary-Beth Harker. A probable cerebral aneurysm."

"Joe Harker's girl?"

"That's right."

"Aw, shit. Shit. When'd it happen?"

"Last night."

"Shit. She's not, what, eighteen, nineteen?"

"Nineteen."

"Shit. That's his only daughter."

Jake felt cold spread through him like a winter gust. Kimmy. God, what if it was Kimmy? How could a man go on living if something like that happened to his kid?

He turned away and walked toward another table. The body on this one was covered with a blue cloth. "This Smeltzer?" he asked without looking around.

"That's Smeltzer, Ronald. I'll get to Smeltzer, Peggy, later today."

I killed this guy, he told himself, wanting to feel the guilt, wanting it to come and take away the terror of imagining Kimmy dead. I killed this guy. He's dead because of me.

His mind began the replay. Fine. Smeltzer raising his head, tearing a flap of skin from his wife's belly, turning in slow motion to reach for the shotgun.

"I've never seen anything like this," Steve said, pulling Jake out of the memory. He drew back the cover.

Smeltzer was facedown. Jake's bullets had left five exit wounds on his back and splayed open the side of his neck.

"Good shooting," Barney commented.

Jake was looking at the gash that ran from the nape of Smeltzer's neck, down his spine, over his right buttock and down his right leg to the outer side of his ankle. The raw, bloodless gash was bordered by about half an inch of blue-gray skin. "What's this?" Jake asked.

"Something of a puzzle," Steve said. With the tip of his cigar, he pointed at the quarter-sized ankle wound. "Know anything about it?" he asked Jake.

Jake shook his head.

"When I stripped him down this morning, I found it along with the hematoma—that discoloration you see there. Frankly, I didn't know what to make of it. A bruise is usually caused by blunt trauma that breaks capillaries in the skin. So I asked myself what could've hit this man in such a way as to follow the curves of his body this way."

"Something flexible," Jake said.

"A whip," Barney suggested. "Maybe a hose."

"That occurred to me. The problem is, the epidermis showed no evidence of injury, which you'd expect if the man had been struck by that kind of instrument. And the ankle wound made me suspicious. So I made an incision at the wound and followed the track of the hematoma to his neck. What I found was a two centimeter separation between the fascias and—"

"Spare me the jargon, huh?" Barney said.

"Along the entire length of the bruise, the connecting tissue between the skin and underlying muscle was no longer connected. It's as if approximately an inch-wide area of skin had been forcibly raised from the inside."

"What are you gettin' at?" Barney asked.

"Something entered this man's body via the ankle wound and burrowed its way up to his neck."

"Y'mean like somethin' *alive*?"

"That's just what I mean."

"Balls."

Steve tapped some ash off the end of his cigar. It dropped into a gutter at the foot of the table. "I found considerable trauma to the brain stem. Appears that it had been chewed into."

Jake stared at the body. "Something tunneled up his body and bit his brain?"

"That's sure the way it looks."

"Jesus," Jake muttered.

"Okay," Barney said. "So where's it at, this *thing*?"

"Gone."

"Gone where?"

"After this man was deceased, it chewed through the posterior wall of his esophagus, traveled down to his stomach, chewed through the stomach wall and made a beeline for his colon. Chewed through that, and exited through his anus."

"You gotta be kiddin'."

Steve punched his cigar dead in the metal gutter. Then he bent down and picked up a pair of boxer shorts that had been turned inside out. The seat was smeared with feces and blood.

Barney wrinkled his nose.

Steve picked up a pair of blue jeans, also pulled inside out. Down the right leg was a narrow trail that diminished as it neared the cuff. "Kidding?" he asked.

Barney shook his head slowly from side to side.

"What could've done something like this?" Jake asked.

Steve shrugged. One side of his mouth stretched upward. "An ambitious snake?"

"Yer a festival a' laughs," Barney said.

"I haven't the faintest idea what did this, but it appears to have been something *shaped,* at least, like a snake."

"I never hearda' snakes doing shit like that."

"Who has?" Steve said.

"Smeltzer was alive when this thing got in him?" Jake asked.

"Definitely."

"How can you tell?"

"The amount of subdural bleeding and the quantity of blood on his right sock. I'd guess, from the degree of coagulation of his ankle wound, that the thing got into him only minutes prior to his death."

"And it left his body after his death? How do you know that?"

"Again, the amount of bleeding. Very little in the areas that it chewed through on the way out."

"Fuckin' 'Twilight Zone,' " Barney said.

"So what do you make of it?" Jake asked.

"I couldn't say."

"We're talking, here," Jake said, "about a guy who blew off his wife's head and started to eat her. And you're saying that, before he went at her, this snake-thing burrowed up his leg and bit him in the brain?"

"That's sure the way it appears."

"And after I shot him, it took off."

"Didn't see it, did ya?" Barney asked.

"I didn't stick around long. I took a quick look through the restaurant to make sure there wasn't a third person, then I headed back to my car to call in. I must've been gone close to fifteen minutes. I guess that gave it time to get out."

"The poop-chute express," Barney said.

"It might still be in the restaurant," Jake said.

"I already searched around here," Steve said, "and the van that brought him in. Didn't want that thing sneaking up on *me.*"

Barney sidestepped, reached over, pinched a leg of Steve's white trousers and lifted. "I already checked that, myself," Steve said. He raised both cuffs above his socks.

Barney crouched for a close look, then turned to Jake. "How 'bout you?"

"I took three showers after—"

"So y'got hygiene. Lift your pants."

Jake drew them up to his knees. Barney squatted beside him, took a long look, then slid Jake's socks down around his ankles.

"Okay, so now we know you guys aren't gonna start munchin' on me."

Jake nodded. "So I'm not the only one who thinks this snake-thing made Smeltzer go haywire."

"It don't make sense, but it makes sense."

"I'm afraid I have to agree," Steve said. "It sounds mad but the possibility is certainly there . . . some kind of creature that sustains itself through a symbiotic relationship with its human host. A parasite. But it doesn't simply take its nourishment from its host, it somehow controls his eating habits.''

Barney smirked. ''Less Smeltzer was in the habit a' eatin' his wife.''

''So we're talking,'' Jake said, ''about a snakelike creature that burrows into a person, takes control of his mind, and compels him to eat human flesh. That *is* what we're talking about here, right?''

''Can't be,'' Barney said. ''Last time I looked I wasn't nuts.''

''If there's another way to interpret this situation,'' Steve said, ''I'd be more than eager to hear it.''

''Yeah. You guys are figments a' my fuckin' nightmare.''

''Neither of you, I take it, has ever heard of a similar situation.''

''You gotta be kiddin'.''

''I've heard of cannibalism,'' Jake said, ''but never anything about a snake or whatever that gets inside you and turns you into one.''

''Gentlemen, I think we've got a situation.'' Steve slipped a fresh cigar from a pocket of his white jacket, stripped off its wrapper, and bit off its end. He spat the wad of leaf into the table gutter. He licked the whole cigar. Then he poked it into his mouth and lit up.

''I drove over to Marlowe, yesterday, at the request of a colleague, Herman Willis. Thursday afternoon, the nude body of a twenty-two-year-old female was found. It had been buried in a field just east of Marlowe. Might never have turned up, except a kid happened to be out playing in the field with his dog. The dog found the grave. The kid ran home for a shovel, apparently thinking he had stumbled onto a buried treasure. He dug for a while, then ran home yelling.''

"Musta' gave'm a good turn."

"Here's the interesting part: the body had been eaten. Quite a lot of the skin had been torn off, portions of muscle devoured." The cigar in Steve's hand was shaking. "She had bite marks all over her body. Some were just enough to break the skin, others took out chunks of her. Her torso had been ripped open. Her heart had been torn out and partly eaten. Her head . . . she had been scalped. Her skull had been caved in with a blunt instrument, possibly a rock. Her brain was missing."

"Holy fuckin' mayonnaise," Barney muttered.

"Willis had never seen anything like this. I think he called me in more for moral support than for my professional opinion. At any rate, the teeth marks and the saliva samples we took from the wounds indicated that her assailant was human."

"Yer sayin' she was a victim of this thing."

"Of someone 'occupied' by this thing."

"When was this person killed?" Jake asked.

"Wednesday, around midnight. Willis was able to pinpoint the time of death pretty accurately based on her stomach contents. She'd been seen at a local pizza joint at eight that night. The degree to which the pizza had been digested—"

Barney flicked the back of his hand against the hip of the body stretched in front of him. "So, where was Ronald Smeltzer Wednesday night?"

"I don't think Smeltzer did it," Jake said. His heart was beating fast. "That van, the one that tried to run down Celia Jamerson, was coming from the direction of Marlowe. Thursday afternoon. Someone, some*thing,* got out of the van alive. There was blood on the pavement behind the rear door. I followed the traces into the field, but couldn't . . ." He shook his head. "Where the van crashed was only a few hundred yards from the Oakwood Inn.

Suppose what I tried to follow was this snake-thing and it found its way to the restaurant, got into Smeltzer that night?'' Jake turned to Steve. ''You got that John Doe from the van?''

''This way.''

They followed Steve out of the autopsy room, down the corridor, and into a room with a dozen refrigerator compartments. He checked the drawer labels, then slid one open. The body that rolled out was covered by a sheet. Jake was grateful for the aroma of Steve's cigar, though it wasn't enough to mask the odor of burnt flesh and hair.

''If you'd prefer not to see this,'' Steve said, ''I think I know what we're looking for.''

Jake, who had seen the charred corpse hanging out the windshield of the van, wasn't eager for a close-up view. But he didn't want to look squeamish in front of Barney, so he kept quiet.

''Let's see'm,'' Barney said.

Steve drew back the sheet. Jake stared at the edge of the aluminum drawer. Though he didn't focus on the body, he saw it. He saw a black thing vaguely shaped like a human.

''I'll have to turn him over,'' Steve said.

''Manage?'' Barney asked, sounding reluctant to help.

''No problem.''

Jake swung his gaze over to Steve and saw that he was wearing surgical gloves. He watched Steve bend over the body. Jake heard papery crumbling sounds. He heard himself groan.

''Guy's a real flake,'' Barney muttered. ''Fallin' apart over ya.''

Steve grinned rigidly around the cigar in his teeth. Lifting and pulling, he wrestled the black lump onto its front. When he finished, the front of his white jacket looked as if someone had rubbed it with charcoal.

"Jake, you were right."

Jake let his eyes be guided by Steve's pointing finger to the gray knobs of spinal column laid bare from the nape of the corpse's neck to midway down its back.

"Looks like the thing was positioned the same as in Smeltzer," Steve said.

"Only didn't take a sneaky way out," Barney added.

"With all this damage, it's hard to be sure exactly what happened, but it appears that the thing made an emergency exit by splitting open the skin all the way up."

"Must be awfully strong," Jake said, "to do that."

"Yeah," Barney said. "And to open the van's back-door."

"The impact probably popped the door open," Jake told him.

"Yeah, maybe."

"I'll take a mold of this man's teeth and draw a blood sample," Steve said, "and make a run over to Marlowe. I'll call from there and let you know if it's a match, but I'd be willing to bet on it."

"Call me at home," Barney told him. "I got a hot poker game goin'."

"If this *is* the guy who killed the woman in Marlowe," Jake said, "it pretty much clinches our theory."

"I think we can assume it's clinched."

"Yeah," Barney agreed. "So we got us a snake that gets inta guys an' turns 'm into cannibals. Y'believe it?"

Jake stepped away from the corpse. He leaned against the wall of drawers, scooted sideways to get a handle out of his back, and folded his arms. "The thing killed on Wednesday. It tried for Celia Jamerson on Thursday afternoon, then started to go for Peggy Smeltzer on Thursday night. That looks like maybe it goes for a new victim daily."

"Give us this day our daily broad," Barney said.

"This is Saturday. I wonder if it got someone yesterday."

"Can't do it on its own," Barney said, "or it wouldn't be climbing inta guys."

"We'd better check out everyone who was at the restaurant Thursday night, everybody who's come into contact with Smeltzer's body."

"Y'got yourself a job. Get on it. Do whatcha can on yer own, we'll see where it gets us. Nobody knows but us three, we'll keep it that way. Folks hear about this thing, they'll go apeshit. Yer our task force, Jake. Stay on this till we got it nailed. Report t'me."

"What about Chuck?"

"I'll reassign him till yer done. I want y'workin alone. That's the only way we're gonna keep this quiet."

"Are you sure we should keep this quiet?" Steve asked. "If people are aware of the danger, they'll take precautions."

"They'll go apeshit. Or they'll say *we* got loose screws. Or both."

"I'm aware of that, but—"

"Keep yer drawers on, Apple. We don't nail this down in a day or two, we'll let the whole suck-head world in on it. Okay? Y'can hold a press conference. But let's take a crack at it before we start tellin' folks they're on the fuckin' menu."

Chapter Sixteen

ALISON DIDN'T KNOW WHY SHE WAS HERE. SHE HAD left the house after lunch and started walking with no destination in mind, just the desire to be alone and to be outside.

The wandering had taken her down Summer Street, to within sight of Evan's apartment. She was finished with him, but she gazed across the street at his building as if to punish herself. She saw two windows on the second story that belonged to his rooms. The shades were open. Was he inside? Was Tracy Morgan with him? Was he alone and would he see her passing by and come after her?

He didn't come after her.

Alison had walked on, feeling empty.

Not knowing why, she'd ended up here—in the woods above Clinton Creek. The creek was swollen and rushing.

It washed around islands of rock. Occasionally, it carried along tree limbs, casualties of last night's storm.

Alison made her way carefully down the steep embankment. At the water's edge, she noticed a familiar, flat-topped rock. During her years in Clinton, especially when she'd been a freshman and an emotional wreck, she had spent a lot of time on this very rock. Standing on it, sitting on it, sometimes with her bare feet in the water. She used to think of it as Solitary Rock. It was where she always came to be alone when she was feeling low.

She had forgotten about it. She had been down here several times over the past few months, had probably seen Solitary Rock and maybe even stood on it without remembering that it used to be so special.

Now she remembered. She stepped onto it and sat down, drawing her knees up and hugging them against her body.

This is nice, she thought. No wonder I used to come here all the time.

She heard a car cross the bridge, a sound much like that of the rushing water. She looked toward the bridge, but it was hidden by trees beyond the bend in the stream. She looked the other way and saw only the stream sluicing around a rocky curve. The slopes on both sides were heavy with bushes and trees. She saw no one, but wondered if there were couples concealed in nooks among the foliage or rocks, making love.

It was just around that bend where she and Evan . . .

It was a secluded, sunlit pocket with waist-high rocks on both sides and the stream at one end. A dense bramble at the other end sheltered them from anyone who might be looking down the slope. They could've been seen from the opposite embankment, but nobody ever went over there. They sat on the blanket that Evan always kept in the trunk of his car. They ate sharp cheddar on crackers and drank white wine from Alison's bota, squeezing the bag to squirt it into their mouths, into each other's mouths, laughing when they missed. When her blouse was soaked, she took it off and lay back on the blanket. Evan, kneeling between her legs, spurted the cool wine onto her neck and chest and breasts. It trickled down her skin, tickling. The laughter had stopped. He aimed at her nipples, the thin stream of wine hitting and splashing off one, then the other. Then he licked her. He made a puddle of wine in the hollow of her navel, and as he lapped at that he opened her jeans.

That had been Sunday afternoon. A week ago, tomorrow.

How could things have gone wrong so fast?

Don't idealize it, she told herself. It had been great—fun and thrilling and then incredible. But not quite right. You only planned on a picnic by the stream. You never intended to have sex with him, not there where anyone could show up and find you at it. But when he soaked your blouse with wine, you knew what he wanted and you went along with it. For Evan, not for yourself. Because you didn't want to disappoint him. And that is not the best of all possible reasons.

Hell, she thought, it sure didn't bother you much at the time.

Shortly afterward, though.

If there *are* regrets, they start in fast, before you even have time to get your clothes back on. If there aren't regrets, you know that, too. There had been times when Alison felt right afterward. Not recently, though. Not with Evan. Maybe not since Jimmy, the summer after high school graduation.

Jimmy. It was missing him, more than anything else, that had brought her so often to Solitary Rock during her freshman year. Especially after the letter that began, "I will always cherish the memories of what we shared together, but . . ." But she was eight hundred miles from

Jimmy and he'd fallen for Cynthia Younger in his world civ class.

Sitting on Solitary Rock with the sun warm on her head and back, Alison didn't feel the loss of Jimmy. She had finished with the pain and bitterness a long time ago. Instead, she inspected the memories of Jimmy and the way her life had gone since then.

The guys she had dated. The guys she had been serious about. The ones she had slept with.

Four of those, she thought, but only three if you don't count Tom and you shouldn't count Tom because that was only once and we were drunk. So three after Jimmy—Dave, Larry, and Evan. And it hadn't been really right with any of them.

Good, but not right. Not wonderful. Not without those regrets sneaking in.

She wondered how she would feel about Nick Winston, the guy she'd met last night at Wally's. Thinking about Nick, she felt no eagerness to see him again. Probably a nice guy, but . . .

Her rump was starting to hurt. She changed positions, lowering her legs and crossing them. Leaning back, she pressed her palms against the rock and braced herself up. She lifted her face into the sunlight. The heat felt wonderful. She imagined going now to the secluded place where she had been with Evan, taking off her clothes, and feeling the sun all over her body.

No way, she thought.

But she leaned forward and pulled her skirt up high on her legs. She unbuttoned her blouse, lifted its front, and tied it around her ribs. Then she leaned back again, bracing herself on stiff arms. That was better—feeling the sun on her chest and belly and thighs. The sun, and the mild breeze.

So I've struck out a few times in the man department,

she thought. It's not the end of the world. I'm twenty-one, not bad to look at. No reason to let this stuff get me down. I'm better off without Evan, better off alone than getting stuck with a guy who isn't exactly right. Hold out for the one who *is* right and don't lie to myself when one isn't. That's the main thing.

Later, when Alison left, she didn't return to Summer Street. She felt peaceful, and had no need to tease or punish herself by walking past Evan's apartment. She walked the length of the wooded park, saw a few strolling couples. She spotted lovers leaning against a tree deep in the shadows, and felt only a moment of sorrow.

At the house, she found Celia asleep on the sofa with her headphones on. The quiet tapping of a typewriter came from beyond the closed door of Helen's room. Alison stepped to the door and knocked. "Yo," Helen said.

She opened it. Helen scooted her chair back, turned it around, and looked at Alison from under a transparent green visor.

"Anything exciting happen while I was gone?"

"Just Celia bitching about her aches and pains, though I don't believe I would call that exciting."

"Any calls?" she asked. Why do I care? she wondered. I don't. But she felt a letdown when Helen shook her head.

"Nary a one. Your public must be otherwise occupied."

"Just as well."

"I thought you were finished with Evan."

"I am. I was just curious, that's all."

"Celia got a call from Danny Gard, wanted to go out romping with her tonight. You should've heard her pissing and moaning." Helen scrunched her face. " 'No, I can't. No, I wasn't just fine last night, I was in aaaagony. Maybe next week. Maybe next month. No, it's not you, it's meeee. I'm in pain. I can hardly moooove.' "

"Celia isn't really going to stay home on a Saturday night," Alison said.

"Nah. She's just waiting for a better offer. I guess she didn't have a great time with him last night."

"He's a gross character. Last time I saw him, he was at Wally's engaged in a belching contest with Lisa Ball."

"He's a Sig," Helen said, as if that explained it.

Alison nodded. "His idea of a high time is lighting farts."

Grinning, Helen asked, "You know that from personal experience?"

"I've heard him pontificate on—" The sudden jangle of the telephone stopped her words. She felt herself go tight. "I'll get it," she muttered, and hurried into the living room.

Don't let it be Evan, she thought.

Her hand trembled as she picked up the phone. "Hello?"

"Celia?"

Thank God. "Just a moment, please," she said. Celia, still on the sofa, had her eyes closed. The music from the headset had probably covered the blare of the ringing phone. Alison wondered if she was asleep.

Helen appeared in the doorway of her room. She raised her bushy eyebrows.

Alison covered the phone's mouthpiece. "It's for Celia."

"A guy?"

"Yeah."

"Find out who it is."

"Who may I tell her is calling?" Alison asked.

"This is Jason Banning."

"Thank you. Just a moment." She covered the mouthpiece again. "Jason, the actor, that scuzzball's roommate."

"The freshman."

Nodding, Alison set down the phone and hurried to the sofa. She nudged Celia's shoulder. The girl frowned and mumbled and kept her eyes shut. Alison lifted one of the mufflike speakers off her ear. "Hey, snoozy, you got a wakeup call."

"Huh?"

"You got an admirer on the phone."

A single eyelid struggled upward. "Huh? Who is . . . ?"

"Jason."

She raised her other eyelid. Her gaze slid sideways to Alison. "Jason? Jason *Banning?*"

"That's the one."

"Be damn," she mumbled.

"Want me to tell him you can't come to the phone?"

"Eat my shorts." She pulled the headset off and slowly sat up, groaning. "God, I'm death warmed over."

Alison brought the phone closer. She placed it on the coffee table and handed the receiver to Celia.

"Hi, Jason," Celia said. She sounded cheerful and friendly and in tip-top shape.

Alison looked at Helen. Helen shook her head and chuckled.

"Yeah, some bastard ran me off the road. . . . No, not too bad. I'm not too pretty to look at, but . . . Well, that's just 'cause you haven't *seen* me. . . . Oh? Well, I wouldn't mind seeing you either. . . . Tonight? . . . No, I don't have any plans that I can't get out of. . . ."

Helen, still shaking her head, swiveled her eyes upward.

"That'd be great. What time? . . . Okay. Great. . . . Terrific. See you then." She held out the phone, and Alison hung it up for her.

"Are you sure you're up to a date?"

"He's taking me to the Lobster Shanty, I'm up to that."

"Decent," Alison said. The Lobster Shanty was the finest restaurant in Clinton.

"That should be a real thrill," Helen said, "going out with a freshman."

"A *gorgeous* freshman," Celia amended.

"Robbing the cradle."

"Floss your butt." She lay down again on the sofa and crossed her ankles. "Besides, he's twenty-one, same as us."

"Sure."

"He is."

"What'd he do, flunk three times?"

"He worked after high school. Modeled, did commercials, that sort of stuff."

"What about his girlfriend?" Alison asked. "I thought you said he was going with some gal."

"Yeah, he was. Guess he saw the error of his ways."

"Maybe he likes to date cripples," Helen suggested.

"Wants to use her for a base," Alison said.

"Wants to slide in," Helen added.

"You two are a riot."

"We're just jealous," Helen told her. "We just wish *we* could go to the Lobster Shanty with a freshman."

"I'll call him back," Celia said. "Maybe he can set up one of you guys with Roland."

"I'm not selfish, Alison can have him."

Celia turned her head on the cushion and smiled at Alison. "We'll make it a double date, just like junior high."

"Pardon me while I heave."

"I realize Roland probably isn't as handsome and worldly as Evan, but hey, it's Saturday night, you don't want to sit around alone on Saturday night, do you?"

"Besides," Helen added, "he's obviously got a good case of the hots for you."

"A case of the hards," Celia said.

"Way he was eyeing you yesterday . . ."

"Stripping you with his eyes . . ."

The talk made Alison feel squirmy. "I'd really like to double with you, Celia, but I happen to know that Roland has other plans. He's got this *ménage à trois* scheduled for tonight."

Helen snorted.

"Chortle, chortle," Celia said.

Alison eyed Helen. "She thinks I'm joking. Don't you find it a trifle *peculiar* that Jason, who has never before asked Celia out—in spite of her beauty and wit—should invite her to dinner the very *day* after her chance encounter at the shopping mall with his roommate, Roland?"

Helen stroked her heavy lower lip, and nodded. " 'Tis passing strange."

Celia smirked. "Tell you what, Roland shows up for dinner, I'll give him my house key and tell him I got two horny roommates just dying for a piece of him." She winked at Helen. "And I'll advise him to bring chips."

"So what do you think?" Celia asked.

Alison, on the recliner, set her yellow highlighting pen into the gutter of the Chaucer text she had been studying for the past two hours, and looked up. "Not bad."

The bandage was gone from Celia's brow. Tied around her head was a blue silk scarf that concealed the abrasion. The scarf was knotted over her left ear, and its ends hung almost to her shoulder. She wore big, hoop earrings.

"You look like Long John Silver," Alison said.

"Cute, huh?"

"Matter of fact, you look great."

"You'd never know I was damaged goods, would you?"

"Just by your reputation," Helen said, coming in from the kitchen with a stein of beer and a can of peanuts. She held the can toward Celia.

"No thanks, I'm saving all my room for dinner."

"Where's your sling?" Helen asked.

"I'm not going to the Lobster Shanty with a goddamn sling on my arm." She lifted the arm stiffly away from her side. "I've got a bandage on the elbow. And both knees."

"I'm surprised you have an outfit that'll cover them," Helen said.

"It's the best I could do."

The blue gown had sleeves to her forearms and its skirt reached well below her knees, covering her bandages but not entirely hiding them. They showed, Alison noticed, because of the way the glossy fabric clung to every inch of her. She appeared to wear three bandages beneath the gown, and nothing else.

Celia looked down at herself. "I would've preferred something that showed a little in front," she said, fingering the neck band at her throat.

"Cellophane might show more," Helen said, and dropped onto the sofa. "Peanut?" She tossed one to Alison. Alison snatched it out of the air and popped it into her mouth.

"This is a problem," Celia said, "but I don't know what I can do about it." She turned sideways and took a step. Her right leg, bare to the hip, came out of a slit in the gown. The knee was wrapped with a brown elastic band. "I tried taking off the bandage, but the knee *really* sucks without it."

"You could try a body stocking," Alison suggested.

"Har!" Helen blared.

"The thing is," Alison said, "he knows you were hurt. There's no big deal if he happens to see your bandages."

"He'll see them all anyway," Helen said, "once you throw your dress on the floor."

"She won't throw her dress on the floor," Alison said. "Roland'll hang it up for her."

"Comedians up the wazoo. What time is it?"

Helen checked her wristwatch. "Six-twenty."

"Good. He's picking me up at ten till seven. I think I'll have a little—"

"I'd want to get drunk too," Helen said, "if I was going out in public wearing that."

"You went out in public wearing this," Celia said, "the public should get drunk." She grinned at Alison. "Get you something?"

"Thanks. Whatever you're having."

Celia went into the kitchen.

"God, she looks fabulous," Helen whispered. "I looked ten percent as good as her . . ." She shook her head and sighed. "Life's tough, then you die."

"Let's send out for a pizza after she's gone."

Helen raised her thick eyebrows. "Well, maybe life ain't so tough."

A few minutes later, Celia returned carrying a tray with her left hand. Two tumblers were balanced on the tray. "Double vodka gimlets," she announced as Alison took one of the glasses.

"You're going to be polluted before he even gets here," Helen said.

"Just a little something for what ails me. Besides, *he's* driving." She set the tray carefully on the table, then lowered herself onto the sofa and lifted her glass.

Alison took a sip. The drink was very strong. She frowned at Celia. "Are you sure about tonight?" she asked.

Staring into her glass, Celia shrugged one shoulder.

"I'm not going to call off my life just because some bastard wracked me up."

"Maybe you need some time."

"Sit around and think about it?"

"I think it hit you pretty hard."

"You're telling me?"

"Emotionally, I mean."

"Alison's right," Helen said. "You can't just pretend it didn't happen. You almost got killed and that guy died. It's pretty heavy stuff."

"I'm handling it, okay? What're you trying to do, ruin my appetite?" She took another drink. "I'll be fine. And I'll be a lot finer after a couple of drinks and a lobster dinner with a nice guy who likes me and happens to be a hunk even if he is a freshman. I appreciate your concern, but knock it off, okay? I'm fine."

"It's a good drink," Alison said. "Pretty soon, we'll both be fine."

"Yeah, but I'll be with a charming gorgeous man and you'll be with Helen. Eat your heart out."

"Hey," Alison said, "you're depressing me."

A peanut bounced off her forehead and plopped into her drink. It floated on her vodka. She picked it out. Grinning, she flicked it into her mouth. The salt was gone. She fished an ice cube out of her glass and studied it.

"Hey, no," Helen pleaded. "Come on, you could hurt somebody with that."

"You're right. What could I have been thinking?" She tossed it at Helen.

Squealing, Helen hunched her shoulders and twisted in her chair. She flinched when the ice dropped onto her lap. Her hand jerked. A foamy tongue of beer slurped over the edge of her stein and flopped onto her breast. "Yeee-ah!"

"Woops," Alison said.

"Golly," Celia said. "Maybe I'll phone up Jason right

now and call it off. I can see that it'll be a lot more fun around here tonight."

Helen clamped the peanut can between her knees. Scowling down, she plucked the wet fabric away from her skin. She was wearing the same faded, stained, shapeless dress that she had worn only yesterday when they went to the mall. Or a different one, Alison thought, that looked the same. She had several. They were hard to tell apart. She sniffed a fistful of the wet cloth. "A definite improvement," she said.

"They're gone," Alison called from her recliner.

Helen's bedroom door eased open and she looked around as if to make sure the coast was clear before venturing out. Satisfied, she approached Alison. "So, how was he?"

"He looks like an after-shave commercial."

"Huh." Helen ran the back of a hand across her nose. "He's probably a jerk. Every guy she goes out with is a jerk, you ever noticed that?"

"I don't know," Alison said.

"They are. Someday, she's going to be sorry."

"I hope not."

"You go out with enough jerky guys, sooner or later . . ."

"What kind of pizza we going to get? Salami, sausage?"

"I got some menus in my desk."

"Get 'em."

Chapter Seventeen

JAKE WAS STILL TREMBLING WHEN HE CLIMBED OUT OF his car. With the flashlight in his left hand and the machete clamped under his arm, he stepped to the trunk. The point of the key missed the lock hole a few times before he managed to fit it in. He turned the key. The trunk opened. He put the machete and flashlight inside, next to the can of gasoline, then slammed the trunk shut.

On the front stoop of his house, he clutched his right hand with his left to hold it steady and got the key into the door lock. Inside, he engaged the dead bolt, then slipped the guard chain into place. Though evening light still came in through the windows, he made a circuit of the living room and turned on every lamp. Along the way, he found himself checking each window and looking behind the furniture.

"Nerves of steel," he muttered.

In the kitchen, he hit the light switch. He checked the windows and backdoor to make sure they were secure. Bending at the waist because his leather pants were too tight for squatting, he opened a cupboard and took out a bottle of bourbon. A drop of sweat fell from his chin and splashed on the toe of his boot.

Stepping to the sink, he yanked a yard of paper towel off its roll. He mopped his face and wet, stringy hair.

Then he filled a glass with bourbon. He took a few swallows and sighed as the liquor's heat spread through him.

He carried the glass down the hallway, turning on lights as he went, and entered his bedroom.

He turned on his bedroom light. He looked around. The curtains were shut. The closet door was open, just as he had left it. Taking another drink, he stepped past the closet and looked in. He wandered to the other side of his bed. He had an urge to get down on his hands and knees and peer under the bed.

Don't be a jerk, he thought. You're home now. This isn't the goddamn Oakwood Inn, this is home and there's nothing under your bed except maybe some dust bunnies.

Besides, it'd be too much effort in this outfit.

After taking another swallow of bourbon, Jake set his glass on the dresser. He unzipped his leather jacket and pulled it off. His blue shirt, dark with sweat, clung to his skin. He tried to open the buttons, but his fingers shook so badly that after getting the top button undone he yanked the shirt up and pulled it over his head.

He unbuckled his gun belt, swung it toward the bed and let go. The holstered revolver bounced when it hit the mattress. He stared at it while he opened his pants and tugged them down to his knees. Sitting on the bed, he popped open the leather strap and slid the revolver free. He placed it close to his right leg, then bent down and pulled his boots off. His socks felt glued to his feet. He peeled them off. He slid the tight pants down his calves and kicked them away.

In the lamplight, his legs were shiny with sweat. He rubbed the clammy skin of his shins, turned his legs and looked behind them.

There were no quarter-size holes.

Hell, of course not. Nothing could've gotten through the boots and leather pants. Not without me knowing it.

Jake stood up. His rump had left sweat marks on the pale blue coverlet. He drew down his sodden shorts and stepped out of them.

Okay, I'm a jerk, he thought.

Picking up his revolver, he dropped to his knees and elbows. He lifted the hanging edge of the coverlet and peered into the dark space under his bed.

A pair of eyes looked back at him.

He yelped. He jabbed the gun barrel toward the eyes. He almost pulled the trigger before he realized he was looking at Kimmy's Cookie Monster doll.

Stretching out an arm, he pulled it out from under the bed. He pressed it to his cheek.

God almighty, what if I'd shot it?

Just a stuffed animal, he knew that. But, like all of Kimmy's dolls, it was somehow more. It was part of Kimmy, as if she had breathed some of her own life into it. He could hear her say in a low grumbly voice, "Me want *cookie!*"

Jake had a tight lump in his throat.

"Close call, Cookie," he whispered.

He pushed himself to his feet. With the chubby blue doll in one hand and his revolver in the other, he headed for the door. He planned to put Cookie Monster back in Kimmy's bedroom. Then he changed his mind and set it on his nightstand next to the telephone.

Barbara's side of the closet still had her full-length mirror on the outside of the door. He swung the door shut and looked at himself.

You'd know if it got you, he thought.

Maybe it can make you forget. If it can turn you into a cannibal . . .

There were no wounds on his legs. His scrotum was shriveled and his penis looked as if it wanted to disappear. He slipped a hand between his legs, checking on both sides of the tight sack and behind it. He prodded his navel, and shivered as he imagined his finger going in all the way. But his navel was okay. The rest of his front appeared all right, though the knife scar under his right nipple looked a little more white than usual.

He turned around. He looked over one shoulder, then the other. He probed between the sweaty cheeks of his rump.

You're all right, he thought, unless the damn thing went up your butt. Couldn't have done that, though, without going through the leather pants, and the pants didn't have any holes.

Satisfied that the thing hadn't invaded him, Jake took another drink of bourbon. The glass was almost empty. He carried it, along with his revolver, into the kitchen. After refilling the glass, he opened a drawer and took out a large, clear plastic freezer bag.

He wondered if he'd flipped his lid.

Nobody will ever know about this, he told himself. It makes you feel better, so do it.

Some kind of cop, scared as a kid.

He slipped his revolver into the bag and pinched the zip-lock top shut along its seam.

Jake locked himself into the bathroom. He searched the floor, the walls and ceiling, the sink, the tub. Then he turned on the shower. He had a couple of drinks while he adjusted the heat of the spray, then set the glass on the toilet seat and climbed into the tub. He slid the frosted glass door shut.

The built-in soap dish had a metal bar above it for holding a washcloth. He slipped the barrel of his bagged revolver between the bar and the tile wall, wiggled the weapon until he was sure it wouldn't fall, then picked up the soap and began to wash himself.

The strong, hot spray felt good. Jake told himself that he couldn't be much safer: the door was locked, he'd checked the bathroom, he was shut behind the shower doors, and his revolver was within easy reach. Nothing could get him.

Then he noticed the sudsy water swirling down the drain.

Gooseflesh crawled up his back.

Don't be crazy, he told himself. There's a metal drain basket down there, nothing could come up.

He dropped to his knees. His fingertip went into the drain only as far as the first knuckle before it touched the obstruction.

Okay. No problem.

Your only problem, pal, is your head.

Two hours alone, searching that damned restaurant.

If it was going to get you, it would've gotten you then.

It didn't come home with you. It's probably already found a new home—in whoever broke into the restaurant between Thursday night and this afternoon. Some lucky bastard is running around with the thing up his back, looking for a meal. *Give us this day our daily broad.* Good old Barney, he can joke about it. He should've gone in there. He might be worried about drains, himself.

Jake stayed in the shower until the water started turning cold. Then he climbed out, dried himself, took another drink of bourbon and took the revolver out of the bag. In his bedroom, he combed his hair and put on a robe. He carried his drink and revolver into the living room. Sitting on the sofa, he crossed his legs to keep his feet off the floor. He rested the gun on his lap. Then he swung the telephone over from the lamp table and dialed Barney's home.

Barney answered by saying, "Higgins."

"It's Jake." His voice sounded all right. "Did Applegate get back to you?"

"Sure did. Y'were right on the John Doe from the van. Perfect match on the teeth 'n blood type. How'd it go from yer end?"

"I checked out everyone who was at the crime scene Thursday night. Nobody was carrying."

"How'd y'make sure?"

"Strip searches."

"They musta liked that. Tell'm why?"

"Damn near. I said Smeltzer had a parasite infestation. They were pretty cooperative."

"Coulda told'm I'd ordered a circumcision survey."

Jake ignored the remark. "After I finished with them, I went out to the Oakwood. Somebody's been in there. The front and back doors had both been forced. I found a bag of flour on the kitchen floor."

"A bagga what?"

"Flour. Like you use for cooking. You know."

"Somebody makin' cookies?"

"I doubt it. No oven. There were some footprints, too. Somebody had stepped in the blood and left tracks. A bare foot. About a size seven. And somebody had polished off a bottle of vodka the Smeltzers had left out in the bar area."

"What d'ya make of it?"

"Maybe a derelict. The size of the footprint, though, makes me think a girl was in there. Maybe a couple of kids from the college had themselves a party."

"But no sign of a' old Sneaky Snake?"

The skin on Jake's thighs and forehead seemed to go stiff and tight.

"Y'looked, didn't ya?"

"I looked. I spent more than two hours looking. I checked every inch of that place."

"No luck, huh?"

"I didn't find it—"

"M'I hearin' a but on the way?"

"Yeah. But." He felt breathless, a little dizzy. He sat up straight and filled his lungs. "Down in the cellar, behind the stairs, I found a half a dozen eggs."

"Eggs?"

"Yeah."

"Like chicken eggs?"

"No, not like chicken eggs."

Barney whistled softly into the phone. "Like *its* eggs?"

"I . . . yeah, I think so. They were clear. Like . . . almost like jelly beans, but soft. Red, but clear. I could see inside them. And each one of them had a little . . . like a little worm."

"You puttin' me the fuck *on*, Corey?"

"Little gray worms."

There was a long silence from Barney. Then he said, "Where're they, these eggs?"

"Still there."

"You *left* 'em!"

"I stomped them flat."

"You crazy? Shit!"

"What was I supposed to do, bag them for evidence?"

"We coulda' had tests run, found out—"

"I know. I know that. I . . . I freaked out a little, Barney."

There was another long silence. "Y' all right?" Barney asked in a soft voice.

"I'm managing."

"Yer not a guy loses it."

"Oh, I can lose it pretty good."

"I shouldn'ta had y'go in there alone. I'm sorry. Y'gonna be okay?"

"Sure."

"Y'mashed the little fuckers."

"Yeah. I'm sorry."

"Well, maybe just as well. Guess we don't want'a be takin' any chances." Jake heard him sigh. "So momma wasn't there, huh?"

"I think . . . it could be anywhere, but there's a good chance it went out of that place with whoever it was that broke in."

"The party kids."

"It's just a guess."

"No idea who they were?"

"Just that one was probably a female, and I don't imagine she went in that place by herself. Probably with a guy. We might lift prints off the door handles and the vodka bottle. I bagged the bottle, so we might as well check it. But I don't think that'd get us much of anywhere. We've got three thousand students at Clinton U., about five hundred more at the high school, print cards in our files on maybe two dozen."

"How 'bout strip searchin' every kid in town? I'll help y'out 'n do the gals myself."

"Yeah, sure. I almost wish we could. That or print them all, it's about the only way we'd find the thing."

"No guarantee the woocha got one a' the kids, anyhow," Barney said.

"Whoocha?"

"A bad-ass whatchamacallit. Coulda gone off 'fore the kids showed. Gotta move in mind?"

"Not really. Maybe stake out the Oakwood. I'm pretty

sure the thing's gone, but there's always a chance that the kids might return."

"Slim t'none. Y'better get some rest. Our whoocha got into someone, maybe it'll fly the coop and be outa' our hair. It sticks around, then we'll have us a missing person or a dead body next day or two, and maybe we'll get lucky."

"Either way," Jake said, "we'll have to go public with it."

"Y'had to remind me," Barney muttered.

"If I didn't, Applegate would."

"Yeah. We talked it over when he called. We're gonna hold off till noon Tuesday. Then it's press conference time if we haven't nailed it. You, me 'n him, we'll be instant celebrities—the three stooges that panicked the nation. Oh, what fun. We better get that fucker by then."

"I hate to just wait around."

"No point wastin' yer time, you haven't got any leads. Just sit tight, try t'get yer mind off it."

"Yeah."

After hanging up, Jake finished his bourbon. He went into the kitchen to start dinner and was peeling a potato over the sink when he realized that he had left his revolver on the sofa. He didn't go after it. For some reason, his jitters had gone away.

Maybe it was the bourbon. More likely, it was talking to Barney—talking about the thing and its eggs, and about the break-in. Especially about the break-in. He had no doubt, any more, that the creature had found a new host. It wasn't slithering around, looking for a chance to sneak up on him. It wasn't ready to lurch out of the garbage disposal in a burst of potato peelings and bite his neck.

It was up the spine of a kid who'd gone looking for fun in the wrong place.

Jake wondered if the kid was getting hungry.

Chapter Eighteen

"IT WAS A LOVERLY DINNER," CELIA SAID AS THEY LEFT the Lobster Shanty. "And you are a loverly person."

"My pleasure," Jason said.

She swept an arm around his back and pressed herself against him and kissed him. They were standing in the light beneath the restaurant's portico, but the parking valet was nowhere in sight. Neither was anyone else. Jason held her, feeling the wet heat of her mouth, the soft push of her breasts, her belly flat against his belly. He was getting hard. He knew she could feel it. She squirmed, rubbing him. He slid a hand down her back. There was only smoothness through her gown, not even a band at her waist. He caressed the firm mounds of her rump.

He thought about Dana and felt guilty. I'm doing it for you, he told her.

For me, right, he could almost hear her say. You're turned on, you bastard.

So who's going to tell on me? he asked himself. Dana might even be dead.

Don't think that. Jesus.

A car pulled into the restaurant's driveway, so they parted. Holding Celia's hand, Jason led her to the sidewalk. "Would you like to go somewhere?" he asked.

"Sure thing."

"I know a nice, secluded place."

"The secludeder, the better," she said, bumped his side, staggered, turned her ankle and said, "Ow! Shit. Hang on." She kicked off her high heels. Keeping her knees straight, she bent at the waist to pick up her shoes. Jason stared at the way the gown clung to her buttocks. Thoughts of Dana prevented him from stroking her. Celia straightened up, holding her shoes. "Tough enough, walking in these things if you're sober."

"You mean you're not sober?"

"Not entirely," she said, speaking the words slowly and precisely. "Nor am I entirely polluted." She made a lopsided grin. "Are you entirely polluted?"

"I am *un peu* polluted."

They arrived at his car. He opened the passenger door, helped Celia in, then went around to his side. The overhead light came on when he opened the door. Celia's left arm was hooked over the seat back, drawing her dress taut across her breast. Her nipple made the glossy fabric jut. Her left leg had found its way through the gown's slitted side. Except for a flesh-colored elastic band wrapping the knee, it was bare to her hip. The fabric draped her inner thigh. I'll get a nice shot, Jason thought, if that little bit of cloth moves slightly farther to the right.

Celia grinned as if she knew what he was thinking. "Are you getting in, or what?"

"Yeah." He sat down behind the steering wheel and pulled the door shut. The light went off. He fumbled the key into the ignition and started the car.

Celia's hand found the back of his neck, rubbed gently. "You tense?" she asked.

"A little, I guess." He pulled away from the curb.

"How come?" she asked, massaging his neck muscles. "You aren't nervous about me, are you?"

"I think it's excitement more than nerves," he said.

"Mmmm."

But it's nerves, too, he thought. Christ. It hadn't gone the way he'd planned. He'd planned to get her smashed, and that part of it had worked fine; she was plenty loaded. But he hadn't planned on feeling anything. He was to play a role in the melodrama cooked up by Roland to save Dana. That's all. Act a part. Act interested and affectionate while he plied her with fine food and plenty of booze until she was plastered mindless and totally helpless.

She's just the way I want her, he told himself.

But I'm not.

It had started to go wrong the moment he saw her and thought, Dana never looked this good. Feeling like a traitor, he had tried to push the thought out of his mind. All through the evening, however, he compared the two and found Dana the loser. Celia was far more beautiful than Dana. She seemed to listen, to care about what he said. She wasn't conceited. She was wittier than Dana, sometimes breaking him up, but even her sharpest remarks seemed good-humored and without the malice that made Dana's sarcasm a little ugly. She had a warmth, a softness, that was totally alien to the other girl.

While they ate, he had found himself more and more attracted to Celia. And he felt poisoned by guilt. He was betraying Celia by using her this way; he was betraying Dana by wanting to trade her for Celia.

"That light's . . ."

Red, he thought. But it was too late to stop, so he sped on through the intersection.

Celia's hand went away from his neck. "You'd better concentrate on your driving," she said. "If you get stopped in your condition . . ."

"Yeah." For the next block, he watched the rearview.

"Are you all right?"

"Yeah."

"Something on your mind?"

"You."

"Me. I know, you're overwhelmed by my cheauty and barm."

Jason smiled. "Right, your cheauty and barm."

"And dizzy with anticipation."

"You're very perceptive."

"But what is it, really? I mean, has it got something to do with Dana?"

Jason felt a jump inside his chest.

"You two were going at it pretty hot and heavy, and suddenly she's out of the picture and I'm in. Do you want to talk aboud . . . about it? I mean, this isn't some kind of ploy to get back at her or make her jealous or something, is it?"

A ploy, all right.

He was thankful for the darkness hiding his hot face which was probably scarlet.

"It's not that at all," he said. "We broke up, but she didn't dump me. I dumped her. I just couldn't stand her any longer, she's such a bitch. I don't know what I ever saw in her in the first place."

Sorry Dana, he thought.

Eat shit, he imagined her snapping. You meant every word of it. I was never anything to you but snatch. But fair's fair, you were nothing to me but a hard cock.

He turned onto Latham Road.

"I finally realized," he said, "that I was missing a lot. I mean, a relationship needs to be more than screwing."

"Two entirely different things," Celia said.

"I don't know. I want to at least *like* the person I'm with, and it was getting so I didn't even want to be around her. She was hard and crass and mean . . . not like you. You're really a sweet person."

"Yeah, I'm an angel."

"Compared to her, you are." So why am I taking you out there? I don't owe Dana a damn thing. Besides, she might already be dead (I almost hope . . . No!) and I shouldn't be talking about her like this, thinking about her like this—even though it's the truth.

I've got to do what I can for her. I owe her that much.

It's a stupid plan, anyway. It'll never work.

So if nothing happens, I take Celia home and she never has to know she was bait.

And if it works, fat chance, nobody gets hurt anyway. We nail the guy, he takes us to Dana.

Takes us to her body, hanging naked from a rafter, mutilated and dead.

But nothing will happen to Celia, either way.

Take her someplace else. Forget the whole thing. A motel, maybe. That'd be nice. Don't do this to her.

"Just up ahead," Celia said, "is where that guy tried to run me down."

"Do you want a look?"

She shook her head. "I don't even like being this close. My bike's still there. I haven' even gone back for it."

"Should we pick it up? We could put it in the backseat." Say yes, he thought. We'll get the bike, we'll forget about the Oakwood.

"Iss too messed up. Even if it could be repaired, I

wouldn't want it anyway. I'll ged a new one if I ever want to go riding again.''

''You sure?''

''Yeah.''

Jason slowed down, flicked the arm of the turn signal, and swung the car onto the narrow road leading to the Oakwood Inn. He looked at Celia. She was staring at him.

''Where're we going?'' she whispered.

''There's a parking lot. It'll be good and deserted.''

''This's where those people got killed Thursday night.''

He nodded. ''Yeah. I read about it. If you'd rather go someplace else . . .''

''No.'' That was all she said. She didn't explain.

''I think we won't have to worry about being disturbed,'' Jason said. ''Nobody'll come out to a place like this after what happened.''

''Maybe for the thrill.''

The road flared out. Jason steered to the right. He drove in a circle, watching his head beams sweep around the parking lot. There were no other cars. The beams met a corner of the restaurant and moved across its dark front, flashing off the windows. When they lit the door, he stopped.

''Go closer,'' Celia whispered.

''Are you . . . ? Okay.'' He let the car roll forward almost to the porch stairs. Then he stopped it, turned off the engine, and set the emergency brake. He left the headlights on.

Celia leaned forward, a hand against the dash, and peered out the windshield. ''Weird,'' she whispered.

''What?''

''Being this close to where it happened. Get the lights, okay?''

He pushed the knob.

Celia stared through the darkness. "Think we could get in?" she asked.

So easy. She *wanted* to go in. Let's do it, get it over with.

"I don't know," Jason muttered.

"Scared?" she asked. Her voice sounded a little shaky.

"Yeah. Aren't you?"

She didn't answer. She eased back into her seat. Looking at Jason, she lifted his hand and placed it on her bare thigh. "Can you feel the gooseflesh?"

He moved his hand lightly up her leg. Yes, he could feel the gooseflesh. She must've shaved, but the nubs of hair were standing and just a bit bristly along the top of her thigh. He curved his hand down the inner side. There, the skin was smooth, incredibly smooth and soft. The fabric brushed the edge of his palm. Another inch, he thought, maybe two . . .

She'll let me, I know she will.

No. You can't mess around with her, not if you're going ahead with it.

So forget the plan. It's a dumb plan.

What if Dana's alive, maybe being kept somewhere, being raped and tortured by some maniac, and this is her only chance? You can't just write her off.

Damn it, what'll I do?

He took his hand away from Celia's leg. "Yeah," he said, "gooseflesh. Are you scared or cold?"

"I got the willies," she said. Jason could see the white of her teeth. "You think that's racist? The willies?"

"Why would it be racist?"

"Wasn' Willy a black guy in the old movies, like in the thirties? He'd get in a haunted house and go all buggy-eyed and shaky?"

"Gee, I don't know."

"I think tha's where the expression came from. The

willies. But don' hold me to it. Wherever it came from, I got 'em."

"I've got just the thing," Jason said, "for getting rid of the willies."

"Not sure I wanna get rid of 'em. Kind of *like* the feeling. Y'know? I'm all shivery inside. It's almost sexual."

"Well, maybe this'll make you feel even more shivery inside." Huddling down against the steering wheel, he reached under the car seat and pulled out a bottle of champagne.

"Well now," Celia said. "That's what I call class."

He nodded and began to peel the foil off the top of the bottle.

The champagne had been Roland's idea. Insurance, Roland had called it. Fill her up with bubbly, you won't have any trouble at all getting her inside. With any luck, she'll pass out. You can carry her in.

It was insurance that Jason didn't need.

But he wanted time to think, to decide.

If we do go in, he told himself, it'll work better if she's totally smashed.

As he twisted the wire seal, Celia turned away from him. Reaching across her body, she used her left hand to roll the window down. She faced him again. "You can shoot the cork out my window."

"Don't want to hit you with it."

"On a good day, I could catch the cork in my teeth."

"This isn't a good day?"

"It's dark and I'm a trifle tipsy. So try to miss me."

Jason pulled off the wire basket, clamped the bottle against his chest, and began to twist the knob of cork. It squeaked quietly. He aimed well in front of Celia's face and gave the cork a final turn. With a hollow pop, it shot past her nose and sailed out the window. He heard her laugh as he rushed the erupting bottle to his mouth, spilling foam down his hand and shirt. He gulped the airy froth and choked.

"You okay?"

A few moments later, he was okay. He took a sip of the champagne, then passed the bottle to Celia. She raised it high and tilted back her head. He watched her throat work as she swallowed. With a sigh, she passed the bottle back to him. "That's good stuff," she said.

She faced Jason, sitting sideways and sliding her leg onto the seat. Her knee touched the side of his leg. The inner side of her thigh was turned upward. He followed the pale skin with his eyes and glanced at the patch of shadow beneath the edge of her gown. Then he raised the bottle. He took one swallow, closed his lips and pretended to drink more before handing the bottle back to her.

"Still feeling shivery?" he asked.

"Yessiree. More'n ever." She took a drink. "Bring any cheese and crackers?"

"Afraid I didn't think of that."

"Maybe there's some in there," she said, and nodded toward the Oakwood. Then she took another drink. "It *is* a restaurant."

"You can't be hungry."

"Hungry, all right." From the way she said it, Jason knew that she wasn't talking about food. She looked over the seat back. "That's a blanket there," she said.

Jason nodded.

"Grab it and follow me."

Before he could object, Celia slid her leg off the seat, turned away from him, and opened her door.

"Hey, what're you doing?" he asked as she climbed out.

"I've gotta go in there."

"Are you nuts?"

"Yup." She swung her door shut.

Jason threw his door open and jumped out. Over the roof of the car, he saw her standing in the moonlight, her back arched, the bottle high as she drank from it.

"I don't want to go in there," he said.

She lowered the bottle. "Come on, it'll be a trip."

"It might be dangerous."

"The blanket," she said. She waved the bottle at him, then walked unsteadily, limping slightly and weaving, to the porch stairs.

Jason grabbed the blanket off the backseat and hurried after her.

She waited for him at the door of the Oakwood. After taking a drink, she handed the bottle to him. "Ladies first," she said in a trembling whisper. Then she opened the door. Taking hold of Jason's elbow, she led him inside and shut the door. "Oh God, dark in here."

"I've got matches," Jason whispered. His heart was sledging.

"We don' need no steenking matches," she said with a Mexican accent.

"Don't you want to see wh—?"

"I like zee dark." Her left arm went around Jason. He let the blanket fall. He put his arms around her, the champagne bottle in his right hand pressing against her back.

She felt warm, but her body shivered. When they kissed, he realized that even her chin was trembling. Her tongue went into his mouth. Her right hand caressed his rump while her left untucked the back of his shirt and went under it and roamed his back.

He eased his mouth away from her. Her face was a vague pale shape with black holes instead of eyes and a mouth. He didn't like seeing it this way. "I've gotta get rid of the bottle."

"Polish id off."

"I don't want any more."

"Give." He brought it to the front. Her hand covered his, then took the bottle. A moment later, he heard her swallowing. He reached through the darkness to the area below her dim face. One hand found a shoulder, the other an armpit. Once he knew what he was touching, he had no trouble locating her breasts. He took them in his hands. Celia stopped swallowing and moaned. She took a quick breath when he gently squeezed her stiff nipples.

The champagne bottle thunked to the floor, startling Jason. He flinched. Celia gasped sharply, "Ah!"

"I'm sorry," he whispered.

"Never mind."

A hand pressed the front of his pants. He squirmed against it, aching. He felt a small pull, then heard his zipper clicking downward.

He wished he could think. He wanted her. But not here. He wanted to get her out of here, but he wanted to feel her cool fingers on him and he wanted to put his hand through the open side of her gown and follow the smooth warm skin of her thigh upward. And then we're naked and we spread the blanket and it's not supposed to be this way. It's not the plan.

We're here now, we should go by the plan.

She didn't reach in. She tugged at his belt, instead. He could hear her breathing heavily as he rubbed her breasts.

"Wait," he gasped in a husky whisper.

"Wha'?"

"I've gotta use the john."

"Lemme have the matches. I'll ged the place ready."

"I'll need one to find the john." He took the matchbook from his pocket, peeled out a match and struck it. The brightness hurt his eyes. Celia squinted against the glare.

He gave the matchbook to her, then headed for the alcove at the far end of the bar where the rest rooms were located. He stepped around the card table. The match was hot on his fingertips, so he shook it out. Hands in front of him, feeling the air, he made his way slowly forward.

Behind him, a match snicked. He hurried the rest of the way to the alcove, then looked back. Celia was standing midway between the front door and the corner of the bar, straddle legged, looking down at the blanket. She staggered and almost fell when she bent over to pick it up. With one hand, she shook the blanket open. Very slowly she raised the match and puffed it out. She vanished.

Jason stared into the darkness, waiting for another match to flare. It didn't happen. Finally, he turned around and felt his way along the wall. He found the door to the men's room. He turned the handle, stepped inside, and flicked the light switch.

Roland, sitting on the toilet, grinned up at him.

Chapter Nineteen

"HOW'S IT GOING?" ROLAND WHISPERED.

Jason shook his head.

Roland pointed at his open fly. "I assume, from that, that you're not alone."

"She's here." He pulled his zipper up and fastened his belt. Then he leaned back against the rest room door. He took a deep breath. He rubbed his face. "I've got my doubts, Ro."

"What do you mean?"

"She's a nice girl. This seems like a rotten way to use her."

"You want to help Dana, don't you?"

"Of course. I wouldn't be here if I didn't. But it's a stupid idea, anyway. What are the chances that the guy'll come back tonight?"

"He was here last night," Roland pointed out. "And

he made a good catch. So why wouldn't he come back and try for another?''

''It's crazy.''

''When he comes, we'll nab him.''

Jason shook his head. Pushing himself away from the door, he stepped to the sink and turned on a faucet. ''Don't want her hearing us,'' he said.

''Where is she?''

''Over near the front door. She was spreading the blanket.'' Jason splashed water onto his face, wiped himself dry with the front of his shirt, and stepped backward until he was leaning against the door.

''Did you get her soused?'' Roland asked.

''She's demolished.''

''Great.''

''I feel like a shit.''

''Nothing's going to happen to her.''

''If the guy comes—''

''We'll nail him. And he'll take us to Dana.''

''Celia, she'll know I used her if the guy really shows up.''

''What do you care? She can't do anything about it. It's not like you kidnapped her or something, she came here of her own free will.''

''She didn't plan to get used for bait.''

''Tough toenails. So maybe she'll be pissed. But you'll find Dana. It'll be worth it, right?''

''I guess.''

Roland stood up. ''We'd better get out there,'' he said, and turned off the faucet. ''Don't want our madman running off with her while we're in here gabbing. You go over to her, but be quiet about it. Don't say anything. If this is going to work, she needs to conk out.''

''She was pretty wired when I left her.''

''Turned on?''

"Yeah, and jittery."

"If she's awake, fuck her. That'll calm her down. Soon as she's asleep, get back here. She won't be much of a decoy if you're right there with her."

"I don't know," Jason muttered.

"You don't know what?"

"This whole thing. Maybe I'll just take her home."

"Don't be a jerk."

"Ro, she's *nice*. I like her."

"Just going to let Dana turn in the wind?"

Jason twisted his face as if he had a gut-ache. That phrase got him, Roland thought—turning in the wind. "I'll see how it goes," he muttered.

Roland waved him away from the door, then flicked off the light and slowly turned the knob. The latch disengaged without a sound. The hinges were silent as he eased the door open. He grinned. He'd thought of everything. Earlier, after popping open the lock with a simple twist of his knife point, he had sprayed oil on the latch and knob and hinges.

His bare feet were silent on the hardwood floor. He could hear Jason's footsteps behind him, but they weren't very loud. Running a hand along the wall, he found the entryway and stopped beneath it.

Jason put a hand on his shoulder.

The light in the bathroom had messed up Roland's night vision. Except for gray areas near the windows, everything looked black. He listened, but heard only his own heartbeat and Jason breathing close to his ear. Jason sounded like he'd just finished a sprint. His breath smelled of liquor.

Roland turned sideways, his back to the edge of the entryway. He found Jason's shirt and gave it a slight tug. Jason stepped past him and started through the room.

Going great, Roland thought.

He hoped that Celia was still awake. He hoped that Jason would fuck her. If that happened, he'd sneak up close have a ring side seat. Nothing to see, but plenty to hear. And he'd be able to imagine the rest. He'd looked her over good yesterday at the mall—her and her friend, the cute one.

Could've been that one tonight. But this was fine. This was great. The date gimmick might not have worked on Celia's friend, and he liked the date gimmick. The bait-date. What a laugh. People were so damned fun to manipulate. Mess around some with their heads, they'll do whatever you want.

So how's it going Jason, old pal? Ready to pork her?

Pork.

Roland laughed softly, caught himself and pressed his lips together hard.

He heard quiet footfalls.

Jason was coming back.

"She's zonked," Jason whispered.

Shit. So much for the good-time show. "Great," Roland said.

"So where do we hide? We should probably get closer. Maybe one of us should wait behind the bar?"

"Good idea."

"You got the handcuffs?"

"Right here." Roland patted a front pocket of his jeans.

"What about my hammer?"

Roland didn't answer.

"You had it when I dropped you off."

"I'm thinking."

"I'm not gonna jump the guy bare-handed."

"Must've left it in the john," he said. "Yeah."

"Well, go find it. Christ."

Roland made his way back to the rest room. He entered and quietly shut the door. He turned on the light. The claw hammer was propped against the wall beside the toilet. He had placed it there, out of sight, intending to return for it once Jason realized he was without a weapon.

He picked it up. It still had a price sticker on its handle. They had bought it that afternoon at a hardware store for Jason to use against the fabricated maniac.

Roland pushed its wooden handle under his belt.

He popped open the snap of his knife case, removed the knife, and folded out the blade. It made a quiet click as it locked into place.

Facing the rest room door, Roland flipped off the light. He opened the door. "Jase?" he asked in a loud whisper.

"Find it?"

"Yeah, but come here."

He listened to the shuffle of Jason's shoes on the floor.

"What?"

"Come in here a minute, we've got to talk."

Jason stepped inside and shut the door. "What is it?"

"I'm getting scared."

"Oh, for Christ—"

"No, really. He reached out with his left hand, found Jason's shoulder, and gripped it. "I never really believed the guy'd show up, but I don't know anymore. What if he does, and we can't handle him? I mean, he might kill us all."

"Calm down, Ro. My God. There's two of us, and we'll have the element of surprise, and besides which, he isn't gonna show up anyway. We'll wait for a couple of hours, then I'll take Celia home and—"

Roland punched the knife into Jason's belly. The impact slammed him against the door. Roland twisted the knife hard, pulled it out and shoved it in again. Jason grabbed his wrist. Roland jerked the knife back, freeing his bloody hand from Jason's grip. Before he could strike again, a blow to his chest knocked him backward. He staggered through the darkness and started to fall. The edge of something—the sink?—pounded his rump. His feet slid forward on the wet tiles. He was going down. Throwing back his arms, he caught the sink with both elbows and braced himself as he struggled to get his legs under him. His feet kept sliding away.

The light came on.

He saw Jason on his knees, a shoulder against the door. The wall around the light switch was smeared with bloody handprints, as if Jason had found it essential to get the light on, to *see* what was happening. Jason turned his head and looked at Roland. His face was the color of dry ashes. His eyes were bugged out, his mouth so wide open that the corners of his lips had split and blood trickled down the sides of his chin.

Most of the floor between Jason and Roland was coated with a spreading red puddle. Roland, legs stretched out, had his heels in it. Still braced, he bent his knees and drew in his legs until they were directly beneath him. Carefully, he stood up. With his left hand on the sink, he held himself steady.

Jason clutched the doorknob and started to get up. His feet slipped away. He landed on his rump with a quiet splash of blood.

Roland switched the knife to his left hand. He pulled the hammer from his belt and started forward slowly, not daring to lift his feet, sliding them instead, skating over the slick tiles. Jason gaped at him and raised a hand to ward off the blow. Roland swung, hammering the back of his wrist. The arm flopped aside. He brought the hammer down with all his strength on top of Jason's head. It went in only half an inch. Lifting it, he saw a quarter-size indentation with matted hair inside. Blood began to fill the hole. He pounded once more, trying for the same place. The hammer, slightly off target, nicked a half-moon of skull off the edge of the original hole, smacked up a quick spray of blood and sank in deep.

Roland left the hammer embedded. He slid himself backward to admire his work. Jason was seated on the floor with his back against the door, his legs stretched out, his arms hanging at his sides. His pants and the lower half of his shirt were sodden with blood. His head, streaming blood, hung forward, chin against his chest. He wore the hammer like a weird party hat.

Though Jason didn't move, the amount of blood spilling out from under the hammer meant that he wasn't dead yet.

Some folks don't die easy, Roland thought.

The thought surprised him. After all, Jason was only his second victim and Dana hadn't been a problem.

But he knew there had been others—some who'd been very tough to kill. No big mystery, he told himself. The memories of the other kills had to be coming from his friend. Smiling, he rubbed the bulge on the back of his neck. He felt it squirm, and a small wave of pleasure washed through him.

Get on with it, he thought.

He skated closer to Jason. Hanging onto the doorknob, he squatted and slashed open Jason's throat.

He stood up, tugged the hammer free and jammed its handle under his belt. He closed his knife and pushed it into its leather case, but didn't bother to snap the case shut. Digging a hand into a front pocket of his jeans, he took out the handcuffs.

Jason's weight was against the door. He tumbled onto his side when Roland opened it.

Roland flipped off the light, stepped out, and shut the door.

At first, his feet were slippery against the floor. But they became less slippery with each step. He stopped beneath the entryway to wait for his eyes to adjust to the darkness.

As he stood there, he felt a few tentative beats of pleasure. They came from his friend. Hints of the maddening ecstasy it would blast through him just a few minutes from now. Licking his dry lips, he wondered why it hadn't given him a good zap for wasting Jason.

He wondered, then he knew. Jason had simply been in the way—an obstacle, not the real target. You just get a little boost for taking him out, the biggy is saved for when you deliver Celia.

Makes perfect sense, he thought, and was rewarded with a small thrill.

You don't know, he thought. Shit, maybe you do, maybe you do. This is just my thing. I've always wanted to pull this kind of stuff, just never had the guts till you came along. I don't need your zaps to get a charge out of it.

But the zaps are great.

Oh yes, oh yes. And I'll get one soon.

His heart was thudding, his mouth dry, his breath trembling, his penis growing hard.

It was almost time. He could see a few things, now, in the darkness: the vague shape of the card table with a few bottles and glasses on top, the long flat surface of the bar counter, and a corner of something dark—maybe Jason's blanket—caught in a spill of gray light from a window.

He couldn't see Celia.

She had to be there. Asleep on the blanket.

He couldn't hear her, either. Just his own heart and breathing.

She's there unless she heard us in the can, he thought.

We didn't make much noise. Jason hardly made a sound. There hadn't been anything to hear except maybe a couple of thuds. If she was good and plastered, she should've slept through all that.

Roland touched his knife case. The flap was loose. Beneath it, the brass butt of the knife handle felt gummy. He left the knife inside its case. He wouldn't be needing it for a while.

He only needed the cuffs.

On the seat of his jeans, he wiped as much blood as possible off his hands.

He held one bracelet in his right hand, letting the other dangle by its chain, and started forward.

His bare feet snicked each time he lifted one off the floor. With each step, his heart pumped harder, his breath grew more raspy. Sweat stung his eyes and trickled down his sides. He walked with a slight stoop to ease the pressure of his erect penis against his jeans. He grinned. He felt so good now, and he wasn't even getting any new surges from his friend. Those were yet to come.

He halted at the foot of the blanket. He still couldn't see Celia.

What if she's gone!

Then he heard her. She was taking long, slow breaths.

Roland crouched. He reached out carefully until his hand met the blanket. He felt something through its softness—probably a leg—and realized that Celia must have covered herself after lying down.

On his knees, Roland moved to her side. He searched with one hand for the edge of the blanket, found it and lifted it. As he uncovered her, she mumbled something but didn't awaken.

He could see her now, in spite of the darkness. She was naked, and enough light found her skin to give it a vague, dusky hue. She lay on her back. Her legs were slightly apart, bare except for darker wrappings at her knees. Her right arm, inches from Roland's knee, lay against her side. The wrapped elbow was bent slightly, and her hand rested with curled fingers just above the jut of her hipbone. Her other arm was high, elbow pointing off to the side, hand beneath her head for a cushion.

Roland stared at the small patch of darkness between her legs. She didn't have a bush like Dana. She must trim her hair down there, he thought.

He gazed at her breasts. They were dim mounds, tipped with darkness. They rose and fell slightly as she breathed.

With his left hand, he reached forward and touched the nearer breast. It was so smooth. It felt like velvet. The nipple, too. But the nipple seemed to squirm under his touch, rumpling and rising stiff.

Celia's breathing changed.

"Hi, there," she whispered in a groggy voice. "Wha' took you so long?"

Roland squeezed her breast, then took his hand away.

Oh God, he ached! He was getting surges now, waves that pounded through him, shaking him.

"Jason?" Celia asked.

"Jason's not here. Jason . . ." and Roland suddenly shrieked, *"had some dying to do!"* He grabbed her wrist and snapped a cuff around it.

In an instant, before Celia could begin to struggle or scream, he whipped the other cuff around his own left wrist.

Chapter Twenty

ALISON WOKE UP. THERE WAS SUNLIGHT ON HER BED. The warm breeze drifting through her open window smelled of flowers and grass. A raucous bird was squawking as if annoyed by the pleasant chirping of its neighbors. The bells of a church, somewhere in the distance, pealed a tune. Alison imagined a congregation singing along—"In the sweet, bye 'n bye, we will meet on that beautiful shore . . ."

Feeling good, she stretched beneath her sheet. Then she slipped the sheet aside and was surprised for a moment to see that she was wearing her new blue negligee.

She had planned to save it for a special occasion. Maybe last night had counted as one, somehow.

She remembered coming up to her attic room after playing Trivial Pursuit and watching *The Howling* on television with Helen, remembered sitting at her desk and staring at the snapshots of Evan pinned to her bulletin board, feeling empty and alone, wondering about him. He was probably making it with Tracy More-Organ Morgan. The bastard. Wishing for a way to hurt him, she had taken down all the photos and started to rip one into tiny pieces. The snapshot showed her holding Evan's hand. Celia had taken it two weeks ago on the lawn behind Bennet Hall. Evan was wearing a T-shirt with the logo, "Poets do it with rhythm." He had a silly look on his face because Celia, instead of telling them to say cheese, announced, "Say, 'I'm a cunning linguist.' "

By the time Alison had ripped the photo apart and watched its tiny bits float down into the wastebasket, she was in tears. She couldn't bear to destroy any more, so she had made a neat stack of the rest, put a rubber band around them, and dropped them into the top drawer of her desk.

Hurting, she had taken off her clothes and opened her dresser. She had planned to wear one of her regular nightgowns, but the new one, blue and glossy, caught her eye. There was no reason to save it, no one to save it for. She might as well enjoy it. So she put the negligee on, sighing as it slid over her skin. She wiped her eyes and gazed at her reflection in the mirror. Her breasts were plainly visible through the gauzy top. She shrugged so that one of the spaghetti straps slipped off her shoulder. Eat your heart out, Evan, she thought. You'd go ape if you ever saw me in this, but you never will. Tough luck, shithead.

The memories brought back some of last night's pain, stealing pleasure from the good feel of lying on the sunlit bed with the breeze sliding over her.

Alison got up and went to the window. It looked beautiful out there. She needed to *do* something, find a way to enjoy herself. Sundays had been fine before Evan, and they could be fine again.

This would be a great day for a long walk. Go to Jack-in-the-Box for one of those crescent rolls with cheese, sausage, and egg inside. Forget about studying, pick up a brand new paperback at the newsstand—a good, juicy thriller. Later on, head over to the quad with the book and a radio and spend a couple of hours lying in the sun. Or go to the park for your sunbathing, go down by the stream. You'd have privacy there. The quad was bound to be lively on a day like this. Would you rather be alone or have company and maybe meet someone? There'd be a lot of guys at the quad. Just decide when the time comes.

She crossed the bedroom, enjoying the feel of the clinging negligee. She felt pretty fine again.

What was that Hemingway story? A kid, probably Nick Adams, went to bed at night feeling awful because he had broken up with his girlfriend. Saw her with another guy? The thing of it was, the last line. He went to bed feeling rotten, and the next morning he was awake half an hour before he remembered that he had a broken heart.

Great stuff.

Nick Winston didn't know what he was talking about, dumping on Hemingway.

Maybe drop by Wally's tonight. Maybe Nick'll be there.

Do I really want to see him again?

She peeled the negligee over her head, folded it neatly, and placed it in the dresser drawer. She rolled deodorant onto her armpits. A bath would be nice. Save it for this afternoon when you're finished lying out.

She put on panties, went to her closet and slipped a sleeveless yellow sundress over her head. Then she stepped into sandals. She took her shoulder bag from the dresser top and left her room.

At the bottom of the attic stairs, she entered the bathroom. She used the toilet, washed, brushed her teeth, brushed her hair, and hurried out.

She found Helen sitting cross-legged on the living room carpet with the newspaper spread in front of her, a box of powdered doughnuts on the lap of her rather tattered pink nightgown, and a mug of coffee on the floor near one knee. "What-ho," Helen greeted her, looking up.

"Morning."

"You're looking perky."

"Perk, perk. And how are you this fine morning?"

"Fine, is it?"

" 'God's in his heaven, all's right with the world.' "

"Yog. What's with you, a midnight visitor sneak into your room?"

"No such luck."

Helen lifted the box off her lap and held it toward Alison. "Doughnut?"

"Thanks anyway. I'm going to hike over to Jack-in-the-Box and get a sausage crescent. Want to come along?"

Helen shook her head, cheeks wobbling. "I don't think so. I'd have to get dressed."

"You could just throw on your rain gear."

"Har." She bit into a doughnut, crumbs and white powder falling onto the exposed tops of her breasts and between them.

"Celia up yet?"

Helen shrugged. She chewed for a moment, then took a drink of coffee. "Celia may or may not be up, but wherever she is or isn't up, it isn't here."

"She didn't come back?"

"It would appear that she found a more suitable abode for the night."

"That bodes well for her."

Helen rolled her eyes upward. "Spare me."

"She and Jason must've hit it off," Alison said.

"Not necessarily. They could've been in a traffic accident."

Alison ignored the remark. ''I just hope it turns into something.''

''No doubt it turned into an orgy.''

''No, I mean it. She likes to pretend she enjoys going through one guy after another, but she only got that way after Mark dumped her.''

''Yeah, that's when she started screwing around.''

''It'd be nice if she'd get really involved with someone.''

''But a freshman?''

''He must have something going for him,'' Alison said, ''or she wouldn't have spent the night. She almost never stays over with a guy.''

Grinning, Helen said, ''Think they stayed in his dorm room with *el weirdo*, Roland? Wouldn't that be the height of funzies?''

''The height of vomitus.''

''Maybe Roland joined in. A big juke sandwich with them as bread and Celia as the meat.''

''You're a very disturbed person, Helen.''

''Think about it.''

''I'm sure they didn't go to Jason's room. Not if that disgusting yuck was going to be there. They probably shacked up in a motel, or maybe they just parked someplace.'' Or rolled out a sleeping bag in a field, she thought, like Robert Jordan and Maria. The warm night would've been fine for that.

''When she gets back,'' Helen said, ''I'm sure she'll tell us all about it.'' With that, she stuffed the remaining chunk of doughnut into her mouth and picked up the comic section.

''See you later,'' Alison said.

Helen nodded.

Alison stepped to the front door and pulled it open. On the wooden landing stood a glass vase filled with yellow daffodils. An envelope was propped against the vase. She stared at the bright flowers, at the envelope. Frowning, she stroked her lips.

They're probably not for me, she thought.

But her heart was beating fast.

Crouching, she lifted the envelope. Her name was written on it. Hands trembling, she tore open the envelope and pulled out the papers inside. They fluttered as she unfolded them.

Three typed pages. Signed at the end of the last page by Evan.

> Dearest Alison,
>
> I am loathsome scum, a worm, a maggot. You would be perfectly justified in spitting on this missive and flushing the flowers down the nearest toilet. If you are still reading, however, let me tell you that you certainly could not detest me more than I detest myself.
>
> There is no excuse for my behavior of Friday night. It was childish and vile to show up at Gabby's with Tracy. What can I say? I was blinded by the pain of your rejection, and I desired to punish you. It was a foolish, contemptible gesture. Let me assure you, however, that the maneuver backfired. As much torment as I may have caused you, I caused myself more.
>
> Let me also make it clear that I have no interest in Tracy. The sole reason I invited her out was to rub her in your face and, hopefully, to make you jealous. I do not care for her at all. Though you may find this difficult to believe (due to her well-deserved reputation and your opinion that I have nothing on my mind except sex), we did not indulge in any in-

timacies whatsoever. I even avoided a good-night kiss when we parted.

I spent last night alone in my apartment, miserable, wanting to be with you but too ashamed to telephone or come over and see you. I thought about you constantly, remembering how you look and the sound of your voice and the way you laugh. I thought about the many good times we shared, and no, not just the sex (though I couldn't help thinking about that, also—especially how it feels when we are so sweetly joined, as if we are one). I even spent some time gazing at your photographs in the school yearbooks, but it was unbearable to look at frozen images of your face and know that I had possibly lost you forever.

When I slept, I dreamed of you. I dreamed that you came into my room and sat down on the edge of my bed and took hold of my hand. In my dream, I began to weep and tell you that I was sorry. I said that I never meant to hurt you, that I loved you and would do anything for your forgiveness. You said nothing, but you bent down and kissed me. I woke up, then, and I was never so sorry to wake up from any dream. My pillow was wet with tears. (I realize that all this must sound maudlin, but I want you to know everything, no matter how embarrassing it may seem in the light of day.)

Right now, it is three in the morning. I got up, after that dream, and sat down at my typewriter to let you know how I feel. I am sure it is too much to hope for easy forgiveness. The dream was a fantasy, the wishful thinking of a tormented mind. I realize that my treatment of you was rash and abominable, and that you probably prefer never to see me again. I wouldn't blame you at all.

If you wish to have nothing to do with me, I suppose I will learn to live with it. I suppose I will have no choice, short of shuffling off these mortal coils with a bare bodkin. (Forget I said that; I don't believe I am that desperate, though morbid thoughts along those lines have crossed my mind.)

Perhaps I won't deliver this to you. Perhaps I'll burn it, I don't know.

I miss you, Alison. I wish that I could make everything right again, that I could turn time backward to Thursday afternoon when I started all this stupid, disgusting behavior. But life doesn't work that way. You can't just make the bad things go away, no matter how much you may want to. (There, I'm so distraught that I've ended my sentence with a preposition—now I *know* I'll burn this.)

I love you.

I hope that you don't hate me.

I am miserable without you, but it's all my own fault and I know that I deserve the misery.

If this is the end, it is the end.

Have a good life, Alison.

All my love,
Evan

Alison's mind felt numb. She folded the letter, slipped it inside the envelope, and picked up the vase of daffodils. She carried it into the house, nudging the door shut with her rump.

"What's the deal?" Helen called.

Alison shook her head. She didn't trust herself to speak; her voice would shake and she might cry.

"Well, all *right*, flowers. Told you he'd see the light."

She climbed the stairs to her room, placed the vase on her dresser, and sat on her bed. She pulled the pages out of the envelope and read them again.

He wrote about a dream. *This* was like a dream. She almost couldn't believe that he had written such a letter. The anguish in it, the desperation. Even a threat, in the Hamlet allusion, of suicide—which he was quick to retract but which remained, nonetheless.

Alison told herself that she ought to be delighted. Isn't this what she had wanted; to have him repent and plead for her to take him back? But she wasn't delighted. The letter was almost disturbing. Could she mean that much to him?

Did she *want* to mean that much to him.

He sounded almost obsessed.

Alison lay down on her bed, the letter pressed to her belly, and stared at the ceiling. She kicked off a sandal, heard it thump the floor, then kicked off the other. She felt exhausted, as if she had just come back from a long walk. She took a deep breath. Her lungs seemed to tremble as she exhaled.

You wanted him back, didn't you? Well, he's yours. If you want him.

You'll have to do something.

Something.

Evan's probably sitting in his apartment, starting at the telephone, waiting, wondering if you sneered when you read his message, or if you wept. And very possibly thinking he had been a fool to open himself up that way.

It's cruel to make him wait.

I should go downstairs, right now, and call him. Or walk over to his apartment. Make it like his dream. Don't say anything when he opens the door, just kiss him.

Don't make it that easy on him.

Maybe I don't want to go back to him at all.

What should I do? Maybe pretend I didn't get the flowers and note, go along as if nothing happened.

Alison lay there, wondering. She felt stunned, confused, hopeful but a little bit frightened.

She pulled the pillow down over her face. The dark was nice. The soft pillow felt good.

Later, she thought. I'll do something about it later.

Chapter Twenty-One

ROLAND COULDN'T UNDERSTAND. HE HAD TAKEN OFF the cuffs before pushing her down the cellar stairs, and he hadn't put them back on because she was beyond struggling and he needed both hands free. So how come, now that he was done, he was suddenly cuffed to her again? It didn't make sense.

He knew that he hadn't attached the manacles again.

Had *she* done it? No. Huh-uh. She's dead.

Then how?

He felt a tingle of fear.

As he dug into the pocket where he kept the key, he wondered vaguely why he was wearing clothes at all. Hadn't he left them upstairs?

The key wasn't there.

Don't worry, you'll find it. You've *got* to find it.

Fighting panic, he searched every pocket. The key was gone.

This can't be happening to me, he thought.

Fortunately, he had turned on the overhead light before following Celia into the cellar. The bulb cast only a dim yellow glow, but it should be enough. Getting to his knees, he scanned the concrete floor. The area surrounding them was pooled with blood. Could the key be *under* the blood? He began to sweep his free hand through the wet layer.

Out of a corner of his eye, he thought he saw Celia grin.

No.

He looked directly at her. She was scalped, her skull caved in (and brain gone, don't forget that), her eyes shut, her face a mask of blood, and she was *grinning*.

Her eyelids slid up.

"*You're dead!*" he shrieked.

Her jaw dropped. Her tongue lolled out. The handcuff key lay near the end of her tongue.

He reached for it.

Celia's teeth snapped shut on his fingers. Crying out in agony, he jerked his hand back. The stumps of three severed fingers spouted blood.

In horror, he watched her chew his fingers.

The cellar suddenly went dark.

He heard the stairway creak.

"Who's there?" he yelled.

No answer came, but Roland knew who was there. He knew. He began to whimper.

"Leave me alone!" he cried. "Go away!"

In a mocking sing song, a voice in the darkness chanted, "I don't *thinnnk* sooo." Dana's voice.

"Youuu are go-ing to diiie noww," sang Jason.

The voices came from high on the cellar stairs but something grabbed the front of Roland's shirt (Celia's hand?) and tugged him. He toppled forward. Onto her.

Her legs locked around him. Her hands (why wasn't one cuffed to him anymore?) clutched his hair and forced his face down. Down against her face. She pressed his mouth against her mouth. She huffed. Into Roland's mouth gushed the mush and splintered bones of his half-masticated fingers.

He started to choke.

And he woke up, gasping for air. For a moment, he thought he must still be in his dream.

But the bulb still glowed from the cellar ceiling. He wasn't on top of Celia's body; he was sprawled on the concrete floor beside it. Quickly, he lifted his hands. Though they both trembled violently, neither was cuffed and he still had all his fingers.

He glanced toward the cellar stairs. Nobody there. Of course not.

Just a nightmare.

As Roland sat up, his bare back came unstuck from the floor.

He looked around and picked up his knife, but he didn't see the handcuffs. Then he remembered leaving them upstairs with his clothes.

He groaned as he struggled to his feet. His body felt tight and chilled. His muscles were sore. It had been madness, allowing himself to fall asleep down here. What if he had slept through the night?

He was confident, however, that he had only been asleep for an hour or two. There would still be plenty of time to sneak away under cover of darkness.

He climbed the cellar stairs as quickly as his stiff muscles permitted, and opened the door. The brightness of day stung his eyes. He cowered, shielding his face. Sickened, he saw himself shrivel and crumble to dust like a vampire. He wanted to turn away from the light, rush down into the comforting gloom of the cellar.

But the warmth felt good. As he stood hunched in the doorway, the deep chill seemed to be drawn out of his body. As the chill diminished, so did his panic.

Major fuck-up, he told himself. Not the end of the world, though.

Consider it a challenge.

Right.

He looked down at himself. His naked body was crimson and flecked with gore.

A challenge.

He was no longer cold, but he felt shivery inside as if he might start to cry.

If anybody sees me like this . . .

I'll figure out something.

Oh God, how could I have fallen asleep? How could I have slept till *morning*?

He rubbed his sticky face, let out a trembling sigh, and stepped to the kitchen's bat-wing doors. Before opening them, he scanned the dining area. He listened. Satisfied that he was alone in the restaurant, he pushed through the doors.

Near the front, along with the stepladder, vacuum cleaner, toolbox and cans of cleaning fluids, he found several rags and old towels. The few rags were filthy, but two of the towels seemed reasonably clean. He took them with him.

He stepped to a window and looked out. His heart gave a sick lurch when he saw the car in the parking lot.

Just Jason's car.

He turned away from the window. His shirt, pants, and handcuffs were on the floor near the rumpled blanket. Celia's neatly folded gown lay on top of the bar counter.

Roland picked up his T-shirt. It was one of his favorites, orange with the slogan, "Trust me," printed beneath a colorful, monstrous face. It was stiff with dried blood. He was about to throw it down when an idea came to him.

Why not *wear* his bloody clothes? He could probably walk right up to his dorm room in them. With his reputation, anyone seeing him would just assume it was another gag.

But he might be seen on the way back to campus. Townies didn't know about his reputation for bizarre behavior.

Muttering, "Shit," he threw the shirt down.

He knew that he could wash the blood from his hair and body. No problem, there. But he needed clothes. Jason's, he knew, were even worse off than his. Only Celia's gown was bloodless. No way, he thought. Talk about conspicuous.

If he'd had any brains, he would've stripped before he opened up Jason.

He felt trapped.

There *must* be a way out. Think!

Where there is a problem, there is a solution. There has to be.

Problem. I can't leave here in bloody clothes. I can't leave here naked. I can't wear Celia's gown.

Why is it a problem? Because if I'm seen by the wrong people, I might get arrested.

Solution?

Obvious. Don't get seen. Stay here. Until say three o'clock in the morning.

Somebody might come. Like that guy yesterday.

Roland shuddered.

That guy yesterday.

That guy *knew.*

Roland had been inside the restaurant no more than ten minutes when he heard a car and rushed to the window. Out of the car stepped a man in boots and leather clothes, a man wearing a gun on his belt and carrying a machete.

The sight of him sent an icy surge along Roland's spine. Memories filled his mind of other men, in other times, dressed in protective garments and carrying sharp weapons: axes, scythes, sabers, long-bladed knives. Other men who knew, just as this one did.

Confused and terrified, Roland had fled out the rear door and hidden in the field behind the restaurant. Lying in the weeds, he had waited until his panic subsided. Then he had crept through the field, keeping low, working his way around the restaurant until he could see the parking lot.

Who *was* this man?

A cortez.

What the hell is a cortez? Roland wondered, and his mind suddenly reeled with images of carnage: bearded soldiers with swords and battle-axes slaughtering Indians beneath a blood-red sky. In the background stood a strange pyramid. As quickly as the images had come, they were gone.

That Cortez, Roland thought. My God. He remembered reading an article in *National Geographic* a few years ago. His parents had a subscription, and he always used to look through the magazines for bare-breasted natives. But this article had caught his attention, and he'd read it. All about the Aztecs, how they not only offered the hearts of their victims as sacrifices to the sun god, but also how they ate the captured warriors. The greatest delicacy was the brain, and it always went to the high priests.

The writer of the article theorized that primitive cultures such as the Aztecs turned to cannibalism because they required protein and had no cattle. He was wrong, Roland realized, and grinned. Boy, was he wrong. The Aztecs had friends up their necks.

And Cortez, with his conquistadors, made mincemeat out of them.

So that's why this guy who went into the restaurant with the machete is a cortez. One who knows, and therefore threatens the existence of my friend—and me.

Lying in the field, Roland understood why he feared the man so much. The man should be killed, but he felt no urge to attempt it. Better to remain hidden.

After the man finally left, Roland entered the restaurant. He climbed down the cellar steps. Finding a gooey smear on the concrete behind the stairway, he trembled with rage and sorrow at what the cortez had done.

I'll get him, he thought.

No, he's too dangerous. Better to get far away from one who knows. Leave town.

Not tonight, though. Stay tonight for Celia.

What about her girlfriend? I want that one, too.

We'll see.

She would be worth a little risk, he thought. He remembered how she had looked when he saw her at the mall—that lovely, innocent face, that jumpsuit with the zipper down the front, the way the fabric hugged the mounds of her breasts.

His friend gave him a quick surge of pleasure.

Roland came out of his reverie and found himself standing over the blanket and bloody clothes. His penis was stiff, but it shrank quickly as he once again confronted his plight.

If he stayed here to wait for dark, he would be risking a return of the cortez.

I'll think of something, he told himself.

He straightened the blanket, tossed his T-shirt and jeans and Celia's gown into its center, rolled it up and carried it into the rest room. The air in the rest room was heavy with odors of blood and feces. He shook open the blanket, the clothes falling out, and spread it over Jason's corpse.

The sink had a mirror above it. Except for pale skin

around his eyes, as if he had worn goggles last night, Roland's face was painted with blood that had dried and turned a shade of red-brown. Locks of hair were glued to his forehead. A bit of something clung to one eyebrow. He picked it off, but it adhered to his finger. He flicked it with his thumbnail and watched it stick to the wall under the mirror.

He turned the faucet on, bent over the sink, and began to clean himself, using one of the towels as a washcloth. He didn't like the noise of the splashing water. It deafened him to other sounds. A car could drive into the parking lot, someone could sneak up behind him . . . He shut the water off. As he listened, he straightened enough to see himself in the mirror. His face and neck were clean.

He turned the faucet on again and resumed washing himself, this time standing back from the sink, flooding the towel with warm water and slopping it against himself. The water spilled down his body, sluicing off blood. He rubbed his skin vigorously, wrung the pink residue from the towel, wetted the towel again and repeated the process. Soon, he was standing in a shallow pool of water and blood but the front of his body was almost spotless.

He shut off the faucet, listened, fought an urge to venture into the bar area for a glance out a front window, and turned the water on again. He began the task of washing his back. This was more difficult.

Restaurants ought to have showers, he thought, for occasions like this. He grinned.

When he supposed he must've gotten most of it, he splashed across the floor until he was standing almost at the rest room door. There, he looked over his shoulder. He was far enough from the mirror so that it reflected his back all the way down past his rump. The green-yellow bruise ran down his spine and angled across his right buttock, but he saw no blood.

He used the other towel to dry himself. Now that he was clean and dry, he was very careful not to slip on the puddled tiles. He skated slowly along as he worked at his few remaining chores.

After draping the towel over one shoulder, he spent a few minutes at the sink washing his knife and handcuffs. He retrieved his shoes and socks from the space behind the toilet, and carried them, along with the knife and cuffs, to the rest room door. He opened the door and tossed them onto the hardwood floor outside.

Crouching beside Jason's covered body, he flung the blanket aside and took the car keys from a pocket of Jason's trousers. His hand got bloody again, doing it, and he sighed. He found Jason's wallet in a rear pocket, removed the student ID and the driver's license with its phonied birth date. After making sure that nothing remained in the wallet to identify its owner, he flushed the cards down the toilet.

He picked up his jeans. In the dorm yesterday, he had removed everything from his pockets that could be used to identify him. (The Skidrow Slasher, he knew, had been caught because the idiot had lost his wallet, driver's license and all, on a hillside while fleeing from a break-in.) He took the handcuff key from the right front pocket and was about to toss the jeans down again when it occurred to him that they didn't look too bad.

They were wet from lying on the floor. They were matted with blood. But they *were* blue jeans.

He spent a while at the sink, scrubbing them with hot water and wringing them out. When he shook them open, he found that the stains were not especially noticeable.

He left the rest room with them. Leaning against a wall by the door, he cleaned his feet. He stepped into the damp, clinging jeans and pulled them up.

You're in business, pal.

A warm, sunny day like this, nobody would think twice about seeing a guy shirtless. And nobody except the cortez would react to the bruise up his back.

Roland put on his shoes and socks. He folded his knife shut and slipped it into the case on his belt. He stuffed Jason's car keys, the handcuffs, and their key into a front pocket of his jeans.

All set.

He was about to leave when he remembered that he had left the spray can of oil in the rest room behind the toilet. It would have his fingerprints.

Fuck it, he thought. I've already got my shoes on. I'm not going back in there.

His prints were probably all over the restaurant. Big deal.

The area in front of the bar looked okay. There were some smears on the floor, but no large quantities of blood. He pulled the towel off his shoulder, spent a few moments scrubbing the area, then tossed the towel behind the bar. He picked up the empty champagne bottle and set it on the card table.

Was he forgetting anything?

Probably.

Who cares? Even if someone finds the bodies today, it'll take a while to identify them. They won't have a clue as to who did this until they've figured out who Jason and Celia are. By then, I'll be on the road.

Roland shut the door behind him, saw Jason's car, and went back into the restaurant. He walked quickly around the corner to the dining area, crouched and opened the toolbox. There were several screwdrivers inside. He took out the largest, and went outside again.

It took only a few minutes to remove both license plates from Jason's car. He took them to the edge of the parking lot and sailed them into the weeds.

Then he returned to Jason's car. He opened the trunk, looked inside, and shut it. He opened a back door and looked along the seat and floor. Fine.

He climbed in behind the steering wheel. The warmth of the car felt good. On the floor in front of the passenger seat was Celia's purse. He opened it and found her wallet. Rather than taking time to search it, he stuffed the entire wallet into a back pocket of his jeans. He found her key chain and pocketed it. Then he inspected the rest of the purse's contents, making sure that nothing remained to identify its owner.

He searched the car's glove compartment. A registration slip gave Jason's name, so he put it into his pocket.

That appeared to be it.

Unless he had missed something, Jason's car was now stripped of everything that might lead to a quick identification of its owner or last night's passenger.

Roland drove away from the Oakwood Inn.

Yesterday afternoon, he had parked Dana's VW bug on a residential street and hiked the final mile or more to the restaurant. Now, he drove back to the place where he had left the car. It was still there, along a lengthy stretch of curb between two expensive-looking ranch style houses. Across the street, an Oriental man in a pith helmet was rolling a power mower down a couple of boards leading from the tail of his battered pickup truck. Otherwise, the neighborhood looked deserted.

Roland turned down a side road and parked near the far corner. He stuffed Celia's purse under the front seat. Then he pushed down the lock buttons of all the doors and climbed out.

He strolled back to Dana's car. It was unlocked, just as he had left it. Feeling around beneath the driver's seat, he found Dana's keys. The engine turned over without any trouble, and he drove it away.

You did it, he thought. You pulled it off.

He let out a deep sigh, rolled down the window, and rested his elbow on the sill. The warm air came in, caressing him.

He liked this neighborhood. Finding himself in no hurry to return to campus, he drove the peaceful streets. The homes along here must cost a pile, he thought. Inside, they were probably nicer than any he had ever known.

Not now, but someday, I'll take care of a family and spend a few days in a really nice house like one of these. Do it over a holiday when the father won't be expected at work and the kids don't have any school. Really live it up.

Ahead of him, a girl stood at a corner. A real beauty, no older than four or five. Her blond hair, blowing in the breeze, looked almost white. She wore a pink blouse and a lime green skirt that reached only halfway down to her knees. A Minnie Mouse purse hung from her shoulder by a strap.

Even though Roland had a stop sign, the girl waited without attempting to cross in front of him.

She was alone.

A hot beat coursed through Roland.

Slowing the car as he neared the stop sign, he looked all around. He saw nobody, just the girl.

No, he thought. This was crazy.

Take her back to the Oakwood.

It's too risky.

But he was breathless and aching and he suddenly didn't care about the risk.

He eased closer to the curb, stopped, and rolled down his window.

The girl's eyes widened. They were very blue.

"Hi," Roland called to her. "I'm sorry to bother you. I'll bet your parents told you never to talk to strangers, but I'm lost. Do you know where Latham Road is?"

The girl frowned as if thinking very hard. Then she raised her right arm. In her hand was a small, dingy doll. It looked like it might be a kitten. She shook the kitten toward the east. "That way, I'm pretty sure," she said.

"What's your kitty's name?" he asked.

"Clew."

"He's cute."

"Clew's a she."

"I had a kitty named Celia. Celia had beautiful green eyes. What color are Clew's eyes?"

"Blue."

"Would you let me pet her?"

"Well . . ."

"I'm feeling awfully sad, 'cause my kitty, Celia, got run over yesterday."

The girl's face clouded. "Did she get killed?"

"I'm afraid so."

"Was she all mooshed?"

"Yeah. It was awful."

"I'm sorry."

"I'd feel a whole lot better if you'd let me pet Clew. Just for a second, okay?"

"Well . . ."

"Please? Pretty please with sugar?"

She shrugged her small shoulders.

Oh, beautiful and young and tender.

Roland pulsed with need.

Chapter Twenty-Two

JAKE, DRIVING HIS PATROL CAR ALONG THE STREETS OF Clinton, felt helpless. This was getting him nowhere.

Earlier, he had taken the vodka bottle to headquarters, dusted it for prints, lifted some good latents with cellophane tape and fixed them onto a labeled card. He had then spent a while comparing the prints with those of juveniles and the few college students in the department's files. He had expected no match, and he had found none.

Nothing to do, then, except spin his wheels and wait. Either the creature and its human host had gone off seeking greener pastures in a different jurisdiction, or they were still in the area and would strike again. So it came down to waiting for a missing person report, or for a body to be found.

By then, it would be too late for someone.

But we might get lucky.

Jake hated the waiting. He wanted to *do* something. But what?

Where do you start when you've got nothing to go on?

The Oakwood Inn.

In spite of the warmth inside his patrol car, Jake felt a chill on the back of his neck.

No reason to go back out there, he told himself once again. You searched the place thoroughly yesterday.

The thing left its eggs.

Yeah, but . . .

Yeah, but . . . yeah, but. Face it, Corey, you know you ought to be out there, should've probably been there all last night staking the place out, you just let Barney talk you out of it because you're scared shitless of going back.

There's nothing to *find* out there.

Sure, keep telling yourself that. You're doing nothing now but wasting time. The thing left its eggs in that place. Maybe it'll go back to them.

I don't *want* to. Besides, I'm not dressed for it and I haven't got the machete.

That's no excuse, he told himself. The thing isn't slithering around, it's in someone. Probably.

There's no point. It won't be there.

If it won't be there, what're you scared of?

Even as Jake argued with himself, he was circling the block. He returned to Central Avenue, turned left, and headed in the direction of Latham Road.

Okay, he thought, I'll check the place. Won't accomplish anything, but at least I'll have done it and I can stop condemning myself.

He started to drive past the campus. A lot of students were out: some strolled the walkways; others sat on benches beneath the trees, reading or talking; a couple of guys were tossing a Frisbee around; quite a few coeds were sprawled on blankets or towels, sunbathing in bikinis and other skimpy outfits.

Jake pulled to the curb and stopped.

Hardly a back among the whole bunch, males and females alike, that wasn't bare.

Through the broad gap between Bennet Hall and Langley Hall, he could see into the campus quad area. Even more students were gathered there—most of the men shirtless, nearly all of the women in swimming outfits or halter tops.

Jake considered leaving his car and wandering among the students. Sure thing, he thought. In uniform.

Go home and change into your swimming trunks. Then you could blend in, check them out, ask a few questions.

It didn't seem like a bad idea.

Anything to avoid going out to the Oakwood?

Whoever has the telltale bulge up his (or her) spine won't be showing it off. Maybe not, but that narrows the field. He'll be one of the few wearing a shirt.

If he's out here at all.

You'd have nothing to lose by conducting a little field investigation.

You're procrastinating. Move it.

Jake sighed, checked his side mirror, then swung away from the curb.

I'll come back in my trunks, he decided, as soon as I've checked out the damn restaurant. Nothing better to do, and who knows? I might learn something.

When he turned onto Latham Road, he began to tremble. His heart quickened. The steering wheel became slick in his sweaty grip.

He wished Chuck was with him. Some company would be nice, and his partner's banter always had a way of keeping the mood from getting too heavy. Barney shouldn't have reassigned Chuck. What difference would it make, anyway, if one more person knew what was going down?

Why the hell can't *Barney* be riding with me? Who does he think I am, the Lone-fucking-Ranger?

Calm down.

Try to think about something pleasant. Like what? Like Kimmy. And how you were cheated out of being with her yesterday? Great. Pleasant thoughts. You had to work yesterday, anyway.

After today, you only have to go four days and then it'll be Friday and she'll be with you. Four days. Seemed like forever. And what if all this crap is still going on?

We're letting it all out of the bag on Tuesday. After that, it won't be on my shoulders anymore. Anything still going on by Friday, someone else can handle it.

Jake glanced to the right as he drove past Cardiff Lane. On the way back, maybe he would make a detour past the house. Not much chance of seeing her, though. If she was outside, she'd be in the backyard behind the redwood fence.

Maybe I could drop in. Barbara hates surprise visits, but she shouldn't begrudge me this one. After all, I gave up my rightful time yesterday so Kimmy could be there for her birthday.

Maybe give Kimmy a ride. Not much traffic along here. Let her turn on the siren and lights. She'd love that. Tell her, "Don't turn on that siren." She'd get that look on her face and reach for the switch.

Jake's smile and good feelings faded as he spotted the sign for the Oakwood Inn. He turned onto the narrow road. Kimmy, he thought, would like this road with its rises and dips. If he took it fast, the car would drop out from under them after each crest and she'd get "fluffies." This was one road, however, that he would never take her on. Not a chance.

At the top of a rise, Jake saw the restaurant and felt something similar to a fluffy himself—a sinking sensation in his stomach. But there was nothing fun about this one. This one made him feel sick and didn't go away. It got worse as he drove closer to the restaurant.

The parking area was deserted.

What did you expect, he wondered, a frat party?

Something like that. He had hoped, he realized, to find at least one car on the lot; the car belonging to the guy (or maybe girl) who had the thing up his back. Go in and maybe find him down in the cellar kneeling over the smear of demolished eggs.

Just a faint hope. He hadn't actually expected that kind of luck.

He stopped his car close to the porch stairs. He wiped his sweaty hands on the legs of his trousers. He stared at the door.

Nobody's here, he thought. What's the point of going in?

To see if anything has changed since yesterday. Maybe someone was inside after you left.

Jake rubbed a sleeve across his lips.

You made it this far, he told himself. Don't chicken out now.

Just take a quick look around and get out.

He tried to swallow. His throat seemed to stick shut.

At least go in and get a drink. You can use the kitchen faucet.

He saw Peggy Smeltzer sprawled headless on the kitchen floor, Ronald tearing the flesh from her belly. He saw the way the skin seemed to stretch as Ronald raised his head.

Just do it, he thought.

He levered open the driver's door and swung his left leg out. As he started to rise from the seat, the car radio hissed and crackled.

Sharon, the dispatcher, said in her flat voice, "Unit two, unit two."

He picked up his mike and thumbed the speaker button. "Unit two."

"Call in."

"Ten-four." Jake jammed the mike onto its hook.

The Oakwood has a phone, he remembered. But he'd tried to use it Thursday night and it hadn't been connected. It wouldn't be working now.

"Too bad," he muttered.

He shifted to reverse and shot his car backward away from the restaurant.

He had passed a gas station about two miles back on Latham. It had a pay phone.

He swung his car around and sped out of the lot, feeling as if he'd been reprieved but tense, now, with a new concern. The message from headquarters could mean only one thing: a new development in the case. Any other matter was to be handled by Danny in unit one.

He floored the accelerator. The car surged over the road, flying off the rises (some real fluffies for you, honey) and hitting the pavement hard on the down slopes.

You're flying, he thought. Flying away from that damned place. But toward what? Maybe toward something worse.

He braked, slowed nearly to a stop at the junction with Latham, made sure no cars were approaching, then lunged out.

A car ahead. He gained on it quickly and he raced past it.

Seconds later, Jake spotted the service station. He slapped a front pocket of his uniform trousers to make sure he had change. Coins jangled. Of course he had change. He'd made sure before leaving home, knowing that he would need to phone Barney if he got a "call in" message. The procedure seemed excessive to Jake, but

Barney had insisted that, for the sake of keeping a tight lid on the matter, the car radio was not to be used.

For some reason, Jake had expected to get through the day without needing the coins.

I was wrong, he thought.

At least the timing was good.

Shit. Someone probably turned up dead, and all you care about is getting saved from the Oakwood.

He whipped across the road, cut sharply onto the station's raised pavement, and mashed the brake pedal to the floor. The car lurched to a stop beside the pair of public phones. He killed the siren, rammed the shift lever to Park, left the engine running, and threw open the door. He fished a quarter from his pocket as he ran to the phones.

The phone on the right had a scribbled "Out of Order" note taped to its box.

He muttered, "Shit." He grabbed the handset of the other phone and listened to the earpiece. A tone came out, indicating that this instrument was operational. Because of the tremor in his hand, he knew he would have trouble poking the quarter into its slot. So he jammed the coin to the metal plate, as close as he could come to the slot on the first try, and skidded it sideways, pressing its edge hard against flat surface until it dropped in. The sound of a ding came through the earpiece.

He dialed as fast as he could.

The phone didn't finish its first ring before Barney answered. "Jake, it might be nothing. I don't want you jumping to conclusions."

Barney didn't sound right. His voice seemed stiff and tightly under control, and he wasn't pronouncing his words like a thug.

This is bad, Jake thought. Very bad.

I don't want to hear this!

"Barbara phoned in. She's concerned about Kimmy.

Apparently, Kimmy has been missing since about thirteen hundred hours."

Jake looked at his wristwatch. For a moment, he had no idea *why* he was looking at it. Then he realized that he wanted to know what time it was. Two thirty-five. Kimmy had been missing for . . .

"Jake?"

He didn't answer. Kimmy had been gone for . . . thirteen hundred was one o'clock, right?

"She probably just wandered off," Barney said. "You know kids. There's no reason to think this has anything to do with . . . the other matter. Jake?"

"Yeah, I'm on my way."

"Keep me posted."

Jake hung up. In a numb haze, he returned to the patrol car. He started to drive.

Kimmy.

She's all right, he thought. She has to be all right. Just wandered off. Maybe got lost.

He saw Ronald Smeltzer in the kitchen, down on his knees, teeth ripping flesh from the belly, but it wasn't Smeltzer's wife being eaten, it was Kimmy. Shrieking "No!" he blasted the man dead.

She's all right. Nobody got her. She just took a walk or something.

Gone more than an hour and a half.

He saw Harold Standish open the door, playfully stick up his hands and say, "Don't shoot." Jake shoved his piece against Harold's forehead and blew out the fucker's brains. Barbara came running. She wore the blue silk kimono. She cried, out, "It's not our *fault*!" Three bullets crashed through her chest. Then Jake stuck the barrel into his mouth and pulled the trigger.

That's how it's gonna play, assholes, he thought. That's

just exactly how it's gonna play if anything happened to Kimmy.

Better calm down.

Fuck that.

You bastards, why weren't you *watching* her!

He swung onto the driveway behind BB's Toy, resisting an urge to slam into it. Then he was out of the car, striding toward the front door.

His right hand was tight on the walnut grip of his Smith & Wesson .38. He flicked off the holster's safety strap.

What am I doing?

He pulled his hand away and clenched it in a fist.

The door of the house opened before he could ring the bell. Barbara, pale and red-eyed, threw herself against him and wrapped her arms around him. He pushed her away. She looked surprised, hurt, accusing.

"Okay," he said, "how'd it happen?"

Barbara shook her head. "I don't know." Her voice was whiny. "She was sitting on the front step. We'd come back from brunch. At the Lobster Shanty? And she was pouting all the way home 'cause I wouldn't let her have ice cream. She'd already *had* chocolate cake, I didn't want her to make herself sick. Don't *look* at me that way!"

"Sorry," Jake muttered, glaring at her. He wasn't sorry. He wanted to grab the front of her blouse and smash her against the doorjamb. Ice cream. Kimmy wanted ice cream and Barbara had to play Boss Mommy and tell her no and now she's gone.

Barbara sniffed. She backhanded a slick away from under her nose. "So Kimmy was pouting and she plonked herself down on the stoop and said she wouldn't come in. So I left her there. I mean, you know how she gets. What was I supposed to do, drag her in by the ears? So I left her. I figured she'd come in in a couple of minutes. But then when she didn't, I came out to get her and she was gone. I'm *sorry*, all right? God, she's my daughter, too!"

"We can put on her tombstone, 'Mommy wouldn't let me have ice cream.' "

"You shit!" she cried out. She swung at Jake, fingers curled to claw his face.

He caught her wrist and clamped it tightly. When he saw her other hand flashing toward him, he gave her wrist a quick twist and she dropped backward. He rump hit the marble floor of the foyer. Clutching her face, she rolled onto her side and curled up.

Jake stepped inside, kicked the door shut, and stood over her. "Where's that dick-head you married?"

"He's . . . looking for Kimmyyyyy."

Jake stared down at her. She was sobbing so hard that her whole body shook. "Hope you're happy. Wasn't enough for you to run out on me, you had to . . . did you want her dead, is that it? I'm sure she was in the way a lot, always underfoot. Well now maybe you won't have to put up with her anymore. You'll like that."

Barbara curled up more tightly.

Why don't you just kick her a few times, Jake thought.

He suddenly felt sick.

What am I doing? he thought. Kimmy's out there and maybe she'll be okay if I get to her in time, and I'm standing here tormenting this woman I used to love.

He felt as if a terrible blackness had cleared away from his mind.

Crouching, he put a hand on Barbara's bare shoulder. She flinched. "Hey, come on," he said. "I'm sorry."

She kept on sobbing.

"You couldn't have known," he told her, stroking her upper arm. "I know you love Kimmy. I know you'd never do anything to hurt her."

"I'll . . . kill myself," she gasped.

"Kimmy'll be all right. She was upset, she probably decided to run away from home. You know kids." Jake realized he was echoing Barney's empty platitude. "Maybe she went to a friend's house."

Barbara shook her head. "We . . . no. Called everyone."

"She'll be all right. I'll find her. I promise."

"You think . . . someone took her."

That was exactly what he thought. Someone took Kimmy—someone with a beast up his back. "Let's not jump to conclusions," he said. "I'm sure Kimmy's fine. Did you check everywhere in the house? She might've come in when you weren't looking, and . . ."

"Everywhere. Her room, closets . . . everywhere." Barbara rolled onto her back. She wiped her wet cheeks with open hands, then let her arms flop to the floor. She stared at the ceiling. She was no longer sobbing, but she struggled to catch her breath. Her green blouse had come untucked in front. Her short skirt was twisted around her thighs. She looked as if she had been the victim of a recent assault, except that she wasn't bruised and bloody. Not where you can see it, Jake thought.

He took hold of her hand and gently squeezed it.

She glanced at him, then quickly shifted her eyes away. "We looked all around for her," she said. "I walked around to all the neighbors. Nobody saw her. Harold went out in his car." She sniffed. She used her other hand to wipe her eyes again. "I kept thinking he'd come back any minute with Kimmy. I kept praying. But he came back without her. That's when I called the police. Barney talked to me. He . . . he was very nice. I always thought he was such a jerk, but he was very nice."

"What was Kimmy wearing?"

"A short-sleeved blouse. Pink. A green skirt. Pink socks and black shoes. And . . . that necklace you gave her. The one with the snap-together beads. And she had Clew. And her Minnie Mouse purse. She kept Clew in the purse while we ate, and she snuck some pieces of cracker into the purse . . . for Clew.'' Barbara's voice trembled. ''She looked so . . . so beautiful.''

''I'll be right back,'' Jake said.

In the living room, he placed a call to headquarters. Barney said that he had already contacted all the off-duty officers. They were on the way to help in the search. Jake gave him a description of Kimmy. ''We're all pulling for you,'' Barney told him. Jake thanked him and hung up.

Barbara was still on the floor of the foyer, but now she was sitting up, knees raised, arms wrapped around her shins.

Jake crouched beside her. ''In a few minutes,'' he said, ''the whole department will be out looking for her. We'll find her. Don't worry, okay?''

She answered with a bleak nod.

''I'll bring her back to you.''

She lowered her forehead against her knees.

Chapter Twenty-Three

ALISON FELT HERSELF BECOMING MORE NERVOUS AS SHE approached home. She had hoped that Evan would show up while she was sunbathing on the grassy quad and save her from the necessity of calling him. It would have been so much easier, that way.

Naturally, he hadn't put in an appearance. He'd probably spent the whole afternoon in his apartment, waiting for his phone to ring.

I've got to call him right away, Alison thought as she climbed the outside stairway. The longer I put it off, the worse it will be.

At the top of the stairs, she found the door standing open. She stepped inside and took off her sunglasses.

On the television screen was some horror movie with a teenage girl running through the woods, chased by a maniac. Helen was asleep on the sofa, wearing only a white bra and panties. The panties were so old that the fabric had torn away from the elastic waistband at one hip and drooped, showing a crescent of skin that looked like uncooked dough.

Alison went over to the television and turned it off.

"Hey, what're you doing?"

"I thought you were asleep."

"Just resting my eyes."

Alison turned the TV on again and stepped out of the way.

"The door was wide open," she said. "Good thing I'm the one who came in, and not some nut off the street."

"Had to get some breeze. In case you didn't notice, it's hotter than a hooker's twat in here."

"Any calls?"

"You mean lover boy? Nope, he didn't call. I suspect that's intended to be your move."

"No doubt," she said, the knot in her stomach seeming to tighten. "Celia back yet?"

"Guess she just can't get enough of that freshman meat."

"She call or anything?"

"Nope."

Alison frowned. "I hope she's all right."

"She must be raw, by now."

"This is a long time to be gone."

"Maybe it's love. Isn't that what you wanted for her?"

"Sure," Alison said.

"Any minute, she'll come limping in. So, you gonna give Evan a buzz, or what?"

"I think I'll get cleaned up first."

"Keep putting it off, he'll forget who you are."

"Oh, I don't think so." With a smile, Alison turned away. She went up to her room, grabbed her robe, and trotted down the stairs again.

In the bathroom, she hung her robe on the door and took off the oversized shirt she had worn as a cover-up. Her bikini was damp with perspiration and stained by suntan oil. Since she might want to wear it again before laundry day, she left it on when she stepped under the shower.

The hot, pelting spray felt good. She turned slowly beneath it. As her bikini became wet, its thin fabric clung to her. She liked the way it hugged her breasts and groin and rump, so she left it on while she shampooed her hair. With sudsy hands, she rubbed the bikini to clean it.

Tonight, she thought, the hands on me will be Evan's.

What happened to celibacy?

We'll see.

If you go at it with him, you'll be back where you started. You'll never find out if there's anything more.

I'll try to hold off.

Rinsing the shampoo from her hair, Alison thought, it's like going to a party where you know there'll be drinking. You have to make up your mind, before you start out, that you won't get drunk. If you just go unprepared, it sneaks up on you, one drink leads to another, and before long you're blotto.

Or before long, as the case may be, you're naked and he's slipping into you.

Which might not be all that bad.

Alison untied the wet cords of the bikini top and peeled the clinging fabric off her breasts. She held it up close to the nozzle. The spray caught it and tugged at it. After a few moments, she turned to the shower, wrung out the excess water, and draped the top over the curtain rod.

She didn't think that she had burned, but with the bikini top off she could see that her skin had a light pink hue that looked as if it had been sprayed on, leaving a well-defined line that angled across the tops of her breasts. On the other side of the line, her skin looked bleached.

Real cute, she thought. Boobs like bugging eyes.

I don't think Evan will complain.

Evan ain't gonna see them, is he?

You'd better decide.

Later. If I try to decide now, it won't bode well for abstinence.

She untied the cords at each hip. The triangle of fabric in front was so small that the weight of the hanging cords was enough to pull it down. She plucked the seat away from her buttocks and the garment came away. She rinsed it, wrung it out, and hung it on the rod beside her top.

Alison picked up a slick bar of soap and began to lather her body.

If you see Evan tonight, she thought, he'll expect you to come across. Nice phrase, come across.

Too bad you're not here right now, Evan old pal. There wouldn't be much of a fight. Hell, there wouldn't be *any* fight. You might be the wrong guy, but you'd do in a pinch. Just catch me any time after I've been lying out in the sun for a while.

Maybe the sun's an aphrodisiac. Or maybe it's the feel or smell of the oil. Or maybe it's just that you're sprawled out almost naked, and the sun is hot on your bare skin and you can feel it through your bikini and sometimes a breeze comes along, caressing you.

I ought to write a paper on it for Dr. Blaine next time he asks for a descriptive passage. Give the guy a hard-on. He'd put it in me if I gave him half a chance. Horniest prof I've ever seen.

Let's not disparage horny.

But let's get over it before we make the big call to Evan.

How's about the old cold shower trick?

Thanks, I'd much prefer to stay horny.

But the house was hot. If she didn't force herself to undergo the torment of a cold shower, the sweat would pop out as soon as she had dried herself, and she'd stay dripping for a long time.

Laughing a little, Alison turned the hot water faucet. The spray became cool, then chilly. She clenched her teeth. She felt goose bumps rise on her skin. She stood rigid with her back to the cold shower, buttocks flexed tight, fists pressing her cheeks. After a while, the cold deluge didn't feel so bad on her back. She turned around and shuddered. Finally, she lowered her head into the spray. She felt as if someone had dumped a pitcher of ice water on her.

When she climbed out, the towel felt wonderful. She hugged it to her body, savoring the warmth and softness. As she started to dry her hair, a knock on the door made her flinch.

"Telephone," Helen called.

Alison felt as if her breath had been knocked out. "Who is it?"

"It's Helen, who do you think?"

"Very funny. Who's on the phone?"

"Three guesses."

"Oh, Jesus," she muttered.

"Wrong. One down, two guesses to go."

"Tell him I'll be right there."

"I could tell him you'll call back."

"No!" Alison draped the towel over her head and rushed to the door. She jerked the robe off its hook and put it on. The velour clung to her wet body. Helen stepped out of the way as she hurried into the hall.

"Slow down. I'm sure he isn't going to hang up on you."

Alison rubbed her hair with the towel a few more times on her way toward the living room. She rushed the rest of the way hunched over, sweeping the towel up and down her legs. She was a little breathless by the time she reached the telephone.

"Hello?"

"Hi," Evan said. In that one word, Alison heard a tension and weariness that seemed completely unlike him.

"How're you doing?" she asked, trying to keep her own voice calm in spite of the tremor she felt inside. Water drops ran down the backs of her legs. She sat down in a chair. Her robe blotted some of the trickles.

"I'm okay, I guess," Evan answered after a pause.

"I was planning to call you in about five minutes," she said. "The flowers are lovely."

"I'm glad you like them."

She tried to think of what to say about the letter. Her mind seemed hazy. She rubbed her wet thighs with the towel. Helen came in from the corridor, grinned and made an O sign with her thumb and forefinger, then went into her room and shut the door.

The silence stretched out.

I've got to say something about the letter, Alison thought.

"I suppose you read my . . . apology."

"Yeah."

"What do you think?"

She felt as if the air were being squeezed from her lungs. Arching her back, she managed to take a deep breath. "I don't know," she said.

"I was such a jerk. About everything. I should've respected your decision. I was just . . . hurt and confused. But that's no excuse. There is no excuse."

"Temporary insanity?"

He made a feeble laugh.

"I'll come over, if you want." Alison could hardly believe she had said that. There had been no decision. At least not a conscious one.

"Really?" He sounded alive again. "Tonight?"

"What time?"

"Oh, God, Alison. I can't believe it."

"We'll see how it goes."

"It'll go great. I promise. How about five?"

"Okay."

"I'll make us something terrific for dinner. I'll pick up some champagne. It'll be great. You're incredible, did you know that?"

"I don't want any hassles, though, okay? We'll just have a friendly dinner and talk and see how it goes."

"I've missed you so much."

Alison's throat tightened. "I've missed you, too. A lot. See you at five."

"Would you like me to pick you up?"

"No. Thanks anyway. I think I'll walk over. I need to stop by Baxter Hall for a second."

"The freshman dorm?"

"I just need to talk to someone. Don't worry, I haven't thrown you over for a freshman. Or for anyone else, as a matter of fact."

"Well, that's good to know. Not that I'd blame you, after the way I treated you."

"No more apologies, all right? Let's just start out, from right now, with a clean slate. All that other stuff is water under the bridge, or over the dam, or wherever the hell the water is supposed to go."

Like down your chest, she thought, and slid the towel over her wet neck and breasts.

"That's fine with me," Evan said.

"Okay. See you in a while."

"If you can make it over sooner than five, that'd be fine."

"We'll see."

"Take it easy, Al," he said.

"Yeah. You, too."

She hung up the phone, leaned back in the chair, and pulled her robe shut. A moment later, Helen's door opened. "Did you catch all that?" Alison asked.

"Catch what?" Helen asked. "So what's the verdict?"

"I'm going over for dinner tonight."

"Well, say hey! Score one for love and true romance."

"I don't know about that, but I'm going."

"What was that about Baxter Hall?"

"You *were* listening."

"No. Who, me? But I couldn't help catching a word here and there. You think Celia's over at Baxter?"

"I don't know. But I guess I'll drop by and check things out. She's probably not there, but maybe someone knows what's up."

"Gonna drop in on Roland?"

Alison wrinkled her nose. "He's Jason's roomy. If anyone knows where they are, he should."

"That'll be loads of fun."

"Yeah, fun like the dry heaves."

"You could phone instead. The next best thing to being there."

"It's on the way."

Helen lowered her bushy eyebrows. "You don't think anything's wrong, do you?"

"I'm starting to get a little worried, aren't you?"

"Celia's a big girl."

"She's been gone a long time."

"You want me to go with you for moral support?"

"You'd have to get dressed."

Neither of them smiled.

"It's all right," Alison said. "I can handle it."

"Well, don't let him get you alone. Stay out of the room."

"Yeah, I'll keep that in mind." She pushed herself up from the chair. "I'd better get a move on."

Alison went up to her room. Sitting at her desk, she pulled open the drawer and took out the photographs of Evan.

We used to have great times together, she thought as she looked at the pictures. Maybe it isn't over. Maybe this will be a new start, and everything will be wonderful from now on. Let's hope so.

But don't count on it.

She pinned the photos onto her bulletin board and stared at them.

In one, he was holding her hand.

In another, they were kissing.

In a third, they were seated on a blanket on the grass beneath an oak tree. Evan looked very pleased with himself. Though the photo didn't show it, Alison remembered that his right hand was inside the rear of her shorts and panties, pressed tight against her rump.

Not long after that one was taken, they had gone to his apartment and made love on the living room floor. It was the only time they ever did it with Alison on top. She sat astride him, leaning forward and bracing herself up with stiff arms, Evan fondling and squeezing and sucking her breasts as she squirmed on him, impaled.

The memory of it sent a warm shimmer through Alison.

You have to get through tonight without any of that, she told herself. Even if it's only tonight. One night without sex, no matter how much you both might want it. Otherwise, you'll never know if there's more.

Sex is like the knot that's been holding us together, she thought. I've got to untie it, just once, just to see whether we come apart. Just to see if there's another knot in the rope binding us to each other—a knot like love.

Chapter Twenty-Four

JAKE DROVE PAST THE ELEMENTARY SCHOOL WHERE Kimmy would be attending kindergarten next fall if . . . don't think it, he warned himself. To die before she even . . .

Stop!

He rubbed his forehead. He felt so damn tired. If only he could somehow make all this go away.

When they'd met briefly at headquarters to organize the search, the other six men had all been full of assurances but their eyes gave them away. They expected the worst, and except for Barney they didn't even *know* the true scope of the danger.

Jake saw a blonde girl on a swing of the school playground. His heart lurched. He hit the brake.

From this distance, the girl looked a lot like Kimmy. A man was standing behind the swing, pushing her. She wore blue jeans and a white T-shirt. Kimmy was supposed to be dressed in a pink blouse and a green skirt.

But Jake remembered a news story about a girl who'd disappeared in a shopping mall. Her mother alerted security. The mall exits were immediately sealed. And the girl was recognized by her mother when the abductors tried to take her past the guards. Only she no longer looked like a girl. After grabbing her, the two men had rushed her into a rest room, thrown her dress into a waste bin, put her into jeans and a boy's shirt, cut her hair short, and put a ball cap on her head.

The guy pushing the girl on the swing . . .

Is her father, Jake thought.

Maybe, maybe not.

She *was* about Kimmy's size, with pale skin and hair that looked almost white.

The man pushed her higher and higher. When she flew forward, her hair streamed behind her. When she swung back, it blew across her face.

Watching the man and girl, desperately hoping, Jake slowly cruised to the next street. He turned left. He was closer now, and she still might be Kimmy.

Don't kid yourself, he thought.

At the next street, he turned left again. The swing set was ahead, just beyond the sidewalk and behind a chain link fence. Jake could only see the back of the girl.

Please.

He drove past the swings. Looking over his shoulder, he saw the girl surge forward, down and up. As the hair blew away from her face, Jake's hopes fell apart.

He sped away.

Okay, it wasn't Kimmy. But I'll find her. I will. Or one of us will. Including Harold and Barney, eight men were searching for her.

One of us . . .

Where are you, honey? Where?

Jake was at least a mile from the house. Surely, she wouldn't have wandered this far. But he had been up and down every street and alley, working his way outward in an ever widening circle.

A long time has gone by. She certainly *could* have come this far.

He turned down an alley that ran through the center of the block. Near the far end of the alley, a red Pinto pulled over to the side. A lanky man in a plaid shirt climbed out. His hand went to his face, and he tugged on his long nose.

The man was far away and out of uniform, but the nose-pull gave him away. Mike Felson.

Of course, Jake thought. I'm in Mike's search sector.

Mike didn't seem to spot the cruiser.

He walked toward the closed door of a garage and past the garage and lifted the lid of a trash barrel. He peered into the barrel. He put the lid down, stepped to the next trash can, and took off its lid.

Jake groaned. Hugging his belly, he pushed his forehead hard against the upper rim of the steering wheel. He couldn't stop groaning. He raised his head a few inches and pounded it down on the wheel. Then he did it again.

Chapter Twenty-Five

ROLAND SNAPPED HIS CHECKBOOK SHUT. AT THE START of the semester, his parents had given him $350.00 in addition to the cost of tuition, room and board. Whatever was left after buying textbooks could be used for incidentals such as entertainment, extra food, clothing, (knives and handcuffs, he thought, grinning), and so on. He had $142.55 left in the account.

In the morning, he would withdraw it from the bank and use it for escape money.

It didn't seem like a whole lot.

Roland got up from the chair, stepped over to Jason's desk, and sat down. He found Jason's checkbook in the top drawer. He flipped through the check stubs until he found the last total Jason had entered, then worked his way forward, subtracting the approximate amounts of the several checks Jason had written since then. It looked as if Jason had close to $400.00 left in the account.

A goodly sum.

Roland would have to practice Jason's signature . . .

You dumb shit, you flushed his driver's license down the toilet at the Oakwood. Remember? Not only that, you didn't even take whatever cash he had in his wallet.

He wondered if Celia had any money in her purse.

He had left her purse in Jason's car.

Go back and get it?

No, too risky.

Bending down, he pulled open the bottom drawer of Jason's desk. He lifted the *Penthouse* and *Hustler* magazines, removed the envelope containing the snapshots of Dana (why not take those along as a souvenir?) and searched under a few more magazines until he found Jason's stash. The money was folded in half and fastened into a packet with rubber bands.

Roland took it out. Though its thickness was encouraging, he discovered that most of the bills were ones. Still, the total came to $87.00.

He carried the money and envelope over to his desk, and stuffed the cash into his wallet.

On the corner of his desk stood a framed eight by ten photograph of himself. He'd had it blown up from the negative of a picture taken at Halloween. It was a great shot, showing him wrapped in a vampire cape that he'd rented for the occasion. His plastic fangs were bared. His mouth and chin were smeared with blood.

Roland patted the envelope of Polaroids and grinned as an idea came to him.

He slipped his photo out of its frame. He removed the Polaroids of Dana from the envelope. Then he took scissors and glue from his drawer.

He snipped Dana apart.

A fine, fine way, he thought, to while away the time.

He glued pieces of her to the vampire photo. Soon, his leering face was surrounded by floating body parts.

A work of art, he thought when he was done.

I ought to name it.

Call it ''Private Dreams.''

He grinned, enjoying the pun.

As he picked up the scraps, someone knocked on his door.

Roland's heart kicked.

Quickly, he slipped the photo into his desk drawer. ''Who is it?'' he asked.

''Alison Sanders. I'm Celia Jamerson's roommate.''

''Just a second,'' he called. His pulse beat fast. Celia's roommate. One of the girls who'd been with her at the mall? What if this is the great-looking one who'd been wearing the jumpsuit?

Quickly, he grabbed his jeans and put them on. Crouching, he closed the suitcase on the floor and pushed it under his bed. He rushed to the closet, took out a sport shirt and slipped into it. With trembling fingers, he fastened a couple of the buttons before opening the door.

It *was* the jumpsuit girl and she looked even better than Roland remembered. She must've been out in the sun since then, for her face had a glow that made the white of her eyes and teeth striking. Even in the shadows of the corridor, her hair shone like gold. She wore a powder blue blouse with short sleeves. It was buttoned close to her throat. At her shoulders, the straps of a bra were faintly visible through the fabric. Pockets covered each breast. The blouse was neatly tucked into the waist of billowy white shorts with rolled cuffs midway down her thighs. She wore knee socks that matched her blue blouse, and bright white athletic shoes. In one hand, she held the strap of a leather purse. The purse swayed, brushing the side of her calf.

"Why don't you take a picture," she said. "It lasts longer."

Cal Taber chose that moment to walk past her. He laughed at Alison's remark, looked over his shoulder and said, "You bite, Rolaids."

Roland flipped him a finger.

"Real cute," Alison muttered.

"Sorry. Some of these guys are such pigs. You want to come in?"

"Here's fine. Do you know where Jason and Celia are?"

Try the Oakwood Inn, he thought. Frowning, he shook his head. "I don't know. The last I saw of Jason, he was taking off from here to pick her up. He planned to take her to the Lobster Shanty."

"You haven't heard from him since then?"

"No." He wondered if Alison always wore her blouses buttoned that high. He imagined slicing off each button with his knife and spreading open the blouse.

Alison's eyes narrowed. Mind reader? Roland wondered. "So you don't have any idea where they might be?" she asked.

"Well, not really. Maybe. I don't want you thinking I'm a snoop, but . . ."

"Don't worry about what I think."

"Well, yesterday afternoon I noticed that Jason had a couple of telephone numbers on his desk. He wasn't around and I was a little curious, so I called the numbers. You know, just for the hell of it. One was the Lobster Shanty. When I called the other number, I got the registration desk of a motel in Marlowe."

"A motel? What was the name of it?"

Roland frowned. "The . . . uh . . ." He shook his head. "Jeez, what was it? I really can't remember. It'll probably come to me later. Anyway, I guess Jason was thinking about taking her there."

"Why all the way in Marlowe?"

"You'd have to ask Jason. I don't have any idea. He did take an overnight bag with him when he left."

"It still seems pretty strange that they'd be gone this long."

Roland smiled. "They must be having a good time."

Alison didn't look amused.

"I'm sure there's no reason to be worried. They'll probably be back pretty soon—unless they decide to stay over another night."

"Yeah," Alison muttered. From the look on her face, she wasn't convinced.

Shit, Roland thought. I should've told her Jason had phoned and *said* they'd be staying over.

He could call Alison later and tell her that. But would she believe him?

It doesn't matter.

She won't be with us long enough to cause any trouble.

"I wouldn't worry," he said, "unless they don't get back tomorrow morning. Jason has a ten o'clock. I'm sure he'll be back in time for that."

Alison nodded. "You're sure you can't remember the name of the motel?"

"I might think of it later. I could give you a call if it comes to me."

"Okay. I probably won't be there, but you can leave the message with Helen. Do you have something to write down my number?"

"It's in the student directory, isn't it?"

"Yeah."

And so is the address. "I'll call if I remember."

"Thanks." She turned away.

Roland watched her walk down the corridor, the loose

fabric of her white shorts pulling lightly across her buttocks with her strides. She began to twist around for a glance over her shoulder, so he stepped back and closed the door.

He rushed over to his bed and stepped into his shoes. He tied them. He felt under his hanging shirt front and touched the knife case on his belt, then patted a pocket to make sure he had his room key.

By the time he opened his door again, Alison was out of sight. He pulled the door shut and raced down the hall. He bounded down the stairs.

"Slow down, jerk-off," Tod Brewster warned as Roland dodged him and his girlfriend on the landing.

"What a dip," he heard the girl say.

Three steps from the bottom, he leaped.

Through the glass doors ahead, he saw Alison outside. She was on the walkway alongside the dorm's north wing.

Roland waited in the lobby until she disappeared around the corner. Then he followed.

He stayed a distance behind Alison as she headed through the center of the campus. She took the walkway along the western side of the quad. Some guys were playing touch football on the lawn. In spite of the late hour, several girls were scattered about, most of them wearing bikinis, some reading, others apparently asleep, some talking in small groups, a few watching the football game. Here and there, couples were sprawled on blankets. One couple was tangled in an embrace. One girl, alone near the walkway, had her top unfastened and was braced up on her elbows, engrossed in a book, and Roland slowed down to stare at the pale exposed side of her breast. He felt a stir of arousal.

I wonder who she is, he thought.

Forget it. You've got other plans for tonight, and you're

hitting the road as soon as you're done. No time for this one, even if you did know who she is.

Things are getting too hot around here.

If you really wanted to play it safe, you'd leave right now and forget about Alison.

Oh, I can't do that. No way.

Alison first, then I'll take off.

Though it's a pity to leave all this behind.

Don't let it worry you. The world is full of delicious young flesh.

At the far end of the quad, Alison turned to the left and made her way through the shaded area between Doheny Hall and the Gunderson Memorial Theater. She walked directly to the street. Then she crossed it.

Roland watched from behind a tree until Alison rounded the corner of the block. Then he rushed to the other side of the street. When he reached the corner, Alison was no more than twenty yards ahead. If she turned around now . . . He quickly back-stepped and ducked behind the shrubbery bordering the lawn of the Alpha Phi sorority house.

He waited for a few minutes, then peered around the bushes. Alison had stopped midway down the block. She was gazing at something high and off to the side. She raised the strap of her purse onto her shoulder. Her back arched and she seemed to take a deep breath. She touched the top button of her blouse. Her hand dropped to the bottom of the blouse and felt around as if to make sure she was tucked in. Then she left the sidewalk.

Roland hurried forward.

He spotted her. She was inside the courtyard of an old apartment building with ivy vines on walls of rust-colored brick. As he watched her, she climbed a flight of stairs to a balcony that ran along the upper story. She walked past two doors, and stopped in front of the third.

Instead of knocking or opening the door with a key, she backed away from it and leaned against the wrought iron railing of the balcony. Her head lowered. For a while, she didn't move. Then, stepping away from the railing, she lifted an arm and twisted around as if trying to see the back of her shorts. She swiped her seat briskly a couple of times. Finally, she stepped to the door and knocked.

A man opened the door. He was bigger than Alison, probably six feet at least. He wore slacks and a clinging knit shirt. Even from this distance, Roland could see that he was powerfully built. He had a flat belly, a big chest, pecs, a thick neck, and bulging upper arms.

This was not a guy to mess with.

The man backed out of sight, and Alison entered the apartment. The door swung shut.

Now what? Roland wondered.

Go up and give it a try?

Don't be stupid.

Wait still she leaves, and nail her while she's walking home?

If the guy's any kind of gentleman, he'll walk her home. Besides, I want her inside somewhere so I won't have to worry about intrusions.

I'll want a long time alone with her.

Go on back to the dorm, he decided, and look her up in the directory.

Yeah.

Roland rubbed his sweaty, trembling hands on his shirt.

"Hurry home, Alison," he whispered.

Then he hurried away.

Chapter Twenty-Six

JAKE SAW A BLONDE GIRL ON A TRICYCLE BEHIND THE chain link gate at the end of a house's driveway. She wore a white blouse.

Kimmy?

He could only see her back.

What would she be doing here, riding a trike? Maybe this is a friend's house. Barbara said she'd phoned all of . . .

The right front of the patrol car tipped upward. Jake forced his eyes away from the girl. He jammed the brake pedal down, but not in time, and the car slammed into the trunk of oak. The impact flung him forward. The safety harness locked, caught him across the shoulder and chest, and threw him back against his seat.

The girl, hearing the crash, looked over her shoulder.

She wasn't Kimmy.

Smoke or steam began rolling out from under the hood. Jake turned off the engine. He released the harness latch. Trembling, he opened the door and got out to see what had happened. He shook his head. He couldn't believe it.

Watching the girl, he'd let the car turn. Its right front tire had climbed the corner of the driveway and he'd smacked into a tree on the grassy stretch between the curb and the sidewalk.

He staggered to the front of the car. It was hissing. The white cloud pouring through the caved-in grill and around the edges of the hood smelled wet and rubbery. He didn't need to open the hood to know what had happened: he'd ruptured the radiator.

Dropping onto the driver's seat, he reached for the radio mike.

"Thanks for the lift," he muttered, and climbed out of unit one.

"Grab some rest before you start looking again," Danny suggested.

"Sure." He swung the door shut. The cruiser pulled away.

Jake walked up the driveway toward his car, digging into a pocket for his keys. He felt exhausted and sick to his stomach. His head throbbed. He needed badly to urinate. On wobbly legs, he turned away from the driveway and crossed his lawn to the front door.

He let himself in. Though it was dusk outside, the house was dark. He turned on a light in the living room.

After using the toilet, he swallowed three aspirin. He rubbed the back of his stiff neck. In the medicine cabinet mirror, he looked as bad as he felt. His hair was mussed. His red eyes seemed strangely vacant. His face had a grayish pallor. Under his arms, his uniform blouse was stained with sweat.

He washed his face, then went to his bedroom. He started to take off his damp clothes.

You thought it was bad yesterday. You thought searching the Oakwood was bad.

You didn't know the *meaning* of bad.

He peeled off his wet socks and underwear and left them on the floor. He took fresh ones from his dresser, knew he would probably fall if he tried to step into them, sat down on his bed, put on the fresh underwear, then the socks. Groaning, he stood up again. He went to the closet for a clean shirt. He slipped into it, tried to fasten a button, and gave up. He took a pair of brown corduroy pants off their hanger and carried them to the bed. Sitting down, he pulled them up his legs.

Yesterday was nothing, he thought. Yesterday it was your goddamn imagination working overtime.

He remembered checking under his bed for the snake-thing and almost blasting Cookie Monster.

Me want cookie!

His eyes burned and tears blurred his vision.

He turned his head to the nightstand where he had placed Cookie after coming so close to putting a bullet between its bobbly eyes.

The doll was gone.

Jake *knew* he'd left it there.

He checked the floor around the nightstand. Then he was on his feet, all the weariness and pain washed away by a cleansing surge of hope, on his feet and pulling up his pants and rushing from his room and across the hall and hitting the light switch and finding Cookie Monster on Kimmy's bed, snug against the side of Kimmy's neck, held there by her tiny hand.

Then Jake was on his knees, his arm across her hot back, his face against her shoulder.

* * *

"Barbara, she's here. She's fine."

"Oh, my God!" For a long time, Barbara said nothing more. Jake listened to her weeping. Finally, she found enough control to ask, "Where is she?"

"Here. At my house."

"Where did you *find* her?"

"Right here. I came back to get the car, and—"

"That's impossible. It's *miles*."

"A little more than three, I guess."

"Oh, damn you! Why didn't you look there *first*!"

"I thought about it. I just . . . it seemed . . . it's so far. I didn't even think she'd know the way, much less walk that far. I still can hardly believe it. But she's here."

"Do you have any idea the *hell* I've been going through?"

"It's over now. She's safe."

"Let me talk to her."

"She's asleep."

"Wake her up, goddamn it!"

"In a while."

"Now!"

"Calm down. I have to call headquarters and get the search called off. Then I'll wake her up. She's probably starving. I'll get her something to eat and bring her over to you in an hour or so. Have a drink or something. Get hold of yourself. I don't want you all hysterical when she shows up."

"Hysterical? Who's hysterical? I had her dead in a ditch somewhere and all the time she's off paying a fucking surprise visit to her fucking Daddy!"

"I have to call headquarters," he repeated. "We'll be along in a while." Then he hung up.

When he was done with the second call, he returned to Kimmy's room. She was still sleeping.

Jake knelt beside her and stroked her head. Her hair

was damp. He put a hand on her back. Her skin was very hot through the fabric of her blouse. He felt the rise and fall of her breathing. She snored softly.

Jake tickled the rim of her ear. Without waking up, she rubbed the itch with Cookie Monster's furry blue head.

He smiled. He had a lump in his throat, but he was better now. Earlier, he'd fallen completely apart. She had slept through all that, fortunately.

Hell, the kid could sleep through almost anything.

With a hand on her shoulder, he gently shook her. "Wake up, honey," he said. He shook her again. "Hello. Anybody home? Kimmy?"

She moaned and rolled onto her side, her back to Jake.

"Armpit attack," he said, and wiggled his fingers under her arm.

Twisting away, she buried her face in the pillow.

"Butt attack!"

She reached back and slapped his hand off her rump, then rolled and faced him. "That's not nice," she protested.

"So sorry. Want to go to Jack-in-the-Box?"

"Can I have nachos?"

"Sure. Let's go."

"You don't have to rush me."

"If we don't get out of here fast, Mommy might show up and take you home, and you won't get the nachos."

Kimmy sat up. Searching under the pillow, she found Clew. "Is Mommy mad at me?"

"I wouldn't be surprised. We were both terribly worried about you. What you did was very dangerous."

"I was very careful."

"Come on." He took her hand. She hopped down from the bed, looked back at Cookie Monster as if considering whether to bring him along as well, then let Jake lead her across the room.

"Can I stay here tonight?"

"I don't think so. Mommy will want you at home."

"Isn't this my home, too?"

"Sure it is."

"Don't you want me to stay with you?"

"I'd love it. But this wouldn't be a good night for it. Besides, I'm on a very important case."

"Somebody toes up?" she asked, and grinned at him.

"That's right."

Outside, Jake lifted her into the car and strapped her into the child seat. He hurried to his side of the car, started the engine and turned on the headlights. As he backed out of the driveway, he told Kimmy, "We looked all over town for you. The whole police department was looking for you."

"Does that mean I'm in trouble?"

"I don't think we'll put you in jail this time. First offense. If you ever do it again, though, I'm afraid it'll be slammer time. Why'd you do it?"

"Mommy wasn't being nice."

"Because she wouldn't let you have ice cream?"

"No, 'cause she socked me."

"What do you mean, socked you?"

"Gave me a knuckle sandwich. Right here." She bumped Clew's small gray head against her upper arm. "It really hurt. You're not supposed to hit little girls, you know."

"So you ran away because she hit you?"

"*You* never hit me."

"That's only because I know you'd pound me if I ever tried." He smiled at her, but blood was seething through him.

Kimmy never lied.

That bitch had punched her.

Didn't even have the guts to admit it.

"So you got mad because she hit you, and you decided to pay me a visit? How did you find my house?"

"Oh, I knew where it was."

"And you walked all the way?"

"Sure. My foots got tired, though."

"There were a lot of people looking for you. I'm really surprised that none of them found you."

"Well, you see, I hid. I'm a good hider."

"What did you do, duck into the bushes every time a car came along?"

"Sometimes there weren't no bushes. I got behind trees and cars."

"Very clever," Jake said.

"Well, you see, I got scared about the man with the cat. He didn't have a cat, for real, 'cause it got smooshed, but he wanted to pet Clew and I ran away."

"What?" Jake asked. My God, he thought, somebody *had* tried to pick her up.

"Daddy, you should've listened the first time. I do not repeat."

"I was listening," he assured her. "You said that a man wanted to pet Clew."

"Only that was just a story. He was going to grab me and take me in his car.'

Jake's heart pounded. "Did he tell you that?"

"No."

"Then what makes you think he wanted to grab you?"

"You can't fool She-Ra."

"When did this happen?"

"Today."

"After you left Mommy's house?"

"Well, of course."

"He was driving a car?"

"Yes."

"And he stopped near you while you were on the way to my house?"

"Yes."

"What did he say?"

"I already told you."

"Press rewind."

Kimmy made a buzzing sound. "Okay, all done."

"What did the man say?"

"His cat got smooshed by a car and he felt sad. I don't think it really did, though. Do you?"

"I don't know."

"I wouldn't let him pet Clew. I ran away."

"Did he drive after you?"

"Well, you see, I ran to a house."

"That was very smart. And what did he do?"

"He drove away fast."

"What did he look like?"

"Are you going to put him in jail?"

"I might."

"Good."

"But I need to know what he looks like, or I won't be able to find him."

"Maybe you should shoot him. I think that might be a good idea."

"How old was he?"

"I don't know."

"Was he younger than me?"

"Yeah, but he was grown-up."

"Did he look old enough to be a student at the college?"

Kimmy shrugged. "He was kind of the same as George."

George was the boyfriend of Sandra Phillips, who used to baby-sit for Kimmy before the marriage broke up. At that time, George was a senior in high school.

"What did he look like?"

"Well, he didn't have a shirt on." In a sly voice, she added, "I saw his beeps."

"Did you see his back?" And did his back have a bulge, Jake wondered, as if he had a snake under his skin?

Kimmy shook her head.

"What color was his hair?"

"Black."

"How about the eyes?"

"I don't *know*," she said, sounding a bit impatient. "Are we almost to Jack-in-the-Box?"

"Just a couple more blocks. Was he skinny, fat?"

"Oh, skinny."

"Did he wear glasses?"

"Nope."

"Sunglasses?"

"Daaaaddy." She sighed heavily. "I'm tired of this."

"You want me to shoot him, don't you?"

"Well . . ."

"What kind of car was he driving?"

"Oh, that's easy. It was just like Mommy's."

"A Porsche?"

"What's a Porsche?"

"Mommy's car that Harold bought her."

"Oh, that. Huh-uh. It was like her old car. Maybe it *was* her old car!"

"Was it exactly the same? The color and everything?"

"Yeah. Only it had a thing on it."

"What kind of a thing?"

"A pointy flag."

"What color was it?"

"Red-orange."

"Like your red-orange crayon?"

"Well, of course."

"Where was this flag? Was it glued to a window, or . . ."

"It was on that thing." Kimmy pointed through the window at Jake's radio antenna.

"That's great, honey. That'll be a real help. Anything else you can remember about the guy or his car?"

"I don't think so. His cat's name was Celia. Only I don't think he really had a cat, do you? I think it was just a story to make me let him pet Clew and grab me. I bet he wanted to do something bad to me. Only I outsmarted him, didn't I?"

"You sure did, honey."

Moments later, Jake swung the car into the crowded lot of a 7-Eleven.

"Hey, you promised Jack-in-the-Box."

"I need to make a call." The parking spaces close to the public telephone were taken, so he had to settle for a spot near the far end.

"Are you going to call Mommy?"

"Nope. Want me to?"

"No!"

"I'm calling the police." He unbuckled Kimmy. She scurried down from her high seat and followed Jake out the driver's door. Taking hold of her small hand, he led her across the parking lot. "I'm going to tell Barney all about the creep in the Volkswagen."

Kimmy's eyes widened with excitement. "Really?"

"Yep. We're gonna nail that guy."

"Can we eat before we nail him? I'm starving."

"We'll eat as soon as I'm done calling."

"Well, make it snappy, buster."

Chapter Twenty-Seven

ROLAND PARKED DANA'S VOLKSWAGEN AT THE CURB halfway down the block and climbed out. He walked past two houses. In the glow of the streetlight, he checked the address he had copied from the student directory: 364 B Apple Lane.

He was on Apple Lane. The porch light of the house across from him revealed the numbers 364 on the front door.

The B on the address undoubtedly meant that Alison had an apartment on the property, either in a different section of the house or in a furnished garage out back.

Light shone through windows on the ground floor and upstairs. Whoever lives in the main part of the house, Roland thought, must be home. I'd better keep it in mind.

A walkway led straight to the front door, but flagstones curved away to the right.

Roland cut diagonally across the lawn. Stepping onto a flagstone at the corner of the house, he saw a wooden stairway to the second story. A door at the top of the stairs was lighted by a single bulb. A railing up there was decorated with potted plants. Girls would have plants like that, he thought.

Near the bottom of the stairs, a mailbox was mounted on the house wall. Roland stopped beside it. The address on the box was 364 B.

Slowly, he began to climb the stairs.

Hearing voices, he stopped and turned around. The sound came from an open window. Though the window overlooked the stairway, it was far to the side so he couldn't see in. He listened for a few moments. The voices had a flat quality—and background music. They came from a television.

So Helen is here, just like Alison said.

Watching the tube.

Alone?

She might have a boyfriend visiting.

Possible. I'll have to be careful, Roland thought.

At the top of the stairs, he removed a plastic bag from the front pocket of his jeans. It was a sturdy translucent wastebasket liner he had taken from his dorm room while planning tonight's activities. Confident that the noise from the television would prevent Helen from hearing such quiet sounds, he unfolded the bag and puffed into it. The bag expanded with his breath.

He took out the keys he had taken from Celia's purse, chose the one that appeared most likely to be the door key, and slipped it silently into the lock. He bit the edge of the bag to free his other hand. Then, using both hands, he slowly turned the key and knob. He eased the door open.

The sound from the television increased. He smelled a pleasant odor. Popcorn.

From where he stood with his face pressed to the gap, he could see only a corner of the living room. No one was there.

He swung the door a little wider and sidestepped through the opening.

He saw the top of her head above the sofa back. Her hair was in curlers.

The furniture arrangement made it easy. If the sofa had been placed flush against the wall, he wouldn't be able to sneak up behind her. But the sofa had a wide space behind it, apparently so people could cross the room without passing in front of anyone who might be sitting there.

Roland considered shutting the door. He decided not to risk making a sound that might disturb her, and left it standing open a few inches.

He took the bag in both hands. Holding it open, he began to walk slowly over the carpet. A slight breeze stirred the bag.

This'll be a cinch, he thought.

Unless there's a guy lying on the sofa with his head in her lap.

Then he was close enough to see that nobody else was there. On the cushion beside Helen rested a big white bowl of popcorn. She reached into it and scooped out a handful of popcorn. She was wearing a red bathrobe. Her legs were stretched out, feet resting on top of a low table in front of the sofa. The robe hung open, revealing thick white legs.

Too bad she's such a pig, Roland thought. This would be much more pleasant if she looked more like Celia or Alison.

No thrill in this.

He raised the bag.

Something thumped off to the side.

He looked. The door had blown shut.

Helen looked, too, her head turning enough to see the door, then turning more and tilting back. Her eyes bugged out when she saw Roland. Half-chewed popcorn spewed from her mouth, some splattering the inside of the plastic bag as he swung it down over her head.

She lunged forward. Roland flung an arm across her face to hold the bag in place. Hugging her head, he was dragged over the back of the sofa. She reached back and tore at his hair. Pain erupted from his scalp.

Helen's shoulder slammed the top of the coffee table. Roland's side hit the surface, knocking her drink out of the way. She squirmed and kicked. Her wild struggle scooted Roland along the table. Its other end flew up. He dropped to the floor, Helen smashing down on top of him.

Pinned beneath her writhing body, Roland clutched the bag tight to her face. With his other hand, he jerked open the snap of his knife case.

No! No blood!

He threw his free hand across Helen. Her robe had come open. He grabbed a breast and twisted it. She squealed into the plastic over her mouth. Letting go, he pounded a fist down hard into her belly. Again. Her body flinched rigid with each blow. Then she seemed to quake. He heard heaving noises. The bag pulsed warm and mushy against his hand and he realized she was vomiting. He fought an urge to pull his hand away. He pressed the bag even more tightly to her mouth. Convulsions wracked Helen's body. She twisted and bucked on top of him, finally throwing herself off.

He rolled with her, but lost his grip on the bag. Vomit slopped out onto the carpet. Her hand slipped in the mess when she tried to push herself up. Roland scrambled onto her back. She was choking and gasping beneath him. But breathing, at least enough to stay alive. As he straddled her and reached for the bag, she tugged it off her head.

Roland wrapped his fingers around her slick neck and tried to strangle her. As he squeezed her throat, Helen pushed herself up. She got to her hands and knees. Whimpering, she began to crawl. Roland rode her. His fingers weakened. He felt a tremor of fear.

Letting go, he scrambled off Helen's back. He staggered a few steps, got his balance, then rushed at her and kicked the toe of his shoe up into her belly with such force that she toppled onto her side. She hugged her belly and sucked breath. She had lost her glasses. Her face was scarlet where it wasn't smeared with vomit.

Roland danced back and forth, looking for the best target. He wondered for a moment what one of those mammoth breasts might do if he punted it. That wouldn't be lethal, though, and he needed to finish this business. She had already proven herself almost too much for him.

He aimed a kick at her throat.

It missed, but knocked her jaw crooked and threw Helen onto her back.

Roland jumped, bringing his knees up high and shooting his feet down, stomping her crossed arms and belly with all his weight. Breath exploded out of her and she half sat up. Roland bounded off her.

Whirling around, he kicked the side of her head.

Her arms flopped onto the floor.

He kicked her head again for good measure.

Then he retrieved the plastic bag. He sat on the soft cushions of her breasts, pulled the filthy bag down over her head, and held it shut around her neck.

As he sat there, he hoped Alison would be spending a long time at her boyfriend's apartment. It would take a long time to clean all this up.

The pig had made a real mess.

Chapter Twenty-Eight

THEY WERE NEARLY DONE EATING AND ALISON GREW uneasy about what might happen once they left the table. To postpone the moment, she asked for coffee. Evan got up to prepare it.

Don't worry so much, she told herself. So far, everything has gone fine. Reasonably fine.

She had been terribly nervous on her way to Evan's apartment, had even come close to backing down. But somehow she found the courage to knock on his door.

She had half expected Evan to look wild-eyed and desperate. If he'd been that way when he wrote the letter, however, he'd had time to recover. The man who opened the door seemed composed and cheerful. Perhaps a bit too cheerful.

"Ah, *la belle dam san merci*," he greeted her. "Make that *avec merci*."

''That's better,'' Alison said.

''Come in, come in,'' He didn't try to hug or kiss her. He backed into the apartment, smiling. ''You look terrific.''

''You don't look so bad, yourself.''

''You got some sun.''

''I was over at the quad for a while.''

Evan lifted a glass off the table in front of the sofa. It was empty except for a few ice cubes that had melted down to nuggets. ''What could I get you? How about a margarita? We're having Mexican.''

''Great.'' Alison took a deep breath, relishing the aromas that filled the apartment.

''I'll just be a minute. Make yourself comfortable.''

He walked past the bookshelves that lined the wall, stepped around the table in the small eating area, and disappeared into the kitchen. The table had been cleared of the typewriter and pile of books and papers that usually covered it. Places had been set. In the center of the table stood a single red candle.

Alison heard the blender whine.

She stepped over to an armchair and sat down.

The gulf between the chair and the sofa, in this small room, looked enormous.

This is no way to start things fresh, she thought. Evan's not contagious.

So she moved to the sofa. On the seat of a folding chair straight ahead was an oscillating fan. It swept a mild warm breeze back and forth. The moving air felt good on her damp face. She leaned forward. The top button of her blouse pressed against her throat. She unfastened it. Arching her back, she reached around and plucked the clinging fabric away from her skin.

It hadn't been *that* hot outside, she thought.

Nerves. Confronting Roland, then coming here.

It can only get better, she told herself.

What makes you so sure?

It's already better, she thought. I'm done with Roland, Evan seems all right, and the fan feels terrific.

Alison looked around the room. She had been here so many times before. Nothing looked different, yet nothing seemed quite the same. This might have been a movie set cleverly made up to *look* like Evan's apartment, and she was an actress in the role of Alison—a role she didn't quite know how to play.

Need a script, she thought. That'd certainly help.

Evan came in with a margarita in one hand and a bowl of tortilla chips in the other. After placing them on the table in front of Alison, he returned to the kitchen. He came back with a bowl of red salsa and another margarita. He put them down, then sat on the sofa beside her.

Beside her, but about two feet away. A good sign, Alison thought. He isn't going to pretend that everything is like it used to be.

They lifted their drinks. "To new beginnings," Evan said. They clinked their glasses and drank.

Alison asked how his dissertation was coming along. He spoke with enthusiasm about its progress, his hopes of developing his study of flight imagery in *Finnigan's Wake* into a full book that could gain him recognition as a Joyce scholar and help insure tenure a few years down the road. While he talked, Alison dipped chips in salsa, ate them, and drank. Occasionally, she made comments or asked questions.

When Evan finally lapsed into silence, Alison asked if he had heard, yet, from any of the universities to which he had applied for teaching positions. He gave her a strange look. "You mean since Thursday?"

"Seems like longer," Alison said.

"Seems like weeks. God, it's good to have you back."

Not all the way back, she thought. Not yet. I'm here, but I'm not back.

Evan took the empty glasses into the kitchen. While he was gone, Alison dipped another chip into the salsa, cupped her hand beneath it in case it dripped, and ate it.

Better stop gobbling these things, she thought, and licked a smear of red sauce off her fingers.

Evan came back with the glasses refilled.

Alison was already feeling somewhat light-headed from the first margarita. Drink this one more slowly, she cautioned herself. Keep at it with the booze and chips, you'll be bloated and drunk by dinnertime.

"You build a mean margarita," she said.

"Wait'll you try my enchiladas." He sat down beside her.

Beside her, and only about one foot away, this time. That's okay, Alison thought. We *are* closer than we were when I got here.

Still not like we used to be, but getting better.

"What have you been doing with yourself?" he asked.

"Not much." She didn't want to tell him that she had spent the past few days thinking about him, often with bitterness, sometimes with longing. "I went to Wally's one night," she said.

"Any luck?" he asked.

"I wasn't there for that," she said, and took a drink. "Saw this far-out video. A woman dancing with a snake. Have you seen that one?"

"I've caught it on MTV. Blue Lady doing 'Squirm on Me.' "

"Pretty far-out," Alison said again.

"Erotic."

"Helen and I played Trivial Pursuit last night. I landed on the Arts and Literature spaces whenever I got the chance. I wiped the floor up with her."

"Sounds like your Saturday night was better than mine."

This keeps straying into areas I don't like, she thought. "I must've gained five pounds. Between the two of us, we polished off a bag of potato chips and a bag of taco chips. Not to mention a six-pack. If I keep spending Saturday nights with Helen, I'll start to look like her."

"Impossible. You could gain a hundred pounds, you'd still be beautiful."

"Oh, sure."

"Your momma could beat you with an ugly stick from now till doomsday, you'd never look like Helen."

Alison laughed, then shook her head. "Come on, she's my best friend."

"I didn't start it."

"She's a great gal. It's not her fault she looks the way she does."

"If she cared, she could fix herself up."

"Not by much," Alison said, and immediately regretted it. "I mean, there's only so much that a hairstyle and makeup and clothes can accomplish. Shit, I don't mean it that way."

Evan was grinning, laughing softly. "No, of course not."

"Anyway, we had a great time. Then today, I took a long walk and I picked up a copy of the new Travis McGee and spent most of the afternoon with that. MacDonald's great to read when you're lying out in the sun."

"What were you wearing?"

"My white bikini."

"Ah."

She took another drink. The second margarita was getting low. "I like all the MacDonalds," she said. "MacDonald, John D.; Mcdonald, Gregory; Macdonald, Ross; McDonald, Ronald."

"I love how you look in the white bikini."

"Is dinner almost ready?"

"Ah, I'll check. Shall I get refills while I'm out?"

"Not for me, thanks."

"No problem. Champagne with dinner. I promised champagne, remember?" Leaving his own empty glass on the table, he stood up. He walked slowly, as if being careful not to weave.

Alison wondered how many drinks he'd had before she arrived.

Don't worry about it, she told herself. Just make sure *you* don't get looped.

She settled back against the sofa and sighed.

So far, so good, she told herself.

She sighed again. It felt good to sigh. She felt pleasantly lazy and light. A great burden had been lifted from her. She was with Evan again, and it was working out fine.

Pretty fine.

He didn't get my McDonald joke.

Too busy thinking about me in my bikini.

Who can blame him?

She laughed softly and closed her eyes.

"Hey, Sleeping Beauty."

She opened her eyes. The room was dark except for the glow of a single candle. The candle was on the table in the dining area. Food was on the table.

Evan was standing above her. "I understand it is traditional," he said, "to awaken the princess with a kiss. However, I showed remarkable restraint and took no advantage of your somnolent condition."

Alison sat up. "How long was I asleep?"

"Oh, perhaps an hour."

"Jeez." It didn't seem possible. "I'm sorry."

"No need to apologize. You're beautiful when you're asleep. Or when you're awake, for that matter."

"I hope dinner isn't ruined."

"I'm sure it'll be fine. In fact, it's just now ready."

"Do I have time to use the john?"

"Help yourself."

She made her way through the darkness and down a short hallway to the bathroom. Though she was embarrassed about falling asleep, the rest had left her feeling refreshed. She turned on the light. She used the toilet. At the sink, she cupped up cold water with her hand and took a few sips. She studied herself in the mirror. Her eyes looked a little pink. Her hair looked fine. The middle button of her blouse had come undone. She fastened it, then washed her hands and left the bathroom.

The kitchen light was on. The enchiladas on her plate were steaming and looked wonderful. Evan pulled out the chair for her and she sat down. He filled her glass with champagne. Before taking his seat, he switched off the light.

"Remember our spaghetti dinner?" he asked. "You were wearing your good white blouse and claimed you didn't want to spill anything on it so you took it off?"

"Evan."

"You were so lovely in the candlelight. Your golden glowing skin, your dusky nipples."

"Stop it."

"Sorry," he muttered. He lowered his head, cut into an enchilada with his fork, and began to eat.

Alison's appetite was gone, but she took a bite. She had a hard time swallowing and washed the food down with champagne.

For a while, they both remained silent.

This is lousy, she thought. What was the real harm in what he'd said? They had a wonderful time, that night. It shouldn't be a crime to remember it, to mention it.

"Good grub," she said.

He looked up from his plate. "Try some sour cream on it."

"Don't mind if I do." She spooned a large glob of sour cream onto her enchiladas. "It was a good thing, too," she said, "that I took off my blouse. I slopped all over myself that night."

She saw Evan smile. "On purpose, I believe."

"Yeah. I'm not, after all, a slob."

"No, indeed."

They returned to eating. Now, the food tasted fine. The cool sour cream added a tangy flavor to the enchiladas. She drank more champagne, and Evan refilled her glass.

"You're really a terrific cook," Alison said.

"I have my specialties. One of them is chocolate mousse pie, but I think we should save it for later. Give us time to digest all this."

"Maybe we should take a walk when we're done," Alison suggested.

He said, "Maybe." He didn't sound thrilled by the idea. "I've got a tape of *To Have and Have Not* I thought you might want to look at on the VCR. Hemingway. Bogart and Bacall. You know how to whistle, don't you?"

"I'd like that," Alison said. "I haven't seen it in years."

"I tought y'might like it, tweet-hot," he said, flexing his upper lip.

He would turn it on and sit with her on the sofa. Soon, his arms would be around her.

We'll be right back where we started before Thursday in Bennet Hall, before the ultimatum, before his date with Tracy Morgan, before the flowers and letter.

And maybe that's not such a bad thing, Alison thought. Why fight it? What's the point?

But what were the last three days all about if you give in tonight? You won't have learned anything.

Sure. You'll have learned that, no matter what, it all comes down to fucking.

It shouldn't have to be that way, damn it.

She pushed her fork under the small portion that remained of her dinner.

Running out of time, kiddo.

She chewed. She swallowed. She drank the rest of her champagne.

Evan lifted the bottle. "Polish it off?"

"No thanks."

He emptied the bottle into his glass and quickly drank the last of the champagne.

"I could use some coffee, if you have some."

"Sure, no problem."

Evan carried two mugs of coffee into the living room and set them on the table in front of the sofa. Then he crouched and slipped his tape of *To Have and Have Not* into the VCR on the shelf below his television. When he started to get up, he stumbled. He staggered a few steps, found his balance, and grinned over his shoulder at Alison. "I meant to do that,' he said.

He's pretty polluted, she thought.

He walked carefully into the kitchen. While he was gone, Alison pushed herself off the sofa and turned on a lamp. As the lamp came on, the kitchen went dark.

She was seated again by the time he wandered in. He had a loose-jointed, swaying walk. He had a bottle of whiskey in one hand, a can of whipped cream in the other. "How about Irish coffee?" he asked, and dropped heavily onto the sofa beside Alison.

Beside Alison, no more than three inches away.

"I think I'll take my coffee straight," she said.

"Fine. Do not let it be said that I attempted to ply you with liquor. When all is written and the story told, let it not be reported that Evan attempted to cloud the fair lady's mind with spirits, opiates, or scorcery."

"You're bombed," Alison said.

"I'm . . . semibombed." Talking out of a side of his mouth in a fairly good impression of W.C. Fields, he said, "She was a gorgeous, delectable blonde and she drove me to drink; it's the only thing I'm grateful to her for."

Alison took a sip of her coffee. "Barf, and I'm on my way home."

"Barf and the world barfs with you." But he left the whiskey on the table. He took a drink of coffee. Then he turned on the movie.

Alison sat on the edge of the sofa, leaning forward, until her mug was empty. Then she settled back against the cushion. She slipped out of her shoes, propped her feet on the edge of the table, and stared between her knees at the television.

She couldn't follow the movie. Her mind was on Evan. She sensed that he was paying no attention to the movie, either.

He was slumped beside her, his legs stretched out beneath the table, his left arm not quite touching Alison but so close that she thought she could feel the heat of it against her arm. His hand rested on his thigh.

The lighted red numbers of the VCR's digital clock showed 9:52.

We've been sitting like mannequins, Alison thought, for almost twenty minutes.

She had an urge to shift her position. But she didn't move. A move might trigger something.

This is crazy.

She lowered her feet to the floor, sat up straight, and stretched, arching her back. She rolled her head to work the kinks out of her neck.

Evan said, "Here." He reached up with one hand and began to massage her neck.

The fingers felt good plying her stiff muscles. Alison turned her back to Evan, sliding a leg onto the cushion.

Now it starts, she thought.

Both of Evan's hands were on her shoulders and neck, rubbing, squeezing, caressing. They eased the tightness. Alison closed her eyes and let her head droop. The massaging hands made her feel weak and lazy.

He worked on the bare sides of her neck, beneath her collar.

Nice. Why not nicer?

Alison unfastened a button. Evan's hands moved outward from her neck, kneading her skin, widening the bare area. Alison felt something loosen and realized, vaguely, that her middle button had popped open on its own. Evan tried to spread the blouse more. It pulled at her. She tugged, untucking it, and the loose blouse rose and opened, exposing her shoulders.

She swayed under the soothing motions of Evan's strong hands. She felt powerless to lift her head or to open her eyes or to protest when, soon, he slipped the bra straps off her shoulders.

His hands no longer massaged, but glided over her bare skin, caressing her from neck to shoulders.

He stopped for a moment. The sofa cushion moved slightly under Alison and she guessed that Evan was changing his position. Getting onto his knees? Yes. From the sound of his breathing, he was higher now. He stroked her shoulders, eased his hands under her blouse and inside the sleeves to caress her upper arms, then slid his hands out and down, down over her collarbones, down her chest, going away instead of touching her through the filmy fabric of her bra, and opening the last buttons.

He slipped the blouse down her back. Alison's wrists

were trapped in the sleeves, but she made no effort to free them.

For a while, his hands roamed her back and sides. Then they unfastened her bra. Evan kissed the side of her neck. He nibbled, making her squirm. Her heart quickened, desire pushing away the lazy weak feeling. He caressed her sides. His hands moved beneath her arms, slipped under her bra, and lightly cupped her breasts. Her nipples stiffened, pressing into his palms.

Reaching back, she rubbed his thighs through the soft fabric of his pants.

He squeezed her nipples.

A hot tremor pulsed through Alison. She caught her breath. She reached higher, intending to caress his penis through his pants, but she found it rigid and bare. Her hand flew from it.

He chuckled softly. ''Surprise,'' he whispered.

How long had he been that way, his penis secretly exposed while he caressed her? It seemed wrong, deceitful, almost perverted.

But he rubbed and squeezed her breasts and what did it matter if he'd jumped the gun a bit? He saved me the trouble, Alison thought. She reached up and stroked him.

Then she turned around. Evan was on his knees. As he slid down his pants, Alison removed her hands from the sleeves of her blouse.

She glanced down at herself. Her bra hung like a flimsy scarf above the tops of her breasts. She began to sweep its strap down her left arm and saw a smudge of red on the white, translucent fabric of one rumpled cup.

She stared at the red stain. It looked like a smear of the salsa they'd been dipping their chips into before dinner.

I must've spilled . . .

It's on my *bra*.

In the bathroom after waking up, she had found the middle button of her blouse unfastened.

After waking up.

Evan, naked from waist to knees, lifted his knit shirt to pull it over his head. It was covering his face. Alison jabbed a fist into his belly. Air whooshed out of him. He folded at the waist. Alison flung herself off the sofa just in time to avoid being struck by his crumpling body.

She rammed her feet into her shoes.

Behind her, Evan was gasping for breath.

"You shit," she muttered. Shaking with rage, she shoved her bra into her handbag. "You filthy shit, you felt me up while I was asleep!" She whirled around to face him. He was on his knees, his forehead pressed against the sofa seat. "That really stinks. *Stinks!*" She thrust a hand down the sleeve of her blouse. "It's *sick* is what it is!"

"I'm sorry," he gasped.

"You rotten bastard." She struggled to find her other sleeve, then shoved her arm through and slung the purse strap onto her shoulder. With palsied fingers, she tried to fasten her blouse as she rushed to the door.

"Alison!"

She jerked the door open and glanced back at Evan. He was still on the sofa, his ass in the air.

"Don't go!" he called. "Please!"

She stepped out and slammed the door.

Chapter Twenty-Nine

I GOT HIM GOOD, ALISON TOLD HERSELF AS SHE HURried along the sidewalk. I got him real good.

Oh, sure you got him good. Maybe he'll have a sore gut for a while, maybe even a bruise, but by morning he'll be almost as good as new and you won't.

How could he *do* a thing like that?

How could I sleep through it?

He probably just slipped his hand in for a quick feel, nothing more.

Yeah, sure thing. A feel here, a feel there.

If he'd cleaned the goddamned salsa off his hand, I never would've been the wiser. What the fuck was he doing, *eating* while he groped me?

Alison heard an engine. Headlights brightened the road on her left. A car moved slowly ahead of her, close to the curb. "I'm sorry!" Evan called through the open passenger window. "Please, can't we at least talk?"

She kept walking.

Evan's car stayed beside her. "At least let me drive you home. We can't leave it like this."

"Oh yes we can."

"I didn't *do* anything!"

"Oh no?" Alison strode across the grass and stepped off the curb. Evan stopped his car. She crossed in front of its headlights and went to his door. The window was down. She clutched the sill and peered in at him. "You didn't do anything? How do you figure that, huh? What do call grabbing my tit, not to mention whatever else you might've grabbed?"

"I didn't *know* you were asleep, damnit! I came back from the kitchen and sat down with you, and you *looked* at me. You opened your eyes when I sat down, and gave me this look as if everything was okay, and I put my arm across your shoulders. You didn't tell me to get lost, so I thought you *liked* it. I thought everything was okay again. That's when I put my hand in your blouse. I didn't know you were asleep. You didn't *act* asleep. My God, you *moaned* when I . . . touched you."

"I don't believe you," Alison muttered. But her outrage had turned to confusion.

What if he's telling the truth?

She lowered her head. Her grip on the car door seemed necessary to hold her up.

"I thought you were awake. I never would've done those things if I didn't think you were awake."

"What things, exactly?"

"You really don't remember any of it?"

"You did more than . . . touch my breast?"

"Yes."

Alison groaned.

"You seemed to like it."

"Christ."

"You were breathing hard, you were kind of writhing . . ."

"My God, I don't—"

"Then suddenly you *snored.* I couldn't believe it. I mean, I was in shock. I couldn't believe you'd been sleeping the whole time, but I thought *what if you were*! I mean, what if you suddenly woke up and found me all over you? So I buttoned your blouse as fast as I could, and decided I'd better pretend the whole thing never happened unless you brought it up first. Which you didn't.

"It was just going to be your dark little secret."

"It was a mistake, Alison."

"Yeah, uh-huh."

"I'd planned to tell you about it, but not until later. I figured that, once everything was patched up between us, it'd be safe to tell you about it. Hell, you probably would've thought it was funny."

"A riot."

"I can certainly understand your being upset. I mean, I know how it must look. But look at it this way: if you hadn't noticed that sauce on your bra, we'd be making love right now. Wouldn't we?"

"Probably," she admitted.

"So what I did . . . it wasn't exactly bad, the timing was just off. If it'd happened before last Thursday or after tonight, it wouldn't even be an issue."

"Murder isn't a fucking issue if you put a bullet through someone's head a minute after he's already dead."

"What the hell does murder have to do with anything?"

"I'm just making a point. About timing."

"I've said I'm sorry, Alison. I've explained that it was a misunderstanding. I thought you were awake."

"Did *I* start to undress *you*?"

He didn't answer.

"Wouldn't that be the standard procedure if I'd been a participant in your little grab-fest?"

"I thought you were just relaxed and enjoying it. Like the way you just relaxed and did nothing while I was giving you the massage."

"Sure," she said. She felt so tired.

"I just want you to understand. I want you to come back with me. Everything was going great, Alison. We owe it to ourselves to give it another try."

"No." She shook her head slowly from side to side. "It's over. It's done."

"We'll talk about it tomorrow, all right?"

"Good night, Evan." She pushed herself away from the car door, staggered backward a few steps, and rubbed her face.

"Tomorrow," Evan said.

"Get out of here," she muttered.

He drove away slowly.

Alison stood in the street for a while. Finally, she willed herself to move. She shuffled her feet along the pavement and managed to step over the curb. She was still several blocks from home. She felt drained. Instead of continuing down the sidewalk, she wandered onto the grass. Soon, the cool dew soaked through her shoes. She wanted to lie down, to shut her eyes and forget, but not on the wet grass. She went to a concrete bench that surrounded the trunk of an oak near Bennet Hall.

At the far side, where she couldn't be seen from the road, she lay down on the bench. She folded her hands beneath her head and let her legs hang off the edge of the circular seat. She closed her eyes.

This is fine, she thought. If Evan comes around again looking for me, he'll never spot me over here.

The concrete hurt the backs of her hands and her shoulder blades, so she used her purse for a pillow and folded her hands on her belly. That was much better.

Something skittered noisily among the leaves overhead. Squirrels, she thought.

She wished she had a sweater. A blanket would be better. If she had a blanket, maybe she would just stay here all night.

Evan's got one in the trunk of his car. His make-out blanket. Shit, he got a lot of use out of it with me.

Never again.

Thought I was awake. Sure he did.

The chill of the concrete seeped through the back of her blouse and shorts and seemed to seep into her skin. She felt a cool breeze sliding over her bare arms and legs. It stirred her hair. It smelled moist and fresh.

Her attic room would be hot.

Another good reason not to move.

I couldn't move if I wanted to, Alison thought. And I don't want to.

Fuck it all. Fuck everything.

Okay, not the squirrels unless one lands on my face. And not Mom and Dad. And not Celia and Helen. And not pizza. Or John D. MacDonald or Ronald McDonald.

That shit didn't even get my joke.

Fuck him. Fuck Evan Forbes. And fuck Roland Whatever and how about Professor Blaine because they both look like they want to rip my clothes off? And who else? How about all of them? How about every man everywhere? Helen's right, they're nothing but walking cocks looking for a tight hole.

Okay, just most of them.

Alison realized she was gritting her teeth and shivering. She wrapped her arms across her chest.

Stick around here, she thought, and they'll find you in

the morning like the frozen leopard on Kilimanjaro. They'll stand around you in awe and say, "What's she doing here?" And some asshole will probably stick his hand in your blouse. Can't let a little thing like rigor mortis stand in the way of a cheap feel.

You're going nuts, Alison.

She rubbed her face. With her arms no longer hugging her chest, the breeze slid over her and stole the warmth from the skin beneath her blouse.

Her attic would be warm, her bed soft.

Enough of this.

She got to her feet and started for home.

The second story windows were dark, but the light at the top of the stairway had been left on. Alison, still shivering, hurried up the stairs and unlocked the door. She stepped inside. The warmth felt wonderful.

Helen must've been burning incense. In spite of the breeze coming in through the open windows, a faint pine odor still hung in the air.

No light came from the crack beneath Helen's bedroom door.

Alison had expected Helen to be waiting up, eager for an account of the night's events. It must be after eleven, though. With an eight o'clock class in the morning, she had probably decided to forget her curiosity and turn in.

By the dim light from the windows, Alison made her way into the corridor and entered the bathroom. She washed her face. She brushed her teeth. She used the toilet.

Standing in the bathroom doorway for a moment, she got her bearings then switched off the light and angled across the dark hall to the staircase. She climbed the stairs slowly, gliding a hand up the banister.

Her room at the top, illuminated by a gray glow from its single window, seemed almost bright after the blackness of the staircase. Its open curtains trembled slightly in the breeze. At this distance, Alison couldn't feel the breeze at all. The room felt stifling, even worse than she had expected.

No middle ground, she thought. You're either shivering or sweating.

She lowered her purse to the floor, out of the way so she wouldn't trip over it if she needed to make a late trip to the toilet.

Then she took off her blouse and dropped it to the floor. She unfastened her shorts. She drew them down, along with her panties, and stepped out of them.

The room was still uncomfortably hot, but she could feel a hint of the breeze on her bare skin.

With a glance over her shoulder, she stepped backward to the door of her closet and leaned against it. The door banged shut. She flinched and caught her breath, shocked as much by the support giving way behind her as by the sharp noise.

She took a deep, trembling breath.

She bumped the door with her buttocks. *Now* it was shut all the way.

The smooth, painted wood felt cool on her skin. Braced against it, she raised one leg and pulled off her shoe and sock. Then the other.

At the dresser, she opened a drawer and moved her hand across the clothing. Her fingers slipped over the filmy fabric of the new negligee. It was lighter than the others, and would feel fine on a night such as this. She took it out, carried it past the end of her bed, and stood in front of the window.

The faint breeze drifted in, roaming her skin. Not long

ago, the cool air had chilled her to the bone. Now, it felt wonderful. It curled around Alison's thighs, slipped between her legs, caressed her belly, slid over her breasts and beneath her arms. She dropped the negligee. She placed her hands high on the window frame and spread her legs and closed her eyes.

The soft touch of the breeze moved over her.

Chapter Thirty

AFTER HEARING THE TOILET FLUSH, ROLAND COUNTED slowly to sixty. He made the count again and again. Then his mind wandered. He pictured Alison in her attic room taking off her clothes, getting into bed. In his fantasy, she wasn't covered by a sheet. She wore only a pajama shirt. He saw himself standing over her, carefully unfastening the buttons as she slept, spreading open the shirt. Her skin looked like ivory in the dim light from the window. He reached down to touch her and suddenly she was obese, she was Helen and she was dead, and she grinned up at him. He lurched, bumping his forehead against the boxsprings.

He lowered his head to the floor.

And held his breath, listening, half expecting Helen to moan or turn on the mattress above him, awakened by the jolt.

Don't be ridiculous, he told himself. She's dead as shit.

But I'm right under her.

He listened and heard nothing. Helen's eyes were open, though. He could see them open. She knew he was under her bed.

Roland must've spent hours in the narrow space only a couple of feet beneath her corpse. It seemed unfair that his mind should start turning against him now, when he was almost done with the wait.

He still heard nothing.

But Helen was listening as she gazed with dead eyes at the ceiling, and *she* could hear Roland under the bed—his quick heartbeat and shaky breath.

"You're dead," he whispered.

Helen rolled over, got to her hands and knees, ripped open the mattress with crooked fingers and tore out great clumps of stuffing. Then she was staring down at him through the mattress tunnel. She bared her teeth. She snarled and thrust her hand down the hole, clawing toward his face.

It isn't happening, he told himself.

But he trembled and gasped. He had to get out. He felt as if spiders were scurrying over his body. He scooted sideways over the carpet, but stopped just beneath the side of the bed frame. Helen was waiting up there. Waiting to grab him when he emerged.

With a stifled whimper, he thrust himself into the open and rolled clear. He sat up. In the dim light from the window, Helen was a motionless mound beneath the covers of her bed.

Watching her, Roland got to his feet. He kept his eyes on her as he sidestepped to the bedroom door. He opened the door, stepped out, and pulled it shut. He backed away from it.

No longer in the presence of the body, his fear slowly

subsided. He felt angry and embarrassed for letting his imagination torment him.

Why, he wondered, had his friend allowed him to lose control that way? Certainly, it could've stopped the horrid thoughts—given him a nice zap to remind him of Alison. Did it enjoy his suffering? Or did it simply not care?

He touched the bulge at the back of his neck.

I'm doing it all for you, he thought.

Then he felt ashamed. This was his friend, who had turned his secret fantasies into reality, who had led him into a new life even more bizarre and thrilling than his most lurid dreams. The fear was his own fault. He had no right to blame his friend.

As if stirred by the reassurance, or perhaps only to remind him of what lay ahead, his friend sent a small tremor of pleasure through Roland.

Had enough time gone by? He wanted Alison to be asleep before he went up to her. Otherwise, she might cry out. Her window had been open when Roland went exploring after he'd finished cleaning the mess in the living room. She wouldn't have closed it; the house was still too hot. With the window open, a scream might be heard by someone outside or even by the people who lived downstairs.

Roland needed to catch her asleep. Then, there would be no scream or struggle.

He went to the sofa, sat down, and waited.

He savored the waiting. Last night with Celia had been incredible. But Alison had stunning beauty along with an innocent, alluring quality that Celia lacked. She would be . . . overwhelming.

It *would* be like a dream.

All night with her.

But he needed to wait. Settling back on the sofa, he folded his hands behind his head and stared at the dark screen of the television. He called up an image of Alison in the mall wearing the jumpsuit with the zipper down the front that he longed to slide down. She'd had a bag in her hand. So had Celia. He wondered what they had bought that day.

Roland grinned. Whatever they'd bought, it cost plenty. It cost their lives and Helen's too. If he hadn't seen them at the mall . . .

He would've chosen someone else, not the Three Musketeers.

Big enough to share with a friend.

His stomach growled.

Desire pulsed through him. Roland writhed, gasping, until it faded.

Okay, he thought. I get the message.

Leaning forward, he pulled off his shoes and socks. He pulled off his shirt and spread it on the top of the table. Standing, he slipped the knife from its case and placed it on the shirt. He removed his handcuffs from a front pocket of his jeans. Digging into the other front pocket, he took out a smashed and flattened roll of duct tape.

He touched the handcuff key which dangled from a thin chain around his neck.

His hands shook badly as he peeled off a six-inch strip of the broad, metallic tape and sliced it off the roll with his knife. He stuck one end of the tape to his chin. It hung down like a strange beard.

He lowered his jeans and stepped out of them.

This time, there would be no problem of blood on his clothes. He would leave them down here and put them on again after showering. He would be clean when he left the house.

I'm learning, he thought. I'm getting good at this.

He sat on the sofa again, picked up his jeans, and pulled the belt out of its loops. He put the knife case back onto the belt, then stood and buckled the belt loosely around his waist. He folded the knife, slipped it into its case.

Now, he would have both hands free for cuffing her and taping her mouth.

He liked the feel of the cool belt and the weight of the knife against his side.

A naked savage.

Drape a cloth over the belt, and he would have a loincloth.

Better like this, he decided.

He slid a hand down the length of his engorged penis, then picked up the cuffs. He stepped around the end of the sofa. His feet were silent on the carpet. He heard only his thudding heart. He began to tremble. With each step, the tremors grew. He wasn't cold; he wasn't frightened. He was shaking with excitement, with delicious shivers of anticipation.

At the bottom of the staircase, Roland shifted the cuffs to his left hand. He curled his right hand over the railing. Slowly, he began to climb.

The staircase was black. But a patch of gray showed at the top.

A step creaked under his weight.

He stopped and listened.

His throat was making an odd, dry clicking sound with each heartbeat. He swallowed, and the sound went away.

He began climbing again. After a few more steps, his eyes were level with the floor of the attic room. The blanket lay heaped on the floor at the foot of the bed. The top sheet hung off the side of the mattress, almost at the end, but still on the bed, ready to be pulled up in case Alison should grow chilly in the middle of the night.

Roland was still too low to see Alison. He climbed. The bed seemed to descend, and there was Alison, sprawled on her back.

He crouched until he could no longer see her. Staying low, he made his way up the final stairs. On elbows and knees, he crawled over the carpet. He stopped close to the side of the bed.

He listened to Alison's soft, slow breathing until he was certain she was asleep. Then he stood and looked down at her.

She was bathed in a glow of moonlight. Her nightie seemed glossed with silver except for the areas over her breasts. There, it had no sheen but was transparent. He could see the creamy skin of her breasts, the dark flesh of her nipples.

Roland licked his dry lips.

He could almost feel the nipples in his mouth, almost taste them.

Alison's pillow rested crooked against the headboard as if she had found it too hot under her head, and shoved it away. Her face was turned toward the window. A few wisps of her hair curled over her pale ear. Her left arm was extended toward Roland, her hand at the very edge of the mattress, palm up, fingers curled. Her other arm lay close to her right side. Her long, bare legs were spread, feet tilted outward. The moon-slicked nightie clung to her thighs.

He bent over, caressed the slick fabric between her legs, pinched a bit of it and lifted, drawing it gently upward.

A hot surge suddenly ripped Roland's breath away. He shuddered with an agony of need, tugging briefly at the gown before it slipped from his fingers. Alison moaned. Her head turned.

Roland, quaking and fogged but somehow alert in spite of the ecstasy, made a quick grab for her left hand. He slapped the cuff around its wrist. Her arm jerked, yanking the other cuff from Roland's grip. Gasping, she rolled for the other side of the bed.

He grabbed her shoulder and hip, stopping the roll, pulling until she was on her back again. He threw himself onto her. He straddled her hips. She bucked and writhed beneath him. He caught her right hand as it lashed at his face. He pressed it to the mattress. He tore her tight left hand away from his throat and forced it down. She flung her head from side to side. She crashed a knee into his back. Roland grunted from the impact.

He jerked her cuffed hand down, pinned it under his knee to free his right hand, and punched her hard in the face. She jerked rigid beneath him, then stopped struggling. She made soft whimpering sounds as she gasped for air.

Roland peeled the duct tape off his chin. He pressed it across her mouth. The sounds of her breathing changed to a frantic hiss as she sucked air through her nostrils.

He should cuff her other hand now.

But Alison wasn't fighting anymore, and he could feel the mounds of her breasts between his thighs. He put his hands on them. The fabric felt like netting. Her skin was hot beneath it.

He no longer heard Alison's hissing struggle for air.

She was silent.

Roland squeezed her breasts.

Her right hand rose off the bed slowly. Suspicious, he watched it. It pressed his hand more tightly to her breast and held it there. She squirmed a little and moaned.

My God, Roland thought. What's going on? Does she *like* it?

Her hand moved upward, caressing his arm, curling gently over his shoulder. She stroked the hair on the side of his head. She stroked his cheek.

The shriek drove spikes into Alison's ears. Her wrist was grabbed and forced down and her thumb popped out of his eye socket with a wet sucking sound. He didn't try to hold her. He clapped a hand to his face and swayed above her.

Alison thrust his knees upward. He tumbled onto the mattress between her legs. She rammed her feet against him, turning him and shoving him away, then kicked a leg high over his body and flung herself off the bed.

She ripped the tape from her face as she backed away. In the moonlight, Roland's naked body looked gray and cadaverous. He was writhing, clutching his face, digging his heels into the mattress and thrusting his pelvis up as he squealed.

Alison whirled around. She grabbed the railing and rushed down the dark stairway. At the bottom, she tried to call out to warn Helen but her voice came out like a choked whisper. She ran through the hallway, rounded the corner, threw open Helen's door and slapped the light switch.

"Helen!"

Helen, under the covers, didn't move.

Alison hurried toward her. "Quick! We gotta . . . Roland's upstairs . . . attacked me!" She jerked the covers down and Helen stared dull eyed through crooked glasses. Her face was torn, scraped, and swollen. Her chin had a crust of dried mess. Alison squeezed the dull, gray-blue skin of her shoulder.

"Helen!" She shook the shoulder. Helen's head wobbled slightly. Her huge breasts quivered. "Helen, come on!"

Alison let go of the shoulder. The skin stayed dented where her fingers had been.

Numb, Alison backed away.

He'd killed Helen.

No. This was some kind of a sick joke. Helen isn't dead. Not Helen. It's a joke.

She's dead.

Alison backed through the doorway. She looked toward the dark hall. *"You bastard!"* she cried out.

And heard quick thuds of footfalls on the attic stairs. They triggered a blast of white-hot fear that sent Alison running to the door. She flung it open, lunged outside, slammed it, and fled down the stairs. The painted wood of the steps was wet with dew and slick under her bare feet, so she slowed down, dreading a fall that might give Roland a chance to catch her. Four steps from the bottom, she leaped. She dropped through the chill night air, her nightgown bellowing up, and landed staggering over the flagstones and grass.

She looked back. Roland wasn't on the stairs. Stepping sideways, she saw that the door at the top was still shut.

She hurried past the stairs to Professor Teal's door. His kitchen was dark beyond the glass panes. She tried the knob. The door was locked, so she pounded the wood hard, shaking the door. "Dr. Teal!" she shouted. Then she yelled, *"Fire! Fire!"* She hammered the door. The kitchen still was dark. With a flick of her right hand, she caught the dangling cuff, clenched it in her fist like a knuckle duster and smashed the glass. She reached in, being careful not to rip her arm on the pointed blades of glass, and turned the knob. With the door ajar, she eased her arm out.

She glanced toward the stairway. Still no Roland.

She shoved the door open. The glass shards on the floor clinked and scraped as the bottom of the door swept over them. Clinging to the doorjamb, Alison swung inside and stretched out a leg as far as she could before placing her foot down. She felt no glass under it. With her weight on that foot, she pivoted and found herself clear of the door. She bent over, fingered its edge, and whipped it shut.

A sudden light blinded Alison.

Squinting, she whirled around.

Under the entry, cane raised like a club, stood Dr. Teal. His white hair was mussed. He wore baggy, striped pajamas. Frowning, he blinked and his mouth started to move.

"Turn off the light," Alison commanded in a sharp whisper.

He didn't ask questions, just hit the light switch.

Alison turned away from him and stared out the door windows.

Still no Roland.

"He killed Helen," she said. "He . . . I hurt him but he's up there."

"Oh my dear God."

Alison heard a quiet clatter. She looked over her shoulder. Dr. Teal's cane was clamped between his knees. He held the pale handset of the wall phone and spun the dial. "Police emergency," he said, his voice as firm and vibrant as if he were standing at the lectern in a hall packed with enthralled students. He waited a few moments, then said, "We have bloody murder at 364 Apple Lane, and the cur is among us. Get here immediately." He hung up the phone.

"Come away from the door," he ordered.

Alison backed away, unwilling to take her eyes from the windows. She halted when the professor's hand curled gently over her shoulder.

"It's all right now, darling. He won't hurt you. The police will be here shortly, I'm sure."

"He killed Helen," she said. Her voice came out squeaky and tears filled her eyes.

Professor Teal patted her shoulder. "Stay here." He slipped past her. He walked toward the door, his cane swinging at his side like a nine iron. Glass crunched under his slippers. He eased the door open.

"Maybe you shouldn't do that," Alison whispered.

Ignoring her, he leaned outside. His head turned, tilted back. Then he brought his head back through the opening and looked around at Alison. "You say that you injured him?"

"I . . . gouged one of his eyes."

"Bully for you. Perhaps you incapacitated the rotter. I'll bash his head to pulp if . . . what about Celia?"

"She's not home."

"Thank God for that."

"I don't know. I'm . . . I think maybe he got her last night."

"Dear God, no."

"She went on a date with his roommate and never came home."

"Two of my girls. Two of my sweet, darling . . . oh, he shall pay dearly, dearly . . ." Professor Teal threw the door open wide and stepped out.

"No!" Alison yelled.

She ran after him, leaped the area of broken glass, and came down on the flagstone outside the door. Professor Teal was already at the bottom of the stairway. "Wait inside," he told her.

"Wait for the cops!" Alison cried out. "Please!"

Ignoring her, he began to trot up the stairs. Alison darted beneath the stairway, reached between the risers, and grabbed the old man's ankle.

"Unhand me!"

"He'll kill you, too!"

"We shall see about that." He tried to shake his foot free.

Alison almost lost her grip. She wrapped her other hand around the man's bony ankle and hung on.

Brakes screamed. Through the gap in the stairs, Alison saw a squad car lurch to a stop, red and blue lights spinning. A man raced around the front of the car. He pulled a pistol from his holster and he ran straight over the lawn toward Alison.

"You win," the professor said.

She didn't trust him. She kept her grip on his ankle until the policeman jangled to a stop, crouched, aimed at him, and shouted, "Freeze, cocksucker, or I'll blow your fucking brains from here till yesterday!"

"He's not the one!" Alison yelled.

She stepped out from under the stairway.

Professor Teal turned around slowly. "I am the owner of this house," he said. "We have every reason to believe that the killer is upstairs."

"Who'd he kill?"

"My roommate," Alison said. "And he tried to get me."

"Is he armed?" asked the burly policeman.

"I don't know. Not that I saw."

"He's still up there?" Without waiting for an answer, he started up the stairs. Professor Teal stepped out of his way and came down as the officer continued to the top.

Alison went to the professor's side and put an arm around his back.

"Silly old bear," she said.

He smiled sadly.

They both flinched as a gun blast shocked the night. Alison's head jerked sideways. She saw Roland at the top of the stairs, arms out. The policeman flopped backward over the rail, yelling with alarm, flapping through the air. His yell stopped short when he hit the ground. For a moment, he seemed to be performing a weird headstand, legs kicking at the sky. Then he toppled. He lay on his back, twitching. There was a knife in his chest.

Roland, at the top of the stairs, turned slowly. He was no longer naked. He wore jeans and an open shirt. The left side of his face was slicked with red from his empty socket, red that dribbled onto his shirt and chest. With zombielike slowness, he lifted his left hand to study it with his one eye. The policeman's bullet hadn't missed Roland completely. Alison saw that his forefinger was gone entirely. His middle finger dangled by a strip of flesh, swinging like a pendulum. He clutched it with his other hand, tore it loose, and sailed it down at Alison like a blunt dart. It dropped into the grass at her feet.

He began to descend the stairway.

Professor Teal pushed Alison away and stepped almost casually to the foot of the stairs. He raised his cane overhead, prepared to strike when Roland came into range.

Alison rushed toward the policeman. He looked dead. She pictured him falling. Had he been holding the revolver? She didn't know. But it was not in either of his hands. She scurried around his body, trying to find the gun.

Where *is* it!

She looked toward the stairway in time to see Roland leap. He dove from high above Professor Teal. The old man swung his cane at the flying body. It missed Roland's head and broke across his shoulder. Roland slammed the professor to the ground.

Alison jerked the knife from the policeman's chest, whirled and ran at the sprawled, struggling men. Roland hammered the professor's nose with a fist. He rolled off. He was on his back, pushing himself up with his right arm. He raised his injured hand as if signaling Alison to halt.

Alison flung herself onto him. He fell back. He tried to push her away, fingers and stumps thrusting at her face. She drove the knife down hard. Roland squealed. Then his right hand clubbed her ear. Stunned by the impact, she felt herself being shoved off him. On her side, she saw Roland grab the knife handle. The blade had pierced his left nipple, but it hadn't gone deep. A rib must've stopped it. Roland yanked the knife free.

His ravaged hand reached for Alison.

She rolled, scurried to her feet, and ran.

She ran for the street.

The dewy grass was slippery, but she ran all out, sprinting, flinging her legs out with long quick strides, pumping her arms. The loose cuff on the end of its chain whipped across her knuckles, her forearm, sometimes lashed her side or breast.

She heard Roland gasping and whimpering behind her. Not very far behind her. She didn't dare to look.

Faint white plumes puffed from the exhaust pipe of the police car.

One foot pounded the sidewalk. The other foot landed in the grass at the other side. She sprang from the curb, rushed past the front of the car. Turning, she glanced over her shoulder. Roland hit the hood belly-first and slid across it, teeth bared, ruined hand reaching for her, knife clenched in his other hand. Alison spun away from the reaching hand. Its two fingertips grazed her belly. Stumbling backward, she grabbed the handle of the driver's door.

She jerked open the door, leaped inside, and slammed the door shut while Roland was squirming off the hood. The window was open. She started to crank it up. Roland stumbled toward her. The glass slid higher. He stabbed. His knife blade pounded the window and skittered down with a grating whine like fingernails on a chalkboard.

Alison released the emergency brake.

Roland opened the door.

Alison cried out, "No!" How could she *not* have locked it.

She rammed the shift lever to Drive and stomped the gas pedal to the floor.

The car surged forward.

Roland yelled.

The door bumped against its frame.

Alison swerved away from the curb to miss a parked Volkswagen.

She looked at the side mirror.

Roland was sprawled facedown on the pavement, half a block away.

Chapter Thirty-One

JAKE ENTERED THE DISPATCHER'S CUBICLE, NODDED A greeting to Martha, who looked back at him with grim eyes, and turned to the girl.

She was sitting on one of the molded plastic chairs that belonged in the waiting area outside the cubicle. It must've been brought in so she wouldn't have to wait alone. She held a plastic coffee cup in both hands. The left side of her face was red and puffy. She wore Martha's old brown cardigan over a blue nightgown. She looked up from her coffee as Jake approached.

"I'm Jake Corey," he said. "I'm in charge of the investigation."

She nodded.

"Would you like to step this way?"

She glanced at Martha, who nodded that it was all right. She stood up.

Jake held the door open for her. She walked stiffly, staring down at her coffee as if concerned about spilling it. Though she must've been about twenty years old, she had the look of a hurt and frightened little girl.

Jake pulled the door shut and stepped to her side.

"Where are we going?" she asked.

"Just over here." He gestured toward Barney's office. "We can't talk about this in front of Martha."

She walked beside him.

"Are you all right?" he asked.

"Yeah."

He opened Barney's door and flicked the switch. Overhead fluorescent lights came on. He followed the girl into the room. "Sit in the chief's seat," he told her.

"Behind the desk?"

"It'll be more comfortable."

She stepped around the desk, set her coffee cup on the blotter, and sat down. The stuffed chair bobbed and squeaked. She rolled it forward as if to take shelter behind the big, protective desk. Her hands curled around the sides of the cup.

Jake sat on a folding chair across from her. "You're Alison?"

"Yes. Alison Sanders."

"Dr. Teal told me what you did. You're a very brave young lady."

"Is he all right?"

"He's fine. He's very upset, of course."

"The policeman, is he dead?"

"Yes."

"I'm sorry."

"So am I," Jake muttered.

"You didn't get him, did you." It wasn't a question.

"Not yet. But we will."

"It was Roland," she said in a steady, low voice. "I

don't know his last name, but he lives in room 240 of Baxter Hall on the campus.''

Jake took a notepad from his shirt pocket. He quickly scribbled the name and room number. ''Was he a friend of yours?''

She shook her head. ''I've only seen him around. He's a freshman.''

''Do you have any idea why he might have done this?''

''I don't know.'' Alison rubbed her forehead. ''He was somehow involved in . . . His roommate took Celia out last night. That's Celia Jamerson. She was living with . . .''

''Celia Jamerson?'' Jake asked, surprised. He saw the slim girl sitting by the road, scuffed and bleeding, holding her tremulous arm. ''A van tried to hit her Thursday?''

Alison nodded. ''She went out with Roland's roommate last night and she didn't come home. I went over to the dorm this afternoon to ask Roland about it. That was the only time I ever really talked to him. He said they'd gone to some motel in Marlowe, but I didn't really believe him.'' She met Jake's gaze with weary, knowing eyes. ''I think Roland killed her. Maybe he killed Jason, too. That's the roommate. Maybe Jason's in on it, but I don't think so.''

''What happened after you spoke with Roland?''

''I went over to a friend's house. We had dinner. Then I walked home. The place was dark. Helen's door was shut. I thought she'd gone to bed, but I guess she must've already been dead. Roland must've been hiding somewhere. I went up to my room and went to sleep. He woke me up. He got a handcuff on me. And he put tape on my mouth. He was naked. I thought that what he wanted to do was, you know, rape me. I mean, I'm sure that *is* what he wanted to do, not just kill me, or he wouldn't have bothered with the cuffs and tape. Anyway, we fought and

I . . . I blinded him in one eye.'' Her right hand left the coffee cup. She lifted her thumb and stared at it. ''I washed,'' she muttered. ''Martha let me wash up. She found a key that opened the cuff. And gave me her sweater. She's very nice.''

''You said that Roland was naked.''

''He had a belt on. That's all.''

''Did you notice anything peculiar about his appearance?''

She looked at Jake and raised her eyebrows. ''You mean like a tattoo or birthmark or something?''

''Did you get a look at his back? Or feel it?''

''I don't think so. Why?''

''I just wonder if he had any kind of a bruise or bulge down his spine.''

''I don't know. Not that I noticed. Why?''

''It's a long story. I'd rather not get into it right now. After you gouged his eye, what happened?''

''I got away. I ran downstairs and went to warn Helen. But she was . . .'' Alison caught her lower lip between her teeth. She shook her head.

''Then you went outside?'' Jake asked.

''Yeah. I went down and broke into Dr. Teal's kitchen, and he came out to help.''

''Okay, fine. He's filled me in from there, up to the point where you ran for the patrol car.''

''That's about all, then. Roland almost got me, but I drove away and . . . he was lying in the street the last time I saw him. I drove here to the police station and told Martha what happened. She sent a car and ambulance to the house and phoned someone.''

''She called the chief. He phoned me, and I went over. Could you describe this Roland?''

''He's . . . eighteen, I guess. Skinny. About five-seven.

Black hair. He's minus his left eye and two fingers of his left hand, and he's got a knife wound on his left nipple."

"He won't go far in that condition."

"I guess not."

"Did you notice if he had a car?"

"I don't know. There was a VW bug on the street by the house. I almost hit it with the police car. It might not have been his, but—"

"A yellow bug with a banner on its aerial?" Jake asked. He felt excited. He felt sick.

"I don't know about the banner, but I'm pretty sure the car was yellow."

"My God," he muttered.

"What?"

"It *was* him. He tried to pick up my daughter this afternoon."

A corner of Alison's lip curled up. "Your daughter?"

"She ran away from him."

"Jesus. She's all right, though?"

"Yeah, fine. It threw a scare into her, but she's fine."

"How old is she?"

"Four and a half. She lives with her mother." Jake wondered why he added that. He stood up. "It's time I go after the guy, Alison. Do you have a place to stay?"

"The house," she said.

"I don't think so."

"Well, Professor Teal has a spare room downstairs."

"The odds of Roland showing up are slim to none, I think, but until he's accounted for . . ."

"You mean I need to disappear for a while?"

"Just to be on the safe side."

"I don't know. I guess I could check into a motel. I don't have my purse, though."

"You're welcome to stay at my place. I'll be out, anyway."

"Thank you, but—"

"It's comfortable. There's food and drink in the fridge. And that way, I'll know where you are and I won't have to worry about you."

She made a small, slightly crooked smile. "You'd worry about me?"

"Yes."

"That's nice," she whispered.

Jake felt his face redden. "Well, you're also our main witness."

Alison picked up her coffee cup. It was still full.

They left Barney's office and returned to the dispatcher's cubicle. "Alison will be coming with me," Jake said.

Alison set the cup on Martha's desk. "Thanks for the use of the sweater," she said. "And for helping."

"No problem, honey," Martha said.

Alison started to unbutton the sweater.

Martha held up a hand. "You keep that on, you'll catch a chill." Grinning, she added, "And you don't want to give Jake any ideas. Not that he's not a perfect gentleman. You can just send it back to me when you're done with it."

Alison thanked her again.

They left, and went outside to Jake's car. Alison climbed into the passenger seat. Walking around to the driver's door, Jake scanned the area. He saw no cars moving on the nearby streets. He saw no parked Volkswagens. He got in and started the engine.

"You didn't notice anyone behind you on the way over, did you?" he asked.

"No. And I was looking. I was afraid he might come after me."

"The shape you left him in, he's probably not coming after *anyone*. He might very well be dead or dying by now."

"I hope so," she muttered.

"I'd like to find him alive," Jake said. Find him dead, he thought, and you probably won't find the damn snake-thing. It's got no use for a dead man. The fucker'll pull a disappearing act and turn up in someone else and you'll be back to square one.

Jake watched the rearview mirror as he drove. The road behind him appeared clear, but Roland could be staying far back with the headlights off.

Jake turned onto a side street, killed his lights, and swung to the curb. "We'll wait here for a while," he said.

"Fine."

He shut off the engine. He smiled at Alison. "I'm sure we're not being followed. This is just a precaution."

He glanced at her bare legs. Her negligee was very short. Her open hands rested on her thighs as if to hold the gown down. An awareness came to Jake, suddenly, that he was alone in the car with a very attractive young woman who was no doubt naked except for the skimpy nightgown and Martha's sweater. And he was taking her to his home. The awareness gave him a warm feeling that threatened to become more than that.

Watch yourself, he warned. The last thing she needs is to get the idea that you're getting turned on.

Turned on? Forget it, Corey.

He rubbed his sweaty hands on his pants, and looked at the side mirror. "Looks all right," he said.

Though he felt sure that Roland wasn't tailing them, he decided to take a roundabout course to his house. He knew that he should make the trip as fast as possible, drop her off, and start searching for Roland.

But he wasn't eager to find Roland.

And he wasn't eager to get rid of Alison.

She was very quiet. Jake wondered what was going on in her mind. Nothing pleasant, probably. She'd gone through hell tonight. Most people never have to face such an ordeal. If they do, they often don't survive to cope with the emotional trauma.

"Things must look pretty bleak," he said.

Alison turned to him. "I'm alive," she said. "I feel pretty lucky."

"It took a lot more than luck."

"I don't know if I deserve it, though. I mean, why me? This must be how people feel when they survive an airline crash. Kind of guilty that they're still alive when so many others aren't."

"I suppose so," Jake said. "Do you have classes tomorrow?"

"I'll probably cut them. I don't think I could handle sitting in a classroom."

"That's probably best. I hope this will all be over by then, but if it's not I won't want you going anywhere. You and I will be the only ones who know where you are, and I'd like to keep it that way until further notice, okay? That's the only way we can be certain you're secure."

"No one to tell," she said.

"What about your parents?"

"They're in Marin County."

"You could call them if you want."

"No reason to stir them up. They'd go hysterical on me."

"Boyfriend?" Smooth, Jake thought. Slipped it right in. He felt vaguely ashamed of himself.

"We broke up," she said. "Tonight, as a matter of fact. It's been a banner night." After a few moments of silence, she added, "I should probably phone him in the morning, let him know I'm okay."

"Fine. Just don't tell him where you are."

"Fat chance of that."

Jake saw his house just ahead. He decided to circle the

block before taking Alison in. Just as a precaution, he told himself.

"You don't think someone *sent* Roland over?"

"No, nothing like that. He could get to someone, though. If nobody knows where you are, nobody can tell him."

"There's more to this than you're letting on, isn't there?"

Jake hesitated, then answered, "Yes."

"And it has something to do with Roland's back."

"You're sharp," Jake said, smiling at her.

"Must be pretty bad, if you're afraid to tell me."

"It's a long story," Jake said. "And we're almost home."

"Maybe it's something I should know."

Jake didn't answer. He steered around the final corner, checked once more to be sure there was no Volkswagen in sight, then swung into the driveway of his house.

Alison held the hem of her negligee to prevent it from sliding up as she scooted off the car seat. Jake shut the door after she was out. He walked backward across his yard, a hand resting on his holstered gun, his head turning slowly, eyes scanning the neighborhood as if he expected Roland to charge out of the darkness.

He didn't seem nervous, though. Just careful. Alison felt safe with him. She didn't like knowing that he would leave just minutes from now.

He opened the house door. Alison followed him inside. The lights were already on, the curtains shut. The warmth of the house felt good after the chill outside.

"Just make yourself at home," Jake said. "The kitchen's over here."

He led the way. Alison began to unbutton her sweater,

but stopped when she realized what she was wearing under it.

Jake turned on the kitchen light. "There's food, soft drinks, beer in the refrigerator. Help yourself." He pointed at a cupboard. "Hard stuff in there, in case you get the urge."

"What's your daughter's usual bedtime?"

"Oh, Kimmy's not . . ." He laughed softly. "What's your hourly rate?"

"In my prime, five bucks per hour. For Kimmy, no charge."

"That's good, since she isn't here." They left the kitchen. "Sofa," he announced, walking in front of it. "Where I'll stretch out when I get back. Television." He bent over the coffee table, picked up the remote control, and turned the TV on and off, demonstrating. He smiled a bit self-consciously.

Alison followed him to the bathroom. He flicked on its light. "Fine if you want to take a bath or shower or something," he said and blushed slightly.

"I could use one."

"There're towels and stuff in the closet here."

He nodded as they passed a dark doorway. "Kimmy's room. Her bed's a little small for you." He opened the door of a linen closet and pulled folded sheets and a pillowcase down from the shelves. Then he stepped into his room. He turned the light on. The bed was unmade. Alison guessed that he had been sleeping when the call came tonight.

He walked over to the bed. "Want to give me a hand with the sheets?" he asked.

"I'll take care of that," Alison told him.

"Well . . ."

"No problem," she said. "It'll give me something to do after you're gone." It was a small lie. She had no intention of taking his bed, forcing him to sleep on the sofa when he returned from hunting down Roland.

Jake set the sheets and pillowcase on the end of the bed. He entered his closet. When he came out, he was holding a shotgun. "Have you ever fired one of these?" he asked.

Alison nodded. "I've gone duck hunting with Dad a few times. Hell, *more* than a few times."

He handed the shotgun to her.

It was a bolt-action .12 gauge. She opened the bolt enough to see a shell in the chamber, then closed it.

"There're three more in the clip," Jake said.

"Okay."

"Keep it close to you. Just don't shoot me when I come back."

Alison smiled.

The color suddenly drained from his face.

"What is it?"

"Maybe that wasn't such great advice." He sat on the end of the bed and frowned up at her. "I want you to brace the bedroom door shut before you turn in. If I try to force my way in, use the shotgun."

"Are you crazy?"

"I don't expect anything like that to happen, but . . . When you come out in the morning, keep me covered if I'm here and have me take my shirt off. Then take a good look at my back. If there's a bulge going up my spine as if I've got a snake under my skin, blow me away. Try to hit the bulge. If you don't nail the thing, it'll probably come out as soon as I'm dead and it might come after you."

She stared at Jake.

He meant it.

"Jesus Christ," she muttered.

"*Invasion of the Body Snatchers*," Jake said. "But it's for real. This snake-thing was up the back of the guy who tried to run down Celia. It got into Ronald Smeltzer over at the Oakwood Thursday night just before he blew off his wife's head. And now I'm pretty sure it's in Roland. It's some kind of parasite that takes control and turns people into killers. It's conceivable that it might get into me when I catch up with Roland. I certainly don't intend for that to happen, but . . . do us both a favor and blast me if I come in with the thing. And try to kill it, too. Or at least make sure it doesn't get close to you.''

Alison was numb.

Jake stood up. ''You okay?''

She stared at him.

He stepped close to her. He put his hands on her shoulders. ''I'm sorry. I had to tell you.''

The weight of the shotgun pulled her arms down.

He lifted it away from her, took her gently by one elbow, and led her down the hall to the living room. He guided her to the sofa. She sank onto it. He propped the shotgun beside her, went away, and came back.

''Maybe this will help,'' he said. He placed a mug of beer with a white frothy head into her hand. He ripped open a bag of potato chips and set it on the cushion so it rested against the side of her thigh. She smelled the pleasant aromas of the beer and chips. From the odor, she knew that the chips were sour cream and onion flavor.

One of Helen's favorites.

She looked up at Jake.

He managed a thin smile, but his eyes were sad. ''Everything will be okay,'' he said. Then he crouched in front of her. ''Alison.''

''Huh?''

''You're acting zoned.''

''I'll be all right,'' she heard herself say. ''In a while.''

''What I just told you, it's a secret. Right? At least until Tuesday. Then we'll be going public with it.''

"Nobody will believe it."

"You do."

"I wish I didn't."

Jake put a hand on her knee. "Get a good night's sleep."

She pressed a hand on top of his. "Watch out," she said. "Come back safe."

Chapter Thirty-Two

THE SECOND FLOOR HALLWAY OF THE DORM WAS DE-serted. Only a few of the overhead fluorescent lights had been left on for the night, giving off a cool, desolate illumination that added to Jake's uneasiness. Bands of light showed beneath some of the doors. Jake heard music coming from one of the rooms and the sound of a shower from the bathroom.

He stopped in front of Roland's door. No light came through the gap at its bottom. Taking out his wallet, he spread the bill compartment and removed a thin plastic case. He slipped the lock pick and torque wrench from the case.

The burglary tools were a gift from Chuck, who had provided lessons for the price of a six-pack.

Jake had never quite planned to use them for an illegal entry. Nevertheless, he'd carried them in his wallet for the past two years, mostly to please Chuck but also telling himself they might come in handy if he ever locked himself out of his house. Lately, he'd picked the house lock several times for Kimmy because she got a kick out of it.

The recent practice paid off. In less than a minute, the lock of Roland's door clicked and Jake eased the door open half an inch.

He put away the burglary tools.

He didn't expect Roland to be in the room. He'd found no yellow VW in the dorm parking area and Roland had to know that Alison would tell the police where he lived. But the guy was hurting. He might go to ground anywhere, even in his own room.

Jake drew his revolver, stepped against the wall for cover, and shoved the door. It swung open and bumped to a stop. He listened and heard nothing.

Reaching around the door frame, he found the switch plate.

Light spilled into the hallway.

He lunged into the room.

Saw no one.

The room had a linoleum floor with a tan, fringed rug spread across the center. Jake saw no blood on the floor or the rug.

There was a bed along each of the long walls. One bed was made, one wasn't. Beyond the head of each bed stood a desk with a straight-backed chair. The far wall had shelves partway up, then windows to the ceiling.

Jake swung the door shut.

He was standing between two wooden partitions which he guessed were the sides of twin closets.

If Roland was in the room, he was hiding. Under a bed or inside one of the closets.

Keeping his back to the door, Jake dropped to his hands

and knees. Both of the beds had suitcases under them. That left the closets.

Jake got to his feet. He rushed forward and spun around, sweeping his revolver from one closet to the other. The sliding doors of both were open. Which left half of each closet out of sight.

Jake stepped to the one on his left, ducked, and peered in beneath the hanging clothes. Nobody there. He side-stepped to the other closet. The hangers were empty, giving him a good view through the dim enclosure.

Satisfied that the room was safe, he holstered his revolver.

If this was Roland's closet, where were the clothes? Had Roland already been here, packed up and fled? It hardly seemed likely that someone in his condition would return for his clothes before taking off. And there was no blood.

Remembering the luggage, Jake crouched beside the nearer bed and pulled out the suitcase. It wasn't latched. He opened it. The case was stuffed with folded clothing. The T-shirt on top was printed with a message. He lifted it, shook it open, and read, "GHOULS JUST WANTA HAVE FUN."

Jake put down the shirt and pushed the suitcase back under the bed.

Obviously, Roland had been planning a trip.

Planning to get out of town before the heat came down on him. Planning, maybe, to travel the roads like the John Doe in the van, killing whenever the opportunity presented itself, leaving a trail of half-eaten bodies in shallow graves.

But he hadn't come back for the suitcase.

Not yet.

He won't be back, Jake decided. He's blind in one eye, maybe brain damaged from Alison's thumb, and less two fingers thanks to Rex Davidson's bullet. He's got a stab wound in the chest, though it sounded as if that might be superficial. At the very least, he has to be in shock and weak from blood loss. The last thing he'll be concerned about is picking up his suitcase.

If he's concerned about anything, at this point. If he's not already dead.

Jake sat on the edge of the bed. On the wall across from him was a poster of the actress Heather Locklear. He stared at her slender, bare legs and his mind drifted to Alison.

Maybe leaving her alone wasn't such a good idea.

She's safe, he told himself.

You can't be sure of that.

Maybe go back.

The best thing you can do for her is nail Roland. Before he dies and the damned snake-thing gets into someone else.

On a shelf below the poster stood a framed family portrait. The young man in the photograph was probably Roland's roommate, Jason, the guy who'd disappeared with Celia.

Maybe Roland has a photo of himself, Jake thought. He looked over his shoulder. The wall was covered with grim pictures that looked as if they'd come from magazines. Most of the subjects weren't familiar to Jake, but he recognized one that showed Janet Leigh in the shower scene from *Psycho.* Another was Freddy, the killer who wore a battered fedora and a glove with long blades on its fingers in *Nightmare on Elm Street.* There was a hideous fat guy holding a chain saw overhead. There was a group of decomposed zombies, one munching on a severed arm.

Jake shook his head. The snake-thing had certainly chosen a compatible host. Coincidence?

He remembered that he was looking for a photo of Roland. Knowing what the guy looked like would help.

He stood and wandered to the end of the room. The desktop was clear except for a bottle of glue and a pair of scissors. Dropping onto the chair, Jake slid open the middle drawer and stared.

He'd found his photo of Roland.

He felt sickened by it.

Body parts floated around the leering face: numerous breasts, torsos, buttocks, vaginas, and a few arms and legs.

These were not cut from magazines. They had the thickness of snapshots.

The only part of the girl's anatomy not cascading around Roland's head was her face.

Maybe Celia Jamerson, Jake thought.

A drop of sweat fell onto Roland's left eye. Jake blotted it with his sleeve, then wiped his face.

He lifted the photograph out of the drawer. Beneath it lay its frame.

So Roland hadn't slipped it back into the frame after finishing his project. Scissors and glue were still on the desktop.

The wastebasket was midway between the two desks, close to the wall. Jake crouched over it. The bottom of its white plastic liner was littered with scraps. He upended the wastebasket, sat on the floor, and searched.

Most of the shots didn't include the girl's face. The photographer, obviously, had been more interested in views of her lower areas—all of which had been snipped out, usually leaving the limbs intact.

Jake found three pictures showing the girl's face. The face in all three belonged to the same girl.

She wasn't Celia.

She wasn't dead. At least not at the time she posed. She smirked; she licked her lips. In one, she sucked her middle finger.

Jake slipped a view of the girl's face into his shirt pocket. He scooped up the remaining scraps and dumped them into the wastebasket.

In the morning, he would get a search warrant. The room would be photographed and gone over, inch by inch, every item studied and catalogued, every surface closely inspected and checked for prints, the whole area vacuumed for stray bits of hair, fabric, and other particles that might incriminate Roland.

Jake took the eight by ten with him, and left.

After leaving Roland's room, Jake cruised the streets around the campus, looking for the yellow Volkswagen bug with the banner on its aerial, not really expecting to spot it, wanting to return home and make sure that Alison was safe but knowing that his duty was to search.

First the streets near the campus, then the Oakwood Inn.

He dreaded the thought of driving out there and entering the dark restaurant. The longer he prowled the streets, however, the more certain he became that the Oakwood was where Roland must've gone. The damned creature seemed to have an affinity for the place. And that's where it had left its eggs.

Jake knew that he was procrastinating.

He turned onto Summer Street, which bordered the campus on the north.

What I'll do, he thought, is go home and get into my gear before heading out there. I'm not going to the Oakwood without my boots and leathers. Roland might be dead. The thing might be loose.

And that'll give me a chance to see Alison.

He wondered if she was asleep yet.

He glanced down a side street, spotted a Volkswagen at the curb, and hit the brakes. He checked the rearview.

Clear behind him. He backed up, stopped, and gazed at the car.

It was parked beneath a street lamp, but the light above it was dead, leaving it in darkness. Jake couldn't make out the color of the VW.

But it had a banner on the aerial.

This is it.

Heart thudding, he turned. He drove straight for the car. His headlights pushed toward it, lit it.

Yellow.

Someone was in the driver's seat.

Jake gazed through the windshield, stunned.

The man in the VW didn't move. The left side of his face looked black in the glare of the headlights.

This had to be Roland.

Jake opened his door. He crouched behind it, pulled his revolver, and took aim. "Step out of the car!" he yelled.

Roland didn't move.

Jake repeated the command.

Roland remained motionless. He was dead, unconscious, or faking.

Jake stepped away from the door. Keeping his handgun pointed at Roland, he walked slowly forward. He tried to watch Roland through the windshield, but found his gaze drawn downward to the pavement.

He wished he had his boots on. His ankles felt bare in spite of the socks.

He remembered the machete in the trunk of his car. Halting, he considered going back for it.

The front bumper of the VW was no more than two yards in front of him. He stared at the darkness beneath it.

Glanced at Roland.

The right eye was open. It seemed to be watching him.

This guy is dead.

The fucking snake might be *anywhere*.

Like under the car, just waiting for me to get close enough.

The skin prickled on the nape of Jake's neck.

He backed away, sidestepped at the rear of his car, and dug into his pocket for the keys. He found the trunk key. He fumbled it into the lock and twisted it. The trunk popped open, blocking his view. He snatched out the machete and rushed clear.

Roland hadn't moved.

Jake saw nothing squirming toward him on the pavement.

With the machete in his right hand, the revolver in his left, he hopped onto the curb and approached the passenger side of the VW. When he could see that the windows were rolled up, he dashed to the middle of the street. The windows on the driver's side were shut too.

Whether Roland was alive or dead, the snake-thing was still in the car. Probably. Either inside Roland, or writhing around loose, trapped.

Jake stepped close to the driver's window and peered in. He glimpsed the gaping hole where Roland's left eye should have been and quickly looked away from it.

Roland was reclined in the seat, the front of his shirt bloody, his head tipped back slightly against the headrest. His position prevented Jake from checking the back of his neck.

The head beams left the lower areas of the car's interior in darkness. If the creature was on a seat or the floor, Jake couldn't see it.

There was only one way to find out whether it was still up Roland's spine: open the door, shove him forward, and look.

No way.

Not a chance.

Jake holstered his pistol. Watching Roland, he walked backward to his car, slid in, and took a pack of matches from the glove compartment. He got out. He back-stepped to the trunk and picked up the can of gasoline.

He poured gas onto the curb beside the VW, onto the pavement behind the car and near its driver's side, then past the front to the curb again, completing the circle. Then he splashed the car, dousing it with the pungent liquid and running trails out to the surrounding gas. Finally, he crouched and flung gas into the space beneath the undercarriage.

He stopped when the can felt nearly empty. He wanted to save some gasoline, just in case.

He capped the can. Hurrying into the road, he stepped over the wet path of the circle. He set the can down behind him, squatted, struck a match, and touched it to the stained pavement.

A low, bluish flame with flutters of yellow and orange stretched out in both directions. It met intersecting paths and rolled toward the car.

Jake picked up the can and backed away. By the time he reached the far side of the street with it, the car was a blazing pyre. He could feel its heat warming his clothes and face. The fire lit the night, shimmering on the leaves of nearby trees, glowing on the walls and windows of the apartment house beyond it, shining on the hood and windshield of his own car.

A car parked behind the VW seemed to be safely out of range.

He wondered if he should move his own car.

Or himself.

Hissing, popping sounds came from the fire. Then a sharp crack made Jake flinch. He heard glass crash on the pavement.

"Christ," he muttered.

He rushed forward until the wall of fire stopped him. Shielding his eyes, he squinted through the flames at the wide, wedge-shaped gap in the driver's window.

Nothing came out.

As he watched, flames enveloped Roland. They crawled up from below, sweeping up his face and igniting his hair. Jake gagged as the face blackened and bubbled. Then dense smoke covered the horror.

Jake heard distant shouts of "Fire!"

He heard more windows burst.

Then he was rushing around the car, brandishing his machete, peering through the blaze at one broken window after another. Smoke poured from the openings. But nothing else came out.

Not yet.

The car's gas tank went up with a muffled boom. Jake staggered back as heat blasted against him. A spike of glass flew past his cheek. Another stabbed his thigh. He pulled it out. The car was still rocking from the impact.

Now, it was an inferno.

The fucker's cooked, Jake thought. Cooked. It's a goner.

For the first time, he noticed a few people watching from the other side of the street. He turned around. More were on the lawn in front of the apartment house. He took a step toward two young men, probably students. One wore a robe, the other wore only boxer shorts. Both men backed away. No wonder, Jake thought. I'm not in uniform, I've got this machete.

"I'm a policeman," he called. "One of you guys call the fire department."

"I already called," said a brunette woman in pajamas. "I hope nobody's *in* that car," she said.

"Nobody alive," Jake said.

"How'd it start?" asked the guy in the boxer shorts.

Jake shook his head. Then he turned away. The fire was still blazing. Several of the spectators from the other side of the street were inching forward for a better view.

When Jake rushed into the road, some of them backed off and one young couple turned and fled, the woman shrieking. Apparently, they had missed the news that he was a cop. Or couldn't bring themselves to trust a guy, cop or not, who was running at them with a machete.

"Everybody stand clear," Jake yelled. "The fire department is on its way."

"Somebody's in the car!" a man shouted, pointing.

"Get back," Jake warned.

A woman turned away, hunched over, and vomited.

"Everybody move back, back to the sidewalk. There'll be fire trucks coming in."

One couple ignored his warning. They were standing over Jake's gas can, frowning at it and muttering to each other. The girl wore a pajama shirt. The guy wore pajama pants. The girl crouched and reached toward the can.

Oh, shit, Jake thought. "Don't touch that!" he snapped. "It's evidence. The arsonist might've left prints."

Clever, he thought.

Dumb asshole, why didn't you put the can back in your trunk?

As the girl backed away, Jake slipped the blade of his machete through the can's handle, raised it, and carried the can toward his car.

No point leaving the thing in sight. The fire boys might not be so easily fooled, and he would have a rough time trying to explain why he torched a vehicle with a suspect still inside.

The gas can and machete were locked safely in his trunk by the time he heard the sirens.

* * *

The firemen rushed the car with chemical extinguishers. Blasting flames out of the way, they pulled Roland's carcass off the seat and dragged it into the road. Two firemen fogged it with their extinguishers, then left it there and joined those trying to knock down the car fire.

Jake looked at the corpse. It was still smoking. It was a charred, featureless hulk that hardly resembled a human being. If he hadn't watched the body being removed from the car, Jake wouldn't have been able to tell whether it was faceup or facedown. He knew it was faceup. But it had no face. Or ears. Or genitals. The surface was a black, cracked crust flecked with frothy white from the extinguishers. Fluids leaked from cracks in the crust.

When the honking blast of the extinguishers went quiet, Jake heard the sizzling sound that came from the body. It sounded like a rib roast.

It didn't smell like one.

Jake stepped back, struggling not to vomit.

A fireman showed up and spread a blanket over the body.

Smoke rose from under the blanket.

Jake kept watch.

The fire was out, the car a smouldering ruin, by the time the coroner's van arrived. The men stayed inside the van, smoking cigarettes, waiting, as instructed, for Applegate to show up.

Soon, Steve arrived in his Lincoln Continental. He climbed out, wearing a warm-up suit and carrying a doctor's bag. He joined Jake. "What's going on?"

"This is our man," Jake said, nodding toward the covered corpse. "Earlier tonight, he killed a girl and tried to nail her roommate. He killed Rex Davidson. There's a good chance he had our snake-thing up his back when he did it."

"Oh, terrific," Steve muttered. "Let me guess: you want a little on-the-scene exploratory surgery to determine whether it's inside him."

"Good guess," Jake said.

"Shit."

Steve went to the van and spoke to the men through its open window. They climbed out.

Wearing gloves, they uncovered the body and lifted it into a body bag. They zipped the bag. One man retrieved a gurney with folding legs from the rear of the van. They hoisted the bagged remains onto the gurney, rolled it to the van, and pushed it in.

"Is this a solo job?" Steve asked Jake. "Or do I get the pleasure of your company?"

"I'll stick with you."

"Good decision. Congratulations. Have a cigar."

Once the cigars were lighted, Jake followed Steve into the rear of the van. He pulled the doors shut. The lights remained on. The smoke from the cigars drifted into vents in the ceiling.

Steve knelt on one side of the body bag, Jake at its end with his back to the doors. He drew his revolver.

"Yes," Steve said. "I was about to suggest as much."

"The thing's probably dead," Jake whispered. "If it's in him at all."

"If it remained between the spine and the epidermis, I would agree with you. But just suppose, when the situation heated up, it took a trip into this fellow's stomach? It passed through Smeltzer's stomach, so obviously it has no problem with the acids."

"This guy must've cooked for fifteen minutes," Jake pointed out.

Steve raised an eyebrow. ''Charred on the outside, rare in the middle. That's how I prefer my steaks.''

Jake squinted at Steve through his rising cigar smoke. ''So if the thing went deep, it might be all right?''

''Very likely fit as a fiddle.''

Jake muttered, ''Shit.''

Cigar clamped in his teeth, Steve opened his satchel and pulled on a pair of surgical gloves. He slid the zipper down the length of the body bag.

In spite of the van's ventilation system and the aroma of the cigars, the stench that rose from the burnt corpse choked Jake. His eyes teared as he gagged, but he watched the bag's opening and held his revolver steady.

Steve seemed unaffected. He bent over the remains. With the tip of a gloved finger, he prodded a blackened crater a few inches above the groin. ''Was this fellow shot?'' he asked, his words slurred by the cigar in his teeth.

''Just in the hand.''

''This might be the creature's exit.''

''Couldn't the fire have made that?''

Steve shrugged. He pushed with his finger. The charred surface in the center of the crater crumbled, and his finger went in deep. He wiggled it around. ''Nope,'' he said. He pulled his finger out.

Then he grabbed the far side of the body bag, lifted and pulled it toward him. The corpse rolled out, bumping face-down onto the gurney. Black flakes fell off it.

Jake switched the revolver to his left hand long enough to wipe his right hand dry on his trouser leg.

Steve spent a while looking at the back of the corpse. Then he took a scalpel from his satchel. He turned his eyes to the barrel of Jake's revolver. ''Try to miss my hands if we have a sudden visitor. They mean a lot to me.''

"What about that exit hole on the other side?"

"If that's what it is."

"Great."

"Ready?"

Jake eased his forefinger over the trigger. "No, but go ahead."

Steve pressed the blade of the scalpel to the nape of the neck, pushed it in, and slid it downward.

"Jesus," Jake muttered, watching the crust of skin crumple at the edges of the incision.

Nothing came bursting out.

Steve brought the blade again to the back of the neck. He inserted its point into the slit and poked around. "I think we may be all right," he said. He grinned at Jake. "Just watch it don't come popping out his arse."

"Thanks."

Setting the scalpel aside, Steve used both hands to spread open the incision. The outer layer of black cracked and flaked off with a sound like dry leaves being crushed. Steve dug in with all the fingers of his right hand. After probing inside the wound for a few moments, he said, "The thing was here, all right. I can feel a definite separation of the lower epidermal layer from the muscle fascia."

Picking up the scalpel again, Steve ran the blade the rest of the way down the spine. He did more exploring with his hands.

"Yep," he said.

"So it was in him, and now it's gone," Jake said.

"That's how it looks. Took a powder through the stomach hole. That's my professional opinion. Of course, the thing *might* still be inside him . . . lying low, so to speak. Won't know that, for sure, until I've done a full autopsy. I'll get the boys to bag him up again. We'll keep him in cold storage and I'll call you over so you can ride shotgun when it's time for the big event. Though, as I said, I'm almost sure it's not in him at this point.''

''If it's not,'' Jake said, ''the thing is either ashes inside his car or else . . . it's not.''

''And looking for a new home,'' Steve said.

''Or already found one,'' added Jake.

Chapter Thirty-Three

THE RINGING OF A BELL WOKE ALISON UP. SHE RAISED her face off the pillow and turned her head. After a moment of confusion, she realized that she was lying on the sofa in Jake's living room. The lamps were on. No light came through the curtains, so it wasn't yet morning.

The bell rang again.

She threw back the sheet and sat up. A strap of her negligee hung off her shoulder. She brushed it back into place.

The front door was open a few inches, the guard pulled taut.

Jake, she remembered, had warned her to barricade herself in the bedroom. Not wanting to take his bed from him, she had chosen to sleep on the sofa. She had heeded his warning enough, however, to fasten the door chain to prevent him from entering while she slept.

"Who is it?" she asked.

"Jake." A belt with a holstered revolver swung through the opening and dropped to the floor. "I'll step away. Bring the shotgun, unchain the door, then back off and keep me covered."

"Just a minute." She lifted the sweater off the coffee table and slipped into it. She fastened the middle button to keep it shut across her breasts. The shotgun was propped against the table. She picked it up and went to the door.

She pushed the door shut. She glanced down at herself.

The negligee was *awfully* short.

Her face heated.

He's seen me in it before, she told herself. Hell, he's seen me in nothing else.

She slid the guard chain to the end of its runner, let it drop, and opened the door.

Jake was standing on the lawn. He shook his head. "That's no way to cover me."

Shrugging, Alison lifted the butt of the shotgun off the floor. She clutched the weapon in both hands. But she didn't aim at him. She backed away.

Jake entered the house and shut the door. A miasma of unpleasant odors came in with him. Though more than two yards in front of him, Alison smelled gasoline, cigar smoke, sweat, and a disgusting, sweetish stench that she couldn't recognize.

Jake's face and clothes were smeared with soot. One leg of his tan trousers was torn at the thigh and matted with dry blood.

"What happened to your leg?"

"Flying glass. No big deal." He untucked his shirt, opened the buttons, and took it off. Then he turned around.

Alison stepped closer. The odors got worse, but his back looked fine. She reached out with her left hand and ran fingers down his spine. She felt no bulges. His skin was cool and damp. "Except for the stink," she told him, "you're fine. What happened?"

Jake turned to face her. "I found Roland. He's dead. He was already dead by the time I found him."

Alison nodded. She suddenly felt sick, and didn't know whether it was the godawful odors from Jake or learning that Roland had died. *I* killed him, she thought.

It's good that he's dead.

I killed him.

It was self-defense. He deserved to die after what he did to Helen . . . what he did, maybe, to Celia.

"Gouging his eye?" she muttered.

"He had a bad stomach wound when we found him. I suspect that was the finishing touch."

"A stomach wound? So it wasn't me who killed him?"

"Wasn't you."

"Thank God."

"I'd better take a shower before you pass out on me. You're looking a little green around the gills."

She nodded. "What *is* that odor?"

"I found Roland in his car parked on a side street near the campus. I didn't want to take a chance of the . . . remember that snake-thing I told you about?"

"I don't think I'm likely to forget that."

"Well, I doused Roland's car with gasoline and torched it. With him in it."

"Christ."

"The idea was to burn the snake-thing. Afterward, I had the coroner cut Roland open to see if we could find it." Jake shook his head. "Wasn't in him. We think it left from his stomach. That's what made the wound that probably polished him off. It knew that Roland was on his last legs, wouldn't be any more use."

"It broke out of him . . . like that monster in *Alien*?"

"Something like that. We're hoping Roland was inside

the car when it happened. All the windows were rolled up. So if the thing was trapped in the car, it almost has to be dead. I searched the rubble afterward. Couldn't find any trace of the thing, but that doesn't mean much. Might've been nothing left but a heap of ashes.''

''It might be dead, then, or it might not?''

''We're going to assume it's alive until we know otherwise.''

''And if it *is* alive?''

''Then it'll try to find someone else to get in, and we're pretty much back where we started. I'm sorry. I wish I could tell you the whole mess is over.''

''But maybe it is.''

''I'd bet a month's salary that the damned thing is dead. But I won't bet your life on it.'' He rubbed the shirt across his face, smearing sweat and soot. ''I'd better take that shower, now.'' He stepped past Alison and headed for the hallway.

When she noticed the sound of the water running, she realized that she hadn't moved since Jake left. She dragged the shotgun over to the door and propped it against the wall. She attached the guard chain.

The disgusting odors still filled the room. In the kitchen, she searched until she found candles in a drawer. She lighted three of them, dripped wax onto paper plates, and stuck them upright. She brought the candles into the living room and placed them on the coffee table.

Sitting on the sofa, she leaned back and propped her feet on the table between two of the candle plates.

She wondered if Jake would come back into the room after his shower. Maybe they could have a drink together.

He'd been through a nightmare of his own, tonight: burning Roland, watching while the coroner cut him open. That one odor, the really bad one . . .

And he apologized to me for not having better news.

Maybe he won't like seeing the candles. They might remind him of what happened earlier.

Alison sniffed. The nasty odors seemed faint. She puffed out the candles and carried them back into the kitchen. Then she went to the front door. She opened it enough to peer out, then shut it again, removed the guard chain, and swung the door wide.

The breeze smelled wonderful. It blew her hair. It felt cool and good on her body. She opened the sweater. The breeze caressed her through the negligee, moved up her bare legs. It felt just as fine as before, when she was standing naked at her bedroom window, and then it stopped feeling fine as the memory surged in of waking to find Roland above her. Moaning, she swung the door shut. She leaned against it, head against her crossed arms.

"Alison?"

She turned around. Jake was standing in the hallway entrance, wearing a robe.

"Are you all right?" he asked.

"Not very. How about you?"

"Better."

"I was just letting in some fresh air."

She saw his gaze stray downward, then back to her face. Just in time to catch my blush, she thought.

"I guess I'd better hit the sack," Jake said. "Don't you want to trade places? I'm sure my bed would be a lot more comfortable for you."

"The sofa's fine. Really."

"It's up to you." He rubbed his chin. "Well, see you in the morning, Alison. Sleep tight, huh?"

"Yeah. You, too."

He turned away. Alison looked down at herself. You sure gave him an eyeful, she thought. He noticed, too, but he didn't get funny. That's good. Would've been awkward if he'd decided it was some kind of an invitation.

Was it some kind of an invitation? she wondered. How come I didn't bother pulling the sweater shut before I turned around? He probably thinks I did it on purpose.

I bet that's why he ran off so fast. He came in, maybe to spend a while talking, saw me like this, and decided he'd better beat a quick retreat.

Scared him away.

Don't flatter yourself, she thought. He left because he's had a long, rough day and he's tired. Probably didn't care, one way or the other, about me and my nightie.

She took off the sweater. Standing there, she folded it slowly and watched the hallway.

Jake was probably in bed already.

Alison moved quietly through the room, turning off lights. There was no need for the lights now that Jake was here.

It felt good, knowing that he was in the house, only a few seconds away.

Alison lay down on the sofa and pulled the sheet up.

He didn't have to rush off like that, she thought. We should've talked for a while.

She imagined herself walking down the dark hallway to his room. Asking if he was asleep. Telling him that she didn't want to be alone, not just yet.

Why not crawl into his bed while you're at it? Sure. You just dumped Evan because he wasn't interested in anything but making it and you're hot to jump in bed with a guy you hardly know.

I am not. I wouldn't do that. Why am I even *thinking* about it, after all that's happened tonight?

What do you *want* to think about—Helen?

She saw Helen on the bed, glasses crooked . . .

The image clenched her with cold, tight fists. She lurched up and gazed through the darkness, gasping.

* * *

When Jake woke up, his room was bright. He squinted at the alarm clock on the nightstand. Almost ten o'clock. But what day was this? Monday.

He rolled onto his belly and pushed his face into the soft warmth of the pillow.

Need to get up, he thought. Need to—what? Go back to where you found Roland, check around, talk to people. What for? See if they saw anything. A snake in the grass.

Shit. It seemed pointless.

Need to do something, though. Need to make sure the thing's dead, is what. Cause if it's not dead, Alison . . .

She's here. Sleeping on the sofa.

And me in my bed. What virtue. Congratulations, Corey.

Missed your big chance.

It would've been wrong. Taking advantage.

I know, he thought. Don't I know. Fell asleep last night telling myself just how wrong it would be . . . and how nice. Even if we'd done no more than hold each other, it would've been fine.

He remembered how small and vulnerable she had looked sitting behind Barney's desk, holding onto the coffee cup as if it were a talisman that would keep harm away. And sitting in the car, that nightie barely covering her legs. And when he came out after the shower and her sweater was open.

Jake's penis was pushing uncomfortably against the mattress. He rolled onto his back to relieve the pressure.

Real nice, he thought. The knight in shiny armor has a hard-on.

Sorry about that, Alison.

Alison, a pretty name. Alison Sanders.

He wondered if she was still asleep. It would be nice to see her sleeping on the sofa, probably looking as peaceful as a little kid. He couldn't go sneaking in and watch her, though. What would she think if she woke up?

Go in and make a pot of coffee. Take a cup to her.

We'll sit for a while, talking. Alison will be all sleepy, her hair mussed. Maybe she'll have the sheet wrapped around her so neither of us will have to be embarrassed about her nightgown.

Take your robe to her. That way, she'll know your intentions are honorable.

Jake pulled the sheet aside. He rolled off the bed and stood up. He was shirtless and wearing his pajama pants. Though his erection had diminished, the front of the pants still bulged somewhat. He headed for the dresser, planning to put on his pajama shirt before venturing from the room, and stopped abruptly at the foot of his bed.

Alison was asleep on the floor.

She lay curled on her side, a pillow under her head, her bare feet protruding from the sheet that covered her to the shoulders.

Jake stared down at the girl, bewildered by her presence. Unless she had walked in her sleep, she had come here on purpose, needing the comfort of being close to him. She must've been suffering, alone in the other room. Needed a friend. So she'd snuck in here and made her bed on the floor to be near him.

I should've stayed up with her, he thought. I should've realized.

He crouched in front of Alison. Wisps of hair hung over the side of her face. Her mouth was open, its lower corner buried in the pillow. The peaceful way she looked reminded Jake of Kimmy.

But Kimmy had never had a swollen, discolored jaw and cheek like Alison.

A bruise on her arm, though. She'd shown it to him when they got to Jack-in-the-Box last night.

Should've given Barbara a bruise for *her* arm.

Ever hurts Kimmy again, it'll be a court order. How could the bitch slug her own daughter like that? How could *anybody* slug a girl like Kimmy?

Or a girl like Alison?

The guy who did that is dead. A hunk of burnt meat.

Deserved it, the bastard. Pounded Alison, tried to rape and kill her.

Reaching out, Jake lightly brushed the hair upward from the puffed and purple side of her face. He slipped it behind her ear.

"Good morning," Alison said, her voice quiet and husky. She turned her head, rolling back slightly until her rump touched the edge of the box springs. She smiled lazily up at Jake, but with only the right side of her face. The punished left side didn't move much.

"I didn't mean to wake you," Jake said.

"You didn't. I've been awake for a while."

"Playing possum, huh?"

"A little bit. Mostly too ruined to move."

"Hard floor," Jake said.

"Least of my problems. I feel like I've been hit by a Mack truck."

"You *look* like you've been hit by a Mack truck."

The right side of her lip curled up, baring some teeth. "That bad, is it?"

"Not that bad. You look pretty fine, all things considered. Did you sleep well down here?"

"Not bad, all things considered. You snore, you know."

"Sorry."

"It was nice. Kept me reminded you were there."

"If you . . . I would've stayed on my own side of the bed, you know. Kept my hands to myself. Especially if I didn't wake up."

She smiled slightly with the working half of her face.

Then the smile faded and she studied his eyes. "We'll never know," she said.

"We'll never know. Could you use some breakfast?"

"Sure."

"You can wear my robe. It's on a chair by the door."

"Thanks."

Jake stood up and went to the dresser. He took out his pajama shirt. With his back to Alison, he put it on and fastened the buttons. Then he turned around.

She was sitting cross-legged, the sheet spread over her lap and knees. She hugged the pillow to her breasts. "If you've got something more elaborate in mind than Trix or Fruit Loops, I'd be glad to make it. I might as well do something useful."

"I'll have you know I'm a pretty fair cook. I haven't burnt anything . . ."

Since last night, he thought.

"I trust you," Alison said. "But I'll help. What's a woman for?" she asked, a gleam of something that might have been mischief in her eyes.

"I'll pick you up a toothbrush. Do you need anything else?"

"I could use some clothes," Alison said, and took a drink of coffee. "I feel like a convalescent, wandering around in my nightgown and your robe."

"I could go over to your place and pick up some things," Jake said.

"How long are you planning to keep me here?"

"As long as possible."

She raised an eyebrow.

"Tonight, anyway," Jake told her.

"It was Roland who was after me," she said. "Not that I have anything against sticking around—you've got a nice floor. But he's dead, and he's the one who wanted to get me. So even if that snake-thing is still alive, there's no reason to think it would try to find *me.*''

''I hope you're right. But it was in the driver of the van when he tried to run down Celia, then it was in Roland when she disappeared. Maybe that's just a coincidence. On the other hand, maybe it's the creature that chooses the targets no matter who it's in.''

Alison curled up her lip. She could've done without that theory. ''So I just have to lay low until you find the thing.''

''Until it's accounted for, one way or another.''

''Okay.''

''I'm sorry.''

''Did you know that you spend a lot of time apologizing for stuff that's not your fault?''

''Sorry.'' He grinned.

Alison liked his grin. She hadn't seen much of it. ''When you get back, am I supposed to keep you covered again and look at your back?''

''Yep.''

''At least it's a good excuse to get your shirt off.''

Jake took a last drink of coffee, set down his cup, and rubbed his mouth with a napkin. ''I'd better get going.''

They left the table. Alison walked ahead of him to the front door. ''Don't you wear a uniform?''

''Usually.''

''I'd like to see you in it, sometime. Bet you look dashing. The fuzz.''

''I crashed a patrol car yesterday,'' he said.

''That was careless.''

''Yeah. Wouldn't look right, I think, driving around in uniform in my own car.''

''What time will you be back?''

He shook his head. ''I have no idea. It'll depend on how things go.''

''Well, should I make supper for you?''

"I don't want you starving. Say if I'm not back by seven, why don't you go ahead and eat without me."

"Okay."

He stepped past Alison and opened the door.

"Watch yourself," she said.

"You, too. If there's any kind of trouble—you see someone suspicious hanging around, anything like that—call the station and ask for Barney. He'll be there, and he knows the whole story."

"All right."

"You know where everything is?"

"I'll be fine, Jake. Don't worry."

Nodding, he hesitated in the doorway as if reluctant to leave. Then he started to turn away. Alison touched his arm. He looked into her eyes. She stepped against him, embracing him, tilting back her head. Jake put his arms around her. Holding her gently, he kissed her mouth. When his lips went away, he cupped the back of her head with one hand. She pressed her face to the side of his neck.

"I'd better get going," he whispered as he stroked her hair.

"I know." Alison squeezed him hard, then stepped back. "See you later," she said.

He stared at her. He kissed her once more, then turned away.

Alison stood in the doorway, watching him until the car moved off down the road. Then she shut the door and locked it. She slid the guard chain into place.

She leaned against the door, closed her eyes, and let herself go back to linger a while with the feel of his body against her, the feel of his lips on her mouth.

Chapter Thirty-Four

AFTER FILLING BARNEY IN ON ALL THAT HAD HAPpened the previous night, Jake returned to his car. He tore up the photograph of Roland. He felt guilty about damaging evidence, but Roland was dead, there would be no trial, and he didn't want to show the picture around with the naked body parts surrounding the guy's head. Once the parts were removed, he drove out to the place where he had burned the Volkswagen.

The car had been towed away, leaving only black smears and ashes. Jake searched there first, spreading the ashes with his shoes. He wasn't sure what he hoped to find. The thing's charred body? The tiny remains of its skeleton, if it had one?

When he finished there, he wandered around the area looking at the pavement, the grass strip between the curb and sidewalk, the sidewalk. Thursday, the thing had left some blood on the pavement of Latham Road behind the burning van and in the weeds on the other side. Today, there was nothing to see.

Jake told himself that the creature had probably died inside the Volkswagen. Maybe he should go over to the yard, later on, and sift through the remains of the car's interior. In the poor light last night, he might easily have missed something. Besides, he'd been tense and eager to get home. He needed to make the search again, thoroughly and in daylight.

Picture in hand, he headed for the apartment house on the corner to begin the door-to-door inquiries.

Alison hung up the telephone after explaining to Gabby that she wouldn't be able to work for the next few days. He'd heard on the radio about the killings and her narrow escape, so he was sympathetic and said she should take off as much time as she needed.

She had another call to make. This one wouldn't be so easy. It was necessary, though.

She misdialed and hung up before the ringing started.

Her stomach hurt. Her heart pounded. The pulsing of it made her face throb. Sweat slid down her sides. She stood up, took off Jake's robe, sat again on the sofa, and dialed Evan's number.

His phone rang once.

"Hello?" He sounded tense.

"Hi. It's me."

"Alison. My God. Are you all right?"

"You heard about last night?"

"Of course I heard about last night. Christ. Are you all right?"

"I'm a little beat up, but I'm okay."

"My God, I couldn't believe it. You could've been

killed. I've just been sick ever since I heard about it. I didn't even go to my classes. You should've called."

"I did call. Just now."

"I've been through hell."

"I'm sorry. It hasn't been a picnic for me, either."

"Who was it? Who did it?"

"A freshman named Roland."

"Some guy you know?"

"I'd met him a couple of times."

"Was he after *you*, or what?"

"I guess so."

"What for? I mean . . ."

"I guess he wanted to rape and kill me."

"Jesus Christ. Did he . . . touch you?"

"He didn't rape me."

"Thank God for that. You, what, fought him off?"

"Yeah."

"Christ, it's my fault. I should've been there. If you'd let me drive you home . . . you shouldn't have left, you know. That business was just a mistake, like I said. You should've stayed at my place, last night. None of this would've happened."

"Would've happened to Helen, regardless," she said. "And even if I'd spent the night with you, I would've gone home sooner or later."

"You should've stayed."

"Well, I didn't."

"Where are you, now?"

"I'm safe."

"Well, I know you're safe—the guy's dead, right? They said on the news he got killed in a fire."

"Yeah."

"So where are you?"

"I'm not supposed to tell anyone."

"That's a crock. Who told you that?"

"A policeman."

"Well, shit. What's the big idea?"

"He thinks I might still be in some danger."

"I don't get it. The bastard's dead, right? So where's the danger?"

"I'm going to do as I'm told."

"Since when?"

"Don't be a creep, Evan."

"I need to see you."

"You can't."

"Alison. We have to talk."

"We *are* talking."

"Face-to-face."

"I'm not up to a confrontation."

She heard him sigh. For a long time, he said nothing. Alison finally broke the silence. "I just wanted to let you know that I'm okay. I figured I owed you that."

When Evan spoke again, he sounded weary. "I honestly didn't know you were asleep last night when I . . . touched you. I love you, Alison. When I think what almost happened to you last night, it kills me. Please, I need to see you. Please. Tell me where you are. I'll come over and we'll talk. Just talk, I promise."

"I'll call you in a day or two."

"No, please. Alison, I'm so wasted. I didn't sleep at all last night. I can't do anything except think about you. I promise, I won't give you any trouble. I just need to see you, to be with you for a while. I'm begging you."

Alison shut her eyes and leaned back against the sofa cushion. This was worse than she'd expected. Evan sounded miserable, desperate.

It's my fault, she thought. I've done this to him.

"I guess we could meet somewhere," she finally said. "How about Wally's?"

Evan said nothing.

"That all right?"

Alison heard a faint sound of ringing. "Someone at your door?" she asked.

"Yeah," Evan whispered. The ringing came again.

"You'd better see who it is."

"I don't care," he whispered. "It can't be you, so I don't care."

"I'll hang on."

"I can't go to the door. I'm not wearing anything. I just got out of the shower."

The bell rang again.

"Probably just a salesman, anyway." After a few moments, he said, "Okay, he's gone."

"I was saying we could meet at Wally's."

"That's awfully public."

"That's the idea. I don't want any hassles."

"Christ, Al. Okay. Wally's. What time?"

"What time is it now?"

"About noon."

"I'll need some time to clean up and walk over there."

"I can pick you up."

"Thanks anyway. How about one-thirty?"

"Okay. I'll buy you lunch."

"Fine. See you then." She hung up.

She didn't want to see Evan.

Some things, she thought, you have to do.

It won't be so bad.

It'll be awful. I'll have to tell him it's over, tell him face-to-face and make him understand it's final.

It'll be awful, but it won't last forever. Then it will be ended and I'll come back here and Jake will show up, sooner or later.

Jake.

Just keep thinking about Jake, and the rest won't be so bad. He'll be here tonight.

* * *

This is getting nowhere, Jake thought. At more than half the doors he tried, nobody responded. The missing occupants, he supposed, were either in class or at work.

Of those people he spoke to, several had watched last night's spectacle, but many claimed ignorance of the entire affair. None admitted to knowing the identity of the young man in the photograph, though three were pretty sure they had seen him on campus at one time or another. Nobody had seen anything, last night or today, that looked like a snake. Nobody had seen or heard anything strange except for the uproar over the car fire.

It seemed pointless, but Jake didn't give up.

He had gone to every door of every apartment building on this side of the block except the one at the corner. Unlikely, he thought, that anyone so far from the scene noticed anything. But he might as well check, anyway, before crossing the road and trying the other side.

At the first two apartments on the ground floor, nobody came to the doors. At the third, he heard music inside. He rang the bell.

A woman in her late twenties opened the door. She was as tall as Jake, with a terry cloth headband around her black hair, thick eyebrows that almost met in the middle, prominent cheekbones, full lips, a jutting jaw, and broad shoulders. Her breasts strained the fabric of a top that looked like two red bandannas knotted together. Her belly was tanned and flat, striped with a few runnels of sweat. Her hips had the breadth of her shoulders. Instead of pants, she wore something that reminded Jake of a pirate's eye patch—a black strap that slanted down from her hips, a black satin triangle not quite large enough to cover her hairless pubic area.

"I'm sorry to bother you," Jake said. "It's police business." He held his wallet open.

She glanced at the badge, ignored the ID card, and licked some sweat from the corner of her mouth. "Come on in out of the cold," she said.

He stepped into the apartment. In spite of the fan and open windows, the heat seemed worse than outside. The woman turned away, and Jake watched her walk to the stereo. A slim black strip clung to the center of her buttocks, leaving the flawless cheeks bare. They flexed as she walked.

She seemed as casual about her attire as if she were wearing a three-piece suit. Jake wished she would put on something to cover herself.

The woman turned the stereo down, and turned around. "Want some iced tea?"

"No thanks."

"I'm Sam. Samantha Summers. Maybe you already know that."

He shook his head. "Jake Corey," he told her. "I'm making inquiries around the neighborhood about a situation last night."

"So you're not here to bust me, huh?"

"For what?"

Her heavy lips curled into a smile. "I'm sure I wouldn't know. Corrupting the staid mentality of minors?"

"You've been doing a lot of that?"

"Some might say so. I'm an associate professor of philosophy at the university."

Jake thought, You're joking. Then he thought, Why didn't *I* ever have a prof like this?

"Maybe I'll sign up," he said.

"Do that. I'll help open you mind to the imponderables."

"I could do without imponderables."

Sam sat on the carpet in front of him. She lay back, folded her hands behind her head, and began doing sit-

Her purse was on the floor beside Jake's feet. I should get it for her, he thought. And maybe some clothes.

There were clothes scattered on the carpet near the purse: white running shoes half covered by knee socks, a rumpled blue blouse, a bra with wispy transparent cups, white shorts with panties still inside them as if she had pulled both down at the same time.

Jake picked up the purse and stood there, staring at the clothes. Less than ten minutes ago, he'd been with Sam. Astonishing Sam in her bandannas and patch. But she hadn't affected Jake a fraction as much as the sight of Alison's discarded clothing on the floor.

For godsake, he told himself, this is no time to get turned on.

Reluctantly, he looked away. He went to the bed, set the purse down, and searched the shelves. In seconds, he found three yearbooks—slim volumes that stood inches taller than most of the other books. He pulled them down. The cover of each was embossed with the title, *Summit,* and the year. The most recent had last year's date. Jake scowled. He wanted the current edition. Then he realized that the *Summit* covering this year probably hadn't been issued yet.

The guy better have been enrolled last year, he thought.

He tossed the books onto the bed.

On his knees, he reached under the bed. He found a suitcase and pulled it out.

You shouldn't do this, he told himself. You should get the books over to Sam.

It'll just take a minute. If I don't, I'll have to make a special trip.

You just want to go through her things, whispered a small voice he didn't like very much.

He carried the suitcase to Alison's dresser, set it on the floor, and opened it.

In the top drawer of the dresser were nightgowns, panties and bras. He grabbed a handful of panties, trying not to think about them, and put them quickly into the suitcase. He was tempted not to get any bras for her, felt guilty about that, and took out two. In the next drawer, he found socks, pantyhose, slips. He took only socks. There were sweatshirts, T-shirts, gym shorts, and a jumpsuit in the next drawer. He took a T-shirt, a pair of red shorts, and the jumpsuit. The bottom drawer held sweaters. He didn't bother with them.

From her closet, he selected a sleeveless sundress, two blouses, and a pair of faded blue jeans. Then he went to the pile of clothing on the floor. He wanted to see her in the white shorts. He picked them up and shook them until the panties dropped through a leg hole. He watched the panties flutter to the floor. He was proud of himself for not touching them. With the shorts in one hand, he gathered up her shoes and returned to the suitcase.

Anything else she might need? he wondered, and scanned the room.

He saw the bulletin board on the wall beyond her desk Snapshots were tacked to it.

She won't need those, Jake told himself. Get going.

But he wanted to look at them, wanted to look at Alison.

He walked over to the desk. Most of the photos showed Alison, but she was with a guy. The same guy. In one, he was pushing her on a swing. In another, they were sitting on a blanket in the shade of a tree. Another showed them kissing.

Jake's stomach hurt.

The guy was handsome, in spite of his glasses, and he looked in good shape.

This is what I get for snooping, Jake thought.

He felt better, however, when he remembered Alison saying she had broken up with her boyfriend last night.

This guy had been dumped.

Good riddance.

Jake hefted the suitcase, picked up Alison's purse and yearbooks, and rushed downstairs.

After soaking in the bath for nearly an hour, Alison felt a little better. The hot water had soothed her tight muscles. It had done nothing, however, to take away the deeper tightness, the cold sick feeling that seemed to grip her insides.

If there was only a way to turn off her mind.

Or change channels. Get rid of the bad shows starring Roland and Helen and Celia and the dead policeman and Evan. Turn to the Jake channel. The Jake show was comforting, sometimes exciting. All the others hurt.

Alison stepped out of the tub, dripping, and began to dry herself with a soft towel.

Everything would be much better if she could just avoid seeing Evan.

You have to go. You have to finish it.

I don't have any clothes.

Alison wanted that for an excuse, but she'd had plenty of time to consider the problem and find a solution.

She hung the moist towel over a bar, and left the bathroom. The air in the hallway felt cool. In Jake's room, the windows were open. A nice breeze came in.

She went to the closet, took out a plaid shirt and put it on. Buttoned, it resembled a dress. A short, loose dress to be sure, but it would have to suffice. She rolled the sleeves up her forearms. Then, she found a belt and fastened it around her waist.

On the inside of Jake's closet door was a full-length mirror.

The shirt didn't look that much like a dress. It looked like a man's shirt. She pulled at it, rearranging the tucks to make it hang more smoothly.

Returning to the bathroom, she brushed her teeth using a finger smeared with Jake's toothpaste.

Finally, she went into the kitchen. On the wall beside the telephone was a notepad and pen. She tore off a sheet and took it to the table.

"That's him," Sam said.

Jake's heart slammed in his chest. "Are you positive?"

"I got a good look at them both. There's no doubt about it. He's the one who was helping Roland into the car." She slid a finger across the page of photographs and stopped it beneath the name. "Evan Forbes."

Alison's dumped boyfriend. The man in those snapshots on her bulletin board.

No need to worry, Jake told himself. They'd split up.

But she'd said she should call him, let him know she's okay.

What if she tells him where she's staying?

"I need to use your phone."

"Help yourself."

Jake dialed his home. He listened to the ringing.

Come on, pick it up. Come on, Alison. Answer the damn phone!

It rang fifteen times before he hung up.

"Do you have a directory?"

Sam rushed from the room. She ran back, clutching a telephone book, and thrust it at Jake.

He flipped through the pages. Forbes was listed. Jake recognized the address: the apartment building in front of which he'd found Roland's car parked last night. He'd already been there, knocking on doors.

"Thanks, Sam."

He ran.

He kicked the door. With a splintering crash, it flew open.

The carpet at his feet was crusted with dried blood.

Chapter Thirty-Five

ALISON WALKED THE L-SHAPED PARKING LOT OF WALly's, looking for Evan's car. It wasn't there. Nor was it parked along the street.

She had left the house at one o'clock, giving herself half an hour to reach the bar. Though she didn't have a wristwatch, she guessed that the walk must have taken no more than fifteen or twenty minutes and that she was early.

To make herself as inconspicuous as possible, she wandered out of the parking lot and headed for one of the elms that lined the street. The grass felt soft and cool under her bare feet. The shade felt good. Leaning back against the tree trunk, she took a deep, shaky breath. She was trembling badly.

She could *see* her legs trembling. They were out in front of her, knees locked to brace her against the tree, thighs pressed together. From the bottom of the shirt to her kneecaps, her skin shimmied over the fluttering muscles. As she watched the shaking, a corner of her shirttail was lifted by a puff of breeze. She swept it down and held the shirt front flat against her thighs. Her open hands felt tremors through the fabric.

Just calm down, she told herself. There's no reason to be so jumpy. I'm just going to have a talk with Evan. It's not like I'm about to get my teeth pulled without benefit of anesthetic.

Maybe Evan's already inside. He might have walked over. I could stay here fretting for an hour while he's inside drinking and thinking I stood him up.

Well, I'm not going in. Bad enough I had to walk over here dressed this way—undressed this way. At least I didn't run into anyone I know.

But even at this hour, Wally's was bound to be loaded with students and Alison was bound to know many of them.

As if to prove her theory, a station wagon slowed in front of the parking lot entrance and started to turn. She spotted Terri Weathers through the passenger window. Luckily, Terri was looking the other way. Alison quickly sidestepped, circling to the other side of the tree.

I should have stayed home is what I should have done.

She heard the car crunch over gravel and stop. The doors bumped shut. She heard footsteps heading away, then the windy sound of another approaching car. Her head snapped to the left. Coming up the street was Evan's blue Granada.

It swung to the curb in front of her, and stopped. Leaning across the seat, Evan opened the passenger door. "You're early," he said.

Both hands holding the shirttails down, she climbed into the car. The seat upholstery was hot against bare rump. Raising herself, she swept the shirt down beneath her. She kept her eyes away from Evan.

"What are you *wearing?*"

"All I could find."

"What is that, a guy's shirt?"

She faced Evan. His hair was neatly combed and he was dressed for the heat in a glossy Hawaiian shirt, white shorts, and sandals. He looked good except for his sallow skin and bloodshot eyes. The eyes had a feverish glaze. Alison didn't like the way they stared down through his glasses, studying her.

"Take a picture, why don't you."

"I could use a drink," he muttered.

"Let's stay here. I really don't feel like going inside. It'll be noisy, and—"

"Aren't you hungry?"

"People will ask questions. About last night. You said it was on the radio."

"Terrible," he said. "Last night." He peered at her face. "You got beat up pretty good."

"Yeah."

"You look great, though."

"Sure."

"You do. A bruise hath no power to diminish the beauty of so sweet a flower."

"Thanks."

"Let's at least get something to eat, okay? We can go someplace that has a drive-up window, so you won't have to worry about meeting anyone."

"Couldn't we just talk here?"

"I'm famished, Al. Really. I haven't eaten all day." He made a grim smile. "I didn't have any appetite. But I'm feeling a lot better, now. You being here. I feel like I've been brought back from the dead."

"I guess it's all right if we pick up something," Alison told him.

"Great." He started to drive.

* * *

The front door of Jake's house wasn't chained. He stepped inside, sensing that Alison was gone.

He called her name as he hurried through the rooms. In the bathroom, he found his bathrobe and Alison's nightgown hanging from a hook. In the kitchen, he found a note. It was on the table, folded in half to stand upright:

Dear Jake,

I had to go out for a little while to see my old boyfriend. I know I was supposed to stay here, but he needs to see me. I'm sure it will be okay, since I'm meeting him at Wally's. There will be plenty of other people around, so please don't worry.

I'll probably be back before you see this, but thought I'd leave a note anyway just in case you dropped by early and wondered what happened to me.

Please don't worry.

I'll be back as soon as possible. Believe me, the sooner the better.

This was just something I had to do.

Alison

Cold and numb inside, Jake lurched to the kitchen phone and dialed directory assistance. He got the number for Wally's, called, and asked for Alison Sanders to be paged.

''She doesn't seem to be here,'' he was told after a long wait.

He hung up and raced for his car.

The note didn't say what time she had left for Wally's. Maybe only a few minutes ago. Maybe hours ago. If she'd walked, she might still be on the way over there. Jake tried to take her most likely route. He scanned the sidewalks for pedestrians.

Evan might have picked her up, he thought. No, the note said she was *meeting* him at Wally's. So she walked. Unless she got a friend to pick her up.

That could be it. She called a girlfriend, asked the girl to bring over some spare clothes and give her a lift to the bar. Maybe the friend will stay with her.

Alison's not *at* Wally's.

So maybe she's still on the way over.

Please.

She might've been there and left. By now, she might be on her way home.

Stupid, wishful thinking. Evan has that fucker up his back and he isn't going to let Alison get away.

Maybe Evan's not the guy she went to see.

He is. But maybe he doesn't have the thing in him.

Then what was that blood on his apartment floor? Roland, half dead, must've staggered up to Evan's door. When Evan opened up, the thing burst out of Roland's belly and nailed him. It took control, got Evan to haul the dead or dying Roland down to the VW. Sam saw them, just thought Roland was plastered.

Why no blood on the sidewalk?

The thing's clever. Maybe it got Evan to bandage the wounds before carrying Roland out. The fire took care of the bandages.

Evan's got it, all right.

And Evan's got Alison.

Evan handed Alison the bags containing their soft drinks, cheeseburgers and french fries. She held them on her lap, glad to have more than her shirttails for covering.

In spite of his frequent glances in that direction, he'd acted all right during the drive over. Alison's jitters had subsided, though she still dreaded telling him that she wouldn't go with him after today.

She would postpone that moment for as long as possible.

Evan pulled away from the drive-up window. Instead of turning in front of the restaurant to circle around to its parking area, he continued ahead and swung onto the road.

"Aren't we going to eat in the lot?" Alison asked.

"That'd be kind of dreary. Let's drive someplace nice. We can have a picnic."

"Evan."

"Don't worry. I'll be a perfect gentleman." He smiled at her. A corner of his mouth trembled. "No more touchy-feely, not unless you start it. I'm a slow learner, but I finally got the message. I've put our relationship in too much jeopardy already. Here you are, convinced I'm some kind of a sex fiend. Well, I'm not. You'll see. From now on, it's hands off. Consider me a eunuch."

Too late for that, Alison thought.

"I came so close to losing you, last night. My boorish behavior, then . . . the attack on you. I had to face how much you mean to me, what it would be like if I never saw you again. I love you so much, Alison. I'll never again do anything to make you doubt me."

"We'll see how it goes today," she said.

"A test. I've always passed my tests with flying colors."

Alison settled back against the seat. She believed him. The lunch would go smoothly. He would make the sacrifice today, knowing this was his last chance. Be a good boy, and there would be plenty of future opportunities to make up for it. So he thought.

He's no mind reader. He doesn't know that, regardless of how wonderfully he behaves, this is it.

By the time he finds out, it'll be over.

He steered onto Latham Road.

"Where are we going?" Alison asked.

"Just out of town a little way. We'll have a picnic, all right? Just like old times. Except no fooling around."

"What'll it be?" asked the bartender.

"I called earlier about Alison Sanders," Jake said.

"Right. She wasn't here."

"Do you know her?"

"Not the name. Maybe if I saw her . . ."

Shaking his head, Jake started to turn away.

"You said Alison Sanders?"

Jake faced a slim young man who was seated on the bar stool beside him, nursing a martini. He looked rather old to be a student. "Do you know her?"

"I met her a few nights ago. Are you a friend?"

Jake showed the man his badge. "I'm also a friend. I need to find her fast. She said she was coming over here today."

"Well, she was here. Around one-thirty or a quarter till two. I was just arriving. In fact, I'd come here in hopes of seeing her." He shrugged. "She was with someone else. I just caught a glimpse of her getting into his car."

"Did you see who she was with?"

"I wasn't looking at the driver."

"Did you tear your eyes away from Alison long enough to notice the car?" Jake asked, not bothering to hide his annoyance.

"A dark blue four-door. I'm not good with cars. I do know that it wasn't a compact. It had a rather squarish shape along the lines of a Mercedes. It wasn't a Mercedes, of course."

"License number?"

"I didn't notice. Nothing suspicious was going on, why would I look at the license plate?"

"Did you see the car leave?" Jake asked.

"It was still sitting at the curb when I came in here."

"This was about one forty-five?"

"Give or take."

Jake checked his watch. Ten after two.

Rushing out of Wally's, he squinted against the sudden glare of daylight and ran to the street. He looked both ways. No blue car.

He leaned sideways against a tree trunk.

Twenty fucking minutes.

If he'd just been quicker.

Groaning, he rammed his elbow hard against the trunk.

Evan slowed the car. As he started to turn, Alison glimpsed a sign on the other side of the narrow road.

The Oakwood Inn.

He's taking me to the Oakwood.

Alison felt herself sinking, going down and down, dropping into an abyss.

It's happening, she thought. Oh dear Jesus, it's happening. It *is* the thing that wants me.

I took care of Roland. I can take care of Evan.

Jesus, I'm going to die.

Maybe Evan just picked this place by accident, just took the first side road that looked interesting.

"Look at that," he said, "a restaurant."

Alison nodded.

"Looks like we're the only ones here."

"It's closed," Alison said. Her voice came out a whisper. "It's where those people were killed."

"Really?" He sounded surprised. "Well then, I guess nobody will mind if we use the parking lot." He steered toward the front of the restaurant.

Alison lifted the bags of food off her lap. Leaning forward, she set them on the floor between her legs.

Evan stopped the car no more than a yard from the porch stairs. "So this is where it happened," he said. "I wonder if we could get inside. It'd be kind of fascinating, wouldn't it? Explore the scene of the crime?"

"Maybe after we eat." She faced him. She stared into his intense, bloodshot eyes.

"What's wrong?" he asked.

"I've been so rotten to you, Evan. All my dumb nonsense. Not wanting you to . . . It all seems so stupid and petty, now. I mean, I was almost killed last night. That sort of thing, it makes a person . . . it made me take a long look at what's important and what isn't. All that really matters is caring for another person. Loving another person. So why have I been putting us both through all this . . . this shit? Will you forgive me?" She put a hand on his shoulder.

"You're kidding," he said, and let out a tiny, nervous laugh. "This part of the test or something?"

"Forget all that. There's no test. I want it to be like it was between us."

"Really? Really?"

She eased him closer. Clear of the steering wheel, Evan turned to her. She kissed his mouth. She put her arms around his back.

The bulge beneath his shirt felt huge.

Her whimper of despair must have sounded passionate to Evan. He clasped a hand over her breast and squeezed. His other hand moved up her thigh. She opened her legs. Shuddering as he stroked her, she muttered, "I've missed you so much, missed the feel of you." She caressed his shorts. His penis felt hard and big. He squirmed as she fondled it. His breathing was ragged. "I'll get the blanket, darling. Is it in the trunk?"

He nodded.

Alison pulled the key from the ignition. ''Bring the food,'' she said. ''We'll eat afterward.''

''You're something else,'' he said.

''I was such an idiot. I never should've screwed things up between us. But that's over.'' She climbed from the car.

She stepped behind the trunk.

Through the rear window, she saw Evan lean over to pick up the food bags.

She whirled and flung the car keys with all her strength toward the weeds at the side of the lot.

Then she sprinted over the hot pavement, heading for the road out.

It was like last night, running from Roland, but this time there was no police car nearby as a goal. Alison could only hope to stay ahead of Evan, to reach Latham Road. Maybe, there, someone in a passing car would stop and help her.

She wasn't even out of the parking lot, yet.

She pumped her arms. She flung her legs out. Her bare feet slapped the pavement. She knew she was moving fast. She could feel her hair flying behind her, her shirttails flapping.

She could hear Evan's shoes pounding behind her.

He had chased her before, always in fun, always catching her easily. But she had never run from him like this. She felt as if she had never run so fast in her life.

Now she heard not only his shoes but his huffing breath.

He's gaining on me!

Tucking her chin down, she pistoned her arms and tried to hurl out her legs even faster than before.

She made it past the parking lot entrance, onto the road that led to Latham.

Evan was tight on her back.

''Leave me *alone!*'' she yelled.

He smashed her between the shoulder blades.

Alison plunge forward in a crazed dance of flinging arms and wild legs. Then she was off her feet. She slammed the pavement, hit it with palms and knees. It knocked away her arms and legs. It punched out her breath. She skidded to a stop. She couldn't get air and her skin burned, but she started to scurry up again.

Evan kicked an arm out from under her. She landed hard on her side. Evan grabbed the numb arm and pulled.

He lifted her. He swung her over his shoulder, turned around, and headed back across the lot.

Chapter Thirty-Six

JAKE SAT IN HIS CAR IN THE PARKING LOT OF WALLY'S, his forehead against the steering wheel.

Don't just sit there, he told himself. Go after her, damn it!

Sure thing. Go where?

Try Evan's apartment.

He wouldn't take her there. Not enough privacy for what he has in mind.

Eating her.

God!

Think!

The apartment is out. He'd take her someplace secluded, where he wouldn't have to worry about neighbors hearing anything, where he could work on her secretly for a long time. A field, maybe, or an abandoned building.

And which abandoned building would that be, you dumb asshole?

You could've been there by now!

Evan's shoulder bounced against Alison's belly as he rushed up the restaurant's porch stairs. He stopped in front of the door. One of his arms went away from Alison, but the other stayed clamped like a tight bar across the backs of her knees, pinning her legs against his body.

He got the door open and carried her inside. The door banged shut. He took a few steps, then bent at the waist to unload her. Alison felt herself start to fall. When she flopped off his shoulder, she reached up fast and clutched the back of his head. For a moment, she held herself up. Then Evan knocked her arm away. He kept her legs pinned until her back slammed the floor. Her head snapped down and hit the hardwood.

Evan bent over her. He tore open her shirt, spread its front, and stepped back. He stared down at her. His mouth hung open. He was panting for air.

Alison lay there, stunned from the blow and straining to breathe. She wanted to close the shirt. She couldn't lift her arms.

"Beautiful," he gasped. "Gotcha now, huh? Beautiful deceitful cunt." He suddenly flinched. Squeezing his eyes shut, he grimaced. His back stiffened and he writhed as if possessed by a terrible ecstasy. He swayed and moaned. Saliva dribbled down his chin. He rubbed his penis through the bulging front of his shorts.

Alison gazed up at him.

He was out of it, caught up in his frenzy.

Now, she thought vaguely. Before he comes out of it. Move!

She found the strength to roll over. She thrust her burning hands and knees against the floor and pushed herself up.

Evan grabbed her ankles. He yanked her legs straight. Her belly slapped the floor. Still holding her ankles, he crossed them and twisted them savagely. Alison flipped onto her back.

"Oh, you're not going anywhere. No party without you." He took a step backward. He wiped his slick chin with the back of a wrist. Then he unbuttoned his shirt. He shrugged it from his shoulders and it fluttered to the floor.

He wore a patch of gauze and tape just to the left of his navel. A band of purple skin at the edge of the patch angled across his belly and around his side.

On his belt was a black case. Alison watched his hand move to the case. He popped open its flap. He slid out a folding knife. He pried out the blade. It locked rigid with a metallic click. Staring down at Alison with half-shut eyes, he licked a flat side of the blade. "Do I taste Celia? Yes, I believe I do. A saucy wench, but tender." He lapped the other side of the blade.

Crouching, he leaned over Alison. The blade was cool and wet on her thigh. He turned it over and wiped the other side on her skin. With a flick of his wrist, he nicked her. She flinched. "Aw, did that hurt? For shame. Poor, poor Alison." He rubbed her cut. The back of his hand came up smeared red. He licked it and sighed.

Alison felt blood trickle down her inner thigh.

Evan stood up. Twisting at the hips, he threw the knife behind him. It thunked the floor. "Plenty of time later for that," he said. "Gotta ream you with something else, first."

He opened his belt buckle. He unbuttoned the waist of his white shorts and lowered the zipper. The shorts dropped around his ankles. He was wearing tight, red briefs. The front jutted with the push of his erection. He slid his thumbs under the elastic at his hips.

Alison lashed out with her foot, catching his left shin. Evan staggered backward, arms waving, feet tangling in the shorts. He started to fall.

Alison flung herself over. She shoved at the floor, got to her hands and knees and scurried up, staggering. In front of her was the bar. She threw her hands against its edge to catch herself. She spun around. Evan had freed himself of the shorts. He was crouched. He sprang at her.

Alison lunged to the right. Straight ahead was the main dining area. Straight ahead, at the end of a long stretch of bare floor, was a window. Crash through it? *That* might kill her. But better the window than Evan. Too far, anyway. Evan was already too close behind her, shoes thudding the floor, breath hissing.

She dodged around the corner.

Had a moment to see the clutter on the floor: cans, rags, toolbox, vacuum cleaner, ladder. A moment to wonder if she could leap clear.

Evan hit her.

His head pounded her rump. His arms wrapped her thighs. His diving tackle drove her forward and down.

She cried out as her body crashed to the floor. Cans overturned. One stayed under her hip. Another pushed at her belly. The edges of the open toolbox dug into her chest. Her left breast was inside the toolbox, pressing cold steel.

Evan squirmed off her. He pulled her by the ankles. As the edge of the toolbox scraped the underside of her breast, she hooked her left arm around the box. It skidded along the floor.

Evan stopped dragging her. He clutched her hips. Growling with effort or rage, he lifted her off the toolbox, swung her sideways, and dropped her. Falling, Alison hugged her belly and turned her face away from the floor. The impact wasn't as bad as she expected.

For a few moments, nothing happened. Alison lay there, gasping.

Evan was nearby, but out of sight as long as she didn't turn her face the other way.

She heard him move closer.

A hand curled over her right shoulder. Another hand hooked her right hip. He tugged at her. She rolled onto her side, rolled onto her back. And kept rolling, opening the arms folded across her belly as she came up onto her left side, facing Evan who crouched on the floor naked, who was staring at her breasts and not at her right hand, not at the screwdriver she'd taken from the toolbox.

She rammed it into him.

It hit him just under the sternum and punched in deep. The force of the blow sent him tumbling backward. Knees in the air, he stared bug-eyed at the ceiling. His mouth was a rictus of agony. He made whiny sucking noises struggling to breathe. A palsied hand pulled at the screwdriver. Its blade started to slide out, but was still deep inside him when his hand gave a spastic jerk, wrenching the screwdriver sideways. His body lurched, heels driving against the floor, thrusting his pelvis high and higher as he yanked the blade the rest of the way out.

Alison had begun to get up while she watched his contortions. She was still on the floor, turning his way, braced on a stiff arm, drawing in her legs, when Evan freed the screwdriver and hurled himself over, twisting, trying for her. She lurched back. Even's arm swung down as his side struck the floor. The tip of the screwdriver buried itself in the wood an inch from her hip.

Alison scooted farther away. Turning over, she crawled toward the toolbox. She watched over her shoulder and saw Evan yank the screwdriver from the floor. He was flat on his belly, writhing.

She took a claw hammer out of the box.

Evan still squirmed on the floor.

She crawled back to him. His twitching arms and legs shuddered against the floor as if he were trying to push himself up.

''Stay down,'' Alison gasped. She raised the hammer overhead. ''Stay down or I'll bash your fucking skull.''

She stared at the bruise that curled around from his side to his back. The discolored skin over his spine, all the way to the nape of his neck, bulged out almost an inch.

It's that *thing,* Alison thought.

She remembered Jake's warnings.

If Evan dies, the thing will come out.

And come after me.

Well, he's not dead yet.

The screwdriver dropped from his hand. He tried to pick it up again, but his jumpy fingers flicked it and sent it rolling.

Alison got to her feet. She was trembling badly and her legs threatened to give out. Ready to fall, she staggered backward to the ladder, dropped the hammer, and grabbed one of the upper rungs to hold herself up.

Evan still writhed on the floor, but not so much anymore.

She would need to go around his body to reach the front door. He was in no shape to stop her, now. She let go of the ladder, took a single step and flinched rigid as blood exploded from the nape of Evan's neck.

The creature surged up through the red spray, sliding out of Evan, darting across his shoulder blade, dropping to the floor, streaking toward Alison's feet.

She lurched backward. Bumped the ladder. Got a heel

onto its first rung. Grabbed the side rails behind her with both hands and climbed. The ladder wobbled. She was only two steps up by the time the creature reached the foot of the ladder. Gazing down at the monstrosity, she moved one rung higher, then clung there, gasping.

The creature slowly circled into a coil.

It resembled a snake, but with its slimy undulating flesh, to Alison the thing looked more like a two-foot length of intestine. Where Evan's blood had rubbed off, it was pale yellow and webbed with veins.

One end of the thing rose from the center of the coil. Not a head so much as an opening. A garden hose with teeth. The opening flattened shut, and Alison saw the dull gray globs of its eyes.

The eyes seemed to gaze up at her, seemed to *desire* her.

Alison's skin crawled. She glanced at herself. The open shirt hung off one shoulder. She had never felt so naked, so exposed, so vulnerable. She ached to close the shirt and clamp a hand between her legs but stood frozen, clutching the sides of the ladder.

The creature stretched upward, uncoiling, and half its length dropped onto the ladder's bottom rung. Its lower end squirmed and flipped. In an instant, the entire length of the creature was stretched along the aluminum step.

Whimpering, Alison climbed higher.

As Jake's car shot over the crest of the road, he saw the Oakwood parking lot. A blue car was parked near the restaurant's front door.

Let me be in time! Please!

His car flew and dropped, pounding the downgrade.

Let me be in time! his mind shrieked. *Please.*

It had taken so damn long. He'd driven as fast as he

could, sped through intersections without regard for red lights or stop signs, twice barely avoiding collisions. But it had taken so long!

Five minutes? Closer to ten.

Oh, God, please. Let her be all right!

The thing kept coming. It kept *coming*.

Alison climbed higher, but so did it. And it seemed to get better at swinging itself from one rung to the next.

Alison sat on the head step, at the ladder's peak, and clutched its edges and stared down between her knees.

She was sobbing. The thing was a vile, jaundiced blur through her tears.

It flopped onto the next rung.

With a whine of despair, Alison carefully let go of the edges and stood up. She climbed backward, arms out for balance. One step, then one more. Then she was standing on the very top of the ladder. She teetered as it wobbled from side to side. When the motion eased, she spread her feet apart and bent her knees just slightly to keep herself steady.

Peering down, she watched the creature mount the rung where her feet had been only seconds earlier. One more, and it would be on the step below the top. From there . . .

Alison heard the roar of a car engine.

A car! It was coming here! It had to be!

Somehow, Jake had figured out . . . God, I hope it's Jake! He'll burst through the door in the nick of the time and blast the fucker to hell.

Brakes squealed.

The corner of the wall blocked her view of the front door.

"*Help!*" she yelled.

Then she looked down.

The creature was already on the next step. The ring of its mouth flattened shut and its gray phlegm eyes seemed to peer up between her legs as its head rose.

Alison leaped.

She kicked her right leg far out, shoved off with her left foot hoping to knock the ladder over, and dropped. She fell for a long time. Fell toward Evan's sprawled body. Her feet hit the floor. Her knees folded. She tumbled forward, outflung hands slapping Evan's back. Her left hand slipped on the blood. As she smashed down on him, something slopped onto her back.

Something long and squirmy.

Rushing up the porch stairs, Jake heard a wild scream.

He threw open the door.

The restaurant seemed dark after the brilliant afternoon sunlight. He snapped his head from side to side. He saw no one, just a knife standing upright, blade embedded in the floor near his feet. But he heard someone sobbing. Then quick footfalls.

He whirled to the left, swinging up his revolver. Alison charged around the corner. Her face was twisted with panic. She clawed the air with one hand as if reaching for Jake. Her other arm was up, elbow high beside her head, hand behind her back. Her open shirt followed her like a fluttering cape as she ran.

Jake lunged sideways to get a clear shot past Alison, but nobody chased her around the corner.

"It's on me!" she cried out. "*In* me!"

She twirled around in front of Jake. The thick, yellowish thing at the small of her back whipped from side to side like a grotesque, misplaced tail.

Jake dropped his gun. He clutched Alison's shoulder to hold her still. With his left hand, he caught the flipping creature and tugged. His hand slipped off its slimy, yielding flesh. He caught it again. Wrapping his hand around it, he felt it moving deeper into Alison. He clenched it in his fist and yanked. Alison shrieked in agony and staggered backward. The creature didn't come off.

"No!" Jake shouted.

He threw Alison to the floor. He jerked the shirt from her shoulders and flung it aside, then dropped onto her writhing body. Sitting on her buttocks, he tore the knife from the floor.

He grabbed the beast, wrapped his left hand around its flacid slick body and pulled it taut. The length of it stretched and thinned, but it kept moving into Alison. The lump under her skin was three inches long and growing longer.

He stabbed Alison in the back.

She yelped, went rigid, dug her fingernails into the floor.

The tip of the blade entered the tunneling front of the bulge. Jake was careful not to stab deep. Half an inch, no more. Blood and a thick yellow syrup flowed from the gash. He drew the blade down, splitting Alison's skin until it parted at the hole, then tore the creature from her back.

"Got it!" he yelled in triumph.

Alison, crying, rolled onto her back and looked up through her tears as Jake leaped to his feet. In one hand was the bloody knife. In the other was the beast. He whirled around, swinging it overhead like a whip. Yellow stuff flew from its ripped body. He lashed it against the wall near the door. It left a dripping smear. He swung it high and whipped it down against the floor. He stomped it with one foot, then with both feet, jumping up and down on the thing until it was mashed flat.

Bending over it, he scraped it up with the edge of the knife. He carried it through the door.

"Jake?"

He didn't answer.

Alison pushed herself up. She crawled to the doorway, wincing as pain swarmed from her ripped back. She grabbed the frame and rose to her knees. Holding on, she watched Jake run to the rear of his car, the flat thing swaying and dripping at his side.

She was hurting and still frightened. She felt blood streaming down her back and buttocks, running down the backs of her legs. She didn't want to be left alone.

Take care of *me,* Jake. I need you.

Shit, she told herself, don't be a baby. He saved your ass. Let him finish whatever he's doing.

He took a red can of gasoline from the trunk of his car. He carried the mashed carcass a few yards, dropped it, and doused it with gas. He emptied the can onto it. A puddle spread over the pavement.

"Wait!" Alison called. She pulled herself up. She staggered onto the porch.

Jake waved her away, but she shook her head.

Setting down the gas can, he rushed toward her. He leaped onto the porch and put an arm around her back. "Alison," he said.

She held onto him. With Jake bracing her up, she climbed down the stairs. He led her to his car. She leaned against the driver's door, then slid down it and squatted as Jake hurried over to the wet patch on the parking lot. He struck a match and touched it to the gasoline.

As the pale flames rose, he came back to Alison. He squatted beside her. She put a hand on his knee. He looked at her. "What happened to Evan?"

"I killed him."

Jake nodded, and turned his gaze toward the fire.

Greasy black smoke swirled up from the remains of the

creature. Alison heard sizzling, popping sounds. When a breeze tore away the shroud of smoke, she glimpsed a bubbling black smear on the pavement.

Jake curled a hand behind Alison's head, and softly stroked her hair.

They watched until the fire burned out.

Chapter Thirty-Seven

JAKE BENT OVER THE BED AND KISSED HER. HE STROKED the back of her head. "Nighty-night honey. Do you want a record on?"

"Not now," Kimmy said, arching an eyebrow. "We are not ready. We're busy."

"Busy, huh? Well . . ." He leered at her ear and licked his lips. "Some mayo," he muttered.

"No!" She hunched up a shoulder. She pressed Clew to her ear. "No earwich. I mean it."

"But I'm hungry."

"You're going to have popcorn. And you'd better save me some."

"We'll see."

She turned to Alison, who was sitting beside her on the bed. "I'll get saved some, won't I?"

"Sure," Alison said.

Kimmy gave Jake a haughty look. "Alison will make sure of it."

Grinning, Jake said, "Good night, honey," and left the room.

Alison lifted the open book off her lap. "Now, where were we? Let's see, Pooh and Piglet were tracking the Woozle through the snow." She started to read, but Kimmy placed a small hand on the page, covering the paragraph. She looked up into Alison's eyes.

"Are you going to be here all the time?" she asked.

"I don't know."

"Well, all your stuff's here."

"Yeah, it is." Alison put a hand on the girl's back. "As long as my stuff's here, I guess I'll be here. Do you think that's okay?"

"I think so," she replied, frowning and nodding. " 'Cause you know, I like how you read. You read a lot better than Daddy. And you know what else? When Daddy used to take me to the moojies and I had to go pee . . ." She covered her mouth and tittered. Pressing a tiny shoulder against Alison, she tilted her head back and took her hand away and whispered, "He made me go in the wrong john and there were men peeing in the sinks! It was so gross!"

"In the *sinks?"*

"Yes!"

"Well, I guess I'd better not let him take you to the moojies anymore without me."

"No more without you."

Alison closed the book. "Now, I'd better let you get some sleep. We need to get up bright and early for the zoo."

"Think we'll see a Woozle?"

"One never knows about Woozles." Alison got up. She

slipped the book onto the shelf while Kimmy crawled between the sheets.

Alison tucked her in, then knelt beside the bed. Kimmy tucked Clew into the top of her nightgown. "Gonna say your prayers?" Alison asked.

Kimmy grinned. "No, you. Do that one you told me. The spooky one."

"Maybe you should do a nice one. I don't want to be a corrupting influence."

"I want the spooky one," Kimmy insisted.

"Well, all right." Alison shut her eyes and folded her hands on the mattress. "From ghoulies and ghosties and long-leggity beasties and things that go bump in the night, oh, Lord, deliver us."

"Neat," Kimmy said.

"Sleep tight." She started to get up.

"You forgot to kiss me."

Alison bent over Kimmy. The girl's arms wrapped around her neck, pulling her down with a tight hug. From the force of it, Alison expected a hard, mashing kiss. But Kimmy's lips pushed against her mouth with such lingering tenderness that tears came into her eyes. "See you in the morning, sweetheart," she said as she stood up.

"Don't forget to save me some popcorn."

"Never fear. Do you want the record on?"

"Side two."

Alison flipped the record and turned on the stereo. She dimmed the lamp on Kimmy's table, looked back at her with Clew tucked into the neck of her nightgown and one arm around Cookie Monster, waved, and left the room.

At the entrance to the living room, she saw Jake on the sofa. A huge bowl of popcorn rested on the cushion beside him. There were two glasses of cola on the table at his knees. Instead of joining him, she went into the kitchen. She took one of Kimmy's cereal bowls from a drawer. It had Charlie Brown and Snoopy on it. She carried it into the living room, bent over the large bowl and started scooping popcorn in.

"Boy, she's got you well trained," Jake said.

"My word is my bond." She carried Kimmy's serving into the kitchen, left it on the counter, and returned.

She'd been hot in her robe. Jake watched as she took it off. She was wearing a red, jersey nightshirt she had bought that day at the university store. "What do you think?" she asked, turning in front of him.

"Nice. Though I have a certain attachment for your blue negligee."

"It brings back some bad memories."

"Not for me."

"Then I'll wear it once in a while." She lifted the popcorn bowl and sat down beside Jake. The nightshirt was very short. She felt the sofa upholstery against her bare skin. Her stomach fluttered. For an instant, she was sliding into the seat of Evan's car, the shirttails too short to cover her buttocks.

"What's the matter?" Jake asked. He was so quick to notice the slightest changes in her moods.

"A little flashback."

"I'm sorry."

She mugged at him. "It's not *your* fault."

"I just hate to see you upset."

"I know." She set the popcorn bowl on her lap. It felt warm against her bare thighs. "It's just that you look so woebegone when you 'sorry' me. Have some popcorn."

He dug in a big hand and took out a fistful.

"What did you rent for tonight?"

"*Halloween* and *The Hills Have Eyes.*"

"Fantastic!"

"I bet you've already seen them."

"Of course," Alison said.

"They do have such things as comedies at the video store."

"They're not nearly as much fun."

Jake grinned, shook his head, and tumbled some popcorn into his mouth. "Amazing," he said, after chewing for a moment. "It really doesn't bother you, watching this kind of thing? After what happened?"

"The movies are pretend."

"I'd think *they* might give you flashbacks."

"They do. Sometimes. But all kinds of things do. It's only been three weeks."

"Three great weeks," Jake said.

"Yeah."

She watched Jake munch some more popcorn. She took a handful, tossed some into her mouth, and flinched. "Ow!"

Jake looked at her, startled.

"It's too damn hot to eat."

Now he looked perplexed.

Alison lifted the bowl off her lap, leaned forward and set it on the table. "I think we'd better let it cool off for a while, don't you? We don't want to burn our tongues while we watch the movies."

"Oh. Right." Jake blushed a little.

Alison pulled the nightshirt over her head. Facing him, she began to open the buttons of his pajama shirt. He swallowed the remains of his popcorn. He stared into her eyes. His gaze roamed downward, lingering on her naked body.

Alison watched his hands move slowly toward her until his fingertips trembled against her breasts. The hand that had held the popcorn felt grainy with salt, and slick. "Woops," he whispered. He took the hand away and rubbed it on his pajama pants, leaving an oily smear.

The oil and butter on Alison's breast gleamed in the lamplight. "You'd better lick it clean," she said.

He did.

As his tongue lapped and swirled, Alison slipped the shirt down his arms. She gasped and arched her back when he sucked.

Then his mouth went to her mouth and his arms went around her.

Alison fell sideways against the sofa back and stretched her legs under the table. Jake pushed his tongue into her mouth. She tugged the waistband of his pajamas. The snaps popped open and she pulled at the pajamas until he was bare against her, smooth and hard.

His tongue left her mouth. He kissed her lips, her chin, the side of her neck. His hands roamed, caressing her shoulder blades, gliding down, curling over her buttocks, moving up again.

They stayed away from the middle of her spine.

Gently clutching his hair, Alison eased his head away and looked into his eyes. "You never touch me . . . *there.*"

His eyebrows lifted slightly.

"Where *it* was."

"I guess not," he whispered. Alison could feel his penis shrinking against her thigh.

"Does it disgust you?"

"No. God, no. Nothing about you disgusts me."

"It was in me."

"Nothing's in there, now. I watched the doctor clean the wound, and—"

"But you're afraid to touch me there."

"No, I'm not."

"Scared you'll catch something?"

"I don't want to hurt you."

"It's healed. All but the scar."

"You want me to touch it?"

"Not if you don't want to."

"It isn't that," he muttered, looking miserable.

"What is it?"

"*I* did it to you. I stabbed you, cut you open. I hurt you, and when I see the wound or touch it, it all comes back, how you cried out and jumped and dug your nails into the floor. It all comes back how much I hurt you."

"You mean it's guilt, just guilt?"

"You might say that."

"Dipshit, you saved my life." Alison pressed her cheek to his and held him tight. "I look at it in the mirror. It's special, Jake. It's you cutting into me and taking out the nightmare."

The tips of Jake's fingers trembled against the flesh of Alison's wound. They gently followed the length of it. They tickled and she squirmed.

"Does it hurt?"

"No. Does this?"

Jake moaned.

"Let's knock off all this small talk," Alison said. "The popcorn's getting cold and we've still got a double feature to watch."

"What am I," Jake asked, "the coming attraction?"

Alison laughed and swung a leg over his hip.